EX LIBRIS

VINTAGE **CLASSICS**

MADAME BOVARY

Gustave Flaubert was born in Rouen in 1821, the son of a distinguished surgeon and a doctor's daughter. After three unhappy years of studying law in Paris, an epileptic attack ushered him into a life of writing. *Madame Bovary* won instant acclaim upon book publication in 1857, but Flaubert's frank display of adultery in bourgeois France saw him go on trial for immorality, only narrowly escaping conviction. Both *Salammbô* (1862) and *Sentimental Education* (1869) were poorly received, and Flaubert's genius was not publicly recognized until *Three Tales* (1877). His reputation among his fellow writers, however, was more constant and those who admired him included Turgenev, George Sand, Victor Hugo and Zola. Flaubert's obsession with his art is legendary: he would work for days on a single page, obsessively attuning sentences, seeking always *le mot juste* in a quest for both beauty and precise observation. His style moved Edmund Wilson to say, 'Flaubert, by a single phrase – a notation of some commonplace object – can convey all the poignance of human desire, the pathos of human defeat; his description of some homely scene will close with a dying fall that reminds one of great verse or music.' Flaubert died suddenly in May 1880, leaving his last work, *Bouvard and Pécuchet*, unfinished.

Adam Thorpe was born in Paris in 1956. His first novel, *Ulverton*, was published in 1992, and he has written ten others – most recently *Flight* – two collections of stories and six books of poetry.

OTHER MAJOR NOVELS BY GUSTAVE FLAUBERT

Memoirs of a Madman
November
Salammbô
Sentimental Education
The Temptation of Saint Anthony
Three Tales
Bouvard et Pécuchet

GUSTAVE FLAUBERT

MADAME BOVARY

Provincial Morals

TRANSLATED, ANNOTATED AND INTRODUCED

BY

Adam Thorpe

VINTAGE BOOKS
London

Published by Vintage 2012

13

Translation, Introduction and editorial apparatus copyright
© Adam Thorpe 2011

First published in Great Britain by Vintage 2011

Vintage
Random House, 20 Vauxhall Bridge Road,
London SW1V 2SA

www.vintage-classics.info

Addresses for companies within The Random House Group Limited can be found at:
www.randomhouse.co.uk/offices.htm

The Random House Group Limited Reg. No. 954009

A CIP catalogue record for this book
is available from the British Library

ISBN 9780099573074

Penguin Random House is committed to a sustainable future for
our business, our readers and our planet. This book is made from
Forest Stewardship Council® certified paper.

Typeset by Palimpsest Book Production Ltd, Falkirk, Stirlingshire

Printed and bound in Great Britain by Clays Ltd, Elcograf S.p.A.

TO

MARIE-ANTOINE-JULES SÉNARD

MEMBER OF THE PARIS BAR
EX-PRESIDENT OF THE NATIONAL ASSEMBLY
AND FORMER MINISTER OF THE INTERIOR

Dear and illustrious friend,

Allow me to inscribe your name in the front of this book and even
before its dedication; for it is to you, above all, that I owe its
publication. On submitting to your magnificent defence in court, my
work has acquired for me a kind of unforeseen authority. Accept
here, then, the acknowledgement of my gratitude, which, as great as
it may be, will never be equal to your eloquence and your devotion.

GUSTAVE FLAUBERT

Paris, 12th April 1857.

TO

LOUIS BOUILHET

CONTENTS

INTRODUCTION

GUSTAVE FLAUBERT WAS BORN IN Normandy in 1821, the son of a renowned surgeon. Brought up in the domestic wing of Rouen's main hospital, the boy was often within earshot of the sick wards' moans and in sight (if he climbed a trellis) of his father at work on the anatomy theatre's corpses. He learnt to read only at the age of eight, despite the efforts of his anxious, migrainous mother. He studied law in Paris for a short time but in his early twenties suffered a probable epileptic attack which curtailed his law career and, with some relief, he devoted himself to writing, 'with the stubbornness of a maniac'. Within two years both his father and his beloved sister, Caroline, had died – the latter in childbirth.

Madame Bovary appeared initially as a serial in the *Revue de Paris* in 1856, and was the author's first published work. An account, based on real cases, of provincial adultery in the flatlands of Normandy, it is also 'brutal' (the author's word) in its realism; notorious for its dissection of the consumerist, industrialising France of the mid-century; prescient in its depiction of a woman alienated from the life that surrounds her; and often, it must be said, piercingly funny. Its author, the *Revue* and the printer were put on trial for the novel's perceived sexual frankness, although this turned out to be an illusion of the book's sensual, meticulous prose: while, for example, the waltz scene was attacked for immorality, the book's fetishistic and phallic content of shoes, feet, gloves, cigars, cactus plants, spires, apricots, pen-knives and so on went unnoticed.

Thanks to Flaubert's abundant letters, particularly to his mistress Louise Colet and to the novelist and feminist George Sand, we know that the novel's five-year composition, inked with a quill (Flaubert hated metal nibs as much as he hated railways), was both agonising and exhilarating. 'We love what tortures us,' he claimed. The trial helped to make the book, and its unknown author, famous overnight. The work's startling newness was immediately recognised: in the words of Maupassant commenting some thirty years later, *Madame Bovary* 'revolutionised the art of letters'. As much as the paintings of Manet or Courbet, Flaubert's work heralds the start of the modern.

THE NOVEL WAS, HOWEVER, WRITTEN against the grain: Flaubert was at heart a romantic in love with exotic tales, realms and ruins – not the gritty, the seedy, the banal. He was no Zola, whose own tale of adultery, *Thérèse Raquin* (1867), takes urban ennui and shabbiness to a gruesome extreme. Flaubert had abandoned his previous work, a seething phantasmagoria concerning the life of Saint Anthony in his desert retreat, after a thirty-two hour reading had numbed his long-suffering friends Maxime du Camp and Louis Bouilhet, who suggested he write something 'down-to-earth'. Flaubert took the hint: a disciple of the master prose stylist Chateaubriand, he may have declared that 'style is everything', yet this time he rooted his fiction in the messiness of the everyday. This would not be easy for a man who wrote, 'Life is such a hideous business that the only way to tolerate it is to avoid it ... by living in Art.' There is something in this of the desert hermit's self-flagellating discipline and denial.

Concerning his new book, he told Louise Colet, 'I'm striving to be buttoned-up and to follow a geometrically straight line.' Yet he would refer to the novel as a poem, and although it borrows from poetry a willed tendency to let language lead the way, this is always in taut tension with the demands of narrative and of the muddy fields, overfurnished rooms, trite conversation and closed minds of the story's rural setting, where Paris remains 'vaguer than the Ocean'. Above all, the author was taking on his greatest enemy: the bourgeois – defined by him as 'anyone who thinks ignobly'.[1]

Here we find a contradiction, part of that inner freedom belonging to the greatest artists. Although Flaubert loathed the ultra-bourgeois, conservative France of the mid-nineteenth century, he was himself both deeply conservative politically ('the whole dream of democracy is to raise the proletarian to the level of stupidity attained by the bourgeois')

---

[1] I'm assuming the term's pre-Marxist connotation.

and passed a thoroughly regulated existence in a riverside *maison de maître*, in the Normandy hamlet of Croisset, living off the proceeds of family land and cosseted by his mother and assorted servants. Apart from occasional bouts of Parisian *libertinage* and travels to, among other places, Tunisia, the Levant, Italy and London, Flaubert did nothing but work at words in his tobacco-fugged study – so obsessively that it led to his final collapse from a stroke in 1880.

Not long before his death, he had advised his friend, the society hostess Gertrude Tennant (who hated *Madame Bovary*), to be 'regular and orderly in your life like a bourgeois, so that you may be violent and original in your work'. The art came first. He detested over-romantic works as exemplified by the poet Lamartine[2] (one of Emma Bovary's favourite authors), yet his professed literary aim was beauty and harmony. Beauty, for Flaubert, was less to do with conventional mellifluousness than the precise matching of word to experience. Recording the reality of human society – including its peevishness, ugliness, hypocrisy and stupidity – meant honouring it with language just as a poet might honour a sunset or the eyes of a lover.

Thus Flaubert's ideal was both a rational fidelity to the truth – an enlightened, quasi-scientific concept – and a desire somehow to match that truth in the parallel and quite fictive universe of words: to reduce the distance between language and things. The heartbeat of that universe, for Flaubert, was rhythm. There is not a sentence in *Madame Bovary* that does not bear its own particular pulse, rippling against the shimmering surface-patterns of assonance and alliteration, in themselves subservient to the lived experience being described – the tap of Hippolyte's wooden leg in the church, a fresh breeze blowing through reeds, the bulkiness of cattle moving back to their stalls, the scoop of a hand in sugar-white arsenic.

The thousands of pages of drafts, now transcribed by the University of Rouen and viewable on the web (www.bovary.fr), are testament to Flaubert's inky struggle: but the process can also be viewed as a highly refined one of condensation – distilling the material to the *mot juste*.

---

[2] Who was nevertheless to tell Flaubert that *Madame Bovary* was the best book he had read in twenty years.

There are alarming excisions. Long and intricate episodes of great poetic power – such as Emma looking at the dawn landscape through panes of coloured glass after the ball at Vaubyessard – are discarded even at proof stage, sometimes leaving an image or even a sentence stranded in ambiguity. When Scott Fitzgerald did something similar to *The Great Gatsby*, he was aided by a brilliant editor: Flaubert seems to have achieved it in isolation, cutting a path into virgin territory.

This self-control extended even to the depiction of characters who would be at home in a period 'sensation' novel or melodrama: the salesman and moneylender Lheureux is all too plausible in his commonplace cunning (his schemes never quite criminal), while the upper-class libertine Rodolphe is closer to nihilism than to fashionable cynicism. As for the minor characters, the servant-boy Justin's story is a miniature masterpiece of tragic infatuation, while even the brief glimpses of the peasant wet-nurse and her scrofulous charge, approached through what can only be described as a remarkable tracking shot of dishevelled ruralism, absorb not a drop of sentiment. As for the 'advanced' pharmacist Homais, a self-righteous Rabelaisian grotesque whose views occasionally sound close to Flaubert's own (particularly about religion), the author never allows his loathing of that type to interfere with the merciless portrayal[3] – an even more remarkable achievement when one knows that *Madame Bovary* was written in a state, as he put it, of 'continual rage'.

In a letter to Louise Colet in 1853, Flaubert worries that, after 260 pages, he has written only descriptions of place and expositions of character, consoling himself with the notion that it is a biography, not a developed event. Or several biographies. Much of Part One is an account, not of farmer's daughter Emma, but of the dull medical officer with an 'almost interesting' face, who timidly loves her and becomes her husband – Charles Bovary. The book's structure is, therefore, unconventional: a lengthy and often slow preparation for Emma's downfall, whose last phase takes place in a breathless rush that feels alarmingly authentic.

---

[3] Except in the last chapter, when he refers to the man's shallow intellect and the 'ne-fariousness of his vanity' ('*la scélératesse de sa vanité*').

DURING THIS FINAL CRISIS, EMMA experiences hallucinations drawn from Flaubert's first-hand knowledge of epileptic attacks (he is always, as in everything, medically accurate). Throughout, *Madame Bovary* skilfully negotiates inner and outer experience with such subtlety that it is only in the modulation of a phrase, a minutely calibrated change of rhythm or vocabulary, that we pass from one to the other, even in the shifting of point of view. Where the latter coincides with the narrator's view, we have what has been termed *style indirect libre* or free indirect discourse, where the narrative is coloured by the tone or vocabulary of one of the characters. It is, in one sense, the overlapping of spoken (or thought) language with the written. Flaubert was probably the first to use it in French literature, where the division had been especially marked.

Although the technique appears in earlier English authors such as Jane Austen, Flaubert uniquely combines it with the complete absence of the authorial 'I', or the kind of moralising commentary we find in Charles Dickens or George Eliot. His revolutionary decision to keep himself out of the picture ('author's personality absent', as he put it), left the job to language alone. It freed him from sounding, as he feared, like '*Balzac Chateaubrianisé*' – that is to say, like a highly stylised social realist. And it offered Flaubert a treasure-house of possibilities: he could play the full range of linguistic and literary devices – parody, pastiche, nuance, irony, wordplay, imitation, contrast, repetition and so on – without any apparent intermediary. This, above all, is why the critic Roland Barthes dated modernism, not from a particular year, but 'from Flaubert'. The way was prepared for James Joyce's multi-tongued *Ulysses*, T.S. Eliot's cubist collage of voices in *The Waste Land*, the subjective fluidities of Virginia Woolf's *Mrs Dalloway*. All that remains of Flaubert's own voice is its insistent and justly famous irony: a tone we come to hear and recognise, nevertheless, and savour for its familiarity.

THERE IS A FURTHER TWIST, however. The first word of the novel (a last-minute alteration) is '*nous*', or 'we'. This sets up two elements: a collusion with the reader, and an apparent narrator. An eye-witness, a schoolboy in a rowdy class, recalls watching the trembling new boy,

Charles Bovary, arrive during term time. A few pages later, the same narrator, his voice popping up without warning, claims to remember 'nothing about him'. Having annulled himself, he vanishes. We then have a supple narrator who seems both limited and omniscient, varying between microscopic intimacy and a disdainful loftiness that apparently reaches its extreme with Emma's unseen coupling in the hackney coach. Jean-Paul Sartre, in his psychoanalytical study *The Family Idiot*, described this as 'copulation in general . . . viewed by a being . . . [who] takes his place outside humanity'. The 'being' is also, surely, the exhausted driver, who sees the world only through street names and the glimpsed details of ivied terrace, spur-stones and a field of red clover.

Furthermore, the opening scene itself was a standard subject for school compositions: thus one of the most sophisticated novels ever written begins with a derivative school exercise. The simple directness of the first paragraph reflects this. These are literature's humble beginnings; the schoolroom's scratch of letters.

But what looks at first like a simple communion between life and language is something much more complex. Flaubert was living in the first period of mass communication, when the combination of newspapers and the railway gave the printed word a new potential for both good and bad: it was certainly more likely to spread stupidity than wisdom, as we see in the go-ahead figure of Homais, both an avid consumer of print and a deadly contributor: his eulogy on the club-foot operation and science in general remains singularly relevant in our own disappointed age. Emma's sentimental reading gives her an inauthentic vision of life's potential, an eternal dissatisfaction with what she has, 'her dreams tumbling into the mud like swallows'. Her first lover, Rodolphe, mimics romantic discourse in his seducer's letter of rupture, reducing words to empty husks, vehicles of lies, in the same way that Léon, the besotted, blue-eyed lawyer's clerk, can spout only poetic clichés. Fragments of poems, stereotypes drawn from literature, technical manuals, medical parlance, scientific facts and statistics, newspaper articles, religious tracts, litter the characters' conversations, making us doubt what they are saying or thinking, or even whether they know what they really think.

Flaubert continually reminds us, then, that what we are reading is itself an artifice, subject to the same critical scepticism as any other verbal matter. There is no such thing as a neutral, omniscient narrator – even in the lyrical glimpses of the Normandy landscape, long used in French schools as stylistic exemplars. The lengthy opening description in Part Two of Yonville l'Abbaye, the country market-town ('this poor village') where Charles has his practice and Emma her emotional prison, is thoroughly Homais-like in its emphasis on utilitarian progress, and climaxes like the authorial signature on the pharmacist's name written 'in letters of gold on a black ground': the place has already been appropriated by the bourgeois mind.

So it is perhaps no coincidence that one of the recurring words in the novel is 'étaler': to put in the window; to display; to show off; to spread or stretch out; to sprawl (s'étaler). Flaubert loved to denigrate his task, to liken himself to an organ-grinder or, like Yonville's tax-gatherer Binet, a turner of napkin rings. The excitement of the modernist experiment was just this thrill of tension, like an electric current, between the two opposite poles of reality and artifice: a self-consciousness that reveals, not surface, but a vertiginous depth, a glorious mise en abîme in which humanity struggles to find meaning.

IN A SECULAR AGE, THIS question of life's ultimate meaninglessness provokes art to its finest efforts; and throughout Flaubert's life, public events conspired to provoke a general ennui in anyone of an idealistic or romantic temperament. At the time Madame Bovary was being written France was still traumatised by the collapse of the ancien régime a half-century earlier, followed by revolutionary experiment and terror; imperial aggression and grandiloquence under Napoleon; a consolidation of both religion and monarchy under the ultra-reactionary Charles X; before a further revolution established a more genial figure on the throne, the bourgeois Louis-Philippe, in 1830 (the novel's action mostly takes place in the 1830s and 1840s). The period continued to be spattered with civilian blood, however, as the disenfranchised, often starving, failed to be included in the utilitarian drive for progress – manned by armies of bureaucrats and businessmen whose generals were members of Flaubert's hated bourgeoisie. By the 1850s, their leader had become an emperor, the farcical little Louis-Napoléon, who dissolved the Assembly in a bloody coup that left hundreds dead in the Paris streets. No wonder democracy, for Flaubert, felt sham; his retreat into his rural study and the creation of a fictive, parallel world was something of a survival technique.

Madame Bovary is, among many other things, a quest for meaning in which only one character searches; the others see no point in setting out, or believe they have already arrived. Part of Emma's plight is the elusiveness of that meaning: between episodes of stasis or '*immobilité*', she races from hedonism to self-denial, from country to town, from grisette-like freedom to bourgeois motherhood, from despair to faith, from charitable works to extravagant shopping sprees, just as she does from man to man. Early in her marriage, she endeavours 'to find out what precisely was meant in life by the words *delight*, *passion* and *intoxication*, which had seemed so beautiful to her in books'.

Her impossible reverie is to be free and happy in a painted backdrop that is always elsewhere – Italy, for preference. Yet these reveries are themselves manufactured – cheap, hand-me-down versions that she fails to evaluate as fraudulent. She is an embedded product of her culture, as helpless in that guise as the ancient, work-crippled farm servant shuffling in front of the Agricultural Show's worthies. And yet few characters in fiction feel more real to us than Emma Bovary, endlessly evoked since in other media, including those Flaubert would have deemed 'vulgar'.

While taking her fate into her own hands[4] and embarking on daring affairs, Emma lacks the superhuman force needed to break free imaginatively from a world in which women were relegated to roles dictated by men (and it was almost impossible for middle-class women to go out and work); the novel has three 'Madame Bovary', after all – each nominally subsumed. When Emma briefly flirts with bohemianism in the streets of Rouen, she feels disgusted, even fearful. For a provincial woman like Emma, a farmer's daughter who dislikes the countryside

---

[4] She does so in a very different and more plausible way to, say, the remarkable and headstrong Magdalen of Wilkie Collins's *No Name* (1862).

yet does not know the town, this would mean an inevitable slide towards social rejection, prostitution and death.

A moment of genuine insight comes in the chateau at Vaubyessard, the apogee of her social pretensions, when she recalls her widowed father (one of the few sympathetic characters) on the family farm, and the simple sensuousness of her lost existence. The register, for once, is not ironic, but touching: it is set brilliantly at the very moment it seems furthest off, against a window (a central leitmotif in the novel) that has just been shattered by a servant to let in the night air on a stifling ballroom.[5] Yet there is never any implication that she has somehow strayed from her natural milieu, as a conventional novelist might have suggested; instead, her memory remains a painful emotional truth, a shard of loss made more poignant by its context, and from which she is separated by the 'lightning-flashes' of the present.

This truth certainly fails to save Emma, exiled from herself as much as from the 'imbecilic petty burghers' or the 'tedium' of her surroundings – which are not only cultural, but stickily physical: her rendezvous with Rodolphe survives on her footwear in the form of mud which, when the servant-boy Justin longingly reaches for the boots to clean them, 'came off in powder under his fingers, and which he would watch gently rising in a beam of sunlight'. It is a very rare writer who can combine illicit sex, a boyish crush, precise observation, time's merciless passage and lyrical beauty in a single image: Shakespeare comes to mind.

'I am pledged to contradictory ideals!' the author complained to George Sand in 1869, '*living* is a métier for which I am not cut out!' Emma, had she a more articulate insight, might well have cried the same. Yet she acts her various roles – daughter, wife, mother, housewife, secretary, lover, bohemian – to perfection, at least briefly (her failure to feel maternal love for more than short bursts is perhaps the most painful thread in the book); even her cultural accomplishments – drawing, playing the piano – make Charles marvel. The realism of the novel includes its emotional truth: Flaubert's understanding of

---

[5] On writing the first lines of the novel, Flaubert wrote to Louise Colet: 'This is my third attempt. It's high time I succeeded or jumped out of the window.'

human nature is not only complex but, for all his grumpiness and bluster, deeply compassionate; Emma is no material for a sympathetic heroine, but in keeping her true to herself and her situation, Flaubert renders her fate not only moving, but genuinely shocking.

One of Emma's difficulties is that life itself is not conveniently categorised into genres or registers, high, middling or low, but is a dishevelled entity on which we struggle to impose order; it may travel in one direction (Flaubert's 'geometrical straight line'), but it is continually disrupted by dissonant elements, and confused by the interpenetration of the subjective and the objective. Even the performance of a great romantic opera barely holds its own against the whiff of gas and bad breath, a husband's clumsiness, or inward feelings of worthlessness heightened by the bright stage romance and its inflated characters.

As for direct dialogue, which like most novelists Flaubert found especially challenging and which he crucially reserved for key scenes, it becomes as much about a failure to communicate as an occasional penetration of solitude (Emma is lonely as well as bored). The characters hear what they want to hear, or mishear, or do not listen at all: Emma's spiritually anguished conversation with the priest being the clearest example: 'You are troubled? . . . doubtless that's the digestion.' In the celebrated scene in the Agricultural Show, in which Rodolphe's seduction of Emma in stock phrases is comically interspersed with the equally stock phrases ('For good general husbandry!') of the farming prizes, Flaubert's collage technique empties both of meaning, reduces both to simple techniques of persuasion and oppression.

Everywhere in the novel, then, the exquisitely conjured physicality of ordinary life at a particular historical moment is ready to deflate human pretension and roughen its frail hopes, just as Flaubert's breathtaking descriptions – whether of Rouen's dawn cityscape or a door's latch-bar knocking a wall – allow us to marvel at the closing gap between words and things; at the miraculous and, finally, the salving possibilities of art.

Adam Thorpe
Nîmes, June 2011

A NOTE ON THE
TRANSLATION

I WAS LUCKY ENOUGH TO FIND a battered copy of the two-volume first edition (Michel Lévy, 1857) with the characteristic typos of the first printing. It was affordable only because a page had been torn out, I presume by the reader who had scrawled '*oeuvre immorale*' ('immoral work') with a quill pen on its flyleaf. The missing page described the senile Duc de Laverdière, bedder of queens (pp.45–46 of the present edition): particularly upsetting for a royalist.

Alongside this magical relic, I have used the modern edition edited by Jacques Neef (Le Livre de Poche, 1999), which is based on the so-called 'definitive edition' (Charpentier, 1873), and draws on Claudine Gothot-Mersch's magisterial critical edition (Garnier, 1971). It has long been recognised that the punctuation of the first edition is often clearer and suppler. Alexander Spiers's celebrated *General English and French Dictionary* (Paris, 1853) has been my stalwart desk-companion.

The peculiar difficulties that *Madame Bovary* presents for the translator include the author's fondness for the imperfect tense, varying levels of pastiche, and his habit of extending a certain lexical field (legal, military, etc) through a whole paragraph;[1] any translation has to be alert to changes of nuance and tone that are micrometrically calibrated, as well as the changing shades of irony, and attempt to find an equivalent for Flaubert's verbal mimicry of wordless states or experiences.[2]

This last is part of Flaubert's complex music: what he referred to

---

[1] See, for instance, the accounting vocabulary on p.103: 'So she carried over to him . . .'
[2] A striking example being the waltz scene on p.49, when the words blur and all but decompose as Emma is whirled: '*Ils tournaient: tout tournaient autour d'eux . . .*' See also the blending of palm ('*paume*') and 'pommel' ('*pomme*') when Emma cools her hands on the iron firedogs after refreshing her hot cheeks (p.21).

as 'style'. No novel, except perhaps Joyce's *Finnegans Wake*, has been more carefully composed at the level of sound and rhythm: the action seems to seep from the words themselves, and in real time (when Flaubert occasionally lapses into the present, it is not the historical present used by Dickens).

I made two decisions before embarking on this task some three years ago: that I would track the original syntax wherever possible (without producing 'translationese') in order to preserve its pressure, weight and balance; and that I would only use pre-1857 vocabulary and expressions. To avoid the feeling of period pastiche, my principal models were Henry James and early James Joyce, both later than Flaubert but best corresponding, in my view, to the modernity of his style.

My reasons for keeping strictly within the period lexicon are various, the most important being that the novel's startling or even shocking nature can only be appreciated when placed back in its own context. If we cannot hope to read this reverberating masterpiece with purely nineteenth-century eyes, that furious '*oeuvre immorale*', scratched on the flyleaf, urges us to honour the attempt.

ACKNOWLEDGMENTS

MY GRATEFUL THANKS TO LAURA Hassan, my editor at Random House, for her patience and support, and to her assistant Frances MacMillan; to Alison Samuel for her remarkable close-reading editorial work – and without whose suggestions and corrections this translation would have been much the poorer; and to Alison Hennessy and the original instigator of the project, Liz Foley. Numerous people have provided encouragement and untied knots at various critical moments: these include Jean-Louis Habert, David Owen, Niek Miedema, Bernard Péchon, Patricia and Laurent Decornet, Simon Elmes, Julian Barnes, Anne-Marie Privat, Corinne Pinferi, Robert Chandler, my late father Barney Thorpe, my daughter Anastasia Thorpe and my tireless agent Lucy Luck. Finally, a special thank you to my wife Jo Wistreich for putting up with Emma for so long and with such tolerance, and for seeing her through.

PART ONE

PART ONE

WE WERE IN STUDY-HOUR, WHEN the Headmaster entered, followed by a *new boy* dressed in his everyday clothes and by a classroom servant carrying a big desk. Those who were asleep woke up, and each of us rose as if caught working.

The Headmaster nodded at us to resume our seats; then, turning to the usher:

'Monsieur Roger,' he said to him in a near-whisper, 'here is a pupil I entrust to you, he will start in the fifth class. If his work and behaviour are deserving, he may go *up to the seniors*, as befits his age.'

Remaining in the corner, behind the door, so much so that we could scarcely make him out, the *new boy* was a country lad, about fifteen years of age, and taller than any of us. His hair was cut straight across the forehead, like a village cantor, and he looked sound enough and exceedingly embarrassed. He was not broad-shouldered, but his short green woollen coat with its black buttons must have been tight at the armpits and revealed, through the slits in the back of its cuffs, red wrists used to being exposed. His legs, in blue stockings, emerged from yellowish trousers hitched up tight by the braces. He was wearing stout shoes, poorly polished and studded with nails.

We started reciting our lessons. He was all ears, as if attending to a sermon, not daring even to cross his legs or lean on his elbow, and when the bell went, at two o'clock, he had to be alerted by the usher to join us as we lined up.

It was our trick, on coming into class, to toss our caps on the floor so as to have our hands freer afterwards; right from the doorway, you had to hurl them under the bench, so that they hit the wall and made lots of dust: that was the *thing*.

But, whether he had failed to notice this stratagem or had not dared succumb to it, when prayers were over the *new boy* was still holding his cap on his lap. It was one of those composite types of headdress, which hints at bearskin, chapka,[1] round hat, otterskin hat and cotton bonnet; one of those sorry contraptions whose dumb ugliness has certain expressive depths, like the face of an imbecile. Egg-shaped and bulging with whalebone, it began with three circular sausage-shapes; then came alternate lozenges of velvet and rabbit-skin separated from each other by a red band, followed by a sort of bag ending in a pasteboard polygon covered with a complicated piece of braid, and from which hung, at the end of a long and too-slender string, a little criss-cross of gold thread by way of a tassel. It was brand-new; the peak shone.

'Stand up,' said the teacher.

He stood up; his cap fell off. The whole class started to laugh.

He bent down to retrieve it. A neighbour made it fall with a jab of the elbow, he picked it up yet again.

'Do get rid of your helmet,' said the teacher, who was a witty fellow.

A loud burst of laughter from the pupils disconcerted the poor boy, so much so that he had no idea whether he should keep hold of his cap, leave it on the floor or put it on his head. He sat down again and placed it on his lap.

'Stand up,' resumed the teacher, 'and tell me your name.'

The *new boy* pronounced, mumbling, an unintelligible name.

'Again!'

The same mumble of syllables could be heard, showered with hoots from the class.

'Louder!' the master shouted, 'louder!'

The *new boy*, coming then to a drastic decision, opened an enormous mouth and hurled forth at the top of his voice, as if calling out for someone, this word: *Charbovari*.

A roar shot up, rose in a *crescendo* on bursts of high-pitched shrieks (we yelled, we barked, we stamped our feet, we repeated: *Charbovari! Charbovari!*), then kept itself going on single notes, dying down with great difficulty, only to revive at times all of a sudden along a bench's row, where it gushed forth here and there in a stifled laugh, like an ill-snuffed firework.

Nevertheless, beneath a rain of extra lines, order was restored bit by bit in the classroom, and the teacher, managing to understand the name Charles Bovary by having it dictated, spelt out and reread, ordered the poor devil to go and sit on the idlers' bench, at the foot of the rostrum. He started to move, but, before heading off, hesitated.

'What are you looking for?' asked the teacher.

'My ca . . .' said the new boy, casting worried eyes around him.

'Five hundred lines for the whole class!' – delivered in a furious voice – quelled, like the *Quos ego*,[2] a new squall. 'So now keep quiet!' the indignant teacher continued, and wiping his forehead with a handkerchief that he had just drawn from beneath his headpiece: 'As for you, *new boy*, you will copy out for me, twenty times, the verb *ridiculus sum*.'[3]

Then, in a softer voice, 'Well now, you'll find your cap, it hasn't been stolen.'

All calmed down once more. Heads bent to books and for two hours the *new boy* behaved in an exemplary fashion, even if, from time to time, the odd paper pellet launched from a pen nib splattered his face. But he wiped himself with his hand, and remained completely still, eyes cast down.

In the evening, at study-time, he pulled his sleeve-guards from his desk, set his little pile of belongings in order, painstakingly ruled his paper. We could see him working hard, looking up every word in the dictionary and going to great trouble. Thanks, no doubt, to the willingness he showed, he avoided dropping down a class; because, though he knew his rules of grammar tolerably well, he had scarce any elegance in his turn of phrase. It was his village priest who had started him in Latin; his parents, for reasons of thrift, sending him to college only at the last possible moment.

His father, Monsieur Charles-Denis-Bartholomé Bovary, former assistant-surgeon-major, compromised around 1812 in some conscription scandal and forced at about that time to leave the service, had then turned his personal attractions to advantage by grabbing as it passed a dowry of sixty thousand francs, which presented itself in the shape of a bonnet merchant's daughter, who had fallen in love with his bearing. A handsome man, boastful, loudly ringing his spurs, sporting side whiskers that met his moustache, fingers forever bristling with rings, dressed in gaudy colours, he had the look of a gallant, with the facile gusto of a commercial traveller. Once he was married, he spent two or three years living off his wife's fortune, dining well, rising late, smoking large porcelain pipes, coming back in the evening only after the theatre and forever in and out of the cafés. The father-in-law died and left hardly a thing; he was furious, launched out *into fabrics*, lost some money there, then retired to the country, where he wished to *exploit the land*. But, as he knew scarcely more about cultivation than about printed calico, and rode his horses rather than turning them out to plough, drank his cider in bottles rather than selling it in the cask, ate the finest poultry from his yard and greased his hunting boots with the lard of his pigs, he soon saw that it would be better to give up all speculation.

Averaging two hundred francs a year, he then found, on the borders of the Caux and Picardy country, a dwelling that was a kind of half-farm, half-mansion; and – despondent, gnawed by regrets, blaming the heavens and envious of everyone – he shut himself up from the age of forty-five, disgusted by men, as he put it, and determined to live in peace.

His wife had doted on him once upon a time; she had loved him with innumerable cringings[4] that had weaned him from her all the more. Previously cheerful, out-going and entirely loving, on growing older she had (in the way a stale wine turns vinegary) become testy, screechy, nervous. She had suffered so, without at first complaining, when she saw him running after all the village strumpets and that a score of disreputable places sent him back to her in the evening, worn out with pleasures and reeking of drunkenness! Then her pride had revolted. So she had kept quiet, swallowing her rage in a mute stoicism that she kept to the day she died. She was endlessly out shopping and on business. She went to the solicitors' office, to the tribunal president, remembered to settle bills, won delays; and, at the house, she ironed, sewed, laundered, watched over the workers, settled the memorandums; so much so that, without worrying about a thing, Monsieur, perpetually benumbed in a sullen stupor from which he only stirred to say unkind words to her, stayed puffing in the chimney corner, hawking on the cinders.

When she bore a child, it had to be put out to a wet nurse. Returned home, the brat was spoilt like a prince. His mother fed him jams; his father let him run around without shoes, and, acting the philosopher, even said that he could go about naked, like the young of animals. To counter any maternal leanings, he had in his head a certain virile ideal of childhood by which he endeavoured to mould his son, wanting him to be brought up the hard way, in the Spartan manner, to give him a sound constitution. He sent him to bed without a fire, taught him to take great swigs of rum and to insult the church processions. But, being naturally easy-going, the child responded poorly to his efforts. His mother was always dragging him after her; she would cut up pasteboard boxes for him, tell him stories, converse with him in unending monologues, full of melancholic gaieties and babbling blandishments. In the loneliness of her life, she transferred onto this child's head all her scattered, broken vanities. She dreamed of high positions, she saw him as already tall, handsome, witty, established in civil engineering or in the magistracy. She taught him to read, and even, on an old piano of hers, to sing two or three sentimental ballads. But, to all this, Monsieur Bovary, who cared little for the arts, objected that it *was not worth it!* Would they ever have what was needed to support him at a government school, buy him a practice or a business? *Besides, if he has the cheek, a fellow always succeeds in the world.* Madame Bovary bit her lip, and the child roamed the village.

He followed the ploughmen and, with clods of earth, would drive off the crows that flew away. He ate blackberries all along the ditches, kept watch over the turkeys with a stick, tossed the hay at harvest, ran in the woods, played hopscotch in the church porch on rainy days, and, during the main festivals, would beg the verger to let him ring the bells, so that he could hang full length from the great rope and feel its peals carry him away.

And he shot up like an oak. He acquired strong hands, a healthy bloom.

When he was twelve, his mother was finally allowed to start him on his studies. They assigned these to the priest. But the lessons were so brief and so poorly followed, that they could serve little purpose. They were given at spare moments, in the sacristy, standing up, in a rush, between a baptism and a burial; or else the priest would send for his pupil after the evening Angelus, if he had not to go out. You went up to his room, you settled down: the midges and the moths swirled around the tallow. It was hot, the child fell asleep; and the old fellow, dozing off with his hands on his belly, was soon snoring, mouth agape. At other times, when Monsieur le Curé, returning from giving the eucharist to some sick person or other in the neighbourhood, spotted Charles up to mischief in the open fields, he would call him over, give him a good talking-to for a quarter of an hour and use the opportunity to make him conjugate his verbs at the foot of a tree. Rain would come to interrupt them, or an acquaintance passing by. Yet he was always pleased with him, even saying that the *young fellow* had an ample memory.

Charles could not stop there. Madame was insistent. Ashamed, or weary rather, Monsieur yielded without resistance, and they waited one more year until the boy had made his first communion.

Another six months went by; and, the following year, Charles was sent for good to school in Rouen, taken there personally by his father, towards the end of October, at the time of the Saint-Romain fair.

It would be impossible now for any of us to remember a thing about him.[5] He was an even-tempered boy, who played at break-time, worked in the study-hour, listened in class, sleeping well in the dormitory and eating well in the refectory. He had a wholesale ironmonger in the Rue Ganterie as guardian, who took him out once a month, on Sundays, after his shop was shut, would send him off to walk around the harbour to look at the boats, then take him back to school as soon as it was seven o'clock, before supper. Each Thursday evening, he wrote a long letter to his mother using red ink and three bars of sealing wax; then he would go over his history exercise books, or read an old volume of *Anacharsis*[6] lying about in the school-room. On walks, he chatted with the servant, who was from the country just like him.

By dint of application, he always remained around the middle of the class; once, he even gained a first certificate of merit in natural history. But at the end of his fourth year, his parents took him out of school to have him study medicine, convinced that he could make his own way up to the baccalauréat.

His mother chose a room for him, on the fourth floor, along the Eau-de-Robec, with a dyer of her acquaintance. She concluded the arrangements for his board and lodging, bought some furniture, a table and two chairs, had an old cherrywood bed sent from home, and in addition bought a little cast-iron stove, with a supply of wood to keep her poor child warm. Then she left at the end of the week, after innumerable recommendations to behave well, now that he was to be left to his own devices.

The curriculum, which he read on the noticeboard, made him feel giddy: lectures in anatomy, lectures in pathology, lectures in physiology, lectures in pharmacology, lectures in chemistry, in botany, and in clinical and therapeutic medicine, not to mention hygiene and *materia medica*, all names of whose etymologies he was ignorant and which were like so many sanctuary doors full of august shades.

He understood nothing; he listened in vain, he did not grasp it. Yet he worked, he had well-bound notebooks, he would follow all the lectures, he missed not a single ward round. He performed his little daily task like a mill horse, that turns on the same spot blindfold, ignorant of what it is crushing.

To spare him expense, his mother sent him, each week, by messenger, a piece of roast veal, on which he would breakfast in the morning, when he returned from the hospital, all the while beating his feet against the wall to warm them. Then he had to run to classes, to the amphitheatre, to the hospice, and come back home, right across town. In the evening, after his landlord's meagre dinner, he went up again to his room and got back down to work, in wet clothes that steamed on his body, before the glowing stove.

On beautiful summer evenings, when the warm streets are empty and the servant girls play battledore on the front step, he would open the window and lean on his elbows. The river,[7] which made a vile little

Venice of this area of Rouen, flowed below, right beneath him, yellow, violet or blue between its bridges and its railings. Workers, crouched by the edge, washed their arms in the water. On poles protruding from the lofts, hanks of cotton dried in the open air. Opposite, beyond the rooves, the great pure sky stretched, with a red setting sun. How good it must be over there! How cool under the beech grove! And he opened his nostrils wide to breathe in the good smells of the countryside, which did not reach him.

He thinned out, he grew taller, and his face took on a sort of doleful expression which made it almost interesting.

Naturally, out of indolence, he began to release himself from all the resolutions he had made. Once, he skipped a ward round, the next day his lecture, and, savouring the laziness, little by little, returned there no more.

He became a tavern-regular, developing a passion for dominoes. Shutting himself up every evening in a squalid public bar, tapping the little black-dotted sheep-bones on marble tables, seemed to him a precious act of liberty, which gave him back his self-esteem. It was his initiation into the world, his admittance into forbidden pleasures; and, on entering, he would place his hand upon the door-knob with a joy that was almost sensual. Then a lot of things that were squeezed in him began to expand; he learnt little songs by heart that he sang at the initiation drinks, was infatuated with Béranger,[8] learnt how to make punch and knew what love was at last.

Thanks to these preparatory labours, he completely failed his medical officer's exam. They were waiting for him that very evening at the house to celebrate his success!

He set off on foot and stopped at the entrance to the village, where he sent for his mother, told her everything. She forgave him, shifting blame onto the unfairness of the examiners, and stiffened his resolve a little, taking it upon herself to sort things out. It was another five years before Monsieur Bovary knew the truth; it was hoary old news, he accepted it, not being able to imagine, anyway, that his male issue could be a dunce.

So Charles went back to work and revised for his exams without

10

a break, learning all the questions in advance by heart. He passed with quite a good mark. What a wonderful day for his mother! They gave a huge dinner.

Where would he go to practise his skills? To Tostes. There was only an old doctor there. For a long time Madame Bovary had been on the watch for his death, and the gentleman had not yet turned up his toes when Charles was installed opposite, as his successor.

But it was not enough to have raised her son, to have had him study medicine and to have found a practice for him in Tostes: he needed a wife. She found him one: the widow of a Dieppe bailiff, who was forty-five and worth twelve hundred livres a year.

Although she was ugly, thin as a rake and pimply as a goose, it has to be said that Madame Dubuc did not lack for choice when it came to a match. To achieve her ends, Mère Bovary had to oust them all, and she foiled – and very skilfully too – the intrigues of a pork butcher who was backed by the priests.

Charles had dimly envisaged in the marriage the advent of a better life, imagining that he would be freer and could have at his disposal her person and her money. But his wife was the master; in front of people he must say this, must not say that, had to abstain from meat on Fridays, dress as she thought fit, harass on her instructions those clients who were not settling up. She unsealed his letters, spied on his every move, and put her ear to the partition wall as he was giving consultations in his surgery, when there were women.

She must have her hot chocolate every morning, and his never-ending attentions. She would complain ceaselessly of her nerves, her chest, her fluids. The noise of footsteps gave her pains; you went away, and the solitude grew hateful to her; you came back to her side, and it was to watch her die, no doubt. In the evening, when Charles returned, she produced her long, scrawny arms from under the sheet, slipped them around his neck, and, having made him sit on the edge of the bed, set about telling him her sorrows: he was forgetting her, he loved another! People had indeed told her she would be unhappy; and she ended up asking him for a syrup for her health and a little bit more love.

II

ONE NIGHT, AT ABOUT ELEVEN o'clock, they were woken by the noise of a horse which stopped just in front of the door. The maid opened the attic skylight and argued things over for some time with the man still down below, in the street. He had come looking for a doctor; he had a letter. Nastasie descended the steps shivering, and went to open the lock and slip the bolts, one after the other. The man left his horse and, following the maid, appeared behind her all of a sudden. From his grey-tasselled cotton bonnet he pulled out a letter wrapped in a piece of rag, and daintily presented it to Charles, who leaned his elbow on the pillow to read it. Nastasie, near the bed, held the light. Madame, out of a sense of decency, stayed with her back turned, facing the wall.

This letter, sealed with a little seal of blue wax, begged Monsieur Bovary to go immediately to the farm at Les Bertaux, to set a broken leg. Now, between Tostes and Les Bertaux, there are a good eighteen miles to cross, by way of Longueville and Saint-Victor. The night was black. Madame Bovary the younger was fearful of accidents befalling her husband. So it was decided that the stable boy should set off first. Charles would leave three hours later, when the moon rose. They would send a child to meet him, in order to show him the way to the farm and open the gates ahead.

At about four o'clock, Charles, wrapped up well in his cloak, set off for Les Bertaux. Still drowsy from the warmth of sleep, he let himself be lulled by the peaceful trot of his beast. Whenever it stopped of its own accord before those thorn-wreathed holes they dig on the boundaries of ploughed fields, Charles, waking up with a start, would remember the broken leg, and endeavour to remind himself of all the fractures he knew. The rain was no longer falling; day was breaking, and, on the leafless apple trees, the birds stayed motionless, ruffling their little feathers in the cold morning wind. The flat country stretched out as far as the eye could see, and the clumps of trees around the farms made, at rare intervals, deep violet patches on this vast grey surface that fused at the horizon with the gloomy tint of the sky. Charles, from time to time, opened his eyes; then, his mind wearying and sleep returning of its own accord, he soon slipped into a kind of slumber where, his recent feelings merging with his memories, he perceived himself in duplicate, both student and married man, lying in his bed as he had been just now, crossing an operating room as in the past. The hot smell of poultices blended in his head with the fresh scent of the dew; he heard the beds' iron rings trundling on their curtain-rods and his wife sleeping . . . As he came through Vassonville, he noticed, on the edge of a ditch, a young boy seated on the grass.

'Are you the doctor?' the child asked.

And, at Charles's reply, he took his clogs in his hands and began to run ahead.

Along the way, the medical officer[9] understood from the chatter of his guide that Monsieur Rouault must be among the better-off farmers. He had broken a leg, the evening before, on his way back from a Twelfth Night revel at a neighbour's house. His wife had been dead two years. He had only his *young lady* with him, who helped him keep house.

The ruts grew deeper. He was approaching Les Bertaux. The little lad, slipping through a hole in a hedge, vanished, then reappeared at the bottom of a courtyard to open the gate. The horse slipped on the wet grass; Charles ducked down to pass under the branches. The guard dogs barked in a kennel, tugging on their chain. When he entered Les Bertaux, his horse took fright and shied.

It was a fine-looking farm. In the stables, through the open upper doors, heavy plough horses could be seen, feeding calmly from new racks. An ample muck-heap stretched the length of the buildings; steam rose from it, and, among the hens and turkey cocks, five or six peacocks pecked about on top, a luxury of Caux farmyards. The sheepfold was long, the barn was high, its walls smooth as your hand. Inside the shed were two large carts and four ploughs, with their whips, their chains, their full harness, whose blue wool fleeces were being soiled by the fine dust that fell from the haylofts. The yard sloped upwards, planted with evenly spaced trees, and the happy chatter of a gaggle of geese rang out by the pond.

A young woman, in a blue merino dress trimmed with three flounces, appeared at the door of the house to receive Monsieur Bovary, whom she showed into the kitchen, where a great fire blazed. The servants' meal bubbled around it, in little pots of uneven size. Wet clothes were drying in the chimney's recess. The fire-shovel, tongs and bellows, all of massive proportions, shone like polished steel, while along the walls stretched a copiousness of coppers and pans, in which the clear flame of the fireplace glittered unevenly, mingling with the sun's first gleams arriving through the panes.

Charles went up to the first floor, to see the patient. He found him in his bed, sweating under the covers and having tossed his cotton bonnet a fair distance. He was a fat little man of fifty, white-skinned, blue-eyed, bald at the front, and wearing earrings. At his side, on a chair, he had a large carafe of brandy, which he poured for himself now and again to buck himself up; but, as soon as he saw the doctor, his intense excitement dropped away, and instead of cursing, as he had been doing for the last twelve hours, he began to moan feebly.

It was a simple fracture, with no complications whatsoever. Charles could not have hoped for anything easier. So, recalling how his teachers behaved at the bedside of the injured, he comforted the patient with all sorts of kindly words, surgical endearments that are like the oil with which they lubricate the scalpels. For the splints, a bundle of laths was fetched from the cart-shed. Charles chose one of them, cut it into pieces and polished it with a sliver of glass pane, while the maidservant ripped up sheets to make bandages, and Mademoiselle Emma endeavoured to sew some pads. As she took a long time to find her box, her father grew impatient; she said nothing in reply; but, while sewing, she kept pricking her fingers, that she would then bring to her mouth to suck.

Charles was surprised by the whiteness of her nails. They were glossy, fine at the tips, buffed more thoroughly than the ivories of Dieppe,[10] and almond-shaped. Yet her hand was not beautiful, not pale enough perhaps, the knuckles a little dry; it was too long as well, and its outline had no soft curves. What was beautiful about her, was her eyes; although they were brown, her lashes made them appear black, and her glance reached you candidly with a guileless daring.

Once the dressing was done, the doctor was invited, by Monsieur Rouault himself, to *take a bite* before he left.

Charles went down into the ground-floor room. Two places had been set with silver goblets on a little table, at the foot of a great canopied fourposter bed covered in calico printed with characters representing Turks. A smell of iris-root and damp sheets could be detected, escaping from the tall oaken wardrobe, facing the window. On the floor, in the corners, placed upright, stood sacks of corn. They were the overflow from the nearby barn, which was reached by three stone steps. For decoration, hooked onto a nail in the middle of the wall whose green paint was being lifted by the saltpetre, the room had a head of Minerva in black pencil, gilt-framed, and which bore at the bottom, written in Gothic lettering: 'To my dear papa.'

The talk at first was of the invalid, then of the weather, of the hard winters, of the wolves that roam the fields at night. Mademoiselle Rouault did not really enjoy herself in the countryside, above all now that she was in almost sole charge of the farm's affairs. As the room was chilly, she shivered as she ate, revealing something of her full lips, which she had a habit of nibbling at in her silent moments.

Her neck emerged from a white, turndown collar. Her black hair, so smooth that its two bandeaux[11] each seemed to be of a single piece, was separated in the middle by a fine parting, that sank slightly along the curve of the skull; and, leaving the tip of the ear scarcely visible, it eventually coalesced behind in a thick chignon, with a flowing movement around the temples, which the country doctor noticed there for the first time in his life. Her cheeks were pink. She wore, like a man, slipped between two buttons of her blouse, a tortoiseshell lorgnon.

When Charles, after going up to say farewell to Père Rouault, came back into the room before leaving, he found her on her feet, forehead against the window, and looking into the garden, where the poles for the runner beans had been blown over by the wind. She turned round.

'Are you looking for something?' she asked.

'My riding crop, please,' he replied.

And he started to ferret about on the bed, behind the doors, under the chairs; it had fallen on the floor, between the sacks and the wall. Mademoiselle Emma spotted it; she leaned over the sacks of corn. Charles, out of gallantry, rushed forward and, as he was also stretching his arm out in the same movement, he felt his chest brush against the back of the young woman, bent under him. Blushing, she straightened up and looked at him over her shoulder, handing him his lashed whip.[12]

Instead of returning to Les Bertaux in three days' time, as he had promised her, he came back the very next day, then consistently twice a week, not counting the surprise visits he made from time to time, as if by accident.

As for the rest, it all went well; the healing proceeded according to the rulebook, and when, at the end of forty-six days, Père Rouault was seen trying to walk on his own in his *barton-yard*,[13] they began to consider Monsieur Bovary as a man of great abilities. Père Rouault said that he would not have had better treatment from the leading doctors of Yvetot or even of Rouen.

As for Charles, he never attempted to ask himself why coming to Les Bertaux was so pleasurable. Had he considered it, he would no doubt have attributed his zeal to the seriousness of the case, or perhaps to the advantage he was hoping to draw from it. Was that really why his visits to the farm were, among the meagre occupations of his life, such a delightful exception? On those days he rose early, left at a gallop, rode his animal hard, then dismounted to wipe his feet on the grass, slipping on his black gloves before entering. He liked to see himself arrive in the yard, to feel the gate against his shoulder as it opened, and the cock crowing on the wall, the boys coming to meet him. He liked the barn and the stables; he liked Père Rouault, who would clap him on the palm and call him his saviour; he liked Mademoiselle Emma's little clogs on the kitchen's scrubbed flags; the raised heels made her taller, and, when she walked in front of him, the wooden soles, coming up swiftly, slapped with a sharp snap against the boot leather.

She would always escort him down to the bottom of the front steps. If they had not yet brought his horse, she would stay there. Their adieus had been said, there was no more talking; the open air wrapped her about, lifting pell-mell her neck's little downy hairs, or tossing the apron's ties at her hip, making them writhe like streamers. One time, during a thaw, the trees' bark oozed in the yard, the snow melted on the rooves of the buildings. She was on the threshold; she went to look for her parasol; she opened it. The parasol, of dapple-grey silk, which the sun penetrated, lit the white skin of her face with a darting shimmer. She smiled beneath it at the balmy warmth; and the drops of water could be heard, one by one, falling upon the taut moire.

In the early days of Charles's visits to Les Bertaux, Madame Bovary junior made sure she kept herself informed about the invalid, and in the accounts book, that she kept by double-entry, she had even selected a fine white page for Monsieur Rouault. But when she learnt that he had a daughter, she made inquiries; and she learnt that Mademoiselle Rouault, brought up in a convent, with the Ursuline nuns, had received, as they say, *a good education*; that she was acquainted, as a consequence, with dancing, geography, drawing, could do needlework and play the piano. It was the last straw!

'So that's why,' she said to herself, 'he has such a beaming face when he goes to see her, and dresses in his new waistcoat, at the risk of spoiling it in the rain? Ah, that woman, that woman!'

And she detested her, instinctively. At first, she assuaged her feelings in hints; Charles did not catch on; then, by dint of casual remarks which he let pass for fear of a storm; finally, through outbursts at point-blank range to which he was at a loss for an answer. 'How is it that he kept returning to Les Bertaux, seeing that Monsieur Rouault was healed and these people had not yet paid up? Aha! It's because over there lay *a certain person*, someone who knew how to converse, an embroideress, a cultivated soul. There lay what he was partial to: so now he has to have the young ladies of the town!' And she went on:

'The daughter of Père Rouault, a young lady of the town! Indeed! Their grandfather was a shepherd, and they have a cousin who all but went on trial for a nasty thump, during a quarrel. Not worth her while cutting such a *dash*, nor exhibiting herself at Sunday church in a silk dress, acting the countess. Wretched fellow, moreover, who, without last year's rapeseed, would have been hard put to it to pay his arrears!'

Charles stopped going back to Les Bertaux, from sheer weariness. Héloïse made him swear that he would no longer go there, hand on his prayer book, after a great many sobs and kisses, in a vast explosion of love. So he obeyed; but the boldness of his desire protested against the slavishness of his behaviour, and, by a sort of innocent hypocrisy, he considered that this prohibition from seeing her gave him the right to love her.

And besides, could the widow rub away with her touch, the picture stuck to her husband's heart?[14] The widow was thin; she had long, hungry teeth;[15] all the year round she wore a little black shawl whose tip came down between her shoulder blades; her stiff waist was sheathed in dresses cut like a scabbard, too short, that revealed her ankles, with the straps of her broad shoes criss-crossing over grey stockings.

Charles's mother came to see them now and again; but, after a few days, the daughter-in-law seemed only to sharpen her on her own cutting-edge; and so, like two knives, they would be busy making little incisions in him with their remarks and observations. He was wrong to eat so much! Why always be offering a drop to the first arrival? What pigheadedness not to want to wear flannel!

It happened that at the beginning of spring, a solicitor of Ingouville, holder of widow Dubuc's assets, sailed off, on a favourable tide, taking with him all the money from his practice. It was true that Héloïse still owned, apart from a share in a boat valued at six thousand francs, her house in Rue Saint-François; and yet, of all this fortune that had been jangled so loudly in his ears, nothing, apart from bits of furniture and a few old togs, had appeared in the house. Matters had to be cleared up. The Dieppe house was found to be eaten by mortgages right down to the foundation piles; what she had placed with the solicitor, God alone knew, and the share in the boat came to no more than a thousand écus. So the good lady had lied! In his exasperation, Père Bovary, smashing a chair against the flags, accused his wife of bringing misery on their son by hitching him up to such a nag, whose harness wasn't worth the leather. They came to Tostes. Matters were discussed. There were scenes. Héloïse, in tears, throwing herself on her husband, entreated him to defend her from his parents. Charles tried to speak up for her. They took offence, and left.

But *the blow had been struck*. Eight days later, when hanging out the washing in her yard, she began to spit blood, and the following day, while Charles had his back turned to close the curtains, she said: 'Ah! my God!' – let out a sigh and fainted. She was dead! What a shock!

When all was over at the cemetery, Charles returned home. He found no one below; he went up to the first floor, into the bedroom, saw her dress still hanging at the foot of the alcove; then, leaning on the secretaire, he remained until the evening lost in a sorrowful dream. She had loved him, after all.

III

ONE MORNING, PÈRE ROUAULT CAME bringing Charles the payment for his mended leg: seventy-five francs in forty-sou coins, and a turkey. He had learned of his calamity and consoled him as best he could.

'I know its nature!' he said, slapping him on the shoulder; 'I've been as you are, I have indeed! Upon losing my dear departed, I went into the fields to be all alone; I fell down by a tree, I wept, I called on the good Lord, I said foolish things to Him; I'd have rather been like the moles I saw up in the branches, with worms a-swarm in the belly, stone dead, in a word. And when I thought that others, at that very moment, were with their little missus and hugging her tight, I gave the earth some fair old thumps with my stick; I was well nigh mad, so much so that I no longer ate; the very thought of going alone to the café disgusted me, you wouldn't credit it. Ah well, very gradually, one day chasing out another, a spring after a winter and an autumn atop a summer, all that slipped past grain by grain, crumb by crumb; it all went away, it's gone, gone down, rather, for you'll always have something left at the bottom, as it were . . . a weight, there, on the chest! But, as that's everybody's lot, one can't be letting oneself waste away, and, just because others are dead, wishing to die oneself . . . You have to be shaking yourself up, Monsieur Bovary; it'll pass! Come and pay us a visit; my daughter thinks of you from time to time, I'll have you know, and she says as you've forgot her, just like that. Spring's around the corner; we'll have you shooting a wild rabbit up in the woods, to take your mind off matters a bit.'

Charles took his advice. He returned to Les Bertaux; he found everything as it was the day before, as it was five months ago, that is to say; the pear trees were already in flower, and old man Rouault, now up and about, kept coming and going, which made the farm livelier.

Believing it his duty to lavish as many courtesies as possible on the doctor, owing to his woeful situation, he urged him not to take off his hat, spoke to him in hushed tones, as though he had been ill, and even pretended to get angry over the fact that they had not prepared something for his benefit that was a little lighter than all the rest, such as some little cream pots or stewed pears. He told stories. Charles found himself laughing; but the memory of his wife, coming back to him all of a sudden, filled him with gloom. A coffee was brought to him; he thought no more of her.

He thought about her less, the more he grew used to living alone. The fresh charm of independence soon made solitude more bearable to him. Now he could change the times of his meals, come and go without giving a reason, and, when he was truly weary, stretch out with all four limbs, the full width, on his bed. So, he pampered and coddled himself, and accepted the consolations that he was offered. Furthermore, his wife's death had not served him so badly in his job, as for a whole month people kept saying: 'That poor young man! What a misfortune!' His name spread, his clientele increased; and then he would go to Les Bertaux without a qualm. He felt an aimless hope, a vague happiness; he would find his face more pleasant-looking when brushing his whiskers in the mirror.

He arrived one day at about three o'clock; everyone was in the fields; he entered the kitchen, but failed to spot Emma at first; the shutters were closed. Through the cracks in the wood, the sun stretched out its long thin rays on the flagstone floor, shattering against the corners of the furniture and trembling on the ceiling. Flies were climbing the length of the glasses left on the table, and buzzing as they drowned at the bottom, in the cider's dregs. The daylight that came down the chimney, giving a velvet sheen to the fireback's soot, turned the cold cinders slightly blue. Between the window and the hearth, Emma was sewing; she wore no shawl; you could see on her bare shoulders tiny drops of sweat.

As was the custom in the country, she offered him something to drink. He refused, she insisted, and finally suggested, laughing, that he have a glass of liqueur with her. So she went to fetch a bottle of curaçao from the cupboard, reached for two small glasses, filled one to the brim, poured scarce a drop in the other, and, having clinked glasses, brought it to her mouth. As it was almost empty, she leaned back to drink; and, head tipped up, lips pushed forward, neck tensed, she laughed that she could not taste a thing, while the tip of her tongue, slipping between her fine teeth, took little licks at the bottom of the glass.

She sat down and picked up her work again, a white cotton stocking that she was darning; she worked with her head down; she did not say a word, and neither did Charles. The draught, slipping in under the door, thrust a little dust onto the flags; he watched it creep along, and all he could hear was the inward throbbing of his head, with the cry of a hen, in the distance, laying its eggs in the yard. Emma, from time to time, would refresh her cheeks by pressing on them the palms of her hands, which she cooled again afterwards on the iron pommels of the massive firedogs.

She complained of being afflicted, since the start of the season, with dizzy spells; she asked if sea bathing might be helpful; she began to chat about the convent, Charles about his school, the phrases came easily. They went up to her room. She let him look at her old music notebooks, the little volumes she had been given as prizes and the crowns of oak-leaves, abandoned at the bottom of a wardrobe. She spoke to him again of her mother, of the cemetery, and even showed him the flower-bed in the garden from where she would pick blooms, every first Friday of each month, to place on her grave. But their gardener understood nothing; one was so badly served! She would have liked, even if it was only for the winter, to live in town, although perhaps the length of the fine days made the country even duller during the summer; – and, depending on what she was saying, her voice would be clear, high, or turn languid all of a sudden, would drawl in a sing-song that finished almost as a murmur, when she spoke of herself, now joyful, opening innocent eyes, now with lids half-closed, her gaze drowned in weariness, her thoughts wandering.

In the evening, on his return, Charles took up the phrases one after another that she had uttered, trying to recall them, to complement their meaning, in order to imagine the portion of existence she had lived through in the period when he had not yet known her. But he could never picture her in his thoughts, differently from how he had seen her the first time, or as she was when he had left her just now. Then he asked himself what would become of her, if she were to marry, and to whom? Alas! Père Rouault was very well off, and she! . . . so lovely! But Emma's face kept swimming back in front of his eyes, and something monotonous like the hum of a spinning top droned in his ears: 'If you were to marry, even so! If you were to marry!' At night, he could not sleep; his throat felt squeezed, he was thirsty; he got up to drink from his water-jug and opened the window; the sky was covered in stars, a warm wind was blowing, dogs barked from afar. He turned his head towards Les Bertaux.

Thinking that after all he had nothing to lose, Charles resolved to pop the question when the occasion offered itself; but, each time it offered itself, the fear of not finding the right words sealed his lips.

Père Rouault would not have been sorry to have been relieved of his daughter, who was scarce any use to him in the house. He excused her in his own heart, finding that she was too intelligent for cultivation, a calling cursed by heaven, as no millionaire ever came of it. Far from making his fortune, the old fellow made a loss every year; for, if he excelled at bargaining in the markets, where he relished the wiles of his trade, the actual farmwork, on the other hand – along with the day-to-day running of the property – suited him less than anyone. He did not readily take his hands out of his pockets, and spared no expense for anything that concerned his creature comforts, wanting to be well fed, well warmed and well tucked up. He loved rough cider, shoulders of mutton done rare, and properly-whipped coffees laced with brandy. He took his meals in the kitchen, alone, in front of the fire, on a little table that was carried to him all laid out, as in the theatre.

So as soon as he noticed that Charles's cheeks went rosy near his daughter, which meant that one of these days he would ask her to marry him, he chewed the whole matter over in advance. He certainly found him a bit of a *runt*, and not the son-in-law he would have wished for her; but they said he was steady, careful with money, well educated, and doubtless wouldn't be cavilling too much over the dowry. Now, seeing as Père Rouault was going to be forced to sell twenty-two acres of *his property*, that he owed a lot to his builder, to his saddle-maker, that the shaft on the cider-press needed replacing: 'If he asks me for her,' he said to himself, 'I'll give him her.'

At Michaelmas, Charles came to spend three days at Les Bertaux. The last day went by just like the previous days, as he deferred from one quarter of an hour to the next. Père Rouault went to see him off; they were walking in a sunken lane, they were about to separate; the moment had come. Charles gave himself as far as the corner of the hedge, and at last, when they had passed it:

'Maître Rouault,' he murmured, 'I would very much like to have a word with you.'

They stopped. Charles held his tongue.

'Let's hear all about it! Don't I know everything already?' said Père Rouault, laughing softly.

'Père Rouault . . . Père Rouault . . .' Charles stammered.

'I'd like nothing better,' the farmer went on. 'Though doubtless the little chit will be of like mind, we ought to ask her opinion of it. So you be off, then; I'll be heading back home. Listen close: if it's a yes, you won't need to come back, because of the other folk about, and, besides, that'll be too much for her. But so as you don't fret, I'll push the shutter wide open against the wall: you'll see it from the back, if you lean over the hedge.'

And he moved off.

Charles tethered his horse to a tree. He ran to position himself on the path; he waited. Half an hour went by, then he counted nineteen minutes by his watch. All of a sudden came a clap against the wall; the shutter had been thrown back, the catch was still trembling.

The next day he was up at the farm by nine o'clock. Emma blushed when he came in, all the while endeavouring to laugh a little, discomposed. Père Rouault embraced his future son-in-law. They put off discussing the settlement of assets; there was lots of time in hand, as the marriage could not decently take place before the end of the mourning period, in other words around the spring of next year.

Winter was spent in anticipation. Mademoiselle Rouault busied herself with her trousseau. A part of it was ordered from Rouen, and she made up nightgowns and nightcaps, following fashion drawings she had borrowed. During Charles's visits to the farm, they chatted about the wedding preparations; they wondered which room should host the feast; they dreamed of the number of dishes needed and what the entrées would be.

Emma had, on the contrary, wished to be married at midnight, by the light of flaming torches; but this idea baffled Père Rouault. So there would be a wedding, attended by forty-three guests, in which sixteen hours would be spent at table, to begin again on the morrow and a little more over the following days.

IV

THE GUESTS ARRIVED EARLY IN carriages, one-horse covered carts, two-wheeled pleasure cars, old hoodless gigs, spring carts with leather curtains, and the young folk of the nearest villages on dung carts in which they stood, in a row, hands resting on the stave-sides to stop themselves falling, trotting along and severely shaken about. They arrived there from thirty miles distant, from Goderville, from Normanville and from Cany. All the relations from both sides had been invited, quarrels patched up between friends, long-lost acquaintances written to.

From time to time, the crack of a whip could be heard from behind the hedge; shortly the gate would open; it was a cart coming in. Galloping right to the foot of the front steps, it would draw up abruptly and empty out its crowd who would issue forth from all sides, rubbing their knees and stretching their arms. The ladies, in bonnets, had town dresses, gold watch-chains, tippets with their crossed ends tucked into their belts, or little coloured fichus fastened at the back with a pin, revealing their necks from behind. The young lads, dressed identically to their fathers, seemed troubled by their new apparel (many that day were even breaking in their first-ever pair of boots); beside them could be seen, not breathing a word in her white communion robe let down for the occasion, some tall lass between fourteen and sixteen, no doubt their cousin or elder sister, red-faced, stupefied, hair greasy with rose pomade, and in great fear of soiling her gloves. As there were not enough stable boys to unyoke all the carriages, the gentlemen rolled up their sleeves and set to it themselves. In keeping with their differing social position, they had on dress coats, frock coats, jackets, cutaways: — best clothes, hemmed about with all the respect of a family, and which left the wardrobe only on formal occasions; frock coats with great skirts flapping in the wind, with cylindrical collars, with broad pockets like sacks; jackets of coarse cloth, that would generally accompany some cap or other with a brass rim on its visor; very short cutaways, with two buttons at the back set side by side like a pair of eyes, and whose panels seemed to have been cut straight from the same block, by a carpenter's axe. Several more still (but these, of course, had to dine at the bottom end of the table) wore formal smock-frocks; the type, that is to say, whose collar would be turned down on the shoulders, the back gathered in tiny folds and the waist attached very low down by a stitched belt.

And the shirts swelled out like breast-plates! Everyone was newly shorn, with stuck-out ears and heads cropped close; there were even some who, rising before dawn and not seeing clearly enough to shave, had diagonal gashes under the nose, or, along the jaw, flaps of skin as broad as a three-franc piece, and which the open air had inflamed along the way, marbling with little pink blotches all these huge, white, beaming faces.

The Mairie being a mile and a half from the farm, they went there on foot, and returned in the same manner, once the ceremony was accomplished at the church. The procession, close-knit at first in a single scarf of colour that fluttered in the fields along the narrow path snaking between the green corn, soon stretched out and divided itself into different groups, lingering to chat. The fiddler walked at its head, his violin's scroll adorned with ribbons; the newly-weds came next, then the relatives, then the friends any old how, and the children stayed at the back, having fun plucking the little bell-flowers off the oat stalks, or playing amongst themselves, without being seen. Emma's dress, too long, dragged a little at the hem; from time to time, she stopped to pull it up, and then delicately, with her gloved fingers, picked off the coarse grasses and tiny spears of thistle, while Charles, empty-handed, waited for her to finish. Père Rouault, a new silk hat on his head and the cuffs of his black coat covering his hands to the fingertips, gave his arm to Mère Bovary. As for Père Bovary, who, deeply contemptuous of all these types, had come simply in a military-style frock coat with a single row of buttons, he was babbling smoking-room gallantries to a blonde young peasant-girl. She nodded, blushed, had no idea what to reply. The remaining wedding guests chatted about business or played tricks behind each other's backs, excited in advance by the jollity; and, listening out, one could still hear the screaking of the fiddler who went on playing among the open fields. When he realised that they were far behind him, he stopped to catch his breath, rubbed his bow with rosin for a long while, so as to make the strings squeak better, and then set off again, lowering and raising the neck of his violin by turns to beat time correctly, for himself. The noise of the instrument chased the little birds from a long way away.

It was under the wide shelter of the cart-shed that the table had been laid out. Upon it were four sirloins, six chicken fricassées, some stewed veal, three shoulders of mutton, and, in the middle, a pretty roasted suckling pig, flanked by four dishes of chitterlings sprinkled with sorrel. On the corners stood decanters of brandy. The sweet bottled cider was urging its thick froth up around the corks, and all the glasses had been filled with wine to the brim. Great dishes of yellow cream, which swayed by themselves at the slightest knock of the table, displayed the initials of the newly-weds, drawn on their plain surfaces in arabesques of tiny comfits. A pâtissier from Yvetot had been sought for the tarts and nougat. As he was just starting out in the area, he had taken great pains; and he himself brought along a tiered wedding cake, for dessert, which made everyone cry out. The base, first of all, was a square of blue pasteboard featuring a temple with porticoes, colonnades and stucco statues all around, in niches spangled with stars of gilded paper; then, on the second tier, there stood a keep in Savoie cake, surrounded by minute fortifications in candied angelica, almonds, raisins, quartered oranges; and finally, on the uppermost shelf, which was a green meadow with rocks and lakes of jam and hazelnut boats, a little Cupid could be seen, playing on a chocolate swing, whose two posts were finished with two real rose buds, by way of balls, at the summit.[16]

They ate until the evening. When they were too tired to stay seated, they went for a stroll round the farmyards or to play a game of corks in the barn; then back to the table they came. Towards the end some fell asleep there, and snored. But at coffee-time everything revived; they broke into songs, they did feats of strength, they lifted weights, they ducked under their own thumbs, they tried to lift waggons onto their shoulders, they cracked coarse jokes, they kissed the ladies. In the evening, when it was time to leave, the horses, stuffed to the nostrils with oats, found it hard to pass between the shafts; they kicked, reared, broke the harness, their masters swore or laughed; and all night, by the light of the moon, by the country roads, carts swept along at full gallop, bouncing in the drainage ditches, leaping the pebble-stone heaps,[17] catching on banks, with women leaning out of the doors to grab the reins.

Those staying in Les Bertaux spent the night drinking in the kitchen. The children had fallen asleep under the benches.

The bride had begged her father that they should spare her the usual jests. Nevertheless, a wholesale fish merchant among their cousins (who had even brought along a pair of soles as a wedding present) started to blow water with his mouth through the keyhole, when Père Rouault arrived just in time to stop him, and explained that his son-in-law's important standing did not permit such improprieties. The cousin, however, had difficulty in going along with these excuses. Privately, he accused Père Rouault of being stuck-up, and went into a huddle with four or five other guests who, having accidentally received, several times running during the meal, the scraggier bits of meat, also deemed that they had been poorly entertained, whispered about their host and wished ruin on him in veiled terms.

Mère Bovary had not opened her lips the entire day. No one had consulted her on either the daughter-in-law's clothes, or the arrangements for the banquet; she retired early. Her husband, instead of following her, sent for cigars from Saint-Victor and smoked until daylight, all the while drinking kirsch grog, a mixture unknown to the present gathering, and which was the source of even greater respect for him.

Charles was not the jocular type, he had not shone during the wedding. He responded indifferently to the witticisms, puns, double-entendres, compliments and wanton words that others felt it their duty to let fly at him from the soup course on.

The next morning, on the other hand, he seemed like a new man. It was he, rather, who might have been taken for the virgin of the previous day, whereas the bride gave nothing away, by which she might have given rise to conjecture. Even the craftiest guests had no idea how to respond, and they studied her, when she passed close to them, straining their mental powers to the limit. But Charles hid nothing. He called her my wife, used the informal *tu* to her, asked her whereabouts of everyone, searched for her everywhere, and kept dragging her off into the farmyards, where he could be seen from afar, between the trees, his arm around her waist, continuing to walk half leaning on her, all the while ruffling his head against the lacy front of her bodice.

Two days after the wedding, the spouses left: Charles, because of his patients, could not absent himself for longer. Père Rouault had them taken back in his covered cart and acccompanied them himself as far as Vassonville. There, he kissed his daughter one last time, dismounted and retraced his steps. When he had gone around a hundred paces, he stopped, and, as he saw the cart leaving, its wheels turning in the dust, he let out a great sigh. Then he recalled his own wedding, the times past, his wife's first pregnancy; he was truly joyful, likewise, the day he brought her to his father's house, when she rode pillion with him, as they trotted over the snow; for it was around Christmas-time and the countryside was all white; she held on to him with one arm, her basket hanging from the other; the wind fluttered the long lacy ribbons of her Cauchoise head-dress, so that now and again they brushed against his mouth, and, when he turned his head, he saw close to him, upon his shoulder, her little rosy countenance silently smiling, under the gold badge of her bonnet. From time to time, to warm them up, she placed her fingers against his chest. How long ago all that was. Their son would be thirty, now! And he looked behind him: he saw nothing on the road. He felt as sad as an unfurnished house;[18] and, fond memories mingling with black thoughts in his mind dimmed by the junketing's fumes, he had a sudden longing to take a turn about the church. Yet, as he was afraid that this sight might make him sadder still, he went straight back home.

Monsieur and Madame Charles arrived at Tostes, towards six o'clock. The neighbours gathered at the windows to look at their doctor's new wife.

The old maid introduced herself, curtsied, apologised for the meal not being ready, and encouraged Madame, in the meantime, to become acquainted with her house.

V

THE BRICK FAÇADE WAS RIGHT on the line of the street, or rather the road. Behind the door hung a cloak with a little collar, a bridle, a black leather cap, and, in a corner, on the floor, was a pair of spatterdashes still covered in dry mud. To the right was the parlour, that is to say the room used for dining and sitting. A canary-yellow paper, set off at the top by a garland of wan flowers, shivered all over[19] on its badly-stretched canvas; white calico curtains, edged with red, overlapped each other across the windows, and on the narrow chimney-piece glistened a clock-faced head of Hippocrates, between two silver-plated lamp-holders under oval globes. On the other side of the corridor lay Charles's consulting room, a little apartment about six paces wide, with a table, three chairs and an office armchair. The tomes of the *Dictionnaire des sciences médicales*,[20] uncut, but whose stitching had suffered in all the successive sales they had passed through, adorned almost single-handedly the six shelves of a pinewood bookcase. The smell of brown butter sauce made its way through the wall during consultations, just as from the kitchen one could hear the patients coughing in the surgery and pouring out their whole sorry tale. Next came a large and dilapidated room with an oven, opening immediately onto the courtyard where the stables stood, and which served nowadays as wood-shed, cellar, warehouse, full of scrap iron, empty casks, unserviceable farm implements, with a mass of other dusty stuff whose use was impossible to fathom.

The garden, longer than it was wide, went up, between two walls of pugging mortar covered in espaliered apricots, to a thorn hedge that separated it from the fields. In the middle was a slate sundial on a stone pedestal; four narrow beds embellished with thin dog-rose plants symmetrically framed the more useful patch of serious-minded vegetation. Right at the end, under the little firs, a plaster priest was reading his breviary.

Emma went up to the bedrooms. The first was unfurnished; but the second, being the matrimonial chamber, had a mahogany bed in an alcove hung with red drapes. A shell-work box decorated the chest of drawers; and, on the writing-table near the window, there stood a bouquet of orange-blossom in a carafe, tied with ribbons of white satin. It was a wedding bouquet, the other one's bouquet! She stared at it. Charles noticed this, picked it up and conveyed it to the attic, while

Emma, seated in an armchair (their belongings were being placed around her), reflected on her own wedding bouquet, wrapped up in a box, and wondered, dreamily, what would be done with it, if she happened to die.

She busied herself, in the first few days, contemplating changes in the house. She removed the lamp-holders' glass globes, had new paper hung, the staircase repainted and benches made for the garden, all round the sundial; she even asked how to set about having an ornamental pond with an artificial fountain and some fish. Finally her husband, knowing how she loved to take a ride in a carriage, found a second-hand *buggy*, which, once new lamps and splashboards in stitched leather had been added, all but resembled a tilbury.

So he was happy and without a care in the world. A meal alone together, an evening walk on the high road, a gesture of her hand on the side of her hair, the sight of her straw hat hanging from a window fastening, and yet more things in which Charles had never suspected delight might be found, now made up his unbroken happiness. In bed, in the morning, their heads side by side on the pillow, he would watch the sunlight thread through the down on her fair cheeks, half-hidden by the scalloped ties of her bonnet. Seen from so close, her eyes seemed to him magnified, especially when she opened her lids several times over on waking; black in shadow and deep blue in daylight, it was as though her eyes had successive layers of colour, and which, thicker deep down, grew clearer as they rose to the enamelled surface. His own eye lost itself in these depths, and he saw a little version of himself to the shoulders, with the silk kerchief[21] on his head and the top of his nightshirt half-open. He got up. She stood at the window to watch him leave; and she stayed leaning on the sill, between two pots of geraniums, robed in her dressing gown that fell loose about her. Charles, down in the street, was buckling his spurs on the mounting-stone; and she continued to talk to him from above, all the while plucking off with her mouth scraps of bloom or greenery that she blew in his direction, and which, fluttering about, floating, making semi-circles in the air like a bird, would catch themselves, before falling to earth, on the uncombed mane of the old white mare, motionless by the door. Charles, in the saddle, blew her a kiss; she replied with a wave, she closed the window again, he went off. And so, upon the highway that stretched forth its long, endless ribbon of dust, by way of sunken tracks arboured by bowed trees, on paths where the corn came up to his knees, with the sun on his shoulders and the morning air in his nostrils, his heart full of the night's delights, his soul calm, his flesh contented, he rode away ruminating on his happiness, like those who, digesting after dinner, still masticate the flavour of the truffles.

Up until now, what fun had he had in life? Was it his time in school, where he stayed shut up between those high walls, alone amidst his fellows who were richer than he or more able in their lessons, who laughed at his accent, who mocked his clothes, and whose mothers came to the parlour with pastries in their muffs? Was it later, when he was studying medicine and never had a purse full enough to dance the quadrille with a little working girl who might have become his mistress? Then he lived for fourteen months with the widow, whose feet, in bed, were as cold as icicles. But now, he was in lifetime possession of this pretty woman whom he adored. His universe was bounded by the silky turn of her petticoat; and he reproached himself for not loving her, he needed to see her again; he rushed back, climbed the stairs, his heart thumping. Emma was in her bedroom, dressing; he stepped up soundlessly, he kissed her on the back, she cried out.[22]

He could not stop himself continually touching her comb, her rings, her fichu; sometimes he would give her fat, full-lipped kisses on the cheeks, or a row of little kisses up the entire length of her bare arm, from finger-tips to shoulder; and she would push him away, half smiling and half annoyed, as one does to a child who clings to you.

Before they were married, she had believed herself to be in love; but since the happiness that should have resulted from this love had not come, she must have been mistaken, she reflected. And Emma endeavoured to find out what precisely was meant in life by the words *delight*, *passion* and *intoxication*, which had seemed so beautiful to her in books.

VI

S HE HAD READ *Paul et Virginie*[23] and she had longed for the bamboo house, the negro-boy Domingo, the dog Fidèle, but above all for the tender friendship of a dear little brother, who goes searching red fruit for you in trees higher than steeples, or who runs barefoot on the sand, bringing you a bird's nest.

When she was thirteen, her father brought her to town himself, to place her in the convent. They stayed in an auberge in the Saint-Gervais quarter, where they ate supper off painted plates that represented the story of Mademoiselle de La Vallière.[24] All the written explanations, cut off here and there by the scratching of knives, exalted religion, the tenderness of the heart, and the court's splendour.

Far from finding it tedious at the convent in the early days, she delighted in the company of the nuns, who kept her occupied with visits to the chapel, reached from the refectory by a long corridor. She played scarcely at all during recreation, understood the catechism well, and was always the one to reply to Monsieur le Vicaire when it came to the difficult questions. Living thus without ever leaving the tepid atmosphere of the classes and among these whey-faced women with their beads and copper crosses, she was softly lulled into the mystic languor exuded by the altar's perfumes, by the coolness of the holy-water fonts and the candles' beaming light. Instead of following the mass, she would look in her book at the pious engravings faintly edged in blue, and she loved the sick lamb, the holy heart pierced by sharp arrows, or poor Jesus, who fell beneath His cross as He walked. In an attempt to mortify the flesh, she tried to go a whole day without eating. She searched in her mind for some vow to fulfil.

When she went to confession, she would invent little sins so as to stay there longer, on her knees in the shadows, hands together, face to the grille beneath the priest's whisperings. The similes of the betrothed, spouse, celestial lover and marriage everlasting which recurred in the sermons roused unexpected sweetnesses in the depths of her soul.

In the evening, before prayers, a religious reading would be held in the study. During the week, it would be a recapitulation of a story from scripture or Abbé Frayssinous's *Conférences*,[25] and, on Sundays, passages from *Le Génie du Christianisme*, for diversion. How avidly she listened, the first few times, to romantic melancholy's high-sounding lament renewing itself at every echo of the earth and of the everlasting! If her childhood had been passed in the back-shop of some merchant quarter, she might have been open to the lyrical invasions of nature, which usually reach us only when translated by writers. But she knew the countryside too well; she knew the flocks' bleating, milking-times, the plough. Used to flat views, she was drawn, contrariwise, to the uneven. She liked the sea only for its storms, and greenery only when it was thinly scattered among ruins. She had to be able to derive a kind of personal advantage from things; and she rejected as useless all that did not immediately contribute to her heart's consummation, – being of a temperament more sentimental than artistic, seeking emotions and not landscapes.

There was an old maid in the convent, who came every month, for eight days, to work in the laundry. Recommended by the archbishop as belonging to an old family of gentlefolk ruined by the Revolution, she ate in the refectory at the nuns' table, and would have a little natter with them before getting back to her work again. Often the boarders would escape from their lessons to go and see her. She knew by heart the amorous songs of the last century, singing them half to herself as she plied her needle. She told stories, gave you the latest news, ran errands for you in town, and lent the bigger girls some novel or other on the sly, that she would always have in the pockets of her apron, and whose long chapters were devoured by the good maiden lady herself, during pauses in her work. It was all passions, suitors, sweethearts, persecuted ladies swooning in lonely summer-houses, postillions slain at every staging-post, horses ridden to death on every page, dark forests, troubles of the heart, eternal vows, sobbings, tears and kisses, little rowing boats in the moonlight, nightingales in the bushes, *gentlemen* as brave as lions, as gentle as lambs, as virtuous as no one ever is, always well dressed, and who cry in bucketloads. Thus for six months, at fifteen, Emma soiled her hands on the dust of old circulating-libraries. Later, with Walter Scott, she became smitten by historical things, dreaming of chests, wardrooms and minstrels. She would have liked to have lived in an old manor-house, like those châtelaines in their long dresses, who, under the trefoil of pointed arches, whiled away their days leaning on the stone and cupping their chin, to watch a white-plumed knight on a black horse gallop towards them from the depths of the countryside. She worshipped Mary Stuart during this time, and felt an enthusiast's reverence for illustrious or unhappy women. For her, Jeanne d'Arc, Héloïse, Agnès Sorel, La Belle Ferronière and Clémence Isaure[26] detached themselves like comets from the gloomy immensity of history – where, gushing forth here and there, but cast further back in the shadows and with no connection between them, came Saint Louis with his oak, the dying Bayard, a few of Louis XI's ferocities, a dash of Saint Bartholomew's Day, the Béarnais crest, and always the memory of those painted plates extolling the glory of Louis XIV.[27]

In the music class, in the ballads she sang, there was no question of anything but little golden-winged angels, madonnas, lagoons, gondoliers, peaceful compositions which allowed her to glimpse, through the inanity of the language and the forced notes, the enticing phantasmagoria of sentimental truths. Some of her companions brought keepsake books they had received in their Christmas boxes. They must be hidden; it was no easy matter; they read them in the dormitory. Delicately handling their lovely satin bindings, Emma would fix her dazzled gaze on the name of unknown authors who had signed themselves, more often than not, as counts or viscounts, at the bottom of each piece.

She shivered, lifting with her breath the silvery tissue paper over the engravings, which rose half-folded and relapsed gently against the page. There, behind the balustrade of a balcony, stood a young man in a short coat, clasping in his arms a young girl in a white dress, with an alms-bag at her belt; or else the anonymous portraits of English 'ladies' with blonde curls, who, from beneath their round straw hats, gaze upon you with their big limpid eyes. They were to be seen displayed in carriages, gliding in the midst of parkland, where a hare leapt before the team of horses, being driven at a trot by two little postillions in white breeches. Others, dreaming on ottomans beside a broken-sealed note, were contemplating the moon through the half-open window, partly draped by a black curtain. The artless creatures, a single tear on the cheek, would be pecking a turtle-dove through the bars of a Gothic cage, or, smiling with head on one side, picking the petals off a daisy with their pointed fingers, the ends turned up like poulaine slippers. And you were there too, sultans with long pipes swooning under green arbours in the arms of Hindu dancing-girls, giaours, Turkish sabres, bonnet-grecs,[28] and you above all, wan landscapes of dithyrambic regions, which oftimes and simultaneously show us palm-trees, pines, tigers to the right, lions to the left, Tartar minarets on the horizon, Roman ruins in the foreground, then some squatting camels; all framed by a virgin forest, nicely cleaned and with a great ray of perpendicular sunlight trembling in the water – in which, standing out at scattered intervals as white abrasions on a ground of steel grey, swans glide about.

And the shade of the oil-lamp, hanging in the thick wall above Emma's head, illumined all these scenes of the world, which passed before her one after the other, in the silence of the dormitory and to the distant sound of a belated hackney-coach still rolling along the boulevards.

When her mother died, she cried a great deal for the first few days. She had a funeral picture made incorporating the hair of the deceased, and, in a letter she sent to Les Bertaux, full of sad reflections on existence, she asked that she might be buried later in the same tomb. The old fellow reckoned she was ill and came to see her. Emma was inwardly gratified to feel that she had with her first attempt gained access to that rare ideal of tame lives, which mediocre hearts never attain. So she let herself slide into winding Lamartinian lines,[29] listened to the harps on the lakes, to all the death-hymns of dying swans, all the leaf-falls, the spotless virgins ascending to heaven, and to the voice of the Everlasting descanting in the dales. She grew bored with it, but not wanting to admit this, carried on out of habit, then out of vanity, and was finally surprised to feel soothed, and with no more sadness in her heart than she had wrinkles on her forehead.

The good nuns, who had felt so sure of her vocation, observed with great amazement that Mademoiselle Rouault seemed to be breaking loose from their care. They had, in fact, lavished on her so many prayers, retreats, novenas and sermons, preached so well of the respect due to the saints and martyrs, and given so much good advice on the modesty of the body and the salvation of the soul, that she did as does a horse that one drags along by the bridle: she stopped short and the bit slipped from her teeth. Pragmatic amidst her enthusiasms, loving the church for its flowers, music for its romantic sentiments, and literature for its passionate excitements, her spirit would revolt before faith's mysteries, just as she chafed against discipline, which was something antipathetical to her constitution. When her father removed her from the school, no one was sorry to see her go. The abbess even implied that, of late, she had become wanting in reverence towards the community.

Emma, once home, delighted at first in taking charge of the servants, then took a dislike to the country and missed her convent. When Charles came to Les Bertaux for the first time, she thought herself to be extremely disillusioned, having nothing more to learn, nothing more to feel.

But the anxiety of a new state of mind, or perhaps the nervous irritation caused by the presence of this man, had sufficed to make her believe that, at last, she was in possession of that wondrous passion which up to then had remained like a great bird with rosy feathers soaring through the splendour of poetical skies; – and she could not now imagine that this calm she was dwelling in constituted the happiness of which she had dreamed.

VII

SHE WOULD SOMETIMES CONSIDER THAT this was, nonetheless, the most beautiful time of her life – the honeymoon, as one might say. To relish its fragrance, doubtless they would have had to take themselves off to those countries with high-sounding names where the days following the nuptials are all the more sweetly idle! In post-chaises, behind blinds of blue silk, you climb at walking pace up the steep roads, listening to the song of the postillion, which echoes in the mountains with the bells of goats and the rumbling din of the waterfall. When the sun sets, you breathe by the gulf's shore the scent of lemon trees; then, in the evening, on the villa's verandah, alone and with fingers entwined, you gaze upon the stars, making plans. It seemed to her that certain places on the earth must yield happiness, like a plant peculiar to that soil and growing poorly anywhere else. Why could she not lean on the balcony of a Swiss chalet or confine her sadness in a Scottish cottage, with a husband dressed in a long-skirted coat of black velvet, and sporting soft boots, a pointed hat and ruffled sleeves!

Well may it have been her wish to confide all these things to someone. But how to express an indiscernible disquiet, which alters its shape like the clouds, which whirls like the wind? So she could not find the words, the opportunity, the boldness.

If Charles had wanted it, however, if he had suspected something, if his gaze, just once, had come to meet her thoughts, it seemed to her that a sudden plenteousness would have detached itself from her heart, as the fruit of an espalier falls when a hand is laid upon it. But, as the intimacy of their life pressed them closer to each other, an indifference grew inside that loosened her from him.

Charles's conversation was as flat as a street pavement, and everyone's ideas paraded along it in their ordinary dress, without rousing emotion, laughter or dreams. He had never been curious, he said, while he lived at Rouen, to go to the theatre and see the actors from Paris. He did not know how to swim, to fence, to shoot, and he could not explain a riding term she came across one day in a novel.

On the contrary, ought not a man to know everything, excel in numerous activities, initiate you in the forces of passion, in the refinements of life, in all the mysteries? But this one taught nothing, knew nothing, desired nothing. He believed her happy; and she resented him for this stolid calm, this serene dullness, for the very happiness that she gave him.

Sometimes she drew; and it was a great entertainment for Charles just to stand and watch her leaning on her drawing-board, half-closing her eyes to see her work better, or rolling little pellets of breadcrumbs[30] on her thumb. As for the piano, the faster her fingers played, the more he marvelled. She struck the notes with aplomb, and ran up and down the whole keyboard without a break. Thus tormented by her, the old instrument, whose chords buzzed, could be heard right up at the other end of the village if the window was open, and often the bailiff's clerk, passing by on the highway, bare-headed and in house slippers, would stop to listen to her, a sheet of paper in his hand.

Emma, by contrast, did know how to run her house. She sent the patients their bills, in well-phrased letters without a whiff of the invoice. On Sundays, when they had some neighbour or other to dinner, she found the means to offer a stylish dish, was skilled at setting pyramids of greengages on vine-leaves, served up fruit preserves turned out on a plate, and she even talked of buying mouthwash bowls[31] for the dessert course. Much esteem rebounded from all this onto Bovary.

Charles ended up by rating himself more highly for possessing such a wife. With pride he would show, in the parlour, two little sketches of hers, in lead pencil, that he had had framed in very wide frames and hung against the wallpaper on long green ribbons. Coming out of mass, people would see him at his door in beautiful needle-work slippers.

He would come back late, at ten o'clock, sometimes at midnight. He would ask for something to eat, and, as the maid had turned in, it was Emma who served him. He removed his riding-coat to dine in more comfort. He spoke of all the people, one after another, that he had met, all the villages he had been to, the prescriptions he had made out, and, pleased with himself, he ate the rest of the boiled beef, peeled the rind off his cheese, crunched on an apple, drained his decanter, then went off to bed, lay down on his back and snored.

As he had long been in the habit of wearing a cotton night cap, his silk kerchief would not stay over his ears; and his hair, in the morning, would be pressed higgledy-piggledy over his face and whitened by the down from his pillow, whose ties had come undone during the night. He always wore stout boots, which had two thick folds slanting up from the instep to the ankle, while the rest of the upper leather extended in a straight line, as if stretched over a wooden foot. He said that it was *quite good enough for the country*.[32]

His mother approved of this economy; for she came to see him as before, whenever some slightly violent squall had occurred at her home; and yet Madame Bovary senior seemed prejudiced against her daughter-in-law. She thought *her style too grand for their financial position*; wood, sugar and candles *disappeared as in a great house*, and the amount of embers burning themselves up in the kitchen would suffice for twenty-five dishes! She rearranged her linen in the closets and taught her to look sharp after the butcher when he brought the meat. Emma accepted these lessons; Madame Bovary was prodigal with them; and the words *Daughter* and *Mother* were exchanged all day long, accompanied by a little quivering of the lips, both women casting blandishments in voices trembling with anger.

In Madame Dubuc's time, the old lady still felt herself the favourite; but now, Charles's love for Emma appeared to her as a desertion of his affection, an encroachment on what belonged to her; and she observed her son's happiness in sad silence, as a bankrupt might watch, through the window panes, people sitting at table in his old house. She reminded him, by way of reminiscences, about her pains and her sacrifices, and, comparing them to Emma's negligences, concluded that it was not reasonable to adore her in such an exclusive fashion.

Charles did not know what to say in reply; he respected his mother, and infinitely loved his wife; he considered the judgment of the one unerring, and yet found the other irreproachable. When Madame Bovary had left, he tried timorously to venture, and using the same phrases, one or two of the most anodyne observations he had heard his mother make; Emma, proving to him in a single word that he was mistaken, sent him back to his patients.

Nevertheless, with theories she thought sound, she tried to devote herself to love. By moonlight, in the garden, she would recite all the passionate verses she knew by heart and sing him melancholy adagios, sighing all the while; but she found herself feeling just as flat afterwards as before, and Charles appeared neither more amorous nor more roused.

Once she had thus struck the flint a few times against her heart, without making a single spark fly, incapable still of understanding what she could not feel, just as she was of believing in whatever did not show itself in conventional form, she painlessly convinced herself that Charles's passion no longer had anything exorbitant about it. His effusiveness had become punctual; he would kiss her at such-and-such a time. It was one more habit among others: a dessert anticipated beforehand, after the monotony of dinner.

A gamekeeper, cured by Monsieur of an inflammation on the chest, had given a little Italian greyhound bitch to Madame; she took it with her on walks, for she would leave the house now and again, in order to be alone for a moment and not have the garden with the dusty road eternally before her eyes.

She went as far as the beech copse at Banneville, near the abandoned summer-house at the corner of the wall along the fields. In the ha-ha, among the weeds, there are long reeds with sharp-edged leaves.

She began by looking all about, to see if anything had changed since the last time she was here. She found the foxgloves and the wallflowers in the same places, the tufts of nettles wreathing the big stones, and the veneer of lichen along the three windows, whose ever-tight shutters were dropping off with rot, from their rusty iron bars. Her thoughts, aimless at first, wandered about at random, like her greyhound making circles in the countryside, yelping after yellow butterflies, giving chase to field mice, or nibbling the poppies on the edge of a field of wheat. Then her ideas settled little by little, and, seated on the turf, digging into it with little stabs of her parasol's tip, Emma kept saying to herself:

'Why, dear God, did I marry?'

She wondered if, by other combinations of chance, there might not have been a way to have met a different man; and she tried to imagine what they might have been, these incidents that had never occurred, this other life, this husband that she did not know. Not all of them were like this one, in fact. He could have been handsome, witty, distinguished, engaging, like those whom her old friends at the convent had doubtless married. What were they doing, these days? In town, among

41

the roar of the streets, the buzzing of theatres and the brightness of the ball, their lives would be spent where the heart swells, where the senses bloom. But this life of hers was as cold as a barn in which the dormer-window faces north, and boredom, that silent spider, was spinning its shadowy web in every nook and cranny of her heart. She recalled prize-giving days, when she would mount the rostrum to collect her little crowns. With her hair in plaits, her white dress and her open prunella shoes, she had a pretty manner, and the gentlemen, when she returned to her chair, would lean towards her to pay her compliments; the courtyard was full of barouches, from the carriage doors they bid her farewell, the music master passed, saluting her with his violin case. How far away it all was, how far away!

She called Djali,[33] took her between her knees, ran her fingers over the long slender head and said to her:

'Come, give mistress a kiss, you who are free of sorrows.'

Then, contemplating the melancholy air of the elegant animal as it slowly yawned, she was moved to pity, and, comparing it to herself, talked to it aloud, as though comforting an afflicted soul.

Squalls of wind would come from time to time, sea breezes which, rolling in one bound over the entire Caux plateau, brought a salty freshness some distance into the fields. The rushes hissed close to the ground, and the leaves of the beech trees rustled in a swift shudder, while their summits, ever swaying, went on with their lofty murmur. Emma tightened her shawl against her shoulders and stood up.

In the avenue, a green light dimmed by the foliage lit the creeping moss that creaked softly underfoot. The sun was going down; the sky was red between the branches, and the matching tree-trunks set in a straight line resembled a gloomy colonnade standing out against a backdrop of gold; a fear took hold of her, she called Djali, returned to Tostes by the highway, subsided onto a sofa, and would not speak for the entire evening.

But, towards the end of September, something extraordinary fell into her life: she was invited to La Vaubyessard, the home of the Marquis d'Andervilliers.

Secretary of State under the Restoration, the Marquis, seeking an entry into political life, prepared his candidacy for the Chamber of Deputies over a long period. In winter he distributed firewood left and right, and, in the General Council, called for roads in his district with exaggerated zeal. He had suffered, during the hot summer days, from an abcess in the mouth, which Charles had miraculously relieved him of, by poking it with a lancet just in time. The steward, sent to Tostes to pay for the operation, related that evening how he had seen some superb cherries in the doctor's small garden. So, as the cherry trees at La Vaubyessard grew poorly, Monsieur le Marquis asked Bovary for a few cuttings, made it his duty to thank him personally, spotted Emma, deemed her to have a pretty figure and that her greeting was by no means peasant-like; so much so that up at the chateau it was not thought to be beyond the bounds of condescension, nor to be committing an impropriety, for the young couple to be invited.

One Wednesday, at three o'clock, Monsieur and Madame Bovary, riding in their gig, set off for La Vaubyessard, with a large trunk tied behind and a hat box placed in front of the splashing-board. In addition, Charles had a box between his legs.

They arrived at nightfall, as the lamps were beginning to be lit in the park, so as to light the way for the carriages.

VIII

THE CHATEAU, A MODERN CONSTRUCTION in the Italianate style, with two projecting wings and three flights of steps, was deployed at the bottom of a vast lawn where a few cows grazed between tufts of tall, well-spaced trees, while small clusters of shrubs, rhododendron, syringa and guelder-rose puffed out their clumps of uneven greenery over the curving line of the gravel drive. A river passed under a bridge; through the mist, thatched buildings could be distinguished here and there in the meadow, whose gentle slope bordered two small hills covered in woods, and beyond, in the massed foliage, lay the coach-houses and stables ranged in two parallel lines, the preserved remains of the old demolished chateau.

Charles's gig stopped in front of the central flight of steps; servants appeared; the Marquis came forward and, offering his arm to the doctor's wife, showed her in to the entrance hall.

It was flagged in marble and very lofty, and the sound of footsteps and voices echoed as in a church. Opposite rose a straight staircase, and to the left a gallery, looking out onto a garden, led to the billiard room where, from the door, the cannoning of ivory balls could be heard. As she crossed to go to the drawing-room, Emma saw serious-faced men around the game, chins resting on high cravats and all wearing insignia, smiling silently as they thrust their cues. On the dark panelling of the wainscot, huge gilded frames bore names at the bottom, in black letters. She read: 'Jean-Antoine d'Andervilliers d'Yverbonville, count of Vaubyessard and Baron of Fresnaye, fell at the Battle of Coutras, the 20th of October 1587.' And on another: 'Jean-Antoine-Henry-Guy d'Andervilliers of La Vaubyessard, admiral of France and Knight of the Order of St Michael, wounded at the Battle of Hougue-Saint-Vast, the 29th of May 1692, died at La Vaubyessard the 23rd of January 1693.' She could scarcely make out those that followed, for the light from the lamps, directed down upon the green billiard-cloth, left a shadow hovering in the room. Darkening the long straight row of canvases, it shattered against them into a web of fine lines, following the craquelure of the varnish; and here and there from all these large black squares edged in gold emerged some lighter portion of the painting: a pale brow, two eyes that gazed at you, wigs uncoiling onto the dusty shoulders of red coats, or the buckle of a garter above a plump calf.

The Marquis opened the drawing-room door; one of the ladies rose (the Marquise herself), came forward to meet Emma and bid her be seated by her side, on a small sofa, where she began to talk to her in a friendly fashion, as if she had known her for a long time. She was a woman of around forty, with handsome shoulders, a hook nose, a drawling voice, and who wore, that evening, on her chestnut locks, a simple fichu of threaded lace which fell behind in a triangle. A fair-haired young person sat nearby, in a long-backed chair; and the gentlemen, who each had a little flower in their dress-coat buttonhole, were chatting with the ladies, all around the fireplace.

At seven o'clock, dinner was served. The men, more numerous, sat at the first table, in the hallway, and the ladies at the second, in the dining room, with the Marquis and Marquise.

As she went in, Emma felt shrouded in warm air, a mingling of flower scents and elegant linen, the aroma of meats and the fragrancy of truffles. The flames from the candles in the candelabra lengthened on the silver dish-covers; the cut-glass crystal, dulled by condensation, sent back wan rays; bouquets were lined up the length of the table, and, on the wide-bordered plates, the napkins, tricked out to look like a bishop's mitre, each held between the gape of their two folds a tiny oval loaf. The red claws of lobsters overshot the dishes; fat fruits in openwork baskets climbed in tiers from a moss bed; the quails had kept their feathers, vapours rose; and, in silk stockings, in short breeches, in white cravate, in lace frills, solemn as a judge, the steward, sliding ready-carved dishes between the shoulders of the guests, made the chosen piece leap up with a flick of his spoon. On the great, brass-hooped porcelain stove, the statue of a woman draped to the chin gazed motionless upon the packed room.

Madame Bovary noticed that several ladies had not put their gloves in their glass.[34]

Nevertheless, at the top end of the table, alone among all these women, bent over his heaped plate, and with a napkin tied at the back like a child, an old man ate, letting drops of sauce fall from his mouth. He had blood shot eyes and wore a little pig-tail tied with a black ribbon. This was the Marquis's father-in-law, the old Duc de Laverdière, once the favourite of the Comte d'Artois, back in the days of hunting parties at Le Vaudreuil, *chez* the Marquis de Conflans, and who had been, it was said, the lover of Queen Marie-Antoinette between Messieurs de Coigny and de Lauzun. He had led a boisterous life of debauch, full of duels, wagers, abducted women, had gobbled up his fortune and appalled his entire family. A servant, behind his chair, imparted aloud in his ear the names of the dishes that he would indicate with his finger, stammering away; and over and over Emma's eyes returned of their own volition to that old flap-mouthed man, as to something extraordinary and august. He had lived at court and slept in the bed of queens!

Iced champagne was poured. Emma's whole body quivered when she felt the cold in her mouth. She had never seen pomegranates nor eaten pineapple. Even the powdered sugar seemed to her whiter and finer than elsewhere.

The ladies then went up to their rooms to prepare themselves for the ball.

Emma dressed with the fastidious meticulousness of an actress at her debut. She arranged her hair as the hairdresser had recommended, and she slipped into her gauzy barège dress, spread out on the bed. Charles's trousers were too tight across his stomach.

'The foot-straps will restrain me when I dance,' he said.

'Dance?' rejoined Emma.

'Why, yes!'

'But have you lost your mind? You'll be a laughing stock! Stay in your seat. Besides, it's more seemly for a doctor,' she added.

Charles held his tongue. He walked up and down, waiting until Emma was dressed.

He was looking at her from behind, in the mirror, between two candles. Her dark eyes seemed darker. The smooth sides of her hair, bulging softly over the ears, gleamed with a blue lustre. A rose in her chignon trembled on an unfixed stem, with imitation drops of water on the end of its leaves. Her dress was a pale saffron, set off by three posies of pompom roses with a splash of greenery.

Charles came to kiss her on the shoulder.

'Leave me alone,' she said, 'you're ruffling me.'

They heard a violin's ritornello and the sounds of a horn. She descended the stairs, trying not to run.

The quadrilles had begun. A great many people were arriving. They pushed forward. She seated herself near the door, on a bench.

When the dance had finished, the floor stayed free for the groups of men to stand and chat and the liveried servants to bring large trays. Along the line of seated women, the painted fans fluttered, the nosegays part-concealed the smiles on the faces, and the scent-bottles with their gold stoppers turned in half-open hands whose white gloves traced the shape of the nails and squeezed the flesh at the wrist. The lacework trimmings, the diamond brooches, the medallion bracelets, quivered on the bodices, glimmered on the breasts, rustled on the bare arms. The confections of hair, pressed down in little curls over the brows and twisted at the nape, had, in crowns, in bunches or in branches, forget-me-nots, jasmin, pomegranate flowers, ears of wheat and cornflowers. Peaceful in their own seats, mothers with grim faces wore turbans of red.

Emma's heart throbbed a little when, her partner taking her by the finger-tips, she took her place in line and awaited the stroke of the bow to give the off. But soon the emotion subsided; and, swinging to the musicians' rhythm, she glided forward, her head nodding slightly. A smile rose to her lips at certain finesses of the violin, which played on its own, at times, when the other instruments fell silent; one could hear the clear noise of gold louis pouring out onto the baize tables in the next room; then everything would start up again at once, the cornet sending forth a ringing burst, the feet keeping time as they fell, the skirts swelling out and rustling, the hands proffered, released; the same eyes, lowered before you, returning to fix their gaze on yours.

A few men (fifteen or so) aged between twenty-five and forty, scattered among the dancers or chatting in the doorways, were distinguished from the crowd by a family air, whatever their differences of age, dress or looks.

Their clothes, better made, seemed to be cut from a more supple cloth, and their hair, gathered into curls over the temples, appeared to be glossed by a more delicate pomade. They had the complexion of wealth, that white complexion enhanced by the pale sheen of porcelain, the shimmer of satin, the lustre of noble furniture, and which is healthily maintained by a judicious diet of exquisite foods. Their necks turned comfortably on low cravats; their long whiskers fell on turned-down collars, they wiped their lips on handkerchiefs embroidered with a large initial, from which a sweet fragrance emerged. Those who were starting to age had a youthful air, while a certain ripeness had spread over the faces of the young. The calm sense of passions daily gratified wafted within their indifferent glances; and their gentle manners were pierced through by that particular brutishness, imparted by the domination of semi-compliant things, in which power is exercised and where vanity amuses itself, the handling of blood horses and the company of lost women.

Three steps from Emma, a gentleman in a blue coat was chatting about Italy with a pale young woman, wearing a set of pearls. He was extolling the impressive size of the columns of St Peter's, Tivoli, Vesuvius, Castellamare and the Cascine, the roses of Genoa, the Coliseum by moonlight. Emma lent her other ear to a conversation full of words she was unable to understand. Guests were gathered about a very young man who, the previous week, had beaten *Miss Arabella* and *Romulus*, and won two thousand sous jumping a ditch, in England. One was complaining of his coursers getting fat; another, the printer's errors that had completely altered the name of his horse.

The ballroom's air grew heavy; the lamps were dimming. The crowd ebbed into the billiard room. A servant got up on a chair and broke two panes; at the noise of the splintering glass, Madame Bovary turned her head and noticed, in the garden, faces of gazing peasants pressed against the windows. And so she remembered Les Bertaux. Again she saw the farm, the muddy pond, her father in a smock under the apple-trees, and again she saw her own self, skimming the cream with her finger off the pans of milk, in the dairy. But under the lightning-flashes of the present moment, her past life, so clear up to now, faded away entirely, and she almost doubted that she had ever lived it. She was here; and then, around the ball, there lay nothing but shadow, spread over everything else. So she ate a maraschino ice, that she held with her left hand in a silver gilt shell, with her eyes half-closed, the spoon between her teeth.

Near her, a lady let her fan fall. A dancer was passing.

'Would you be so kind, monsieur,' said the lady, 'as to pick up my fan? It is behind this sofa!'

The gentleman bowed, and, as he made to reach out with his arm, Emma saw the young lady's hand cast something white, folded in a triangle, into his hat. The gentleman retrieved the fan and offered it to the lady, respectfully; she thanked him with a nod and began to inhale the fragrance of her flowers.

After the dinner, where there were Spanish wines and Rhenish wines, rich crayfish bisques and milk-of-almond soups, Trafalgar puddings[35] and all kinds of cold meats set in jellies that quivered in the dishes, the carriages began to ride away, one after the other. On lifting the corner of the fine muslin curtain, you could see the light from their lanterns sliding into the dark. The benches cleared; a few card-players remained; the musicians cooled their finger-tips on their tongues; Charles was half asleep, back propped against a door.

At three o'clock in the morning, the cotillon began. Emma did not know how to waltz. Everyone was waltzing, Mademoiselle d'Andervilliers herself and the Marquise; there was no one left but the chateau guests, around a dozen people.

However, one of the waltzers, known familiarly as the 'Vicomte', and whose gaping waistcoat seemed moulded to his chest, came yet a second time to invite Madame Bovary, assuring her that he would guide her and she would carry it off well.

They started slowly, then proceeded faster. They were reeling round: all reeled round and about them, the lamps, the furniture, the panelling, the parquet, like a disc on a spindle. As they passed near the doors, the bottom of Emma's dress grazed his trousers; their legs interlaced; he glanced down at her, she glanced up at him; a torpor came over her, she stopped. They set off again; and, moving faster, the Vicomte, sweeping her away, disappeared with her to the far end of the gallery, where, panting for breath, she all but fell down, and, for an instant, leaned her head on his chest. And then, still reeling round, but not as fast, he led her back to her seat; she fell back against the wall and put her hand over her eyes.

When she opened them again, in the middle of the drawing-room a lady seated on a stool had three waltzers on their knees in front of her. She chose the Vicomte, and the violin started up again.

Everyone watched them. They whirled past again and again, she with her body motionless and chin down, and he always in the same pose, shoulders thrown back, elbow rounded, chin forward. She could certainly dance, that one! They went on for ages and wore all the others out.

A few minutes more of chat, and, after bidding each other goodnight, or rather good morning, the chateau guests went off to bed.

Charles dragged himself up by the banisters, *on his last legs*. He had spent five hours on the trot, on his feet by the tables, watching the whist game without understanding a thing. So he gave a great sigh of relief when he removed his boots.

Emma slipped a shawl over her shoulders, opened the window and leaned out.

The night was dark. A few drops of rain fell. She breathed in the moist wind cooling her eyelids. The ball's music still hummed in her ears, and she strained to keep awake, prolonging the illusion of this luxuriant life that she must so soon forsake.

First light dawned. For a long time she gazed at the windows of the chateau, trying to guess which were the bedrooms of all those she had noticed the day before. She would have liked to know their reality, penetrated them, become one and the same.

But she was shivering with cold. She undressed and curled up under the sheets against Charles, who slept.

There were a lot of people at breakfast. The meal lasted ten minutes; no spirits were served, which astonished the doctor. Afterwards Mademoiselle d'Andervilliers collected the pieces of brioche in a small hamper, to bear them to the swans on the lake; and a stroll was taken in the hot-house, where fantastical plants, bristling with hairs, tiered upwards in pyramids under hanging vases, which, like nests crammed with too many snakes, had long, green, interlaced cords tumbling down from their rims. The orangery, found at the far end, led under cover right up to the chateau's outhouses. The Marquis, to amuse the young lady, took her to see the stables. Above the basket-shaped racks, porcelain plaques carried the name of the horses in black. Each animal stirred in its stall when they passed close by, clicking their tongues. The wooden floor of the saddlery gleamed like a drawing-room's parquet. The carriage-harness was arranged in the middle on two revolving pillars, and the bridle-bits, the whips, the stirrups, the curb-chains were arrayed in a line the whole length of the wall.

Charles, in the meantime, went off to ask a servant to hitch up his gig. It was brought before the flight of steps, and, all the packages having been stuffed inside, the Bovary couple paid their respects to the Marquis and Marquise, and set off again for Tostes.

Emma, in silence, watched the wheels turn. Charles, perched on the very edge of the seat, drove with his arms spread, and the little horse ambled between the shafts, which were too wide for it. The slack reins, wet with sweat, struck against its croup, and the box, tied on with string to the gig's rear, kept thumping against the frame.

They were on the heights of Thibourville, when all of a sudden, in front of them, some mounted gentlemen passed, laughing and with cigars in their mouths. Emma thought she recognised the Vicomte; she turned and looked back, and saw nothing on the horizon but the move-ment of heads rising and falling, according to the unequal rhythm of trot or gallop.

Three-quarters of a mile further on, they had to stop in order to mend a broken breeching-strap with rope.

But Charles, giving a last glance at the harness, saw something on the ground, between the legs of his horse; and he retrieved a cigar-case embroidered all over with green silk and blazoned in the middle with a coat of arms, like the door of a coach.

'There are even two cigars inside,' he said; 'those can be for this evening, after dinner.'

'You smoke, then?' she asked.

'Now and again, when the occasion presents itself.'

He pocketed his find and whipped up the nag.

When they arrived home, dinner was not ready. Madame railed. Nastasie responded with insolence.

'Leave!' said Emma. 'What cheek! You're dismissed.'

For dinner there was onion soup, with a piece of veal in sorrel. Charles, seated opposite Emma and happily rubbing his hands, said:

'How delightful to be back home again!'

They heard Nastasie crying. He quite liked this poor girl. In times past she had kept him company through many an evening, in the idleness of his widowhood. She was his first patient, his oldest acquaintance in the area.

'Have you sent her off for good?' he said at last.

'Yes. Who's to stop me?' she replied.

Then they warmed themselves in the kitchen, while the bedroom was being prepared. Charles began to smoke. He smoked by pouting his lips, spitting every other minute, recoiling at each puff.

'You'll make yourself sick,' she said, disdainfully.

He put his cigar down, and ran off to swallow a glass of cold water at the pump. Emma, seizing the cigar-case, threw it brusquely into the bottom of the wardrobe.

The next day passed so slowly! She walked in her little garden, going up and down the same paths, stopping before the flower-beds, before the espalier, before the plaster priest, contemplating with amazement all these things belonging to the past that she knew so well. How distant the ball already seemed! What was it then that had set the morning of the day before yesterday so far apart from the evening of today? Her journey to La Vaubyessard had made a hole in her life, like those huge crevices that a storm, in a single night, sometimes scours in the mountains. Nevertheless, she was resigned; she reverently folded away in the chest of drawers her beautiful costume, right down to her satin slippers, whose soles had been yellowed by the parquet's slippery beeswax. Her heart was like them: rubbed against wealth, it had been left a surface deposit which would never wash off.

So the mere recollection of this ball kept Emma occupied. Every time Wednesday came round, she said to herself on waking up: 'Ah! eight days ago . . . , fifteen days ago . . . , three weeks ago, I was there!' And little by little, the faces blended in her memory, she forgot the tunes of the quadrilles, she no longer saw so distinctly the liveries and the rooms; a few details slipped away, but the regret stayed.

IX

OFTEN, WHEN CHARLES WAS OUT, she would go to the wardrobe and take the cigar-case in green silk from where she had left it between the folds of linen.

She would look at it, open it, and even smell the scent of its lining, mingled with lemon verbena and tobacco. To whom did it belong . . . ? To the Vicomte. Perhaps it was a present from his mistress? Embroidered on a rosewood frame, a delicate, pretty ornament it was, kept hidden from prying eyes, filling many hours, and over which the soft curls of the pensive, painstaking woman had leaned. A breath of love had crept between the stitches on the canvas; each stroke of the needle had fixed therein a hope and a memory, and all these interwoven silk threads were no more than a continuation of the same silent passion. And then the Vicomte, one morning, had taken it away with him. What did they talk about, while it stayed on the broad chimneypiece, between the vases of flowers and the Pompadour clocks? She was at Tostes. He was in Paris, now; there, in that very place! What was Paris like? What a name beyond measure! She repeated it in a low tone, just for the pleasure of it; it rang in her ears like a great cathedral bell; it blazed in her eyes, even on the label on her pots of pomade.

At night, when the fish merchants, in their carts, passed under her windows singing *La Marjolaine*,[36] she woke up; and listening to the iron-rimmed wheels, their clatter deadened by the earth as soon as they left the village:

'They will be there tomorrow!' she said to herself.

And she followed them in her thoughts, going up and down the hills, travelling through villages, moving off along the high road by starlight. At the end of an indeterminate distance, there was always a confused spot where her dream expired.

She bought a plan of Paris, and, with the tip of her finger on the map, she went shopping in the capital. She ascended the boulevards, stopping at each corner, between the lines of the streets, in front of the white squares that denoted houses. Her eyes strained by the end, she closed her lids, and in the gloom she saw the gas-lamps' burners twist in the wind, and the footboards of the carriages lining up in front of the theatre colonnades in a great hubbub.

She subscribed to *The Basket*, a woman's journal, and to *The Sylph of the Salons*. She devoured, without missing a thing, all the reports of first nights, of races and parties, taking an interest in a singer's debut, in a store's opening. She knew all about the new fashions, the right addresses for tailors, the days for the Bois[37] or the Opéra. She studied descriptions of furniture in the novels of Eugène Sue;[38] she read Balzac and George Sand, seeking imaginary gratifications for her private lusts. Even at table she would bring her book, leafing through the pages while Charles ate and talked to her. The memory of the Vicomte always recurred in her reading. She drew comparisons between him and the invented characters. But little by little the circle whose centre he occupied widened around him, and that halo of glory he wore, straying from his face, spread itself further off, to illumine other dreams.

Paris, vaguer than the Ocean, thus shimmered to Emma's eyes inside a silvery, gilded haze. The numerous lives that tossed about in this uproar were nevertheless divided into parts, classified in distinct lists. Emma perceived just two or three that concealed all the others from her, single-handedly standing for the whole of humanity. The ambassadorial world walked on gleaming parquet floors, in drawing-rooms panelled with mirrors, around oval tables spread with gold-tasselled cloths of velvet. Here were trailing gowns, great mysteries, distress dissembled under smiles. Then followed the society of duchesses; there, one was pale; one rose at four o'clock; the women – poor angels! – wore Brussels lace on the hem of their petticoats, and the men, capabilities unrecognised beneath frivolous exteriors, rode their horses to death for sport, went to spend the summer season in Baden, and at last, around their fortieth year, married heiresses. In the back rooms of restaurants where supper is eaten after midnight, under bright candlelight, the motley crowd of literati and actresses laughed. These types were as extravagant as kings, full of idealised ambitions and fantastical frenzies. It was a superior way of life, between earth and sky, storm-filled and sublime. As for the rest of the world, it was lost, indefinitely placed, as if non-existent. Besides, the closer things lay, the more her mind averted its eyes. Everything that immediately surrounded her, tedious countryside, imbecilic petty burghers, life's mediocrity, seemed to her exceptional in the world, a particular accident in which she was trapped, while beyond stretched further than the eye could reach the immense land of blissful joys and passions. In her longing, she confused the sensual pleasures of luxury with heartfelt joys, the elegance of social customs with the refinements of feeling. Did love, like an Indian plant, not need well-tilled soil, a precise temperature? So the sighs by moonlight, the long embraces, the tears trickling over forsaken hands, all the fevers of the flesh and the languishings of tender love were inseparable from the balconies of great chateaux replete with leisure, from a boudoir with silken blinds and a good thick carpet, stands filled with flowers, a bed mounted on a platform, or from the sparkle of precious stones and the livery-servants' shoulder-braids.

The postboy, who, each morning, came to groom the mare, would cross the corridor in his big wooden shoes; he had holes in his smock, his feet were bare in list slippers. That was the 'foot-boy' in short breeches with whom she had to be satisfied! When his work was over, he stayed away for the rest of the day; for Charles, on returning, would stable the horse himself, removing the saddle and slipping on the halter, during which time the maid would bring a bundle of straw and throw it, as best she could, in the manger.

To replace Nastasie (who left Tostes at last, in floods of tears), Emma took into her service a young girl of fourteen, an orphan with a sweet look. She forbade her to wear cotton caps, taught her that she must address you in the third person, bring a glass of water on a plate, knock at doors before entering, and how to iron, to starch, to dress her, intending to make of her a lady's maid. To avoid being dismissed, the new servant obeyed without a murmur; and, as Madame usually left the key in the sideboard, each evening Félicité took a little supply of sugar that she ate all alone, in her bed, after saying her prayers.

Sometimes, in the afternoon, she went to chat with the postboys. Madame stayed upstairs, in her room.

She wore a wide-open dressing gown, revealing, between the shawl facings of her bodice, a plaited chemisette with three gold buttons. Her belt was a corded girdle with fat tassels, and her little garnet-coloured slippers had a tuft of broad ribbons that sprawled over her instep. She had purchased for herself a blotting-case, stationery, a penholder and some envelopes, although she had no one to write to; she wiped the dust off her shelves, looked at herself in the mirror, took down a book, then, dreaming between the lines, let it fall in her lap. She had a desire to travel, or to go back and live at her convent. She wished both to die and to live in Paris.

Charles, in rain, in snow, rode along the country ways. He ate omelettes at farm tables, poked his arm into damp beds, got struck in the face by the warm jet of blood-lettings, listened to death-rattles, scrutinised basins, tucked up dirty linen; but he found, every evening, a blazing fire, dinner ready, yielding chairs, and a charming, nicely-dressed wife, smelling so fresh, that it was impossible to tell where the fragrance came from, or whether it was not her skin perfuming her chemise.

She charmed him with a variety of niceties: sometimes it was a new way of making up paper sconces for the candles, a flounce she altered on her gown, or the extraordinary name of a very simple dish, that the maid had spoilt, but which Charles tucked into with pleasure to the last little morsel. In Rouen she saw ladies who wore a bundle of charms by their watches; she bought some charms. She wanted a pair of big blue glass vases on her chimneypiece, and, shortly afterwards, an ivory sewing-case with a silver-gilt thimble. The less Charles under-stood these elegant touches, the more he was seduced by them. They added something pleasurable to his senses and to the sweetness of his home. It was like a dusting of gold scattered all along the little pathway of his life.

He felt well, he looked well; his reputation was entirely established. The rustics cherished him because he was not haughty. He patted the children, never went to the tavern, and anyway inspired confidence by his character. He was particularly successful with catarrh and consumption. Very much afraid of killing his patients, Charles in fact scarcely prescribed anything but soothing draughts, or now and then an emetic, a foot-bath or leeches. It was not that surgery frightened him; he would bleed people abundantly, like horses, and when it came to drawing teeth he had a *devilish keen grip*.

Finally, *to keep himself abreast*, he took out a subscription to *The Medical Hive*, a new journal whose prospectus he had received. He would read a little of it after his dinner; but the heat of the apartment, on top of his digestion, caused him to fall asleep after five minutes; and there he stayed, chin on his hands, hair spread mane-like down to the base of the lamp. Emma shrugged, looking at him. At least she might have had, as husband, one of those intense, silent men, who labour at their books deep into the night, and who, by the time they are sixty and rheumatism is setting in, sport a string of medals on their black, poorly-cut coat. She would have wished this name Bovary, which was her name, to have been illustrious, to see it displayed in bookshops, repeated in the newspapers, known by all of France. But Charles had no ambition! A doctor from Yvetot, with whom he had recently been in consultation, had humiliated him a little, at the patient's very bedside, in front of the assembled family. When Charles recounted the anecdote that evening, Emma inveighed loud and long against the colleague. Charles was touched by this. He kissed her tearfully on the brow. But she was incensed with shame, she wanted to hit him, she went into the corridor to open a window, sucking in the fresh air to calm herself down.

'What a wretched man, what a wretched man!' she said in an undertone, chewing her lips.

She was feeling more exasperated by him anyway. He was putting on weight with age; he kept cutting up the corks of empty bottles during dessert; he would pass his tongue over his teeth after eating; he would make a clucking noise each time he swallowed a mouthful of soup, and, as he was growing stout, his eyes, already small, seemed to be pushed up towards the temples by the bloating of his cheeks.

Sometimes Emma would tuck the red edging of his undervest back into his waistcoat, adjust his cravate, or throw out the faded gloves he was on the point of putting on; and this was not, as he imagined, for him, but for her own sake, in an outpouring of selfishness, of nervous irritation. She also talked to him at times of something she had read: a passage in a novel, a new play, or some anecdote of the *high life* regaled in the feuilleton; for Charles was at least someone happy to listen, ever ready with an approving remark. She confided many secrets to her greyhound! She would have confided them to the chimney's logs and the clock's pendulum.

In the depths of her soul, meanwhile, she was awaiting an event. Like a shipwrecked sailor, she swept a despairing gaze over the solitude of her life, searching afar for any white canvas on the foggy horizon. She had no idea of what this chance happening might be, what wind might push it right to her, towards what shore it might carry her, whether it was a rowing boat or a three-masted vessel, laden with anguish or crammed with joys up to the gunnels. But each morning, when she woke, she would have high hopes for it that day, and she listened to every sound, started up out of bed, was amazed when it did not come; then, at sunset, all the more sad, she would yearn for the morrow.

Spring re-appeared. She had fits of breathlessness during the first warm days, when the pear trees blossomed.

From the beginning of July, she counted on her fingers how many weeks she had left before October came, thinking that the Marquis d'Andervilliers would perhaps be giving another ball at La Vaubyessard. But the whole of September slipped past with neither letters nor visits.

After the tedium of this disappointment, her heart was once more left empty, and then the series of self-same days began again.

Now they were going to follow each other thus in single file, always the same, numberless, and bringing nothing! Other existences, however vapid, at least stood the chance of a denouement. One adventure would occasion an infinity of dramatic turns, and the scenery shift. But for her, nothing was going to happen, God had decreed it! The future was a corridor entirely dark, with a door fast-shut at the end.

She gave up music. Why play? Who would listen to her? As she could never, in a short-sleeved velvet dress, on an Erard piano, in a concert, striking the ivory keys with her slender fingers, feel an ecstatic murmur, like a breeze, circling about her, it was not worth the tedium of practising. She left her drawing portfolios and needlework in the cupboard. What use were they? What use? Sewing exasperated her.

'I have read everything,' she said to herself.

And she stayed turning the fire-tongs red, or watching the rain fall.

How sad she was of a Sunday, when vespers sounded! She listened, in an attentive stupor, to the bell's cracked strokes tolling one by one. Some cat or other on the roof, stepping slowly, arched its back in the wan rays of the sun. The wind blew trails of dust on the high road. Sometimes, far off, a dog howled: and the bell went on with its monotonous ringing, the regular strokes losing themselves in the fields.

Yet out of church they still came. The women in waxed boots, the peasant men in new smock-frocks, the little children skipping before them, they all headed home. And, until nightfall, five or six men, always the same, would stay on to play a game of corks in front of the inn's great door.

The winter was a cold one. Every morning the window panes were thick with frost, and the light, whitish through them, as through sanded glass, would sometimes not vary all day. The lamp had to be lit from four o'clock in the afternoon.

On fine days, she would go down into the garden. The dew had left a lace of silver over the cabbages, with long bright threads stretching from one to the other. There were no birds to be heard, all seemed asleep, the espalier covered in straw and the vine like a great sick snake under the wall's coping where, as you came nearer, you could see woodlice with numerous legs. Under the spruce trees, near the hedge, the breviary-reading priest in the tricorn hat had lost his right foot, and even the plaster, flaking off in the frost, had left white scabs on his face.

Then she went up again, closed the door, spread the coals, and, swooning from the heat of the hearth, would feel the tedium lapping ever heavier over her. She might well have gone down to chat with the maid, but a sense of decorum held her back.

Every day, at the same hour, the schoolmaster, in a black silk hat, opened the shutters of his house, and the village watch would pass by, bearing his sword over his frock coat. Morning and evening, the post-horses crossed the street in threes to drink at the pond. From time to time, a tavern door would jingle its bell, and, when there was a wind, the wig-maker's little copper basins, that served as the sign for his shop, could be heard grating on their two rods. It had a venerable fashion print pasted on a window-pane and, as decoration, the wax bust of a woman, whose hair was yellow. The wig-maker, too, lamented his arrested calling, his ruined prospects, and, longing for some shop in a city, somewhere like Rouen, for instance, on the quayside, near the theatre, he would spend the entire day walking up and down, from the Mairie to the church, gloomily awaiting customers. Whenever Madame Bovary raised her eyes, she would see him always there, like a sentry on duty, with his bonnet-grec over one ear and his jacket of tough wool.

Sometimes, of an afternoon, a man's head would appear beyond the parlour windows, a tanned head with black whiskers, which smiled slowly with a broad, gentle smile, showing white teeth. A waltz began immediately, and, on top of the organ, in a tiny drawing-room, dancers the size of a finger, women in pink turbans, Tyroleans in jackets, monkeys in dress-coats, gentlemen in short breeches, twirled, twirled among the armchairs, the sofas, the pier-tables, reflected again and again in the pieces of mirror joined at their edges by wisps of gold paper. The man cranked the handle, looking to the right, the left and up at the windows. From time to time, while shooting a long jet of brown saliva at the mounting-stone, he raised his instrument with his knee, the hard strap tiring his shoulder; and, sometimes mournful and languid, or cheerful and hurried, the box's music burst forth buzzing through a curtain of pink taffeta, under an arabesque rail of brass. These were airs played elsewhere in theatres, sung in drawing-rooms, danced to in the evening under glittering chandeliers, echoes of a world that reached as far as Emma. Endless sarabandes unrolled in her head, and, like a Hindu dancing girl on a flowery carpet, her thoughts skipped about to the notes, swinging from dream to dream, from sadness to sadness. When the man had received his alms in his cap, he would pull down an old blanket of blue wool, hitch the barrel organ onto his back and wander off with a heavy step. She watched him leave.

But it was above all at meal-times that she could bear it no longer, in that little room on the ground floor, with the stove that smoked, the door that squeaked, the walls that oozed moisture, the damp paving; all the bitterness of existence seemed to be served up on her plate, and, with the boiled beef's reek, there rose other similarly nauseating whiffs from the bottom of her soul. Charles was a slow eater; she would nibble a few nuts, or else, leaning on her elbow, amuse herself in making lines on the waxed cloth with the point of her knife.

She let everything go in her household, and Madame Bovary senior, when she came to spend a part of Lent at Tostes, was most astonished by the change. Indeed, she who was so mindful and dainty in the past, now spent whole days without dressing, wore stockings of grey cotton, used tallow candles for light. She would say over and over that they had to economise, not being rich, adding that she was very contented, very happy, that Tostes pleased her very much, and other novel speeches that left the mother-in-law mute. Yet Emma seemed no more disposed to follow her advice; one time, even, Madame Bovary having taken it into her head to maintain that masters should superintend the religion of their servants, she was replied to with so furious an eye and with such a frosty smile, that the good woman meddled no more.

Emma grew difficult, capricious. She ordered dishes for herself, did not touch them, one day drank nothing but milk on its own and the next day cups of tea by the dozen. Often she would stubbornly refuse to go out, then feel suffocated, opening the windows and putting on a light gown. When she had treated the maid with particular harshness, she gave her presents or sent her off to visit the neighbours, just as she would sometimes toss all the silver in her purse to paupers, although in the meantime she was scarcely tender-hearted, nor easily capable of feeling another's emotions, as is true of most country-bred people, who always keep in their souls something of the callousness of their fathers' hands.

Towards the end of February, Père Rouault, in memory of his recovery, personally brought a superb turkey for his son-in-law, and stayed three days at Tostes. Charles being busy with his patients, Emma kept him company. He smoked in the bedroom, spat on the fire-dogs, chatted about husbandry, calves, cows, poultry, and the municipal council; to such an extent that she closed the door again, when he had left, with a feeling of satisfaction that took even her by surprise. Moreover, she no longer hid her contempt for everything, as well as everyone; and now and again she would start to utter peculiar opinions, censuring what was approved of, and approving of perverse or immoral things: which made her husband stretch his eyes.

Would this misery last for ever? Would she not escape it? She was nevertheless as good as all those women who lived happily! She had seen duchesses at La Vaubyessard who were dumpier and more common-looking, and she cursed God's injustice; she would rest her head against the wall to cry; she envied lives full of tumult, masked nights, the saucy pleasures with all the wild states of mind she knew not of and which they must provide.

She grew pale and her heart would flutter. Charles gave her valerian and camphor baths. Everything he tried seemed to vex her more.

There were days when she prattled with a feverish spontaneity; these exalted moments were abruptly followed by periods of torpor in which she would remain without speaking, without stirring. What revived her then, was to sprinkle a bottle of eau-de-Cologne over her arms.

As she kept on and on complaining of Tostes, Charles imagined that the cause of her malady was doubtless to be found in some local influence, and, fixing on this idea, he seriously considered settling elsewhere.

Then she drank vinegar to make herself slimmer, contracted a little dry cough and lost her appetite completely.

It would cost Charles to leave Tostes after four years' residence and just as he was *beginning to make his mark*. Yet, if he had to! He drove her to Rouen to see his old master. It was a nervous complaint: they must have a change of air.

Having turned this way and that, Charles learnt that in the district of Neufchâtel, there was a large market-town called Yonville-l'Abbaye, whose doctor, a Polish refugee, had decamped just the week before. So he wrote to the local pharmacist to find out what the population figures were, the distance to the nearest colleague, how much his predecessor earned a year, etc.; and, the answers being satisfactory, he determined to move around springtime, if Emma's health did not improve.

One day, while she was tidying up a drawer in anticipation of her departure, she pricked her fingers on something. It was a wire on her marriage bouquet. The orange-blossom was yellow with dust, and the satin ribbons, piped in silver, were frayed at the edges. She threw it in the fire. It blazed up faster than dry straw. Then it was like a red bush on the embers, slowly consuming itself. She watched it burn. The little pasteboard berries flashed, the brass wires writhed, the lace melted; and the paper florets, all shrivelled up, swaying along the fireback like black butterflies, finally flew away up the chimney.

When they left Tostes, in March, Madame Bovary was pregnant.

PART TWO

I

Yonville-l'Abbaye[1] (thus named after an ancient Capuchin abbey of which not even the ruins exist any more) is a market-town some twenty-five miles from Rouen, between the Abbeville and Beauvais roads, at the bottom of a valley watered by the Rieule, a little river which after turning three millwheels near its mouth, flows into the Andelle, and has a few trout in it, that lads amuse themselves angling for of a Sunday.

We leave the main road to La Boissière and continue on the flat until we come to the top of Leux hill, from where the valley can be seen. The river that runs through it forms, as it were, two regions that are physiognomically distinct; everything on the left is put to grazing, everything on the right is put to the plough. The meadow stretches away under low, swelling hills to join up at the back with the pastures of the Bray country, while, on the eastern side, the plain, rising gently, broadens out gradually to display its golden cornfields as far as the eye can see. Flowing along the edge of the grass, the water divides the meadows' colour from that of the tilled fields in a single sinuous white streak, and so the country resembles a great unfolded cloak with a collar of green velvet edged in silver lace.

On the extreme skyline, as we arrive, we have in front of us the oaks of the Argueil forest, with the scarps of Saint-Jean's hill, striped from top to bottom by long, uneven trails of red; these are the marks of rainstorms, and their brick hues, standing out in thin threads from the grey colour of the mountain, derive from the large number of ferruginous springs flowing higher up, in the surrounding area.

Here we are in the border country of Normandy, Picardy and the Ile de France, a bastard region where the language lacks modulation, like the characterless countryside. This is where the worst Neufchâtel cheeses in the entire district are made, and where, on the other hand, farming is expensive, because a lot of dung is needed to fatten these friable soils full of sand and stones.

Up until 1835, there was no passable road serving Yonville; but around this time *a major parish* highway was established, linking the Abbeville and Amiens roads, and sometimes used by waggoners travelling from Rouen into Flanders. Nevertheless, Yonville-l'Abbaye continued to stand still, despite its *new openings*. Instead of improving cultivation, they stubbornly clung here to grazing, however low its value, and the indolent town, turning aside from the plain, continued naturally to expand towards the river. It can be seen from afar, lying all along the bank, like a cowherd having a nap beside the water.

At the base of the hill, after the bridge, begins a road planted with aspens, leading us in a straight line to the first houses of the place. Enclosed by hedges, they are surrounded by dishevelled buildings, presses, waggon-sheds and distilleries scattered under bushy trees with ladders, poles or scythes hooked up in their branches. The thatched rooves, like fur caps pulled over the eyes, come to about a third of the way down the low windows, whose thick, bulging glass is embellished with a knot in the middle, like the bottom of a bottle. Occasionally, on the plaster walls crossed diagonally by black joists, hangs the odd scrawny pear-tree, and the ground-floor doors have a little swing-gate to keep out the chicks, which come to peck on the threshold at crumbs of dark bread soaked in cider. Meanwhile the yards grow narrower, the dwellings draw closer together, the hedges disappear; a bundle of ferns swings on the end of a broom handle under a window; there is a farrier's forge and then a wheelwright's shop with two or three new waggons outside, encroaching on the road. Then, through a wall's opening, a white house appears beyond a circle of lawn adorned by a Cupid, finger to his lips;[2] two cast-iron vases stand at each end of the front steps; brass plates shine on the door: it is the notary's house, the finest in these parts.

The church is on the other side of the road, twenty paces further, at the entrance to the square. The little cemetery which surrounds it, enclosed by a wall at chest height, is so crammed with tombs, that the old stones level with the ground make an unbroken flagging, in which the grass has laid out neat green squares of its own accord. The church was rebuilt as good as new in the final years of Charles X's reign.[3] The wooden vault is starting to rot from the top, and its blue colouring has black cavities in places. Above the door, where the organ should be, clings a rood loft for the men, with a spiral staircase that rings under the wooden shoes.

The daylight, slanting in by the plain glass windows, illumines the rows of pews standing sideways to the wall, adorned here and there with a straw mat nailed above the words in thick letters: 'M. So-and-So's pew.' Further down, where the nave narrows, the confessional is matched by a statuette of the Virgin, dressed in a satin gown, her hair covered in a veil of net strewn with silver stars, her cheeks rouged like a Sandwich Islands' idol; a copy of the *Holy Family, sent by the Minister of the Interior*, dominating the high altar between four chandeliers at the back, finally concludes the vista. The pinewood choirstalls have been left unpainted.

The market-house, that is to say a tiled roof supported by a score of posts, alone takes up about half of Yonville's main square. The Mairie, *built after the plans of a Paris architect*, is a sort of Greek temple on the corner, next to the apothecary's house, with three Ionic pillars on the ground floor and, on the first floor, a semi-circular gallery, while the tympanum which completes the building is filled by a Gallic cock, resting one claw on the Charter[4] and holding the scales of justice in the other.

But what most draws the eye, opposite the *Lion d'Or*, is the pharmacy of Monsieur Homais! – chiefly in the evening, when its lamps are lit and the red and green flasks that adorn its façade throw their two bright colours a long way over the ground; and when, through them, as if by the light of Bengal-flares, might be glimpsed the shadow of the pharmacist, leaning his elbows on his desk. From top to bottom his house is placarded with inscriptions written in a sloping hand, in a round hand, in block capitals: 'Vichy, Seltzer and Barèges Waters, purifying syrups, Raspail's physic, Arabian sweetmeats, Darcet's pastilles, Regnault's paste, trusses, baths, chocolates for health, etc.' And the sign-board, which takes up the entire width of the shop, declares in gold letters: *Homais, Pharmacist*. Then, at the back of the shop, behind the huge scales fixed to the counter, the word *Laboratory* unscrolls above the glassed door which, halfway up its loftiness, repeats *Homais* yet one more time, in letters of gold on a black ground.

After that there is nothing more to see in Yonville. The street (the sole one), the length of a musket-shot and lined with a few shops, stops abruptly where the road turns. If we leave this on our right and follow the bottom of Saint-Jean's hill, we soon arrive at the cemetery.

To enlarge it during the cholera outbreak, a section of wall was knocked down and three acres of land purchased alongside; but this entire portion is almost uninhabited, the graves continuing to pile up near the gate, as before. The warden, who is both grave-digger and beadle to the church (thus drawing a double profit from the parish corpses), has taken advantage of the vacant ground to plant potatoes. From year to year, nevertheless, his little field shrinks, and, when an epidemic unexpectedly occurs, he does not know whether he should rejoice at the deaths or mourn the burial plots.

'You're feeding on the dead, Lestiboudois!' the priest told him finally, one day.

This sombre utterance caused him to reflect; it stayed him for a while; but still today he continues to cultivate his potatoes, and even maintains with aplomb that they grow naturally.

Since the events we are about to relate, nothing, in fact, has changed at Yonville. The tin tricolour still turns atop the church's bell-tower; the novelty shop goes on fluttering its two calico streamers in the wind; the pharmacist's specimens, like lumps of white fungus, decay more and more in their muddy alcohol, and, over the main entrance of the inn, the old golden lion, its colour washed out by the rain, still shows off its poodle frizz to passers-by.

The evening the Bovary couple were due to arrive at Yonville, the widow Lefrançois, landlady of this inn, was so very busy that sweat poured off her as she gave her stewpans a stir. Tomorrow was market day in the town. The meat had to be carved, the chickens drawn, the soup and coffee prepared, all in advance. In addition, she had her lodgers' meal, and that of the doctor, his wife and their maid; the billiard room rang with bursts of laughter; three millers in the snug called for brandy; the wood blazed, the embers crackled, and on the long kitchen table, amongst the quarters of raw mutton, rose piles of plates that trembled at the shocks of the chopping block as the spinach was hashed. The poultry in the yard could be heard screeching as the maid chased after the birds to cut off their heads.

A man in rawhide slippers, his skin a little scarred by smallpox and sporting a velvet cap with a gold tassel, was warming his back against the fireplace. His face expressed nothing but self-satisfaction, and he appeared to be as little ruffled by life as the goldfinch suspended above his head, in a wicker cage: this was the pharmacist.

'Artémise!' cried the landlady, 'break some kindling, fill the carafes, bring some brandy, look sharp! If I at least knew what dessert to offer to the company you're expecting, Monsieur? Sweet heavens! The removal men are starting up their racket again in the billiard-room. And that cart of theirs left in front of the main door! The *Hirondelle*'s arriving'll likely as not knock the bottom out of it! Call for Polyte, girl, tell him to put it in its proper place . . . To think that, since this morning, Monsieur Homais, they have played perhaps fifteen matches and drunk eight jugs of cider. But they're going to tear that baize,' she went on, watching them at a distance, her skimmer in her hand.

'No great harm,' replied Monsieur Homais, 'you'd buy another one.'

'Another billiard-table!' exclaimed the widow.

'Since that one is barely holding together, Madame Lefrançois; I'll tell you again, you're doing yourself no favours, absolutely no favours. And besides, these days the lover of the game wants narrow pockets and heavy cues. They're not playing marbles any longer: it's all changed. One has to go with the times! Consider Tellier, now . . .'

The landlady turned red in the face with spite. The pharmacist added:

'His billiard-table, whatever you say, is prettier than yours; and if it occurred to them, for example, to organise a tournament in aid of Poland or the flood victims of Lyon . . .'

'It isn't rascals like him who scare us,' interrupted the landlady, shrugging her stout shoulders. 'Be off with you, Monsieur Homais: as long as the *Lion d'Or* lives, they'll keep on coming. We have a fair bit tucked away, we do. Instead you'll see the *Café Français* closed one fine day, and with a lovely seizure bill on the shutters! What, change my billiard-table,' she continued to herself, 'when it's so convenient for setting out my laundry on, and slept up to six travellers for me in the hunting season. But still no sign of that dawdler Hivert!'

'Are you waiting for him before starting your gentlemen's dinner?' asked the pharmacist.

'Waiting for him? And what about Monsieur Binet, then! On the stroke of six you'll see him come in: there's none like him on earth for punctuality. He must always have his seat in the snug. He'd rather die than have to dine elsewhere. And finical eater that he is, and so particular about the cider! That's not the case with Monsieur Léon, not him; sometimes he comes in at seven o'clock, or seven-thirty even; he doesn't so much as glance at what he's eating. What a nice young man! Never gives himself airs.'

'There is quite a deal of difference, do you see, between someone who has received an education and a former rifleman turned tax-gatherer.'

Six o'clock chimed. Binet entered.

He was dressed in a blue frock coat, hanging stiff and straight all about his thin body; and his leather cap, its flaps tied up with string on top of his head, revealed, under the raised visor, a bald brow in which the habitual cap had made a dent. He wore a black woollen waistcoat, a horsehair stock, grey trousers, and, all the year round, a pair of well-polished boots that had two parallel swellings, on account of his protruding toes. Not a hair was out of trim in his fair beard that, following the jaw's contours, framed, like the edging of a flower-bed, his long wan face with its tiny eyes and hooked nose. Skilled in all types of card-games, a crack hunter and possessing a fine writing hand, he had a lathe at home, on which he amused himself turning napkin holders and amassing them in his house, with the jealousy of an artist and the selfishness of a bourgeois.[6]

He proceeded to the snug; but first the three millers had to be ousted; and, during the entire time the table was being laid, Binet stayed silent in his spot, near the stove; then he closed the door and took off his cap, as was customary.

'Courtesies won't be wearing out his tongue,' said the pharmacist, as soon as he was alone with the landlady.

'He never talks more,' she replied; 'last week two cloth-salesmen were here, witty lads who told a heap of jokes that made me weep with laughter; ah well! he stayed there, mute as a herring, and not one word.'

'Yes,' the pharmacist said, 'no imagination, no witticisms, nothing that constitutes the society man.'

'It's said that he's clever,' objected the landlady.

'Clever?' rejoined Monsieur Homais; 'Him? Clever? In his own calling, perhaps,' he added, in a quieter tone. And he resumed: 'Ah! That a merchant with considerable connections, that a lawyer, a doctor, an apothecary should be so engrossed, that they grow whimsical and even testy, I can understand; there's many a citable instance in the history books. But they are at least turning something over in their minds. Take myself, as an example: how many times has it happened to me that, on searching for my pen on my desk to write out a label, I find, upon the upshot, that I have placed it above my ear!'

Meanwhile, Madame Lefrançois went to the door to see if the *Hirondelle* had arrived. She gave a start. A man in black entered, all of a sudden, into the kitchen. You could make out, in the last of the twilight, his rubicund face and athletic figure.

'What is your pleasure, Monsieur le Curé?' asked the inn's landlady, at the same time reaching for one of the brass candlesticks on the chimneypiece, ranged there in a colonnade with their candles; 'Can I fetch you anything? A drop of cassis? A glass of wine?'

The clergyman refused most courteously. He had come to look for his umbrella, that he had forgotten the other day at the convent of Ernemont and, having beseeched Madame Lefrançois to have it returned to him at the presbytery that evening, he left to go to the church, where the angelus was ringing.

As soon as the pharmacist could no longer hear the tap of his shoes in the square, he found his late conduct most improper. This refusal to accept refreshment seemed to him the most obnoxious hypocrisy possible; all priests secretly tippled, and were out to restore the days of the tithe.

The landlady sprang to her priest's defence:

'And what's more, he could break four of you across his knee. Last year he helped our folk bring in the hay; he carried up to six bundles at once, he's that strong!'

'Bravo!' said the pharmacist. 'So send your daughters to confess to lively fellows with similar constitutions. Personally, if I was the government, I'd ordain that priests be bled once a month. Yes, Madame Lefrançois, a grand phlebotomy, every month, in the interest of public order and morality!'

'Hush now, Monsieur Homais! You're an infidel! You've no faith!'

The pharmacist replied:

'I have a faith, my faith, and I've even more of it than all of them, with their mummery and their hocus-pocus. On the contrary, I adore God. I believe in the Supreme Being, in a Maker whatever he is, to me it's immaterial, who has set us down here to fulfil our duties as citizen and father of a family; but I do not need to go into a church, kiss the silver plate and out of my own pocket fatten a heap of jokers who thrive better than us! You might just as effectively honour him in a wood, in a field, or even by contemplating the vault of heaven, as the ancients did. My God, as far as I'm concerned, is the God of Socrates, of Franklin, of Voltaire and of Béranger! I stand for the *Profession of Faith of a Savoyard Vicar* and the immortal principles of '89![7] Nor do I acknowledge an old codger of a God who takes a turn in his garden-plot with his walking-stick, entertains his friends in the bellies of whales, expires with a cry and comes back to life three days later: matters preposterous in themselves and completely opposed, moreover, to all the laws of natural philosophy; which proves, by the by, that priests have always wallowed in a vile ignorance, in which they strive to engulf the populace along with themselves.'

He held his tongue, gaze searching round for an audience, because, in his exuberance, the pharmacist had momentarily believed himself to be in the middle of a town council meeting. But the landlady was no longer listening. She was straining to hear a distant rumble. The rattle of a carriage could be discerned, mixed up with a clattering of slack horseshoes hammering the ground, and at last the *Hirondelle* came to a halt in front of the door.

It was a yellow crate carried on two big wheels which, reaching the height of the canopy, prevented the passengers seeing the road and dirtied their shoulders. The little panes of its narrow quarterlight windows trembled in their frames when the carriage was closed, and preserved spots of mud, here and there, amidst their ancient coating of dust that even rainstorms did not entirely wash away. It was drawn by three horses, the first in a leader's traces, and, when alighted from at either side, touched bottom with a bump.

A few worthy citizens of Yonville arrived in the square; they were all talking at the same time, asking for news, explanations and baskets;[8] Hivert was at a loss to know whom to satisfy. He was the one who carried out the local commissions in town. He would go into the shops, bringing back rolls of leather for the cobbler, scrap iron for the farrier, a barrel of herring for the inn, bonnets from the milliner's, toupets from the hairdresser's; and, the whole way back, he would distribute these parcels, throwing them over fences, standing upright on his seat and calling out at the top of his voice, while his horses trotted on by themselves.

An accident had held him up: Madame Bovary's greyhound bitch had run away over the fields. They had whistled after her for a good quarter of an hour. Hivert had even gone back a mile or so, thinking he might spot her at any minute; but they had had to carry on. Emma had wept, flown into a passion; she had blamed Charles for this misfortune. Monsieur Lheureux, cloth-merchant, who was with her in the vehicle, had tried to console her with numerous examples of lost dogs recognising their master after long years. There was one case, he said, of a dog that had returned from Constantinople to Paris. Another had gone a hundred and fifty miles in a straight line and swum four rivers; and his own father had owned a poodle which, after twelve years' absence, had suddenly leapt up at him one evening, in the street, when he was off to dine in town.

II

EMMA ALIGHTED FIRST, THEN FÉLICITÉ, Monsieur Lheureux, a wet-nurse, and they had to wake Charles up in his corner, where he had fallen fast asleep the moment night fell.

Homais introduced himself; he presented his compliments to Madame, his respects to Monsieur, said how delighted he was to be able to render them whatever service, and added with a cordial air that he had dared to invite himself along, his wife happening to be away.

Madame Bovary, once in the kitchen, went up to the fireplace. With the tips of her two fingers, she caught her gown at knee-height, and, having thus raised it to her ankles, she held out to the flame, above the revolving leg of mutton, one foot enclosed in a small black boot. The fire lit her up in her entirety, its raw light penetrating the weave of her dress, the smooth pores of her white skin and even her eyelids that she half-closed from time to time. An intense crimson hue swept over her, whenever a puff of wind came in through the half-open door.

From the other side of the fireplace, a young man with fair hair[9] watched her in silence.

As he was heartily bored at Yonville, where he was clerk to the lawyer Guillaumin, Monsieur Léon Dupuis (he it was, the other regular at the *Lion d'Or*) would often defer the moment of his meal, hoping that some traveller would come to the inn with whom he might chat in the course of the evening. Indeed, on days when his work was done, he was more or less obliged, for want of any other occupation, to arrive punctually, and suffer Binet's conversation from the soup to the cheese. So he accepted with delight the landlady's proposal that he dine in the company of the new arrivals, and they passed into the big parlour, where Madame Lefrançois, out of ostentation, had had the four covers laid.

Homais asked permission to keep on his bonnet-grec, for fear of a head cold.

Then, turning to his neighbour:

'Madame, no doubt, is a little weary? One is so terribly tossed about in that *Hirondelle* of ours!'

'That's true,' said Emma; 'but disturbance always diverts me; I like changing places.'

'It's such a dull affair,' sighed the clerk, 'just to spend one's life confined to the same spot!'

'If you were like me,' said Charles, 'endlessly obliged to be on horseback . . .'

'But,' Léon went on, addressing himself to Madame Bovary, 'there's nothing more agreeable, to my mind; when you're able to,' he added.

'Yet,' said the apothecary, 'the practice of medicine is not overly taxing in our region; for the state of our roads permits the use of the gig, and, generally speaking, one is paid reasonably, the farmers being well off. We have, medically, aside from the normal cases of enteritis, bronchitis, bilious ailments, etc., some sporadic fevers now and again at harvest-time, but, overall, few serious cases, nothing special to note, except for a decent amount of scrofula, no doubt due to the appalling conditions of hygiene in our peasant dwellings. Ah! you will come across much prejudice to battle against, Monsieur Bovary; much routine stubbornness, with which your every scientific effort will clash daily; for they still have recourse to novenas, to relics, to the priest, rather than going as a matter of course to the doctor or to the pharmacist. The climate, however, is not, to tell the truth, bad, and we even count several ninety-year-olds in the commune. The thermometer (I have taken the readings myself) goes down to four degrees in winter, and, in high summer, touches twenty-five, thirty degrees Centigrade at the very most, which gives us a maximum of twenty-four Réaumur, or else fifty-four Fahrenheit (English scale),[10] no higher! – and, indeed, we are sheltered from the northerly winds by the Forest of Argueil on the one side, and by Saint-Jean's hill from the westerly winds on the other; and this heat, meanwhile, on account of the water vapour given off by the river and the considerable presence of cattle in the fields – which emit, as you know, much ammonia, that's to say, azotic gas, hydrogen and oxygen (no, just azotic gas and hydrogen) – and which, sucking up the humus from the earth, blending all these different emanations, reuniting them in a bundle, so to speak, and itself combining with the electricity diffused in the atmosphere, when there is any, can in the long term, as in the tropics, spawn unhealthy miasmas; – this heat, I say, is precisely tempered on the side where it comes from, or rather from where it would be coming, that's to say the south side, by the south-easterly winds, which, themselves being cooled as they cross the Seine, sometimes reach us all of a sudden, like the winds from Russia!'

'Have you at least some walks in the vicinity?' continued Madame Bovary, speaking to the young man.

'Oh, very few,' he replied. 'There's a spot known as the Pasture, at the top of the hill, on the edge of the forest. Sometimes, of a Sunday, I go up there with a book, and stay to watch the sunset.'

'There's nothing I admire more than a sunset,' she resumed, 'but by the seaside, especially.'

'Oh! I adore the sea,' said Monsieur Léon.

'And then, does it not seem to you,' replied Madame Bovary, 'that the mind sails more freely on that limitless expanse, whose contemplation lifts the soul and imparts ideas of the infinite, of the ideal?'

'It's the same with mountain landscapes,' Léon went on. 'I've a cousin who travelled through Switzerland last year, and who told me that you cannot imagine the poetry of the lakes, the charm of the waterfalls, the gigantic effect of the glaciers. You see pines of an incredible size, lying across torrents, cottages hanging above precipices, and, a thousand feet below, entire valleys, when there's a break in the clouds. Such sights must enrapture, be an inducement to prayer, to ecstasy! And I no longer feel astonished by this celebrated musician who, to better stimulate his imagination, was wont to go off and play the piano before some imposing site or other.'

'You play music?' she asked.

'No, but I like it very much,' he replied.

'Ah! don't listen to him, Madame Bovary,' Homais interrupted, leaning over his plate, 'that's pure modesty. – What, my dear boy? Well! The other day, in your room, you were singing *The Guardian Angel* quite delightfully. I heard you from the laboratory; you articulated the words like an actor.'

Léon did, indeed, lodge at the pharmacist's, where he had a little room on the second floor, overlooking the square. He blushed at this compliment from his landlord, who had already turned to the doctor and was enumerating the principal inhabitants of Yonville one after the other. He recounted anecdotes, proffered information; the notary's wealth was not known precisely, *and there was the Tuvache household* which caused great to-do.

Emma took up again:

'And which music do you prefer?'

'Oh! German music, the sort that induces dreams.'

'Do you know the Italians?'

'Not yet; but I shall see them next year, when I go to live in Paris, to finish my law studies.'

'As I had the honour,' said the apothecary, 'to convey to your husband with reference to this wretched Yanoda fellow who took off: you will, thanks to his imprudent actions, find yourself enjoying one of the most comfortable houses in Yonville. Its chief convenience for a doctor, is that it has a door onto the *Alley Walk*, which lets you go in and out without being seen. Moreover, it is furnished with all that's pleasing in a household: wash-house, kitchen with pantry, family parlour, fruit-loft and so forth. He was a jolly fellow who never thought twice about spending! He had built for himself, at the bottom of the garden, beside the water, an arbour expressly for summertime beer-drinking, and if Madame likes to garden, she can . . .'

'My wife scarcely takes an interest in it,' said Charles; 'she prefers, however much we beg her to exercise, to stop in her room the whole time, reading.'

'I'm just the same,' said Léon; 'in fact, what better occupation than to lie by the fireside in the evening with a book, while the wind beats on the panes, the lamp burns . . . ?'

'Isn't it?'" she said, fastening upon him her large dark wide-open eyes.

'Nothing is planned,' he continued, 'the hours slip by. One roams motionless through countries that seem vividly seen and your mind, entwining with the fiction, frolics in the details or pursues the twists and turns of the adventures. It blends with the characters; so that it seems to be you whose heart races under their dress.'

'True! True!' she said.

'Has it sometimes happened to you,' Léon went on, 'that you meet in a book with a vague idea you've had, some dim picture that returns from a long way off, and which is like the total exposure of your shrewdest perception?'

'I have felt that,' she replied.

'This is why,' he said, 'I especially love the poets. I find verse more delicate than prose, it makes you cry more easily.'

'Nevertheless, it's wearying in the long run,' Emma went on; 'and these days, on the contrary, I adore stories where one thing follows another without a breath to spare, that make us feel scared. I detest those commonplace heroes and mild feelings, as exist in life.'

'In fact,' the clerk observed, 'as these works do not touch the heart, they wander, it seems to me, from the real aim of Art. It is so soothing, among life's disenchantments, to be able to turn in your imagination to noble characters, unsullied affections and pictures of happiness. As for me, living here, far from society, it's my sole distraction; but Yonville offers so few resources!'

'Like Tostes, no doubt,' Emma went on; 'I too was always subscribed to a circulating library.'

'If Madame wishes to do me the honour of using it,' said the pharmacist, who had just caught these last words, 'I myself have at her disposal a library composed of the finest authors: Voltaire, Rousseau, Delille, Walter Scott, *The Literary Echo*, etc., and I receive, furthermore, different periodicals, among them *The Rouen Beacon* daily,[12] having the benefit of being its correspondent for the districts of Buchy, Forges, Neufchâtel, Yonville and environs.'

They had been eating for two and a half hours; because Artémise the maid, nonchalantly dragging the selvage of her old slippers on the tiles, would bring the plates one after the other, forget everything, pay attention to nothing and keep leaving half-open the billiard-room door which battered the wall with its latch-bar's tip.

Without realising it, talking all the while, Léon had placed his foot on one of the crosspieces of the chair in which Madame Bovary was seated. She wore a little blue-silk scarf, which held a collar of fluted cambric upright like a ruff; and, depending on how she moved her head, the lower part of her face buried itself in the linen or emerged from it softly. Thus it was, close to each other, while Charles and the pharmacist chatted, that they embarked on one of those vague conversations, in which chance phrases keep bringing you back to the fixed centre of a mutual understanding. Parisian shows, titles of novels, new dances, and the society world they knew nothing of, Tostes where she had lived, Yonville where they had turned out to be, they explored everything, spoke of everything until the end of dinner.[13]

When the coffee was served, Félicité went off to prepare the bedroom in the new house, and the guests soon withdrew. Madame Lefrançois slept by the embers, while the stable lad, lantern in hand, waited to take Monsieur and Madame Bovary home. His red hair was interwoven with bits of straw, and he limped on his left leg. When he had taken Monsieur le Curé's umbrella in his other hand, they set off on foot.

The town was asleep. The pillars of the market-house cast long shadows. The ground was entirely grey, as on a summer's night.

But, as the doctor's house stood only fifty paces from the inn, they had to wish each other goodnight almost immediately, and the company dispersed.

Emma, even from the entrance hall, felt the plaster's chill drop onto her shoulders like a damp cloth. The walls were newly done, and the wooden stairs creaked. In the bedroom, on the first floor, a whitish daylight fell through the curtainless windows. Tops of trees could be glimpsed, and the meadows further off, half-drowned in fog, smoking in the moonlight wherever the river wound.

In the middle of the rooms, piled pell-mell, there were drawers, bottles, curtain-rods, gilt poles along with mattresses on chairs and basins on the parquet – the two men who had carried the furniture having left everything there, carelessly.

It was the fourth time she had slept in an unknown place. The first had been the day of her entry into the convent, the second that of her arrival at Tostes, the third at Vaubyessard, the fourth was this one; and each had acted in her life like the unveiling of a fresh phase. She refused to believe that things could repeat themselves in the same way in different places, and, as the portion already experienced had been bad, what remained to be consumed would doubtless be better.

III

THE NEXT DAY, ON WAKING up, she saw the clerk in the square. She was in her dressing gown. He raised his head and waved at her. She gave a quick nod and closed the window.

Léon waited all day for six o'clock to come; but entering the inn, he found no one except M. Binet, sitting at table.

Yesterday's dinner was, for him, a considerable event; never, until that point, had he chatted for two hours in succession with a *lady*. How then had he been able to expound to her, and in such language, so very many things that he would not have said so well before? He was generally shy and held himself back out of both modesty and dissimulation. In Yonville he was considered to have *proper* manners. He listened to the arguments of older folk, and seemed not to be over-excited politically, a remarkable thing in a young man. He was talented, besides; he painted in watercolours, could read a treble clef, and applied himself willingly to literature after dinner, when he was not playing cards. Monsieur Homais esteemed him for his learning; Madame Homais delighted in his obligingness, for he would often play in the garden with the Homais children, brats who were always begrimed, very badly brought up and of a somewhat phlegmatic humour, like their mother. To look after them, besides the maid, they had Justin, the student in pharmacy, a distant cousin of Monsieur Homais who had been taken into the household out of charity, and served also as a menial.

The apothecary showed himself to be the best of neighbours. He proffered Madame Bovary particulars about tradesmen, had his cider merchant come over expressly, tasted the beverage himself, and saw to it that the cask was properly stowed in the cellar; furthermore he showed how to go about obtaining a cheap butter supply, and concluded an arrangement with Lestiboudois, the sacristan, who, beyond his sacerdotal and mortuary duties, looked after Yonville's principal gardens by the hour or by the year, according to people's inclinations.

The need to take care of others was not all that was prompting the pharmacist to such a degree of obsequious warmth, and there was beneath it a scheme.

He had infringed the law of the 19th Ventôse, Year XI, Article 1,[14] which forbids any individual not holding a diploma from practising medicine; so much so that, denounced by persons obscure, Homais had been summoned to Rouen, before the king's procureur, in his private chambers. The magistrate had received him standing up, begowned, ermine-shouldered and with cap of office on his head. It was in the morning, before the hearing. In the corridor could be heard the sturdy boots of policemen passing, and the turning of great locks like a far-off roar. The apothecary's ears rang as if he was about to have an apoplectic fit; dimly he glimpsed dungeons, his family in tears, the pharmacy sold, all his specimen jars dispersed; and he was obliged to enter a café for a glass of rum and seltzer water, to recover his spirits.

Little by little, the memory of this reprimand grew fainter, and he continued, as before, to give soothing consultations in his back-shop. But the mayor bore him malice, his colleagues were jealous, he had everything to fear; binding Monsieur Bovary through courtesies, was to gain his gratitude, and would stop him from talking later, if he noticed anything. And every morning, Homais would bring him *the newspaper*, and often, of an afternoon, would leave the pharmacy for a moment to go over to the medical officer's for a talk.

Charles was unhappy; the patients were not coming. He remained in his chair for many hours, without speaking, went off into his consulting room to sleep or watched his wife sew. For diversion, he exerted himself at home as a drudge, and even tried to paint the loft with a residue of the colour that the painters had left. But money-matters were bothering him. He had laid out so much for the repairs to Tostes, for Madame's dresses and for the removals, that the whole dowry, more than three thousand crowns, had drained itself away in two years. Then, how many things were damaged or lost in the transfer from Tostes to Yonville, not counting the plaster priest, who, falling from the carriage after an excessively heavy jolt, was smashed into a thousand pieces on the paving of Quincampoix!

A happier care came to divert him, namely his wife's pregnancy. The nearer her term approached, the more he cherished her. It was the establishing of a different fleshly bond, and like the continual reminder of a more complex union. When from afar he caught sight of her sluggish gait and her waist swinging slackly on uncorseted hips, or when the two of them were face to face and he beheld her so utterly comfortable, assuming weary postures as she sat in her chair, then his happiness could no longer contain itself; he rose, he kissed her, stroked her face, called her little mother, wanted to make her dance, and babbled, half laughing, half crying, all manner of tender pleasantries as they came into his head. The idea that he had begot delighted him. He wanted for nothing at present. He was acquainted with the entire span of human existence, and leaned on his elbows serenely there at its table.

Emma experienced a great amazement at first, then longed for the delivery, to know what it was to be a mother. But, not being able to spend what she wanted, to have a cradle with curtains in pink silk and embroidered bonnets, she renounced the baby's outfit in a paroxysm of bitterness, and ordered it all at once from a work-woman in the village, without choosing or discussing a thing. So she never had fun with those preparations on which a mother's love whets its appetite, and her fondness, from the beginning, was perhaps weakened in some way.

However, as Charles, at every meal, would talk about the mite, she considered it in greater depth.

She desired a son; he would be strong and dark, she would call him Georges; and this notion of having a male child was like the anticipated revenge for all her former powerlessness. A man, at least, is free: he can leaf through loves and lands and pass through obstacles, have a taste for the most remote joys. But a woman is continually impeded. Inert and pliant at the same time, against her she has the weakness of the flesh and the law's subjections. Her will, like her bonnet's veil constrained by a ribbon, flutters at every breath of wind; there is always some desire that urges, some seemliness that constrains.

She was delivered one Sunday, around six o'clock, at sunrise.

'It's a girl!' said Charles.

She turned her head and fainted.

Almost immediately, Madame Homais ran up and kissed her, as did Mère Lefrançois, of the *Lion d'Or*. The apothecary, a prudent fellow, merely sent her some provisional congratulations, through the half-open door. He wished to see the infant, and found it well formed.

During her convalescence, she was much occupied in seeking a name for her daughter. At first, she reviewed all those with Italianate endings, such as Clara, Louisa, Amanda, Atala; she rather liked Galsuinde, and Yseult or Léocadie even more so. Charles desired the child to be called after his mother; Emma was against it. They leafed through the calendar from end to end, and outsiders were consulted.

'Monsieur Léon,' said the apothecary, 'with whom I was chatting the other day, is amazed that you have not chosen Madeleine, which is excessively in fashion now.'

But Mère Bovary clamoured vociferously against this sinner's name. As for Monsieur Homais, he had a fondness for all the ones that called to mind a great man, an illustrious deed or a noble notion, and it was by this very system that he had christened his four children. Thus, Napoléon stood for glory and Franklin for liberty; maybe Irma was a concession to romanticism; but Athalie,[15] a homage to the most immortal masterpiece of the French stage. Because his philosophical convictions did not impede his artistic admirings, the thinker in him never smothered the sensitive man; he knew how to differentiate, to make allowances for imagination and for zealotry. In that tragedy, for example, he censured the ideas, but admired the style; he cursed the conception, but applauded all the details and became exasperated by the characters, as he enthused over their speeches. When he read the great passages, he was enraptured; but, when he considered how the Church bigots would take advantage of them to set out their stall, he was disconsolate, and in this confusion of entangled feelings, he would have liked at the same time to have crowned Racine with both hands and to have argued with him for a good quarter of an hour.

At last, Emma remembered that at the Château de la Vaubyessard she had heard the Marchioness call a young lady Berthe; consequently this name was chosen, and, as Père Rouault was unable to come, they begged Monsieur Homais to be godfather. His christening presents were all goods from his business, namely: six boxes of jujubes, a whole jar of Arabian sweetmeats, three little baskets of marshmallow and, furthermore, six sugar-candy sticks that he had found in a cupboard. The evening of the ceremony, there was a great dinner; the priest was there; things warmed up. Monsieur Homais, over the liqueurs, struck up *The God of the Simple Folk*.[16] Monsieur Léon sang a gondolier's song, and Mère Bovary, who was the godmother, a ballad from the days of the Empire; finally Père Bovary demanded that the baby be brought downstairs, and set about baptising it with a glass of champagne that he poured over its head from on high. This mockery of the first of the sacraments roused the indignation of the Abbé Bournisien: Père Bovary responded with a quotation from *The War of the Gods*,[17] the priest wanted to leave; the ladies implored; Homais interposed; and they succeeded in making the clergyman sit down again, he calmly taking up once more, on its saucer, his little half-drunk cup of coffee.

Père Bovary stayed another month at Yonville, dazzling its inhabitants with a superb silver-banded forage cap, which he wore in the mornings, when smoking his pipe on the square. Being likewise in the habit of drinking a deal of brandy, he frequently despatched the maid to the *Lion d'Or* to buy a bottle for him, which they put on his son's account; and, to scent his handkerchiefs, he consumed the entire stock of eau-de-Cologne in his daughter-in-law's possession.

The latter did not find his company at all disagreeable. He had travelled the world: he spoke of Berlin, Vienna, Strasbourg, of his time as an officer, the mistresses he had had, the great luncheons he had given; he proved himself endearing besides, and sometimes, either on the stairs or in the garden, he would seize her around the waist and exclaim:

'Charles, you watch out!'

So Mère Bovary feared for her son's happiness, and, dreading that her husband, in the long run, might have an immoral influence on the young woman, she lost no time in hastening the departure. Perhaps she had graver anxieties. Monsieur Bovary was a man who respected nothing.

One day, Emma was suddenly taken with a need to see her daughter, who had been put out to nurse with the carpenter's wife; and, without checking by the calendar whether the six weeks of the Virgin[18] were over yet, she set out for the Rollet house, which lay right on the edge of the village, at the foot of the hill, between the high road and the meadows.

It was midday: the houses had their shutters closed, and the slate rooves, glittering under the sharp light of the blue sky, seemed to be sending up sparks from the ridges at their gable-ends. A strong wind blew. Emma felt faint, walking; the pavement's stones hurt her; she hesitated whether to return home, or to go in somewhere and sit down.

At that moment, Monsieur Léon came out of a neighbouring door with a bundle of papers under his arm. He came over to greet her and stood in the shade before Lheureux's shop, under the grey awning that jutted out.

Madame Bovary said that she was going to see her child, but that she had begun to feel weary.

'If . . .' began Léon, not daring to go on.

'Have you an engagement somewhere?' she asked.

And, at the clerk's reply, she begged him to accompany her. From that evening, Yonville knew all about it, and Madame Tuvache, the mayor's wife, declared in front of her maid that *Madame Bovary had compromised herself.*

To reach the wet-nurse's house they were obliged, after the road, to turn left, as if making their way to the cemetery, and to pursue, between the small houses and the yards, a little path bordered by privet. This was in flower, as were the speedwell, the dog roses, the nettles, and the slender-stemmed brambles bursting forth from the thickets. Through holes in the hedges, they perceived, in the *barton-yards*, some hog or other on a muck-heap, or wooden-collared cows, rubbing their horns against the trunks of trees. Both of them, side by side, walked slowly, she leaning on him and he curbing his step, measuring his pace to hers; in front of them, a swarm of flies hovered, buzzing in the warm air.

They recognised the house from the old walnut-tree by which it was shaded. Low and covered in brown tiles, it had a string of onions hung outside under the loft window. Bunches of kindling, upright against the thorn fence, surrounded a patch of lettuce, a few lavender plants and some sweetpeas trained up sticks. Dirty water ran straggling over the grass, and all about lay a number of indeterminate rags, knitted stockings, a red cotton night-shirt, and a big sheet of thick canvas stretched lengthwise over the hedge. At the sound of the gate, the wet-nurse emerged, holding a suckling baby on her arm. With her other hand she was pulling a poor wretched mite, his face covered in scrofulous sores, a Rouen hatmaker's son whose parents, too taken up by their business, would leave him in the country.

'Come in,' she said; 'your little one is over there, sleeping.'

The bedroom, on the ground floor, the only one in the dwelling, had a large bed without curtains set against the wall at the far end, while the kneading-trough occupied the window-side, one of whose panes had been repaired with a blue paper sunflower. In the corner, behind the door, half-boots with gleaming studs were lined up under the scullery slab, near a bottle full of oil sporting a feather in its neck; a Mathieu Laensberg almanac[19] drooped on the dusty chimneypiece, between gunflints, candle-stubs and bits of touch-wood. The final piece of superfluousness in this room was Fame blowing on her trumpets, an image doubtless cut out from some perfumery prospectus, and nailed to the wall by six shoe tacks.

Emma's child slept on the floor, in a wicker cradle. She picked her up with the blanket she was wrapped in, and began to sing gently, rocking from side to side.

Léon paced the room; it seemed queer to him to see this lovely woman in a nankeen dress, right in the middle of this wretchedness. Madame Bovary blushed; he averted his eyes, thinking that his look had perhaps betrayed some impropriety. Then she put the baby, which had just vomited over her collar, back to bed. The wet-nurse immediately came to wipe it off, protesting that it would not show.

'She's done a lot worse to me,' she said, 'and just rinsing her off keeps me busy! So if you've the kindness to make an order with Camus the grocer that he lets me take a bit of soap when I need it, as would be easier for you what's more, so I wouldn't be putting you to no bother.'

'It's fine, it's fine,' said Emma. 'Goodbye, Mère Rollet!'

And she went out, wiping her feet on the threshold.

The good woman accompanied her to the end of the yard, all the while talking of the trouble she had in getting up in the night.

'I am that worn out by it sometimes, that I nod off in my chair; also, you ought at least to give me a little pound of ground coffee which'd do me for a month and I'd take mornings with some milk.'

Having endured her thanks, Madame Bovary took herself off; and she was a little way along the path, when the sound of wooden clogs made her turn her head: it was the wet-nurse!

'What is it?'

And the peasant-woman, pulling her to one side, behind an elm, began to talk to her about her husband, who, with his trade and six francs a year which the captain . . .

'Come to the point,' said Emma.

'Ah well,' the nurse took up again, sighing between each word, 'I'm afraid he'll come over all sad when he sees me drink my coffee all alone; you know, these men . . .'

'Since you are to have some,' Emma repeated, 'so I shall give you some . . . ! You're boring me!'

'Alas! My poor dear lady, it's just that, owing to his injuries, he has terrible cramps in his chest. He even says that cider weakens him.'

'Out with it, quickly, Mère Rollet!'

'So,' the latter took up again with a curtsey, 'if it's not too much to ask –' she curtsied again – 'when you like,' – and she gave a beseeching look, – 'a little crock of brandy,' she said at last, 'and I'll rub some on the feet of your little one, hers being tender as a tongue.'

Rid of the wet-nurse, Emma took Léon's arm again. She walked quickly for a while; then she slowed down, and her gaze adrift in front of her alighted on the shoulder of the young man, whose frock coat bore a collar of black velvet. His auburn hair fell over it, smooth and well combed. She noticed his nails, which were longer than were generally worn at Yonville. One of the clerk's major occupations was keeping them in repair; and he kept, for this use, a uniquely appropriate knife in his inkcase.

They returned to Yonville along the water's edge. In the warm season, the broader bank exposed the foundations of the garden walls, where a staircase of a few steps led down to the river. It flowed without a sound, swift and cold to the eye; slender long grasses bowed down there as one, depending on the current that pressed upon them, to spread out like forsaken heads of green hair in its limpidness. Sometimes, on the tips of the rushes or the water-lily leaves, an insect with delicate legs crawled or alighted. A single sunbeam pierced the waves' little blue bubbles as they burst in one another's wake; the lopped and ancient willows mirrored their grey bark in the water; beyond, all around, the meadowland seemed empty. It was lunch-time in the farms, and the young woman and her companion heard as they walked only the rhythm of their steps on the footpath's earth, the words they uttered, and the brush of Emma's gown rustling all around her.

The garden walls, their coping studded with pieces of bottle, were as warm as greenhouse glass. Wallflowers had grown in the brickwork; and, with the edge of her spread parasol, Madame Bovary, as she passed by, made a few of their withered blooms drop their yellow pollen, or else some branch of honeysuckle or traveller's joy hanging down on the outside would trail for a moment on the silk, catching in the fringe.

They talked of a Spanish dance troupe, who were expected soon on the Rouen stage.

'You're going?' she asked.

'If I can,' he replied.

Had they nothing else to say? Yet their eyes were full of a more serious talk; and, whilst they were endeavouring to find trite phrases, both of them felt the same languor invade them; it was like a murmur of the soul, deep and continuous, prevailing over the murmur of the voices. Overtaken with wonder at this novel sweetness, they did not think of telling one another of the sensation nor of discovering its cause. Future joys, like tropical shores, discharge their native indolence, a perfumed breeze, on the immensity leading up to them, and you drowse in this intoxication without even troubling yourself about the horizon that you do not descry.

The earth, at one point, had given way under the tread of cattle; they were obliged to walk on large green stones, carefully spaced apart in the mire. She would frequently stop for a moment to see where to place her lady's boot – and, wavering on the shaky boulder, her elbows in the air, bent at the waist, her glance undecided, she would giggle then, from fear of falling over in the puddles.

When they arrived in front of her garden, Madame Bovary pushed the little gate, ran up the steps and disappeared.

Léon returned to his office. The master was absent; he cast an eye over the papers, then cut himself a pen, put his hat on at last and went out.

He went up onto the Pasture, to the crest of Argueil hill, by the entrance to the forest; he lay down on the ground under the firs, and surveyed the sky through his fingers.

'How bored I am!' he said to himself, 'how bored I am!'

He deserved to be pitied having to live in this village, with Homais for a friend and Monsieur Guillaumin for a master. The latter, completely taken up with cases, sporting spectacles with gold side-pieces and red whiskers on a white neck-cloth, understood nothing of the mind's delicacies, although he affected a stiff, English manner that had dazzled the clerk at first. As for the pharmacist's wife, she was the best spouse in Normandy, gentle as a lamb, cherishing her children, her father, her mother, her cousins, weeping at the ills of others, entirely free and easy with her household, and abhorring stays; – but so slow to stir, so dull to listen to, of so common an appearance and so limited in conversation, that he had never imagined, although she was thirty, and he twenty, and they slept next door to each other, and he talked to her each day, that she might be someone's wife, or own anything else of her sex but the dress.

And after that, who was there? Binet, a few tradesmen, two or three tavern-keepers, the priest, and finally M. Tuvache, the mayor, with his two sons, wealthy folk, peevish, dull-witted, tilling their land themselves, feasting with their families, and bigots besides, and their company nothing less than unbearable.

But on the common back-scene of all these human faces, Emma's countenance stood out lone and yet further off, for between her and him he sensed vague, unfathomable depths.

At first, he had called on her several times in the pharmacist's company. Charles had not seemed exceedingly eager to receive him; and Léon, between the fear of being indiscreet and the desire for an intimacy that he considered almost impossible, did not know what to do.

IV

WITH THE FIRST CHILL DAYS, Emma left her bedroom and took to the parlour, a long, low-ceilinged room where, on the chimneypiece, a tufted coral showed itself off in the mirror. Seated in her armchair, near the window, she could see the village folk passing by on the pavement.

Léon, twice a day, repaired to the *Lion d'Or* from his office. Emma, from far off, would hear him coming; she would bend forward to listen; and the young man glided behind the curtain, always dressed in the same way and without turning his head. But when, at twilight, chin in her left hand, she had abandoned her needlework on her knees, she would often start at the apparition of that sudden shadow passing by. She would rise and order the table to be laid.

Monsieur Homais would arrive during dinner. Bonnet-grec in his hand, he entered on soundless tread so as not to disturb a soul and always repeating the same phrase: 'Good evening everyone!' Then, when he had settled in his place, at table, between husband and wife, he would ask the doctor for news of his patients, and the doctor in turn consulted him on the likelihood of fees. Then they would chat about what had appeared *in the paper*. Homais, by that hour of the day, knew it almost by heart; and he recounted it in its entirety, with the journalist's reflections and every story of individual catastrophe that had occurred in France or abroad. But, the subject drying up, soon enough he would toss out a few observations on the dishes he was examining. At times, half rising, he would even indicate daintily to Madame the tenderest piece, or, turning towards the maid, proffer her advice on the manipulation of stews and the hygiene of seasonings; he spoke aroma, osmazome, juice and gelatine in a manner fit to dazzle. With a head more filled with recipes than his pharmacy with jars, Homais also excelled at making a variety of jams, vinegars and sweet cordials, as well as being acquainted with all the latest contrivances of economical steam-kitchens, along with the art of conserving cheeses and nursing sick wines.

At eight-o'clock, Justin came for him in order to lock the pharmacy. Then Monsieur Homais would look slyly at the youth, above all if Félicité was present, aware that his apprentice had taken a fancy to the doctor's house.

'My young fellow,' he would say, 'has begun to have ideas, and I do believe, the devil take me, that he's in love with your maid!'

But a more serious fault, and one he would reproach him for, was that he continually eavesdropped on conversations. On Sundays, for example, it was impossible to make him leave the drawing-room, where Madame Homais had called him to take away the children, who were nodding off in the armchairs, their backs dragging down the loose-fitting calico covers.

Not many people came to the pharmacist's evening-parties, his backbiting and his political opinions having successively driven away various respectable people. The clerk never failed to be there. The moment he heard the bell, he ran to meet Madame Bovary halfway, took her shawl, and put to one side, under the pharmacy desk, the stout list slippers she wore over her boots, whenever it snowed.

They would begin by playing several games of *trente-et-un*: then Monsieur Homais played *écarté* with Emma; Léon, behind her, giving her advice. Standing up and with his hands on the back of her chair, he gazed at the teeth of the comb sunk into her chignon. Each time she played her hand, the movement made the right side of her dress ride up. From her fastened hair, a dusky tint ran down over her back, and, gradually paling, lost itself little by little in shadow. From there her garment fell away on either side over the seat, puffing out, full of pleats, and sprawling down as far as the ground. When Léon occasionally felt the sole of his boot placed upon it, he moved away, as if he had stepped on someone.

After the card game was over, the apothecary and the doctor played dominoes, and Emma, changing seats, leaned her elbows on the table, leafing through *L'Illustration*.[20] She had brought along her fashion journal. Léon sat down next to her; they looked at the engravings and waited for each other at the bottom of the page. She would often entreat him to read verses to her; Léon would recite them in a drawling manner and was careful to make his voice die away in the love passages. But the click of the dominoes vexed him; Monsieur Homais was good, he beat Charles by a whole double six. Then, the third hundred finished, the two of them stretched out in front of the fire and would not take long to nod off. The fire died in the embers; the tea-pot was empty; Léon went on reading. Emma listened to him, mechanically turning the lampshade, clowns in carriages and rope dancers with their swings painted on its gauze. Léon would stop, silently pointing out his sleeping audience; then they spoke in low voices, and their conversation seemed to them sweeter, because it was not heard.

Thus a kind of confederacy set itself up between them, a continual intercourse of books and ballads; Monsieur Bovary, untroubled by jealousy, found nothing there to surprise him.

For his birthday he received a handsome phrenological head, inlaid all over with numbers down to the chest and painted blue. It was a kind thought of the clerk's. He had many another, going as far as to run errands for him in Rouen; and, a novelist's work having brought into vogue a mania for cacti, Léon bought some for Madame, carrying them on his lap in the *Hirondelle*, all the while pricking his fingers on their hard bristles.

She had a small board with railings fitted, against her casement, to take her oriental pots. The clerk also had his hanging garden; they were aware of each other at their respective windows, tending their flowers.

There was one of the village windows that was occupied even more frequently; for, on Sundays, from morn till night, and every afternoon, if the weather was fine, you could see at an attic dormer-window the lean profile of Monsieur Binet bent over his lathe, its monotonous hum audible as far as the *Lion d'Or*.

One evening, on his return, Léon discovered in his room a wool and velvet coverlet patterned with foliage against a pale background; he called Madame Homais, Monsieur Homais, Justin, the children, the cook, he spoke of it to his master; everyone wished to be acquainted with this cloth; why these *kindnesses* offered to the clerk by the doctor's wife? It did seem odd, and they were of the definite opinion that she must be *his sweetheart*.

He gave you good cause to believe it, so incessantly did he keep on about her charms and her wit, to such an extent that one time Binet responded in the most brutal manner:

'What does it matter to me, since I am not of her society!'

He tortured himself, trying to discover a way to *declare his love*; and, forever hesitating between the fear of displeasing her and the shame of being faint-hearted, he wept from discouragement and desire. Then he would make drastic resolutions; he wrote letters that he tore up, postponed things to a time that he kept deferring. Frequently he would march himself off, with the notion of daring all, but this resolution swiftly forsook him in Emma's presence, and, when Charles, arriving unexpectedly, invited him to climb into his gig to go and see some patient or other in the neighbourhood, he accepted straightaway, gave Madame a bow and went off. Her husband, was he not something of her?

As to Emma, she did not examine her heart to know whether or not she loved him. Love, she believed, should come on all at once, with great claps of thunder and lightning – a hurricane from heaven that falls upon your life, turns it topsy-turvy, tears up intentions like leaves and sweeps your whole heart into the abyss. She did not know that, on the foundation terrace of a house, the rain makes lakes when the gutters are blocked, and so she remained safe and secure, until suddenly she discovered a crack in the wall.

V

IT WAS A SUNDAY IN February, one snowy afternoon.

They had all, Monsieur and Madame Bovary, Homais and Monsieur Léon, set off to visit a flax mill that was being set up in the valley, a mile and a half from Yonville. The apothecary had brought Napoléon and Athalie with him, to give them some exercise, and Justin accompanied them, carrying umbrellas on his shoulder.

Yet nothing could be less curious than this curiosity. A large area of waste ground, where a few gear-wheels, already rusted, lay between heaps of sand and pebble, surrounded a long four-cornered building pierced by a number of small windows. It had not yet finished being built, and the sky could be seen through the roof joists. Attached to the gable beam, a straw bouquet woven with ears of corn snapped its tricolour ribbons in the wind.

Homais talked. He explained *to the gathered company* the future importance of this establishment, calculated the strength of the floor, the thickness of the walls, and deeply regretted not having a metrical ruler, like the one Monsieur Binet had for his private use.

Emma, who gave him her arm, leaned a little on his shoulder, and she watched the sun's far-off disc radiating its dazzling paleness in the fog; but she turned her head: Charles was there. He had his cap pulled down over his eyebrows, and his thick lips were quivering, which added something stupid to his face; even his back, his unruffled back was irritating to look at, and there, exposed on the frock coat, she found all the vapidness of the individual.

While she was considering him, tasting in her irritation a kind of depraved voluptuousness, Léon stepped forward. The cold that made him pale seemed to settle a sweeter languidness on his face; between his cravat and his neck, the shirt collar, a little loose, left the skin visible; an ear-lobe showed below a lock of hair, and his big blue eyes, uplifted to the clouds, seemed to Emma more limpid and lovely than those mountain lakes in which the sky admires itself.

'Wretch!' cried the apothecary all of a sudden.

And he ran to his son, who had just thrown himself into a pile of lime in order to paint his shoes white. Beneath the weight of reproaches, Napoléon set about howling, whilst Justin wiped his shoes for him with a fistful of straw. But a knife was needed: Charles offered his.

'Ah!' she said to herself, 'he carries a knife in his pocket, like a peasant!'

The hoar frost fell, and they turned back for Yonville.

Madame Bovary did not go over to her neighbours that evening, and when Charles had left, and she felt alone, the comparisons began again with the clarity of an immediate sensation and the lengthening of perspective that memory gives to things. Gazing from her bed at the burning fire's brightness, she saw again, as if she were there, Léon standing, flexing his switch with one hand and with the other holding Athalie, who was sucking calmly on a piece of ice. She found him charming; she found it impossible to tear herself away; she recalled other gestures of his on other days, phrases that he had uttered, the sound of his voice, his whole self; and she repeated, putting her lips forward as for a kiss:

'Yes, delightful! Quite delightful! . . . Is he not in love?' she asked. 'With whom then? Why, with me!'

All the little proofs at once spread themselves out, her heart leapt. The blaze from the hearth was sending a merry light quivering over the ceiling; she turned on her back and stretched her arms out wide.

Then began the eternal lament: 'Oh! If the heavens had but wished it! Why isn't it so? Then who prevented . . . ?'

When Charles returned, at midnight, she looked as if she were waking up, and, as he made a noise undressing, she complained of a migraine; then casually asked what had happened that evening.

'Monsieur Léon,' he said, 'retired early.'

She could not stop herself smiling, and she went to sleep, soul filled with fresh enchantment.

The next day, at nightfall, she was visited by 'sieur Lheureux, seller of fancy goods. A sharp fellow, this tradesman.

Born a Gascon, but ending up Norman, he lined his southern loquacity with a Cauchois cunning. His greasy face, slack and beardless, seemed to have been tinted with extract of clear liquorice, and his white hair made the fierce lustre of his tiny black eyes even more intense. No one knew what he had been before: pedlar, some said, banker at Routot, according to others. What was certain, was that he could, in his head, make complicated calculations, enough to give even Binet himself a fright. Polite to the point of obsequiousness, he always held himself crook-backed, in the posture of someone either bowing or beckoning.

Having left his crape-trimmed hat at the door, he placed a green pasteboard-box on the table, and began by complaining to Madame, with numerous courtesies, that up to now he had still not gained her confidence. A poor shop like his was not fit to attract a *fashionable lady*; he laid stress on the term. Yet all she had to do was to bid him, and he would undertake to supply her with whatever she desired, as much in haberdashery as in drapery, hosiery or fancy goods; for he travelled into town four times a month, regularly. He had relations with the most considerable establishments. You could mention his name at the *Trois Frères*, at the *Barbe d'Or* or at the *Grand Sauvage*; all those gentlemen knew him like the back of their hand! So today, he had come to show Madame, in passing, various articles that he happened to have, thanks to the rarest of opportunities. And he took from the box half a dozen embroidered collars.

Madame Bovary examined them.

'I don't need anything,' she said.

And Monsieur Lheureux daintily exhibited three Algerian scarves, several packets of English needles, a pair of straw slippers, and, finally, four cocoa-nut egg-cups, carved in openwork fashion by convicts. Then, hands on the table, neck stretched, bent forward, he followed, mouth hanging wide, Emma's gaze, as it wandered uncertainly among the wares. From time to time, as if to expel the dust, he gave a flick of the nails to the silk of the scarves, unfolded to their full length; and they quivered with a slight rustle, the cloth's gold spangle, in the greenish light of dusk, sparkling like tiny stars.

'How much are they?'

'A trifle,' he replied, 'a trifle; but there's no urgency: whenever you please; we aren't Jews.'

She considered for a moment, and again finished by thanking Monsieur Lheureux, who answered impassively:

'Ah well, we'll get along together later; I have always come to an arrangement with the ladies, though not, however, with my own!'

Emma smiled.

'So what I'm saying here,' he continued with a simple, easy air after his little joke, 'is that it is not the money that bothers me . . . I would give them to you if needs be.'

She made a surprised gesture.

'Ah,' he said sharply and in a low voice, 'I don't have to go far to find you something; count on it.'

And he set about asking for news of Père Tellier, the landlord of the *Café Français*, whom Monsieur Bovary was attending at that time.

'What's the matter with him then, Père Tellier? . . . He coughs enough to shake the whole house, and I'm much afraid he'll shortly be needing a pinewood greatcoat rather than a flannel night-shirt. He went on a fair few jags in his youth! That sort, Madame, they had not the least notion of orderliness. He pickled himself with brandy! But it's disagreeable all the same to see an acquaintance pop off.'

And, while he was buckling up his box again, he continued expatiating on the doctor's patients.

'It's doubtless the weather,' he said, looking on the panes with a glum face, 'which is responsible for all those diseases. I don't feel quite myself, either; one of these days I must also pay Monsieur a visit, about the backache. Still, good day to you, Madame Bovary; at your command; your very humble servant!'

And he closed the door, softly.

Emma had her dinner served in her bedroom, by the fire, on a tray; she took a long time eating; everything seemed good to her.

'How sensible I've been!' she said to herself, thinking about the scarves.

She heard footsteps on the stairs: it was Léon. She rose, and took off the chest of drawers, from among the dusters to be hemmed, the first in the pile. She seemed very busy when he appeared.

The conversation was flat, Madame Bovary abandoning it at every turn, while he himself remained as though completely embarrassed. Seated on a low chair, near the fireplace, he turned the ivory case in his fingers; she plied her needle, or from time to time, with her nail, pleated the folds of the cloth. She did not speak; he said nothing, captivated by her silence, as he would have been by her words.

'Poor boy!' she thought.

'How do I displease her?' he asked himself.

Léon, however, finally said that he had, one of these days, to go to Rouen, on a case for his practice.

'Your music subscription is expired, should I renew it?'

'No,' she replied.

'Why?'

'Because . . .'

And, biting her lips, she slowly pulled a long needleful of grey thread.

This work irritated Léon. Emma's fingers seemed to be flayed at the tips; a gallant phrase came into his head, but he did not risk it.

'You're giving it up then?' he resumed.

'What?' she said sharply; 'the music? Ah, dear God, yes! Haven't I my house to keep, my husband to look after, a thousand things in short, a great many tasks which must be put first?'

She looked at the clock. Charles was late. So she played the anxious wife. She even repeated two or three times:

'He is so good!'

The clerk was fond of Monsieur Bovary. But this tenderness regarding the latter amazed him in an unpleasant way; nevertheless he went on eulogising, as he had heard everyone do, he said, and above all the pharmacist.

'Ah, he's a decent man,' Emma replied.

'Certainly,' answered the clerk.

And they began to talk of Madame Homais, whose badly neglected appearance usually made them laugh.

'What difference does it make?' Emma interrupted. 'A decent mother of a family does not trouble herself about her clothes.'

Then she relapsed into silence.

It was the same over the days that followed; her talk, her manner, everything changed. She was seen to take her housekeeping to heart, go regularly again to church and manage her maid with greater strictness.

She withdrew Berthe from the wet-nurse. Félicité brought her in when visitors called, and Madame Bovary undressed her in order to show her limbs. She declared that she adored children; this was her consolation, her joy, her madness, and her caresses were accompanied by lyrical effusions, which would have reminded anyone other than the Yonvillais of la Sachette in *Notre-Dame de Paris*.

When Charles came in from work, he found his slippers warming by the embers. Now his waistcoats no longer lacked linings, nor his shirts buttons, and he even delighted in surveying in the wardrobe all the cotton caps marshalled into matching piles. She no longer balked, as before, at taking a turn in the garden; whatever he proposed was always granted, although she might not predict what odd fancies she would submit to without a murmur – and when Léon saw him by the hearth, after dinner, hands on his belly, feet on the fire-dog, cheeks flushed by digestion, eyes moist with happiness, with the child crawling on the rug, and this slender wife coming up to kiss his forehead over the back of the chair:

'What madness,' he said to himself, 'and how to reach her?'

Thus she appeared to him, so virtuous and unapproachable that all hope, even the haziest, forsook him.

But, by renouncing her, he vested her with extraordinary qualities. She was disentangled, for him, from the carnal properties he had no means of procuring; and she ran on in his heart, ascending still and detaching herself from him, in the gorgeous manner of a soaring apotheosis. It was the kind of pure unadulterated sentiment that does not trouble the practice of life, cultivated because it is rare, and whose loss is more distressing than the joy of its possession.

Emma grew thinner, her cheeks paled, her face lengthened. With her black swathes of hair, her large eyes, her straight nose, her bird-like walk, and always silent now, did she not seem to pass through life scarcely touching it, and to bear on her forehead the hazy impress of some sublime predestination? She was so sad and so calm, so gentle and at the same time so reserved, that when close to her you felt yourself caught under an icy spell, as in churches when you shiver in the fragrance of flowers dashed with a marble chill. Even the others did not escape this seduction. The pharmacist said:

'She's a woman of great talents and would not be out of place in a sub-prefecture.'

The wives admired her thrift, the patients her politeness, the poor her charity.

But she was full of lusts, rage, hate. That dress with the straight pleats concealed an overthrown heart, and those so-chaste lips would not speak of the torment. She was in love with Léon, and she sought solitude, that she might more easily delight in his image. The sight of him in person troubled this voluptuous contemplation. Emma quivered at the sound of his footsteps; then, in his presence, the emotion fell away, and all that remained to her afterwards was a boundless wonder that ended in gloom.

Léon did not know, leaving her house in despair, that behind his back she would get up to look at him in the street. She was anxious about his proceedings; she secretly watched his face; she fabricated a long story as pretext for visiting his room. The pharmacist's wife seemed to her very fortunate to be sleeping under the same roof; and her thoughts continually alighted on this house, like the pigeons of the *Lion d'Or* who came to dip in its gutters their pink feet and their white wings. But the more Emma became aware of her love, the more she pushed it away, so that it should not be visible, and to abate it. She would have liked Léon to suspect something; and she imagined the risks, the catastrophes that might have made this easier. Doubtless what held her back was indolence or terror, as well as shame. She imagined that she had repelled him too far, that there was no time left, that all was lost. Then pride, the joy of telling herself, 'I am virtuous', and of looking at herself in the mirror as she struck resigned poses, consoled her a little for the sacrifice that she believed she was making.

Then the appetites of the flesh, the lust for money and the gloomy states of passion, all blended into the one single suffering – and, instead of averting her mind from it, she fastened upon it the more, excited by the pain and seeking opportunities for it everywhere. She would become incensed at a poorly-served dish or a half-open door, groaned over the velvet she did not have, the good fortune she lacked, her too-lofty dreams, her too-narrow house.

What exasperated her, was that Charles did not appear to have any awareness of her anguish. His firm belief that he was making her happy seemed to her an idiotic insult, and his confidence about it an ingratitude. For whom then was she being well-behaved? Was he himself not the obstacle to all bliss, the cause of all misery, and like the sharp buckle-tongue of this complex leather strap binding her on all sides?

So she carried over to him alone the sum of hatred which resulted from her vexation, and each effort to lessen it merely served to increase it; for this needless pain would be added to other counts of despair and contribute even further to the separation. Her very gentleness towards herself occasioned revolts. Domestic competence pushed her into luxuriant fantasies, matrimonial tenderness into adulterous desires. She wished Charles would thrash her, that she could have detested him more justly, taken her revenge. She amazed herself at times with the atrocious conjectures which entered her mind; and she had to go on smiling, hear herself repeat how happy she was, feign being so, suffer it to be believed!

She felt moments of disgust, however, at this hypocrisy. She was tempted to elope with Léon, somewhere, far away, to essay a new destiny; but immediately a vague gulf opened in her soul, full of darkness.

'Besides, he doesn't love me any more,' she thought; 'what's to be done? What rescue to expect, what consolation, what relief?'

She stood broken, panting, inert, sobbing under her breath and with tears trickling down.

'Why not speak about it to Monsieur?' the maidservant would ask her, when she came in during these crises.

'It's my nerves,' replied Emma: 'don't speak to him about it, you'll distress him.'

'Ah yes!' Félicité continued, 'you're just like la Guérine, the daughter of Père Guérine, the Pollet fisherman, who I knew at Dieppe, before coming here. She was so sad, so sad, that to see her stood on the front step of her house, she put you in mind of a burial cloth in front of the door. Her trouble, apparently, was a kind of fog she had inside the head, and the doctors couldn't do a thing, nor the priest neither. When it took her too strong, she went off all by herself to the seashore, so that the customs officer, doing his round, would often find her laid out flat on her belly and weeping into the pebbles. Then, after her marriage, it wore off, they said.'

'But, in my case,' Emma rejoined, 'it was after the marriage that it came upon me.'

VI

ONE EVENING WHEN THE WINDOW was open, and seated on the sill she had just watched Lestiboudois, the beadle, pruning the box tree, all of a sudden she heard the angelus ring out.

It was the beginning of April, when the primroses are out; a mild wind rolls across the dug flower-beds, and the gardens, like women, seem to be preparing their finery for the feast days of summer. Through the bars of the arbour and beyond, all around, the river could be seen in the meadow, sketching restless meanders over the grass. The evening haze passed between the leafless poplars, blurring their outlines with a violet tint, paler and more transparent than a delicate gauze pinned on their branches. Far off, cattle were on the move; you could hear neither their steps, nor their lowing; and the bell, still ringing, continued its peaceful lament on high.

At this repeated tolling, the young woman's mind wandered through old memories of youth and boarding school. She recalled the altar's tall candlesticks, higher than the vases full of flowers and the columned tabernacle. She would have liked, as in times past, to be mingled still with the long line of white veils that was marked here and there in black by the stiff cowls of the good sisters bowed down on their prayer-stools; on Sundays, at mass, when she lifted her head, she would perceive the Virgin's sweet face among the bluish eddyings of the incense as it rose. Then a tender feeling came over her; she felt weak and wholly abandoned, like a bird's feather wheeling round and round in the storm; and without being conscious of it she set out for the church, in the mood for no matter what devotion, provided it absorbed her soul and the whole of existence might vanish within it.

On the square she met Lestiboudois, who was on his way back; for, in order not to cut the day short, he preferred to interrupt his task and then to take it up again, ringing the angelus at his own convenience. Besides, rung earlier, the bells warned the children that it was time for catechism.

Some had already arrived, and were playing marbles on the cemetery's flagstones. Others, sitting astride the wall, were jiggling their legs, and with their wooden shoes mowing down the tall nettles that sprouted between the low wall and the most recent graves. It was the only place that was green; all the rest was nothing but stones, and constantly covered in a fine dust, despite the sacristy broom.

The children in list shoes ran about there as if on an inlaid floor made just for them, and the peal of their voices could be heard through the humming of the bell. It diminished along with the vibration of the fat rope which, falling from the heights of the belfry, dragged its end over the ground. House martins swooped past uttering little cries, cutting the air with the edge of their outspread wings, and going swiftly back into their yellow nests, under the drip-stone tiles. At the back of the church, a lamp burned; that is to say, the wick of a night-lamp in a hanging glass. Its glow, from a distance, resembled a whitish stain trembling on oil. A long ray of sunlight crossed the entire nave and made the side-aisles and corners even gloomier.

'Where is the priest?' asked Madame Bovary of a young boy who was amusing himself jogging the turnstile gate in its loose socket.

'He's coming,' he replied.

Indeed, the presbytery door grated, Abbé Bournisien appeared; the children ran pell-mell into the church.

'These little rascals!' murmured the clergyman, 'always the same!'

And, picking up a catechism in tatters that he had just knocked with his foot:

'No respect for anything!'

But, as soon as he noticed Madame Bovary:

'Pardon me,' he said, 'I failed to recognise you.'

He thrust the catechism into his pocket and stood still, continuing to swing the sacristy's heavy key on two fingers.

The gleam of the setting sun that struck him full in the face blanched the tough wool of his cassock, glossy at the elbows, frayed at the hem. Specks of grease and tobacco followed the line of little buttons over his broad chest, becoming more frequent the further they strayed from his clerical collar, on which rested plenteous folds of red skin, flecked with yellow blemishes that disappeared into the coarse hairs of his greying beard. He had just dined and was breathing noisily.

'How are you keeping?' he added.

'Badly,' replied Emma; 'I am suffering.'

'Ah well, me too,' the clergyman replied. 'These first mild days weaken you amazingly, don't they? Still, how can it be helped, we are born to suffer, as St Paul says. But what does Monsieur Bovary think about it?'

'Him!' she said with a scornful gesture.

'What?' rejoined the good fellow, completely astonished, 'he's not prescribing something for you?'

'Ah,' said Emma; 'earthly remedies are not what I need.'

But the priest, every now and then, would peep into the church, where the kneeling youngsters were all pushing each other with their shoulders, and falling over like a house of cards.

'I wanted to know . . .' she went on.

'Stop that, stop that, Riboudet,' cried the clergyman furiously, 'I'm going to warm your ears for you, wicked rogue!'

Then, turning to Emma:

'That's Boudet the carpenter's son; his parents are well off and leave him to his own devices. Yet he'd learn quick enough, if he wanted to, he has the wit. And so sometimes, just for sport, I call him Riboudet (as in the hill you take to get to Maromme), and I even say: "*mon* Riboudet". Ha ha! Mont-Riboudet! The other day, I repeated this joke to His Lordship, who laughed at it, he vouchsafed a laugh. – And how is Monsieur Bovary?'

She seemed not to hear. He continued:

'Still awfully busy, no doubt? For we are certainly, he and I, the two members of the parish who have the most to do. But he's the doctor of the body,' he added with a dark laugh, 'whereas I am that of the soul!'

She fixed beseeching eyes upon the priest.

'Yes . . .' she said, 'you assuage all pains.'

'Ah, don't speak to me of those, Madame Bovary. Just this morning, I had to go over to Bas-Diauville for a cow with *the wind*; they thought it was under a spell. All their cows, I don't know how . . . But, excuse me . . . Longuemarre and Boudet! By Jove, will you have done!'

And, in one bound, he sprang into the church.

At this point, the youngsters were crowding around the great lectern, climbing on the chantry stool, opening the missal; and others, step by stealthy step, were off venturing very nearly into the confessional. But the priest, of a sudden, served them all with a hail of boxed ears. Taking them by the jacket collar, he lifted them off the ground and set them back on their knees on the paving stones of the choir, as vigorously as if he had planned to plant them there.

'Well,' he said, returning to Emma and unfurling his large cotton handkerchief, a corner of which he put between his teeth, 'the farmers are greatly to be pitied!'

'As are others,' she said.

'Certainly. The workmen in the towns, for example.'

'It is not them . . .'

'Begging your pardon, but I have known poor mothers of families there, virtuous women, I can assure you, veritable saints, who even lack bread.'

'But those,' Emma went on (and the corners of her mouth twisted as she spoke) 'those, *Monsieur le curé*, who do have bread, but do not have . . .'

'Fire in winter,' said the priest.

'Oh, it doesn't matter!'

'Come now. Doesn't matter? It strikes me that when you're well heated, well fed . . . for, after all . . .'

'My God, my God,' she sighed.

'You are troubled?' he said, advancing with a worried air; 'doubt-less that's the digestion. You must return home, Madame Bovary, drink a little tea; that will strengthen you, or else a glass of cold water with brown sugar.'

'Why?'

And she looked like someone waking from a reverie.

'You happened to put your hand to your brow. I thought you were taken by a giddy spell.'

Then, thinking better of it:

'But you were asking me about something? What was it now? I've no idea.'

'Me? Nothing . . . nothing . . .' Emma repeated.

And her gaze, turning around her, gradually lowered itself to the old man in the cassock. The two of them considered each other, face to face, not speaking.

'Well, Madame Bovary,' he said at last, 'do excuse me, but duty first, you know; I must be dealing with my rascals. There are the first communions coming up. We shall yet be taken by surprise, I fear! In addition, after Ascension, I keep them *behind* every Wednesday for a further hour. These poor children! They cannot be led too soon into the Lord's path, as He Himself commended us through the mouth of his Divine Son . . . Good health to you, Madame; my respects to your husband!'[21]

And he went into the church, genuflecting from the door.

Emma watched him disappear between the double line of benches, walking with a heavy tread, head leaning a little to one side, and with his hands half-open, facing outwards.

Then she turned on her heel, swivelling like a statue on a pivot, and took the path back to her house. But the priest's rough voice and the bright voices of the boys still reached her ears and carried on behind her:

'Are you a Christian?'

'Yes, I'm a Christian.'

'What is a Christian?'

'He who, being baptised . . . baptised . . . baptised . . .'

Clinging to the banister-rail, she ascended the steps of her staircase and, once inside her room, fell into an armchair.

The whitish light of the panes subsided gently in fluttering waves. The furniture, in its place, seemed to grow increasingly motionless and to be cast away in the shadows as on a murky ocean. The fire was out, the clock still beat time, and Emma let herself wonder at this calmness of things, when there were so many upheavals inside her. But, between the window and the work-table, there was little Berthe, toddling in her knitted bootees, and trying to approach her mother, to catch hold of the end of her apron-strings.

'Leave me alone!' she said, pushing the child away with her hand.

The little girl soon came back even closer, up against her knees; and, using her arms to support herself there, looked up at her with large blue eyes, while a thread of clear saliva ran down from her lip onto the apron's silk.

'Leave me alone!' repeated the young woman, exasperated.

Her face terrified the child, who began to wail.

'Well, leave me alone then!' she said, thrusting her away with an elbow.

Berthe tumbled by the chest of drawers, against its brass rosette; she cut her cheek on it, out came the blood. Madame Bovary rushed to pick her up, snapped the bell-pull, called for the servant with all her might, and was about to curse herself, when Charles appeared. It was dinner-time, he had come home.

'Look, my dearest,' Emma said to him in a calm voice; 'our darling here has just fallen down and hurt herself, while playing.'

Charles reassured her, this was not a serious case, and he went off to find some sticking-plaster.

Madame Bovary did not come down for dinner; she wished to stay on her own to look after her child. Then, gazing at her as she slept, what anxiety remained gradually dissipated, and she seemed to herself very silly and very foolish to have been so troubled just now for so trifling a matter. Berthe, indeed, was no longer sobbing. Now her breathing was imperceptibly lifting the cotton blanket. Fat tears were settled in the corners of her half-shut eyelids, which revealed between their lashes two pale, sunken eyes; the plaster, stuck on her cheek, pulled the stretched skin aslant.

'It's strange,' thought Emma, 'how ugly this child is.'

When Charles, at eleven o'clock that night, came back from the pharmacy (where he had gone, after dinner, to return what remained of the plaster), he found his wife standing over the cradle.

'I assure you it's nothing,' he said as he kissed her on the forehead; 'don't torment yourself, poor darling, you will make yourself ill.'

He had stayed a long time at the apothecary's house. Even though Charles had not appeared very upset about it, Monsieur Homais had nevertheless striven to fortify him, to *raise his morale*. So they had chatted about the various dangers menacing childhood and of the thoughtlessness of servants. Madame Homais knew all about it, still bearing on her breast the marks of a porringer-full of live embers that a cook had, in days gone by, let fall into her frock. So these good parents took a variety of precautions. The knives were never sharpened, nor the rooms waxed. There were iron bars over the windows and strong rails across the fireplace. The Homais children, despite their independence, could not stir a finger without someone supervising them; at the least cold, their father crammed them with cough medicines, and up to more than four years old they all wore, unsparingly, cushioned padding around their heads. This was, in truth, a mania of Madame Homais; her husband was privately distressed by it, fearing the possible effects of such compression on the intellectual organs, and he forgot himself to the extent of saying to her:

'So you want to turn them into Caribs or Botocudos?'

Charles, in the meantime, had tried to break off the conversation several times.

'I would like to have a chat with you,' he had whispered into the clerk's ear, who set off up the stairs in front of him.

'Does he suspect something?' Léon asked himself. His heart pounded and he was lost in conjecture.

At last Charles, having closed the door, begged him to see for himself what the price of a good daguerreotype might be in Rouen; he was preparing a romantic surprise for his wife, something nice and thoughtful, his portrait in black. But he first wanted to *know where he stood*; these proceedings should not trouble Monsieur Léon, since he went to town every week, more or less.

With what aim? Homais suspected some *young man's fancy* lay beneath it, an intrigue. But he was wrong; Léon was pursuing no love affair. He was sadder than ever, and Madame Lefrançois observed this clearly from the amount of food that he now left on his plate. To find out more, she questioned the tax-gatherer; Binet replied, in a haughty tone, that he was *not paid by the police*.

His companion, nevertheless, seemed to him most peculiar; for Léon would often fall back in his chair with outspread arms, and complain vaguely about existence.

'It's because you don't have enough distractions,' the tax-gatherer would say.

'Such as?'

'In your position, I would have a lathe!'

'But I don't know how to work one,' the clerk replied.

'Ah, that's true,' said the other as he stroked his jaw, with an air of disdain mingled with satisfaction.

Léon was weary of loving without any outcome; and he began to feel that extreme depression which the repetition of the same way of living induces in you, when no interests shape it and no hope sustains it. He was so bored by Yonville and by the Yonvillais, that the sight of certain people, of certain houses, irritated him beyond endurance; and the pharmacist, easy fellow though he was, had become completely insufferable to him. Nevertheless, the prospect of a new situation appalled as much as it beguiled.

This fear quickly turned to impatience, and then, in the distance, Paris beckoned him with the fanfare of its masked balls and the laughter of its grisettes. As he had to finish his law studies there, why did he not leave? What was keeping him back? And he set about making mental preparations; he contrived his affairs in advance. He furnished an apartment in his head. There he would lead the life of an artist! There he would take guitar lessons! He would have a dressing gown, a basque beret, blue velvet slippers! And he was already even admiring a pair of crossed foils over his chimneypiece, with a death's-head and the guitar above.

The difficult business was his mother's consent; yet nothing could seem more reasonable. His master was even obliging him to consider another practice, where he might better thrive. Taking the middle course therefore, Léon searched for some assistant clerk's post in Rouen, did not find it, and finally wrote a long detailed letter to his mother, in which he explained his reasons for going to live in Paris immediately. She gave her consent.

He did not hurry, however. Each day, for a full month, Hivert transported for him trunks, valises and parcels from Yonville to Rouen, from Rouen to Yonville; and, when Léon had replenished his wardrobe, he had his three armchairs stuffed, bought a supply of handkerchiefs, in short made more arrangements than for a journey around the world, delaying week after week, until he received a second maternal letter in which he was urged to depart, since he wished to take his exam before the holidays.

When the moment came to embrace one another, Madame Homais cried; Justin sobbed; Homais, acting brave, hid his feelings; he himself desired to carry his friend's great-coat up to the gate of the notary, who was taking Léon to Rouen in his carriage. The latter just had time to bid goodbye to Monsieur Bovary.

When he was at the top of the stairs, he paused, so out of breath did he feel. At his entrance, Madame Bovary rose eagerly.

'It's me again!' said Léon.

'I was sure it was!'

She bit her lips, and a surge of blood coursed under her skin, which turned pink all over, from the roots of her hair to the edge of her collar. She stayed standing, leaning on the wainscot with her shoulder.

'So Monsieur is not in?' he went on.

'He's out.'

She repeated:

'He's out.'

There was a silence then. They looked at one another; and their thoughts, mingled in the same anguish, pressed tighter together, as breast to throbbing breast.

'I would very much like to kiss Berthe,' said Léon.

Emma went down a few steps, and called Félicité.

Quickly he threw a wide glance around him that ranged over the walls, the shelves, the fireplace, as if to penetrate all, bear all away.

But she came back in, and the maid brought Berthe, who was jiggling a windmill upside-down on the end of a string.

Léon kissed her several times on the neck.

'Goodbye, poor child. Goodbye, little one, goodbye.'

And he handed her back to her mother.

'Take her away,' said the latter.

They remained alone.

Madame Bovary's back was turned, her face resting against a window-pane; Léon held his cap in his hand, beating it gently down his thigh.

'It's going to rain,' said Emma.

'I have a coat,' he replied.

'Ah.'

She drew away, chin down and brow forward. The light slipped over it as over marble, to the curve of her eyebrows, revealing nothing of what Emma was looking at on the horizon nor of the thoughts in her heart.

'Well, goodbye,' he sighed.

She raised her head with a brusque movement:

'Yes, goodbye . . . , go!'

They advanced towards each other; he held out his hand, she hesitated.

'In the English fashion then,' she said, yielding up her own and all the while endeavouring to laugh.

Léon felt it between his fingers, and the very substance of his being seemed to go down into this moist palm.

Then he opened his hand; their eyes met each other once more, and he vanished.

When he was beneath the market-house, he stopped, and hid himself behind a pillar, so as to gaze one last time upon that white house with its four green wooden blinds. He thought he saw a shadow behind the window, in the bedroom; but the curtain, unhooked from the retaining peg as though by its own volition, slowly stirred its long, aslant folds, that in one bound all spread themselves out, and then it stayed straight, more motionless than a wall of plaster. Léon began to run.

He perceived from afar, on the road, his employer's gig, and beside it a man dressed in a thick apron, holding the horse. Homais and Monsieur Guillaumin were chatting together. They were waiting for him.

'Embrace me,' said the apothecary with tears in his eyes. 'Here is your great-coat, my good friend; mind the cold! Look after yourself! Take care of yourself!'

'Come on, Léon, into the carriage with you,' said the notary.

Homais leaned on the splash-board, and in a voice broken by sobs, let fall these two sad words:

'Pleasant journey!'

'Good night,' replied Monsieur Guillaumin. 'Cast off!'

They left, and Homais returned home.

Madame Bovary had opened her window onto the garden, and she was watching the clouds.

They were piled up to the west towards Rouen, and were swiftly rolling their black volutes, behind which great rays of sunlight extended, like the golden arrows of a hung trophy, while the rest of the empty sky had the whiteness of a porcelain vase. But a squall of wind made the poplars bend, and all of a sudden the rain fell; it pattered on the fresh leaves. Then the sun reappeared, the hens clucked, the sparrows shook their wings in the wet bushes, and the puddles of water draining on the sand bore away the pink flowers of an acacia.

'Ah, how far he must already be,' she thought.

Monsieur Homais, as usual, came at half-past six, during dinner.

'Well,' he said as he sat down, 'so we have just now seen off our young man?'

'It seems so,' replied the doctor.

Then, turning round in his chair:

'And what's new with you?'

'Not a great deal. Only that, this afternoon, my wife was a little excitable. You know how it is, with women, stirred by a mere trifle. Mine above all! And it would be a mistake to be indignant about it, since their nervous system is a lot more susceptible than our own.'

'That poor Léon!' said Charles. 'How will he live in Paris? Will he get used to it?'

Madame Bovary sighed.

'Nonsense!' said the pharmacist, clicking his tongue; 'Secret pleasure parties in the chop-house! Masked balls! Champagne! 'Tis all going to be fine, I assure you.'

'I don't think he will go astray,' Bovary objected.

'Me neither!' Monsieur Homais resumed sharply, 'although he'll still have to go along with the others, at the risk of passing for a Jesuit. And you've no notion of the life those fellows lead there, in the Latin quarter, with the actresses. Yet students are very well regarded in Paris. If they have the least talent for being agreeable, they're received into the best society, and ladies there are in the faubourg Saint-Germain who even fall in love with them, providing them, subsequently, with opportunities to make a very handsome match.'

'But,' said the doctor, 'I'm fearful that he . . . over there . . .'

'You're right,' the apothecary interrupted, 'that's the dark side of the picture. And one has to keep a hand over one's purse all the time! So, I am imagining you're in a public garden; a certain person appears,

115

well turned out, dignified even, and whom you take for a diplomat; he accosts you; you chat together; he worms himself in, offers you a pinch of snuff or picks up your hat. Then you become more intimate; he takes you to a café, invites you to his house in the country, gets you acquainted, half seas over, with all kinds of types, and three-quarters of the time it's only to swindle you out of your purse or tempt you into taking highly pernicious steps.'

'That's true,' Charles replied; 'but I was thinking mainly of diseases, of typhoid fever, for instance, which attacks students from the provinces.'

Emma gave a start.

'Because of the change of diet,' continued the apothecary, 'and of the resulting disturbance to the general economy. And besides, you see, the Paris water! The chop-house dishes, all those spicy foods end up overheating your blood and aren't a patch, whatever is claimed for them, on a good meat stew. I have always, speaking for myself, liked plain home cooking better: it's healthier! Likewise, when I was studying pharmacy at Rouen, I boarded in a boarding-house; I ate with the lecturers.'

And he then continued to reveal his general opinions and his personal sympathies, right up to the moment when Justin came to fetch him for the preparation of a mulled egg.

'Not a moment of respite,' he cried, 'always in the traces! I cannot go out for a minute. Like a plough-horse, I have to sweat blood and tears! What drudgery!'

Then, when he was at the door:

'Talking of which,' he said, 'have you heard the news?'

'What's that?'

'It seems most likely,' Homais went on, raising his eyebrows and adopting his most serious expression, 'that the Lower Seine's agricultural show is to be held this year at Yonville-l'Abbaye. At least that's the rumour. This morning's paper touched on it a little. That would be of the utmost importance for our area. But we'll discuss it later. I can see my way, thank you; Justin has the lantern.'

VII

THE NEXT DAY WAS, FOR Emma, a mournful one. Everything seemed to her muffled in a gloom which wavered confusedly over the exterior of things, and the heartache sank into her soul with soft howls, such as the winter wind makes in abandoned castles. It was that type of waking dream you experience when something is gone for ever, the lassitude that grips you after each fait accompli, in short the suffering that the interruption of any habitual motion, the abrupt ceasing of a prolonged vibration, brings.

As with the return from Vaubyessard, when the quadrilles whirled in her head, she felt a dull melancholy, a torpid despair. Léon reappeared as taller, more handsome, more pleasant, more vague; although he was separated from her, he had not left her, he was there, and the walls of the house seemed to preserve his shadow. She could not tear her eyes from this rug he had walked on, from those empty pieces of furniture he had sat in. The river still flowed, and slowly drove its little swells along the slippery bank. They had walked there many times, to this same murmur of the waves, on pebbles coated in moss. What lovely sunny days they had had! What lovely afternoons, alone, in the shade, at the bottom of the garden! He would read aloud, bare-headed, seated on a stool made from dry sticks; the cool wind from the meadows trembled the pages of his book and the arbour's nasturtiums . . . Ah he was gone, the sole delight of her life, the sole possible hope of any bliss. Why had she not seized that happiness, while it offered itself? Why had she not held it back with both hands, on both knees, when it wished to flee? And she cursed herself for not having loved Léon; she thirsted for his lips. She longed to run and join him, to throw herself in his arms, to say to him: 'I am here, I am yours!' But Emma fretted beforehand over the difficulties of the undertaking, and her desires, augmented by regret, became still more potent.

Thenceforth, the memory of Léon lay at the centre of her ennui; it crackled there more fiercely than a travellers' fire on a Russian steppe, abandoned in the snow. She hastened towards him, she huddled up against him, she delicately stirred this hearth that had all but died away, she went searching all around her for what might revive it further; and the remotest reminiscences as well as the most recent encounters, her actual experiences along with her imaginings, her scattered cravings for voluptuousness, her plans for happiness that creaked in the wind like dead boughs, her barren virtue, her tumbled hopes, the straw-litter of domesticity, she gathered all, seized all, and let it all serve to rekindle her sadness.

Nevertheless the flames subsided, either because the fuel itself was spent, or its pile too considerable. Bit by bit, love died away through absence, regret was stifled by habit; and that fiery glimmer that empurpled her pale sky was further clouded by shadow and gradually blotted out. In the slumbering state of her conscience, she even took husband-hatred for lover-longing, the scorch of spite for the rekindling of tender love; but, as the storm was still blowing, and her passion burned to ashes, and since no help came, no sun appeared, utter night fell on every side, and she remained lost in a terrible cold that penetrated her through and through.

Then the bad days of Tostes began once more. She reckoned herself as far unhappier now; for she had the experience of grief, with the certainty that it would not end.

A woman who had imposed such great sacrifices upon herself could well be forgiven whims. She bought herself a Gothic prayer-desk, and laid out fourteen francs on lemons in one month for cleaning her nails; she wrote to Rouen, to have a blue cashmere dress; from Lheureux she chose the loveliest of his scarves; she fastened it at the waist over her dressing gown; and with the shutters closed, a book in her hand, she lay stretched on a sofa in this apparel.

She would often vary her coiffure: she adopted a Chinese style, soft curls, tressed plaits; she affected a parting on the side of her head and rolled her hair below it, like a man.

She wanted to learn Italian; she bought dictionaries, a grammar book, a stock of white paper. She tried some serious reading, of history and philosophy. At night, sometimes, Charles woke up with a start, believing that they had come to fetch him out for a patient:

'I'm going,' he mumbled.

And it was the noise of a match that Emma was striking to light the lamp again. But her reading shared something of her needlework, cluttering her wardrobe with its unfinished pieces; she took one up, abandoned it, passed on to another.

She had fits, when she would be easily prompted into wild follies. One day she maintained, in opposition to her husband, that she would definitely drink a large half-glass of brandy, and, as Charles was stupid enough to dare her to do so, she swallowed the brandy to the dregs.

Despite her giddy airs (this was how the good women of Yonville put it), Emma still did not look cheerful, and the corners of her mouth would retain that permanent tenseness which creases the faces of old maids and ambitious failures. She was pale all over, white as a sheet; the skin of her nose was drawn down towards the nostrils, her eyes would look at you in a vague way. Having discovered three grey hairs at her temples, she talked a great deal about her old age.

She would frequently feel a strange weakness come over her. One day, she even spat blood, and, as Charles rushed to help, his anxiety noticeable:

'Oh, nonsense!' she replied, 'what does it matter?'

Charles took refuge in his consulting-room; and he wept, elbows on the table, seated in his office chair, under the phrenological head.

Then he wrote to his mother begging her to come, and they had long conferences together on the subject of Emma.

How to resolve it? What to do, since she rejected all treatment?

'Do you know what your wife needs?' Mère Bovary went on. 'Hard work, manual labour! If, like so many others, she was forced to earn her bread, she wouldn't have these vapours, which come to her from a heap of ideas she stuffs her head with, and from her life of idleness.'

'Yet she keeps herself busy,' said Charles.

'Hah! Keeps herself busy! With what? Reading books, bad books, works that are against religion and where they make fun of priests with speeches taken from Voltaire. But all that has repercussions, my poor child, and someone who has no religion always ends up by turning bad.'

So, it was decided that Emma would be kept from reading novels. The task did not seem an easy one. The good lady took charge of it: when she next passed through Rouen, she would go in person to the book-lender and impress on him that Emma should stop her subscription. Would they not have the right to alert the police, if the bookseller persisted all the same with his poisoner's trade?

The farewells of the mother-in-law and the daughter-in-law were cold. During the three weeks that they had been together, they had not exchanged four words, apart from the usual inquiries and compliments when they met at table, and during the evening before they went to bed.

Mère Bovary left on a Wednesday, Yonville's market day.

The Square, from morning onwards, was encumbered with a line of waggons, each tipped up and shafts on high, stretching the length of the houses from the church to the inn. On the other side, there were canvas booths where they were selling cotton cloths, bed-clothes and woollen stockings, with halters for horses and bundles of blue ribbons, their ends soaring in the wind. Heavy ironmongery was strewn on the ground, between pyramids of eggs and small hampers of cheese, from which emerged sticky tufts of straw; near the threshing machines, hens clucking in flat cages were putting their necks through the bars. The crowd, all jammed into one place yet not wanting to move, threatened at times to break the front of the pharmacy. On Wednesdays, it never emptied and people pushed their way in, less to buy medicines than to seek a consultation, so renowned was Monsieur Homais' reputation in the neighbouring villages. His robust self-possession had captivated the country folk. They looked upon him as the greatest doctor of all.

Emma was leaning on her elbows at her window (she would often be there: the window, in the provinces, replaces theatres and promenades), and was amusing herself contemplating the crowd of rustics, when she caught sight of a gentleman dressed in a green velvet frock-coat. He was gloved in yellow, although got up in stout gaiters; and he was making for the doctor's house, followed by a peasant walking with his head lowered in a most ruminative manner.

'May I see the master of the house?' he asked Justin, who was chatting on the threshold with Félicité.

And, taking him for the house servant:

'Tell him that Monsieur Rodolphe Boulanger de la Huchette is here.'

It was not from territorial vanity that the new arrival had added the nobiliary particle to his name, but with the aim of identifying himself the better. La Huchette, in fact, was an estate near Yonville, whose chateau he had just purchased, along with two farms he was working himself, yet without too much personal bother. He lived as a bachelor, and was reputed to have *a private income of at least fifteen thousand pounds!*

Charles came into the room. Monsieur Boulanger introduced his servant, who wished to be bled because he was feeling *ants all down his body*.

'That'll cleanse me,' he objected, to counter all their arguments.

So Bovary ordered a bandage and a basin to be brought, and requested Justin to hold it. Then, addressing the cotter, who was already pale:

'Don't be afraid, my brave man.'

'No, no,' replied the other, 'you keep on!'

And, in a blustering manner, he held out his thick arm. Under the lancet's puncture, the blood spurted out to splash against the mirror.

'Bring the vessel!' Charles exclaimed.

'*Look'ee!*' said the peasant, 'you'd swear it were a tiny fountain as is running! How red my blood be! That's a good sign, no?'

'Sometimes,' went on the medical officer, 'you feel nothing to start with, then the fainting fit declares itself, and more particularly with people of a strong constitution, like this fellow.'

The rustic, at these words, let go of the small box that he was turning in his fingers. A jerk of his shoulders made the chair-back crack. His hat fell.

'I suspected as much,' said Bovary as he put his finger on the vein.

The basin began to tremble in Justin's hands; his knees wavered, he grew pale.

'Wife! Wife!' Charles called out.

She came down the stairs at a bound.

'Some vinegar!' he cried. 'Oh dear God, two at once!'

And, in his excitement, he had trouble in placing the compress.

'It's nothing,' Monsieur Boulanger said quite calmly, as he took Justin in his arms.

And he sat him down on the table, letting the boy's back rest against the wall.

Madame Bovary began to remove his neck-cloth. There was a knot in the shirt's strings; she spent a few minutes moving her slender fingers over the young man's neck; then she poured vinegar on her cambric handkerchief; she dabbed at his temples to wet them and blew there, delicately.

The ploughman woke up; but Justin's swoon continued, and his eyes disappeared into their pale sclera, like blue flowers into milk.

'We must,' said Charles, 'hide that from him.'

Madame Bovary took the basin. In the movement she made leaning down to put it under the table, her dress (it was a four-flounced summer dress, yellow, long in the waist, broad in the skirt), her dress spread about her on the floor tiles – and when Emma, bent forward as she was, teetered a little as she spread her arms, the fullness of the cloth was crushed in places, following the curves of her bodice. Afterwards she went to fetch a jug of water, and she was dissolving sugar lumps when the pharmacist arrived. The maid had gone to look for him during the explosion; on seeing that his pupil's eyes were open, he recovered his breath. Then, circling the youth, he looked him up and down.

'Fool!' he said; 'little fool, truly. In a word, fool! After all, a phlebotomy's a big thing. And a big fellow like you who's afraid of nothing. A sort of squirrel, you see before you, who climbs up to loosen nuts at dizzying heights. Ah yes! Tell them, brag of it! So here we have a glorious natural aptitude for practising pharmacy later on; because you might find yourself being called up in grave circumstances, before the bench, in order to set the magistrates' minds at rest; and yet you have to keep your temper, answer your superiors, show yourself a man, or else pass for an idiot.'

Justin did not reply. The apothecary continued:

'Who asked you to come? You're forever bothering Monsieur and Madame. Besides, I can spare you even less on Wednesdays. There are now twenty people at the house. I dropped everything in my concern for you. Come on, be off! Run! Wait for me there, and watch the jars!'

When Justin, who was dressing again, had gone, they chatted a little about fainting fits. Madame Bovary had never suffered them.

'That's extraordinary for a lady,' said Monsieur Boulanger. 'Yet certain people are very delicate. Indeed, I once saw, during a duel, a witness lose consciousness over nothing more than the sound of the pistols being loaded.'

'As for me,' said the apothecary, 'the sight of others' blood has no effect; but the mere thought of mine running would be enough to make me faint, if I thought about it too much.'

Meanwhile Monsieur Boulanger despatched his servant, urging him to calm down, since his generous whim had worn off.

'It brought me the benefit of your acquaintance,' he added.

And he stared at Emma as he said this.

Then he put three francs down on the corner of the table, gave a nonchalant bow and left.

He was soon on the other side of the river (it was his route back to La Huchette); and Emma observed him in the meadow, as he walked under the poplars, slowing down from time to time, like someone reflecting.

'She's exceedingly fine!' he was saying to himself; 'She's exceedingly fine, this doctor's wife! Lovely teeth, black eyes, coquettish foot, and a figure like a Parisienne. Where the devil did she spring from? Where did he find her, then, that coarse fellow?'

Monsieur Rodolphe Boulanger was thirty-four years old; he was of a brutal temperament and quick-sighted intelligence, having moreover frequented women a great deal, and knowing them well. This one had struck him as pretty; so he mused on her, and on her husband.

'I think he's very stupid. No doubt she's tired of him. He has dirty nails and a three-day beard. While he jog-trots off to his patients, she stays darning socks. And we're bored with it. We want to live in town, dance the polka every night. Poor little woman! Gasping for love, like a carp for water on a kitchen table. With three gallant words, that type would adore you, I'm certain. It would be delicate! Charming! . . . Yes, but how to get rid of her afterwards?'

Thus the impediments to pleasure, glimpsed in the distance, made him think, by pure contrast, of his mistress. She was a Rouen actress, whom he maintained; and, when he had fastened on this image, whose very recollection left him sated:

'Ah, Madame Bovary,' he thought, 'is a deal prettier than her, and certainly fresher. Virginie is becoming decidedly too fat. She's so tiresome with those pleasures of hers. And, besides, what a mania for pink prawns!'

The countryside was deserted, and all Rodolphe heard around him was the regular flap of the grasses as they lashed his boots, and the crickets crouched far off beneath the oats; he saw Emma in the room again, dressed as he had seen her, and he undressed her.

'Oh, I will have her!' he cried out, crushing a clod of earth in front of him with one blow of his stick.

And straightaway he examined the politic part of the enterprise. He asked himself:

'Where to meet each other? By what means? We shall always have the brat on our backs, and the maid, the neighbours, the husband, all sorts of significant botheration. Bah!' he said, 'too much time lost there!'

Then he started up again:

'But her eyes, they penetrate your heart like gimlets. And that pale complexion . . . I, who adore pale women!'

On the crest of Argueil hill, he came to a resolution.

'All I have to do is look for opportunities. Well, I shall pass by sometimes, I'll send them game-birds, fowl; I'll get myself bled, if needs be; we'll become friends, I'll invite them home . . . Zounds!' he added, 'there's the agricultural show soon; she'll be there, I'll see her. We'll begin, and boldly, for that is the soundest way.'

VIII

I T DID INDEED ARRIVE, THIS famous Agricultural Show! From the morning of the official solemnities, all the inhabitants, on their doorsteps, talked of the preparations; the town hall's pediment had been garlanded with ivy; a pavilion in a field had been erected for the banquet, and, in the middle of the Square, in front of the church, a type of bombard was to signal the arrival of Monsieur le Préfet and the announcement of the prizewinning farmers. The national guard of Buchy (there was none at Yonville) had come to join with the fire-corps, of which Binet was the captain. He was wearing a collar that day that was even higher than usual; and, strapped into his tunic as he was, his chest was so stiff and motionless, that all the vital parts of his person seemed to have descended into his legs, which rose, in time and with a pronounced step, in a single movement. As a rivalry subsisted between the tax-gatherer and the colonel, each of them, to prove his abilities, drilled his men separately. Red epaulettes and black breast-plates were seen passing back and forth in turn. It was never-ending and always began anew! There had never been such a splendid display! Several citizens had washed their houses the day before; tricolours hung from half-open windows; all the tap-houses were full; and, in the fine weather they were having, the starched bonnets, the gold crosses and the coloured neckerchiefs appeared whiter than snow, shimmered in the bright sun, and heightened with their scattered motley the sombre monotony of the frock-coats and blue smocks. Dismounting from their horses, the local farmers' wives removed the stout pin that held their dress, tucked up for fear of mud-spots, tight around the body; and the husbands, by contrast, in order to spare their hats, kept pocket handkerchiefs spread over them, a corner gripped between the teeth.

The crowd arrived in the main street from both ends of the village. They disgorged from lanes, alleyways, houses, and from time to time you caught the return fall of door-knockers behind good women in cotton gloves, venturing out to view the entertainment. Admired most of all, were two tall pyramidal stands covered in lamps flanking a stage where the officials were to sit; and in addition, against the four pillars of the town hall, there were four long types of pole, each carrying a little standard of greenish canvas, embellished with inscriptions in gold letters. On one could be read: 'To Commerce'; on another: 'To Agriculture'; on the third: 'To Industry'; and on the fourth: 'To the Arts'.[22]

But the jubilation broadening every face appeared to fill Madame Lefrançois, the inn's landlady, with gloom. Standing on her kitchen steps, she murmured into her chin:

'What nonsense! What nonsense with their canvas hut! Do they believe that the prefect will be truly comfortable dining over there, under a tent, like a buffoon? They call these embarrassments doing good by the area! Not worth going all the way to Neufchâtel to find a rotten cook, in that case! And all for who? For cowmen! Tramps!'

The apothecary passed by. He wore a black coat, nankeen breeches, beaverskin shoes and, on this rare occasion, a hat — a hat with a low crown.

'Your servant!' he said. 'Do excuse me, I'm in a hurry.'

And as the fat widow asked him where he was off to:

'That seems queer to you, doesn't it? I who always stay more shut up in my laboratory than the gentleman's rat in his cheese.'[23]

'What cheese?' inquired the landlady.

'Oh, nothing, nothing!' Homais continued. 'I wished merely to convey to you, Madame Lefrançois, that I usually remain entirely a recluse at home. Today, however, given the circumstances, I must obviously . . .'

'Oh, you're off over there, are you?' she said with an air of disdain.

'Yes, I'm off,' retorted the astonished apothecary; 'am I not part of the Advisory Committee?'

Mère Lefrançois studied him for a few minutes, and finished by replying with a smile:

'So you are, truly! But what have you to do with farming? You know something about it, then?'

'I most certainly do know about it, as I'm a pharmacist, that's to say a chemist! And chemistry, Madame Lefrançois, having as its object the knowledge of the mutual and molecular action of the entire body of Nature, it follows that agriculture is included in its domain! And, indeed, the composition of compost, the fermentation of liquids, the analysis of gases and the influence of miasmas, what is all that, I ask you, if it is not chemistry pure and simple?'

The landlady did not reply. Homais continued:

'Do you believe it necessary, in order to become an agriculturalist, to have worked the land or fattened poultry oneself? One has sooner to know the constitution of the substances in question, the geological deposits, atmospheric actions, the quality of the ground, the minerals, the water, the density of different bodies and their capillarity, and so forth! And one has to be thoroughly acquainted with all its principles of hygiene, to manage, to reflect upon the construction of buildings, the diet of animals, the feeding of servants! Furthermore, Madame Lefrançois, one has to be a master of botany; be able to discriminate between plants, d'you see – which are the beneficial and which the deleterious, which the unproductive and which the nourishing, whether it is good to dig them up here and sow them again there, to propagate one, and destroy the other; in short, one has to keep abreast of the science through pamphlets and public papers, to be always attentive, in order to point out improvements . . .'

The landlady's eyes never left the door of the *Café Français*, and the apothecary carried on:

'Would to God our farmers were chemists, or at least listen more to the counsel of science![24] I, for one, have recently written a strongly worded tract, a dissertation of more than seventy-two pages, entitled: *On Cider, its Manufacture and Effects; Followed by Several New Thoughts On this Subject*, which I sent to the Agricultural Society of Rouen; this even procured me the honour of being received among its members, agricultural section, pomology class; well, if my work had been published . . .'

But the apothecary stopped, so preoccupied did Madame Lefrançois appear.

'Just look at them!' she said, 'It's beyond belief! A cook-shop like that!'

And, with a shrugging of the shoulders that stretched the stitches of her knitted bodice over her breasts, she thrust both hands towards her rival's tap-house, from which songs were then emerging.

'Anyway, it's not there for long,' she added; 'within eight days, it'll all be up.'

Homais stepped back in astonishment. She came down her three steps, and, speaking into his ear:

'What? You didn't know? It's going to be seized this week. It's Lheureux making him sell up. He's plagued him with bills.'

'What an appalling catastrophe!' cried the apothecary, who could always come up with the appropriate expression for every imaginable circumstance.

Then the landlady began to tell him this story, that she had got from Théodore, Monsieur Guillaumin's servant, and, although she cursed Tellier, she blamed Lheureux. He was a wheedler, a groveller.

'Ah, look,' she said, 'there he is under the market-house; he's bowing to Madame Bovary, in a green hat. She's even on the arm of Monsieur Boulanger.'

'Madame Bovary!' said Homais. 'I must hurry over and offer my respects. She might be very glad to have a seat in the enclosure, under the colonnade.'

And, without listening to Mère Lefrançois, who was calling him back to tell him at greater length, the pharmacist hurried away, bouncing on his toes, a smile on his lips, distributing a host of greetings to right and left and taking up lots of space with the great skirts of his black coat, that fluttered behind him in the wind.

Rodolphe, having spotted him from afar, had set off at a quick pace; but Madame Bovary grew out of breath; so he slowed down and said to her smilingly, in a brutal tone:

'It's to avoid that fat fellow: you know, the apothecary.'

She jabbed him with her elbow.

'What was all that about?' he asked himself.

And he considered her out of the corner of his eye, as he carried on walking.

Her profile was so calm, that nothing could be conjectured from it. It came fully into the light, within the oval of her close bonnet with its pale ribbons like the leaves of reeds. Her eyes with their long curved lashes gazed in front of her, and, although opened wide, they seemed as though kept in check by the cheeks, for the blood throbbed gently under her fine skin. A rosy tint passed through the thin partition between her nostrils. She tipped her head to one side, and the pearly edge of her white teeth could be glimpsed between her lips.

'Is she making fun of me?' he wondered.

This gesture of Emma's had been only a warning, however; for Monsieur Lheureux was alongside them, and from time to time he would talk, as if to enter into conversation.

'What a splendid day! Everyone is out! The winds are easterly.'

And Madame Bovary, like Rodolphe, would scarcely respond to him, while at the slightest movement on their part, he drew closer saying, 'I beg your pardon?' and brought his hand to his hat.

When they were in front of the farrier's house, instead of following the road up to the gate, Rodolphe abruptly dived down a path, hurrying Madame Bovary away; he cried:

'Good evening, Monsieur Lheureux! Until the next time!'

'What a way to get rid of him!' she said, laughing.

'Why,' he resumed, 'let oneself be intruded on by others? And seeing as, today, I'm lucky enough to be with you . . .'

Emma blushed. He did not finish his sentence. Then he talked of the beautiful weather and of the pleasure of walking on grass. A few daisies were springing up again.

'Look at these pretty Easter daisies,' he said, 'plenty to keep the local love-maidens well supplied with oracles.'

He added:

'Supposing I were to pick one. What do you think?'

'Are you in love?' she asked, coughing a little.

'Ah ha, who knows?' replied Rodolphe.

The field began to fill up, and the housewives would knock against you with their big umbrellas, their baskets and their babies. Many a time you had to step out of the way of a long line of countrywomen, maidservants in blue stockings, with flat shoes and silver rings, smelling of milk when you passed near them. They walked holding hands, and so were spread out along the entire length of the field, from the line of aspens to the banquet tent. But the moment had come for the judging, and the farmers, one after the other, entered a sort of racecourse formed by a long cord strung between posts.

The animals were there, muzzles turned towards the twine, and confusedly lining up their uneven rumps. Drowsy pigs buried their snouts in the soil; calves bellowed; sheep bleated; the cows, one leg bent inwards, spread their bellies on the turf, and, chewing slowly, blinked their heavy lids, under the gnats that hummed around them. The carters, arms bared, held on to the halters of rearing stallions, which whinnied with nostrils flared beside the mares. These last remained peaceful, stretching out heads and draped manes, while their foals rested in their shade or came to suckle now and again; and, over the long undulation of all these packed bodies, you could see, like a billow lifted in the wind, a white mane, or else sharp horns jutting, and the heads of running men. Set apart, outside the enclosures, a hundred paces off, was a great black muzzled bull, which sported an iron ring in one nostril and stirred no more than might a beast of bronze. A child in rags held it by a rope.

Meanwhile, between the two rows, gentlemen moved forward heavy-paced, examining each animal, then consulting with each other in a low voice. One of them, who appeared more eminent, was taking a few notes in a book as he walked along. It was the president of the jury: Monsieur Derozerays of La Panville. As soon as he recognised Rodolphe, he rushed up, and said, smiling in a friendly manner:

'What, Monsieur Boulanger, you're abandoning us?'

Rodolphe protested that he was on his way. But when the president had disappeared:

'My word, no,' he went on, 'I won't go; your company is better than his.'

And, continuing to pour scorn on the agricultural show, Rodolphe, in order to circulate with more ease, showed the gendarme his blue ticket, and even stopped occasionally before some handsome *subject* that barely drew Madame Bovary's attention. He noticed this, and so began to joke about the ladies of Yonville, with regard to their dress; then he excused himself for neglecting his own: it was an incongruous mix of the ordinary and the refined, in which, as a rule, the common herd thinks it can glimpse signs of an eccentric existence, dissolute feelings, the tyrannies of art, and always a certain contempt for social conventions, which it finds either seductive or exasperating. Thus his cambric shirt with its pleated sleeves swelled at every random gust blowing through his open grey-drill waistcoat, while his broad-striped trousers revealed at the ankles nankeen half-boots, with their uppers of patent leather. So highly polished were they that they reflected the grass. He trampled the horse-droppings with them, hand in his jacket pocket and straw hat tipped to one side.

'Besides,' he added, 'when you live in the countryside . . .'

'Everything's a waste of effort,' said Emma.

'That's true,' replied Rodolphe. 'To imagine that not one of these good folk is capable of understanding even the cut of a coat.'

Then they spoke of provincial mediocrity, of the lives it stifled, of the illusions lost therein.

'I too,' said Rodolphe, 'am plunging into a dreariness . . .'

'You!' she said, astonished. 'But I thought you very light-hearted?'

'Ah, yes, on the surface, because in the midst of people I know to place a jesting mask over my face; and yet at times, when I see a cemetery, by moonlight, I have asked myself if I would not do better to join those who are sleeping . . .'

'Oh! And your friends?' she said. 'You do not think of them.'

'My friends? Which ones, then? Have I any? Who cares for me?'

And he accompanied these last words with a sort of hiss between his lips.

But they were obliged to swerve away from each other, on account of a great scaffolding of chairs that a man behind them was carrying. So overloaded was he, that you could only see the tips of his wooden clogs, with the end of each arm thrust out straight. It was Lestiboudois, the gravedigger, who was carting the church chairs through the multitude. Full of imagination when it came to anything concerning his own interests, he had discovered this means of turning the agricultural show to account; and his idea succeeded, because he could no longer satisfy everyone's needs. Indeed, the villagers, who were hot, contended with one another for these chairs whose straw seats smelt of incense, and would lean on the heavy backs sullied by candlewax, with a certain veneration.

Madame Bovary took Rodolphe's arm again; he continued as if talking to himself:

'Yes, I lack so many things. Always alone. Ah! If I had had a purpose in life, if I had met with love, if I had found someone . . . Oh, I should have used all my strength to the last drop, I should have overcome everything, smashed everything!'

'It yet seems to me,' said Emma, 'that you have little to complain about.'

'Ah you think so?' said Rodolphe.

'Because in the end . . .' she went on, 'you are free.'

She hesitated:

'Wealthy.'

'Do not mock me,' he replied.

And she swore that she was not mocking him, when the boom of a cannon resounded; immediately everyone pushed forward, pell-mell, towards the village.

It was a false alarm. Monsieur le Préfet did not arrive; and the members of the jury were most embarrassed, not knowing whether to begin the session or else wait longer.

At last, at the far end of the Square, there appeared a large hired landau, pulled by two lean horses, whipped with all his might by a white-hatted coachman. Binet only had time to shout: 'To arms!' and the colonel to echo him. The men ran towards the pile of muskets. They dashed forward. Several even forgot their collar. But the prefectorial carriage seemed to sense this confusion, and the two paired nags, ambling in their lead chains, arrived at a gentle trot in front of the town hall arches, at the very moment when the national guard and the firemen were deploying themselves, drum beating to determine the step.

'Mark time!' shouted Binet.

'Halt!' shouted the colonel. 'Left dress!'

And, after a presentation of arms in which the click-clack of barrel-bands, sliding back and forth, rang out like a copper kettle tumbling down the stairs, all the rifles were lowered again.

Then they saw alighting from the coach a gentleman dressed in a short black coat embroidered with silver, bald in front and with a little tuft at the back, his colour wan and his appearance excessively mild. He half-closed his fat eyes, behind thick lids, in order to survey the multitude, at the same time as he lifted his sharp nose and brought a smile to his sunken mouth. He recognised the mayor by his sash, and vouchsafed to him that Monsieur le Préfet was unable to come. He was himself a counsellor from the prefecture; then he added a few apologies. Tuvache responded with civilities, the other confessed himself abashed; and so they remained, face to face, their foreheads almost touching, with the members of the jury all around, the municipal council, the worthies, the national guard and the crowd. The counsellor, pressing his little black tricorn hat against his chest, reiterated his greetings, while Tuvache, bowed over like an arch, smiled likewise, stammered, searched for words, protested his devotion to the monarchy, and the honour being shown to Yonville.

Hippolyte, the inn's servant, came to take the coachman's horses by the bridle, and limping the whole time on his club foot, led them under the porch of the *Lion d'Or*, where many of the country-folk had gathered to gaze at the coach. The drum struck up, the howitzer thundered, and the gentlemen filed up onto the stage to settle themselves in the armchairs of Utrecht velvet lent by Madame Tuvache.

All these people looked alike. Their slack fair-skinned faces, a little sun-burnt, were the colour of sweet cider, and their puffy side-whiskers burst out of great starched collars, borne up by white and very showy bow-ties. All the roll-collar waistcoats were of velvet; all the fob-watches carried some oval keepsake or other at the end of a long ribbon; and with two hands resting on two thighs, one carefully spread one's trousers at the crotch, the cloth with the sheen still on it gleaming more brilliantly than the stout boots' leather.

The society ladies stayed at the back, under the archway, between the pillars, while the vulgar crowd was in front, standing up, or seated on chairs. In fact, Lestiboudois had carried over all those chairs that he had removed from the field, and was likewise running every minute to fetch others in the church, and causing such an obstruction with his trade, that one had great trouble reaching the little stairs to the stage.

'I think, personally,' said Monsieur Lheureux (addressing the pharmacist, who was passing by on the way to his seat), 'that they should have placed two Venetian poles there: along with something a little austere and opulent in the drapery line, it would have made a mightily pretty effect.'

'Indeed,' replied Homais. 'But, what can one do? The mayor has taken it all upon himself. He has dubious taste, this wretched Tuvache, and is anyway utterly devoid of what one might call artistic spirit.'

Meanwhile Rodolphe, with Madame Bovary, had climbed up to the first floor of the town hall, into the Council Chamber, and, as it was empty, he had declared that they would be well placed there to enjoy the show more comfortably. He took three stools from around the oval table beneath the bust of the monarch, and, having drawn them up to one of the windows, they sat down next to each other.

There was a bustling on the stage, lengthy whisperings, some parleying. Finally, Monsieur le Conseiller rose to his feet. Everyone now knew that his name was Lieuvain, and they repeated it one to another in the crowd. So once he had gathered together several sheets of paper and stuck an eye up close in order to see them better, he began:

'Gentlemen, may I take the liberty first of all (before talking to you of the object of today's reunion, and this feeling, I am certain, will be shared by you all), may I take the liberty, I say, to do justice to the upper chamber, to the government, to the monarchy, gentlemen, to your sovereign, to this much-loved king to whom no branch of public or private prosperity is a matter of indifference, and who guides with such a firm and at the same time wise hand the chariot of State amidst the unceasing perils of a stormy sea, knowing moreover how to ensure that peace is as well respected as war, industry, business, agriculture and the arts.'

'I must,' said Rodolphe, 'move back a little.'

'Why?' asked Emma.

But, at that moment, the Councillor's voice swelled in an extraordinary manner. He declaimed:

'We are no longer of that hour, gentlemen, when civil strife stained our public places with blood, when the landlord, the merchant, the worker himself, sleeping their pleasant slumber of a night, trembled to find themselves woken all at once by the din of inflammatory alarms, when slogans of the most subversive kind brazenly sapped the foundations . . .'

'It's just that they can see me,' said Rodolphe, 'from below; then I'd be making excuses for a fortnight, and, what with my bad reputation . . .'

'Oh, you slander yourself,' said Emma.

'No no, it's quite awful, I do assure you.'

'But, gentlemen,' the Councillor went on, 'if, putting aside these sombre pictures from my memory, I turn my gaze upon the present condition of our lovely homeland: what do I see? Everywhere business and the arts are flourishing; everywhere new means of communication, like so many new arteries in the body of the State, are establishing new relations; our great manufacturing centres have resumed their activities; religion, strengthened the more, smiles in every heart; our harbours are thriving, our confidence reborn, and at last France may breathe . . . !'

'Yet,' added Rodolphe, 'perhaps, from society's point of view, might they be right?'

'How so?' she asked.

'What,' he said, 'aren't you aware that some souls are endlessly tormented? They require both dreams and deeds in turn, the purest of passions, the fiercest of enjoyments, and so one plunges into all sorts of fancies, follies.'

Then she looked at him as you gaze upon a traveller who has come by way of remarkable lands, and she said:

'Not that we've even this diversion, we poor women!'

'Dreary diversion, for there happiness is not to be found.'

'But do we ever find it?' she ventured.

'One day, yes, you hit upon it,' he answered.

'And this is what you have understood,' said the Councillor. 'You, farmers and workers of the fields; you peaceful pioneers of a wholly civilised labour! You men of progress and morality! You have understood, say I, that political storms are in truth even more formidable than atmospheric disturbances . . .'

'One day you hit upon it,' Rodolphe repeated, 'one day, all of a sudden, and just when you have lost heart. Then the horizons yawn asunder, it's like a voice that cries out: "There it is!" You feel the need to confide your life to this person, to give them all, sacrifice all! No need to explain, you divine each other's meaning. You glimpse one another in dreams.' And he looked up at her. 'At last, there it is, this treasure you have sought so long, there, before you; it shines, it glistens. Nevertheless you still have your doubts, you do not dare trust it; you remain dazzled, as if newly emerged from shadows into the light.'

And, completing these words, Rodolphe added a dumb-show to his speech. Over his face he passed his hand, like a man taken with a dizzy spell; then he let it fall onto Emma's. She withdrew her own. But the Councillor was still reading:

'And who can marvel at this, gentlemen? Only he who would be sufficiently blind, sufficiently immersed (I do not fear to say it), sufficiently immersed in the prejudices of another age not to recognise once more the spirit of the farming population. Where meet, indeed, with more patriotism than in the fields, with more devotion to the public cause, with, in a word, more intelligence? And I do not mean, gentlemen, that superficial intelligence, vain ornament of idle minds, but rather that profound and moderate intelligence, which applies itself above all else to the pursuit of profitable aims, contributing thus to the good of each person, to the common betterment and the upholding of the State, fruit of respect for the law and for the observance of one's duties . . .'

'Ah, yet again!' said Rodolphe. 'Always one's duties, I'm wearied to death by these words. They're a heap of old blockheads in flannel vests, and bigoted dames with foot-warmers and rosaries, who go on warbling in our ears: "Duty! Duty!" Pah! Ye gods! Duty is rather to savour what is great, cherish what is beautiful, and not accept every convention of society, along with the infamies it forces upon us.'

'And yet . . . and yet . . .' objected Madame Bovary.

'Ah, no! Why speak out against the passions? Are they not the only beautiful thing on earth, the fount of heroism, of enthusiasm, of poetry, of music, of the arts, indeed of everything?'

'But one really ought,' said Emma, 'to conform to society's opinion a little and obey its morality.'

'Pah! The fact is, there are two,' he responded. 'The petty, the expedient, the morality that belongs to man, that never ceases to change and bawls at the top of its voice, bustling about down below, workaday, like that gathering of imbeciles that you see there. But the other, the eternal one, lies all around and overhead, like the landscape that surrounds us and the open sky that gives us light.'

Monsieur Lieuvain had just wiped his mouth with his pocket handkerchief. He went on:

'And what would be the point, gentlemen, in demonstrating the usefulness of farming to you here? Who provides for our needs? Who supplies our sustenance? Is it not the farmer? The farmer, gentlemen, who, sowing with laborious hand the fertile furrows of the fields, brings forth the wheat which, once ground, is turned to powder by means of ingenious apparatuses, emerging under the name of flour, and, thence, transported to the cities, is shortly taken to the baker's, who turns it into a nutriment for rich and poor alike. Is it not once more the farmer who, for the sake of our garments, fattens his abundant flocks on the pastures? For how to clothe ourselves, how feed ourselves, without the farmer? And is it even necessary, gentlemen, to seek so far for examples? Who has not often reflected on the utmost importance that we reap from that humble animal, ornament of our farmyards, which at the same time furnishes a soft pillow for our beds, its succulent flesh for our tables, and eggs? But I would never come to a close, if I had to enumerate one after another the different types of produce which the well-tilled earth, like a generous mother, lavishes on her children. Here, it is vines; elsewhere, it is cider apples; there, rape; further off, cheeses; and flax; gentlemen, let us not forget flax! Which, over these last few years, has seen a considerable increase and to which I draw your particular attention.'

He had no need to draw it; for all the mouths of the multitude were held open, as though to drink in the words. Tuvache, beside him, listened with a wide-eyed stare; Monsieur Derozerays closed his lids placidly from time to time; and, further away, the pharmacist, with his son Napoléon between his knees, had his hand cupped behind his ear in order not to lose a single syllable. The other members of the jury slowly rocked their chins in their waistcoats, as a sign of approval. The firemen, at the foot of the stage, rested on their bayonets; and Binet, motionless, remained with his elbow out, the point of the sabre aloft. He could perhaps hear, but could not have observed a thing, on account of his helmet's visor which sloped down to his nose. His lieutenant, the eldest son of Monsieur Tuvache, had gone even further with his; for he wore an enormous one that wobbled on his head, leaving an end of his cotton handkerchief peeping out. He smiled beneath with an entirely childlike meekness, and his pale little face, sweat trickling down it, bore an expression of joy, exhaustion and sleepiness.

The Square was packed with people right up to its houses. Folk were to be seen leaning their elbows at every window, others standing in every doorway, and Justin, in front of the pharmacy, seemed stuck in contemplation of whatever he was looking at. Despite the silence, Monsieur Lieuvain's voice was lost to the air. It reached you in scraps of phrases, interrupted here and there by the noise of chairs in the crowd; then you heard, all of a sudden, an ox's drawn-out bellow emanating from behind him, or the bleating of lambs answering one another at street corners. In fact, the cowherds and the shepherds had driven their animals thus far, and they lowed every so often, while tearing off with their tongue some odd end of foliage that dangled on their muzzles.

Rodolphe had approached Emma, and he said, speaking quickly in a soft voice:

'Aren't you revolted by this conspiracy of society? Is there a single feeling it does not condemn? The noblest of instincts, the purest of sympathies are persecuted, slandered, and, if two poor souls do finally meet, all's organised so they cannot consort. Nevertheless they will try, they'll beat their wings, they'll call to one another. Oh, no matter! sooner or later, in six months, ten years, they will be united again, will love each other, because fate demands it and because they are born for one another.'

He sat with his arms crossed on his knees, and, thus lifting his face towards Emma, he gazed at her from close to, fixedly. In his eyes she could make out tiny golden beams darting out all round his black pupils, and could even smell the perfume of the pomade with which his hair gleamed. Then a limpness laid hold of her, she recalled that Vicomte who made her waltz at La Vaubyessard, and whose beard, like the hair in front of her now, gave off this fragrance of vanilla and lemon; and, automatically, she half-closed her eyelids the better to breathe it in. But, as she did so, arching back slightly on her chair, she perceived far off, on the furthermost horizon, the old diligence *Hirondelle*, trundling slowly down the Leux hill, trailing a long plume of dust. It was in this yellow vehicle that Léon had so often come back to her; and by the same road there that he had left for ever! She thought she saw him opposite, at his window; then everything grew confused, clouds passed over; it seemed to her that she was twirling still in the waltz, under the chandeliers' blaze, on the Vicomte's arm, and that Léon was not far, that he was about to arrive . . . and yet she continued to smell Rodolphe's hair beside her. So the sweetness of this sensation permeated her earlier desires, and like grains of sand under a gust of wind, they swirled about in the fine puffs of perfume spreading through her soul. Several times she flared her nostrils, wide, to inhale the cool scent of the ivy around the pillars' capitals. She removed her gloves, she wiped her hands; then, with her handkerchief, she fanned her face, while through the beating of her temples she heard the crowd's murmur and the voice of the Councillor droning on.

He was saying:

'Carry on! Persevere! Heed neither the suggestions of routine, nor the overly premature counsel of a rash empiricism! Apply yourselves above all to the improvement of the soil, to decent manure, to the development of equine, bovine, ovine and porcine stock! May these agricultural shows be for you as peaceful arenas in which the victor, on leaving there, holds forth his hand to the vanquished and fraternises with him, in the hope of greater success! And you, time-honoured servants! Humble menials! Whose painful labours no government up to this day has taken into proper consideration, come and receive the reward for your silent virtues, and be assured that the State, from this time forward, has its eyes fastened upon you, encouraging you, protecting you, that it shall do justice to your rightful demands and shall, to the best of its ability, ease the burden of your painful sacrifices!'

Monsieur Lieuvain then sat down again; Monsieur Derozerays stood up, beginning another speech. Perhaps his was not so flowery as the Councillor's; but was to be commended for its more positive style, that is to say by a more particular grasp of things and a loftier set of reflections. Thus, praise for the government took up less space; religion and agriculture occupied more. One ascertained the affinity between these two, and how they had always concurred in civilisation. Rodolphe, with Madame Bovary, was chatting of dreams, premonitions, animal magnetism. Travelling back to the cradle of society, the speaker was painting for you those fierce times when men lived on acorns, in the depths of the woods. Then they put away the skins of wild beasts, put on cloth, ploughed furrows, planted the vine. Was it a boon, and were there not more inconveniences than advantages in this discovery? Monsieur Derozerays did ask himself this question. From animal magnetism, little by little, Rodolphe had come round to the subject of affinities, and, while the President was quoting Cincinnatus at his plough, Diocletian planting his cabbages, and the Emperors of China inaugurating the year by sowing seed, the young man was explaining to the young lady that these irresistible attractions drew their cause from some previous existence.

'Likewise, with us,' he said, 'why did we meet? What chance willed it? Across the separation, no doubt, like two rivers that flow on to reunite, our own particular inclinations thrust us towards one another.'

And he seized her hand; she did not withdraw it.

'For good general husbandry!' cried the President.

'Just now, for example, when I came to your house . . .'

'To Monsieur Bizet, of Quincampoix.'

'Did I know that I would be accompanying you?'

'Seventy francs!'

'A hundred times, even, I desired to leave, and I followed you, I stayed.'

'Manures.'

'As I shall stay tonight, tomorrow, every day, all my life!'

'To Monsieur Caron, of Argueil, a gold medal!'

'For in no one else's company have I ever found a more perfect sweetness.'

'To Monsieur Bain, of Givry-Saint-Martin!'

'And so I, for one, shall be carrying away your memory.'

'For a merino ram . . .'

'But you'll forget all about me, I will have passed like a shadow.'

'To Monsieur Belot, of Notre-Dame . . .'

'Ah no! Surely I shall count for something in your thoughts, in your life?'

'Porcine stock, prize *ex aequo*; to Messieurs Lehérissé and Cullembourg; sixty francs!'

Rodolphe clasped her hand, and felt its full warmth, its quivering, like a captive turtle-dove that wants to take flight again; but either because she was trying to disengage it or was responding to this pressure, she moved her fingers; he cried out:

'Oh, thank you! You're not spurning me! You are so good! You understand that I am yours! Let me see you, let me gaze upon you!'

A gust of wind coming through the windows wrinkled the cloth on the table, and, on the Square, down below, the large bonnets of the peasant-women all lifted, like wings of fluttering white butterflies.

'Use of oil-seed cake,' continued the President.

He hastened on:

'Flemish manure . . . flax cultivation . . . Drainage . . . long leases . . . domestic service . . .'

Rodolphe no longer spoke. They gazed at each other. An

overwhelming desire made their dry lips tremble; and loosely, without effort, their fingers melded together.

'Catherine-Nicaise-Élisabeth Leroux, of Sassetot-la-Guerrière, for fifty-four years of service in the same farm, a silver medal – valued at twenty-five francs!'

'Where is she, Catherine Leroux?' repeated the Councillor.

She did not come forward, and whispering voices could be heard:

'Go on!'

'No.'

'To the left!'

'Don't be scared!'

'Ah, she's so silly!'

'Is she there, after all?' shouted Tuvache.

'Yes! . . . There she is!'

'So let her step up!'

Then a little old lady of timid bearing could be seen moving across the stage, seemingly shrivelled up in her wretched clothes. She wore stout wooden pattens on her feet, and, about the hips, a large blue apron. Her thin face, surrounded by an untrimmed *béguin* hood, was more frounced with wrinkles than a withered pippin apple, and the sleeves of her red blouse overshot her long, gnarled hands. The dust of barns, the wash's lye and the wool's grease had so deeply encrusted, chafed and hardened them that they seemed filthy despite having been soused in clear water; and, by dint of long service, they were always half-open, as though to tender on their own account the humble witness of such suffering endured. Something of a nun-like severity dignified the cast of her face. Nothing sad nor tender softened that pale look. From a life spent with animals, she had taken on their dumbness and their placidity. It was the first time that she had found herself in the middle of so great a company; and, inwardly scared by the flags, the drums, the gentlemen in black dress and the Councillor's cross of the Legion of Honour, she remained utterly still, not knowing whether to advance or flee, nor why the crowd was pushing her on and why the judges were smiling at her. So stood, before the beaming burghers, that half-century of servitude.[25]

'Approach, time-honoured Catherine-Nicaise-Élisabeth Leroux!' intoned the Councillor, who had taken the list of the laureates from the President's hands.

And examining by turns the sheet of paper and then the old woman, he repeated in a paternal manner:

'Approach, approach!'

'Are you deaf?' said Tuvache, bouncing on his chair.

And he began to shout into her ear:

'Fifty-four years of service! A silver medal! Twenty-five francs! It's yours.'

Then, when she had her medal, she gazed at it. And a beatific smile spread over her face, and you could hear her mumbling as she went off:

'I'll give it to the priest back home, so as he might say masses for me.'

'What fanaticism!' exclaimed the pharmacist, leaning towards the lawyer.

The meeting was over; the crowd dispersed; and, now that the speeches had been read, everyone recovered rank and everything resumed its habitual round: the masters spoke harshly to their servants, and these hit their animals, sluggish triumphators who made their way back to the stall, a green crown between their horns.

Meanwhile the national guardsmen had come up to the first floor of the town hall, with brioche cakes spitted on their bayonets, and the battalion's drum conveying a basket of bottles. Madame Bovary took Rodolphe's arm; he accompanied her to her house; they separated at her door; then he walked alone in the field, awaiting the banqueting hour.

The feast was long, noisy, badly served; so crammed were they, they could scarce move their elbows, and the narrow planks that served as benches all but snapped under the weight of the guests. They ate copiously. Each took a goodly share. The sweat trickled down every brow; and a whitish vapour, like a river mist on an autumn morning, floated above the table, between the hanging lamps. Rodolphe, leaning back against the tent cloth, was thinking so deeply about Emma, that he heard nothing. Behind him, out on the grass, servants were stacking dirty plates; his table-companions spoke, he did not answer them; his glass was filled, and a silence settled on his thoughts, despite the growing clamour. He dreamed on what she had said and on the shape of her lips; her face, as in a magic mirror, shone out from the badge on the shakos; along the walls fell the folds of her dress, and days of love unrolled to infinity through the vistas of the future.

He saw her that evening, during the fireworks; but she was with her husband, Madame Homais and the pharmacist, the latter fretting about the danger of lost fireworks; and, every other moment, he would leave the company to go and give Binet his advice.

The pyrotechnical pieces sent to Monsieur Tuvache's address had, out of excessive precaution, been shut away in a cellar; so the damp gunpowder scarcely ignited, and the principal item, which should have featured a dragon biting its tail, misfired completely. From time to time, a wretched Roman candle went off; then the gaping crowd sent up a clamour in which were mingled the screams of women being tickled round the waist in the darkness. Emma, silent, cowered softly against Charles's shoulder; then, chin lifted, she followed the luminous spurt of the rockets in the black sky. Rodolphe gazed at her by the light of the burning lamps.

They went out little by little. The stars brightened. A few drops of rain began to fall. She tied her shawl over her bare head.

At that moment, the Councillor's hackney-coach emerged from the inn. Its driver, who was drunk, dozed off all of a sudden; and you could discern from a distance, over the hood, between the two lamps, his body's bulk swaying from right to left with the pitch and toss of the carriage braces.

'The truth is,' said the apothecary, 'we must treat drunkenness with proper rigour! I would like to have recorded, on a weekly basis, at the door of the town hall, on a special board, the names of all those who, during the week, had poisoned themselves with alcohol. Moreover, with regard to the statistics, we would have a sort of open record we could go to when the need arose . . . But excuse me.'

And he ran once more towards the captain.

The latter was returning to his house. He was off to behold his lathe again.

'Perhaps it would not be a bad thing,' Homais said to him, 'to send one of your men or to go yourself . . .'

'Leave me in peace,' replied the tax-gatherer, 'since there is nothing amiss!'

'You can rest easy,' said the apothecary, when he had returned to his friends. 'Monsieur Binet has assured me that the proper steps were taken. No spark will fall. The pumps are full. Let's go to our slumbers.'

'My word, I need to,' declared Madame Homais, who was yawning a great deal; 'but, never mind, we've had the most lovely day for our festival.'

Rodolphe repeated in a low voice and with a tender gaze:

'Oh yes. Most lovely.'

And, having bid good night to each other, they went their separate ways.

Two days later, in the *Rouen Beacon*, there was a big article on the agricutural show. Homais had composed it, in a rapture, the following day.

'Why these festoons, these flowers, these garlands? Whence runs this crowd, like the billows of a furious sea, under the torrents of a tropical sun pouring out its heat upon our tilled fields?'

After that, he discussed the condition of the peasants. Certainly the government did much, but not enough! 'Courage!' he roared at it; 'a thousand reforms are absolutely necessary, let us execute them.' Then, broaching the Councillor's entrance, he did not forget 'the martial look of our militia', nor 'our friskier village maidens', nor 'the bald-pated old men, a certain sort of patriarch, who were there, and of whom several, relics of our immortal battalions, felt their hearts throb once more to the manly sound of the drums.' He named himself among the leading members of the jury, and he even recalled, in a footnote, that M. Homais, pharmacist, had sent a dissertation on cider to the Agricultural Society. When he came to the prize giving, he depicted the joy of the winners in dithyrambic strokes of the pen. 'The father embraced his son, the brother his brother, the husband his wife. More than one displayed his humble medal with pride, and without doubt, once returned to his home, beside his good housewife, he will have hung it tearfully on the modest walls of his little thatched cot.

'About six o'clock, a banquet, laid out in M. Liégeard's meadow, brought together the principal persons present at the festival. There the greatest heartiness never ceased to prevail. Various toasts were made: M. Lieuvain, to the king! M. Tuvache, to the prefect! M. Derozerays, to farming! M. Homais, to industry and to the fine arts, those two sisters! M. Leplichey, to improvement! In the evening, a brilliant firework display suddenly lit up the sky; it looked like a veritable kaleidoscope, a genuine opera set, and a moment when our little locality could believe itself transported into the middle of a dream from *A Thousand and One Nights*.

'Let us note that no disagreeable incident came to perturb this family reunion.'

And he added:

'All we did observe was the clergy's absence. Without doubt the vestries take progress to mean something quite different. Entirely up to you, gentlemen of the Loyola strain!'

IX

SIX WEEKS WENT BY. RODOLPHE did not come back. At last, one evening, he appeared.

He had said to himself, the day after the agricultural show:

'Let us not return there so soon, that would be a mistake.'

And, at the end of the week, he had left to go hunting. After the hunt, he thought it would be too late, then he reasoned to himself:

'But, if she loved me from the first day, she should, eager to see me again, love me all the more. On on, then!'

And he understood that his calculation had been correct when, as he entered the room, he noticed Emma turn pale.

She was alone. The day was fading. The little muslin curtains, drawn across the window-panes, thickened the twilight, and the barometer's gilt, struck by a shaft of sun, glimmered fierily in the mirror, between the coral's jagged edges.

Rodolphe stayed standing; and Emma scarcely responded to his first polite phrases.

'I've had business matters to attend to. I have been ill.'

'Seriously so?' she cried.

'Well,' said Rodolphe, sitting down beside her on a stool, 'no! . . . It's just that I did not wish to come back.'

'Why?'

'You cannot guess?'

He stared at her again, but in so violent a way that she lowered her head, blushing. He went on:

'Emma . . .'

'Monsieur!' she said, moving away a little.

'Ah, you see plainly,' he replied in a melancholy voice, 'that I was right not to want to come back; for this name, this name that fills my soul and has burst from my lips, you forbid me to use it. Madame Bovary! . . . Ah, all the world calls you that . . . What's more, it's not your name; it is the name of another!'

He said again:

'Another!'

And he buried his face in his hands.

'Yes, I think of you all the time. The memory of you drives me to despair. Ah, forgive me! I'm leaving you . . . Farewell! I'll go far away . . . so far away, that you will hear of me no longer . . . And yet . . . today . . . some unknown power thrust me towards you again. For we cannot strive against Heaven, we do not resist the smile of angels. What is lovely, sweet, adorable, we allow ourselves to be tempted by!'

It was the first time that Emma herself had heard such things said; and her pride, like someone refreshing themselves in a sweat-house, stretched itself out languidly and at full length in the warmth of these words.

'But, though I did not come,' he continued, 'though I was unable to see you, ah! at least I have looked upon your surroundings. At night, each and every night, I would rise from my bed, I would venture up here, I would gaze at your house, the roof shining in the moonlight, the garden trees waving at your window, and a tiny lamp, a gleam, shining through the window-panes, in the shadows. Ah, you little knew that a poor, miserable wretch stood by, so near and yet so far . . . !'

She turned towards him with a sob.

'Oh, you're so good,' she said.

'No, I love you, that's all. You do not doubt it. Say it to me; one word, a single word!'

And Rodolphe, imperceptibly, allowed himself to slip from the stool onto the floor; but the clatter of wooden shoes could be heard in the kitchen, and the door to the room, he perceived, was not shut.

'Might you be kind enough,' he pursued, rising, 'to gratify a whim.'

This was to visit his house; he wished to know her; and, as Madame Bovary saw no inconvenience in it, they were both rising to their feet, when Charles came in.

'Good day, doctor,' said Rodolphe.

The physician, flattered by this unexpected title, broke out in obsequiousness, and the other man took advantage of this to compose himself a little.

'Madame was talking to me,' he said, 'of her health . . .'

Charles interrupted him: he was extremely anxious, indeed; his wife's dullness of spirits had started again. Then Rodolphe asked if horse-riding would not be beneficial.

'Certainly. Excellent, perfect. Now there's an idea! You should follow it up.'

And, as she objected that she had no horse, Monsieur Rodolphe offered her one; she refused his offer; he did not insist; then, with the aim of stating a motive for his visit, he related how his carter, the man who was bled, was still troubled with giddy spells.

'I'll drop in,' said Bovary.

'No, no, I shall send him along; we'll come together, that will be more convenient for you.'

'Ah! Very well. I thank you.'

And, as soon as they were alone:

'Why do you not accept Monsieur Boulanger's proposition, so kind as it is?'

She adopted a sulky air, sought a thousand excuses, and declared finally *that perhaps it would look strange.*

'Ah, what do I care for that?' said Charles, with a crafty side-step. 'Health before anything. You're mistaken.'

'Well, how do you wish me to ride a horse, since I have no riding-habit?'

'We must order one,' he replied.

The riding-habit decided her.

When the costume was ready, Charles wrote to Monsieur Boulanger that his wife was at his disposal, and that they were counting on his compliance.

The next day, at twelve o'clock, Rodolphe arrived in front of Charles's door with two mounts. One sported pink pompoms behind the ears and a lady's deerskin saddle.

Rodolphe had donned long soft boots, telling himself that without doubt she had never seen the like; indeed, Emma was charmed by his bearing, when he appeared at the top of the steps with his long velvet riding-coat and his white knitted breeches. She was ready, she was waiting for him.

Justin slipped out of the pharmacy to have a look at her, and the apothecary likewise went out of his way. He gave Monsieur Boulanger some advice:

'A misfortune happens so quickly! Take care! Your horses may perhaps be spirited!'

She heard a noise overhead: it was Félicité drumming on the window-panes to distract little Berthe. The child sent a kiss from afar; her mother signalled back to her with the knob of her horse-whip.

'Happy riding!' cried Monsieur Homais. 'Prudence, above all! Prudence!'

And he waved his newspaper as he watched them move off.

As soon as it felt earth, Emma's horse broke into a canter. Rodolphe cantered next to her. At moments they exchanged words. Face lowered, hand held high and right arm stretched, she abandoned herself to the rhythm of the movement that rocked her in the saddle.

At the bottom of the hill, Rodolphe gave his mount its head; they set off together, in a single bound; then, up on the top, all of a sudden, the horses came to a halt, and her long blue veil subsided.

It was early October. There was fog over the flat country. Between the contours of the hills vapours spread to the horizon; and others, tearing away, rose, dissolved. Sometimes, during a break in the clouds, under a shaft of sun, they glimpsed the rooves of Yonville in the distance, with the riverside gardens, the yards, the walls, and the church steeple. Emma narrowed her eyes to pick out her house, and never had this poor village in which she lived seemed so small to her. From where they were on the heights, the whole valley appeared like an immense pale lake, evaporating into the air. The blocks of trees, here and there, jutted out like black rocks; and the tall lines of poplars, reaching above the mist, became strands stirred by the wind.

Nearby, on the greensward, between the pines, a dusky light was circulating in the warm air. The earth, reddish-brown like tobacco powder, deadened the plod of the hooves; and, with the tips of their horseshoes, as they walked, the steeds kicked before them the fallen fir-cones.

In this manner Rodolphe and Emma followed the verge of the wood. She turned away from time to time in order to avoid his gaze, and then saw nothing but the straight lines of pine trunks, whose unbroken succession made her a little dizzy. The horses blew. The saddles' leather creaked.

The moment they entered the forest, the sun came out.

'God is shielding us,' said Rodolphe.

'You think so?' she cried.

'Forward, forward!' he insisted.

He clicked his tongue. The two animals sped on.

Long fronds of bracken, on the side of the track, kept catching in Emma's stirrup. Rodolphe, without stopping, would lean over and pull them out one by one. At other times, to push away the branches, he passed close to her, and Emma felt his knee graze her leg. The sky had turned blue. The leaves did not stir. There were large clearings full of flowering heather; and sheets of violets alternated with the tangle of trees, which were grey, fawn-coloured or golden, in a variousness of leaves. Often they would hear, beneath the bushes, the faint flap of wings darting, or else the hoarse, soft caw of crows flying among the oaks.

They dismounted. Rodolphe tied the horses. She went in front, over the moss, between the ruts.

But the unwieldy length of her dress encumbered her, even though she lifted it up by the train, and Rodolphe, walking behind her, contemplated between that black cloth and the black half-boot, the daintiness of her white stocking, which seemed to him a part of her nakedness.

She stopped.

'I'm tired,' she said.

'Come on, just a little more effort!' he urged. 'Courage!'

Then, a hundred paces further, she stopped again; and, through her veil, which fell obliquely from her man's hat down onto her hips, you could make out her face in a bluish translucency, as though she were swimming beneath azure waves.

'So where are we going?'

He made no reply. She breathed in a jerky fashion. Rodolphe cast his eyes about him and chewed his moustache.

They came to a broader area, where staddles²⁶ had been hewn. They sat down on a felled tree-trunk, and Rodolphe began to speak to her of his love.

At first he did not frighten her at all with compliments. He was calm, serious, melancholic.

Emma listened to him with lowered head, all the while stirring the fallen woodshavings with her toe.

But, at this sentence:

'Are our destinies not mutual now?'

'Of course not,' she replied. 'You know perfectly well. It is impossible.'

She got up to leave. He seized her by the wrist. She stopped dead.

Then, having considered him for several minutes with moist, love-filled eyes, she said sharply:

'Look, let us speak no more of this . . . Where are the horses? We are going back.'

He made an angry, world-weary gesture. She repeated:

'Where are the horses? Where are the horses?'

Then, smiling with a strange smile and a fixed gaze, teeth clenched, he came forward with outspread arms. She backed off trembling. She stammered:

'Oh! You're scaring me! You're hurting me! Let us leave.'

'Since we must,' he went on, with an altered expression.

And immediately he returned to being respectful, fawning, shy. She gave him her arm. They retraced their steps. He said:

'So what was the matter? Why? I cannot make it out. You have doubtless misunderstood? You're in my soul like a madonna on a pedestal, up on high, steadfast and immaculate. But I need you in order to live. I've need of your eyes, your voice, your mind. Be my friend, my sister, my angel!'

And he stretched out his arm and put it around her waist. She strove feebly to break loose. He supported her thus, as they walked.

But they heard the two horses cropping the leaves.

'Oh, once more,' said Rodolphe. 'Don't leave! Stay!'

He drew her further off, around the rim of a small pool, its waters green with duck-weed. Withered water-lilies lay motionless among the rushes. At the sound of their footsteps in the grass, frogs leapt to hide themselves.

'It is wrong of me, wrong of me,' she said. 'I must be mad to listen to you.'

'Why? . . . Emma! Emma!'

'Oh, Rodolphe!. . .' said the young woman slowly as she leant on his shoulder.

The cloth of her dress caught in the riding-coat's velvet. She threw back her white neck, distended by a sigh; and, weakening, all in tears, with a drawn-out shudder and hiding her face, she surrendered herself.

The evening's shadows were falling; the low sun, passing between the branches, dazzled her eyes. Here and there, all about her, in the leaves or on the ground, spots of light trembled, as if humming birds, flying to and fro, had scattered their feathers. The silence was everywhere; something sweet seemed to rise from the trees; she was aware of her heart, that was beating again, and of the blood circling through her flesh like a river of milk. Then, she heard from far and away, beyond the wood, on the opposite hills, an indistinct and protracted cry, a voice that lingered, and she listened to it silently, as it mingled like a snatch of song with the last quiverings of her plucked nerves. Rodolphe, cigar between his teeth, was patching up a snapped bridle-rein with his pocket-knife.

They returned to Yonville, by the same path. They saw again in the mud the prints of their horses, side by side, and the same bushes, the same stones in the grass. Nothing around them had changed; and yet, for her, something had taken place that was more considerable than the shifting of mountains. Rodolphe, from time to time, leaned over and seized her hand to kiss it.

She was delightful, on horseback! Straight-backed, with her slender waist, knee bent on the animal's mane and her colour heightened a little by the open air, in the evening's blush.[27]

Riding into Yonville, she pranced a caracole on the paving-stones. She was being watched from the windows.

Her husband, over supper, thought she was looking well; but she appeared not to be listening when he inquired about her ride; and she rested her elbow next to the plate, between the two glowing candles.

'Emma,' he said.

'What?'

'Well, I spent this afternoon at Monsieur Alexander's; he has an old filly, still very fair, just a little broken-kneed, and which we could have for a hundred crowns, I'm certain of it . . .'

He added:

'Thinking how much that would please you, I reserved it . . . I bought it . . . Have I done right? Tell me now.'

She moved her head in a sign of assent; then, a quarter of an hour later:

'Are you going out this evening?' she asked.

'Yes. Why?'

'Oh nothing, nothing, my dear.'

And, as soon as she was rid of Charles, she went upstairs to shut herself up in her room.

At first, it was like a giddy spell; she saw the trees, the paths, the ditches, Rodolphe, and she still felt the grip of his arms, while the leaves quivered and the rushes hissed.

But, when she glimpsed herself in the mirror, she marvelled at her face. Never had her eyes been so large, so black, nor so deep. Something subtle had spread over her body, transfiguring it.

She repeated to herself: 'I have a lover! A lover!' – delighting in this idea as if at a second puberty that had unexpectedly come upon her. So she would at last possess those joys of love, that fever of happiness she had so despaired of. She was entering into something wondrous where all would be passion, ecstasy, delirium; a bluish immensity surrounded her, emotion's peaks glistened beneath her thought, and ordinary existence appeared only in the distance, far below, in the shade, between the intervals of these heights.

Then she recalled the heroines in the books she had read, and the lyric legion of those adulterous women began to sing in her memory with beguiling, sisterly voices. She became a veritable part of these imaginings and realised the drawn-out dream of her youth, in deeming herself one of those archetypal lovers whom she had so envied. Moreover, Emma felt the gratification of vengeance. Had she not suffered enough! But now she was triumphant, and love, so long contained, gushed forth whole and with a joyful bubbling. She relished it without remorse, without unease, without confusion.

The next day passed by in a fresh sweetness. They exchanged pledges. She recounted her sorrows. Rodolphe would interrupt her with his kisses; and she would beg him, gazing upon him with eyelids half-closed, to call her again by her name and to say once more that he loved her. It was in the forest, as the day before, in a shoe-maker's hut. The walls were of straw and the roof came down so low, they had to stoop. They were seated one against the other, on a bed of dry leaves.

From that day forth, they wrote to each other regularly every evening. Emma would carry her letter to a crack in the wall, at the bottom of the garden, near the river. Rodolphe would come there to fetch it and put in its place another, that she would always accuse of being too short.

One morning, when Charles had gone out before dawn, the whim took her to see Rodolphe instantly. One could speedily reach La Huchette, stay there an hour and be back in Yonville with everyone still fast asleep. This idea made her gasp with lust, and she soon found herself in the middle of the meadow, where she walked at a rapid pace, without a glance behind her.

The day was beginning to break. Emma, from a distance, recognised her lover's house, whose two swallow-tailed weather-vanes stood out blackly against the pale dawn.

After the farmyard, there was a main building which must be the chateau. She entered, and it was as though the walls, at her approach, had stood aside of their own volition. A great flight of stairs rose straight up to a corridor. Emma lifted the latch on a door, and all of a sudden, at the far end of the bedroom, she perceived a sleeping man. It was Rodolphe. She let out a cry.

'There you are! There you are!' he repeated. 'How did you manage to come?. . . Ah, your dress is soaked.'

'I love you,' she replied, circling his neck with her arms.

Having succeeded in this first boldness, each time Charles now left the house early, Emma would dress swiftly and with a stealthy tread descend the flight of steps that led to the water's edge.

But, when the cattle-board was raised, she had to follow the walls that ran along the river; the steep bank was slippery; she hung on with one hand to the bunches of withered wallflower, so as not to fall. Then she took off across ploughed fields, into which she would sink, stumble and entangle her puny lady's boots. Her scarf, knotted over her head, was flung about by the wind in the pasture; she was scared of the oxen, she broke into a run; she would arrive out of breath, cheeks flushed, and breathing from every pore a fresh fragrance of sap, of greenery and the open air. Rodolphe, at that hour, would be still asleep. It was as though a spring morning had entered his room.

The yellow curtains across the windows let through a deep golden light. Emma would grope her way blinking, while the dewdrops suspended from the drawn-back swathes of her hair made a halo of topazes all about her face. Rodolphe, laughing, drew her to him and caught her to his heart.

Afterwards, she would examine the room, she would open the drawers, she would comb her hair with his comb and gaze at herself in the shaving-mirror. Often, she would go so far as to set between her teeth the stem of a stout pipe that was on the night table, among the lemons and the sugar lumps, next to a carafe of water.

A good quarter of an hour was needed for their farewells. Then Emma would weep; she wished never to have to leave Rodolphe. Something stronger than herself thrust her towards him, so much so that one day, seeing her suddenly and unexpectedly appear, he knitted his brows like someone vexed.

'What's the matter with you?' she said. 'Are you in pain? Tell me!'

Finally he declared, in a serious manner, that her visits were becoming indiscreet and that she was compromising herself.

X

LITTLE BY LITTLE, THESE FEARS of Rodolphe's gained on her. Love had intoxicated her at first, and she had thought of nothing beyond it. But, now it was indispensable to her existence, she feared to lose some part of it, or even that it might be disturbed. When she made her way back from visiting him, she would throw anxious glances all about her, closely watching each shape that went by on the horizon and each attic-window from which she might have been observed. She listened to the footsteps, the cries, the clinks of ploughs; and she came to a stop, more pale and shivering than the poplars' leaves swaying above her head.

One morning, when she was returning thus, she suddenly thought she could discern the long barrel of a rifle which seemed to be aimed at her. It extended at an angle beyond the rim of a small tub, half buried among the grasses, on the margin of a ditch. Emma, ready to faint from terror, came forward nevertheless, and a man emerged from the tub, like a Jack-in-the-box springing up from the bottom. He had gaiters buckled up to his knees, his cap pushed down to his eyes, lips shivering with cold and a red nose. It was Captain Binet, lying in wait for wild ducks.

'You should have spoken from further off!' he shouted. 'When one observes a gun, warning must always be given.'

In this way, the tax-gatherer was trying to conceal the fright that he had just had; for, a prefectorial decree having forbidden duck-hunting other than from a boat, Monsieur Binet, despite his respect for the law, was committing an offence. So at every moment he believed he could hear the rural guard arriving. But this worry chafed at his sport, and, all alone in his tub, he congratulated himself on his good fortune and his wiliness.

At the sight of Emma, he seemed relieved of a great burden, and immediately, beginning the conversation:

'Not warm out. *Biting!*'

Emma made no reply. He pursued:

'And there you are, out bright and early?'

'Yes,' she said, stammering; 'I'm coming from the wet-nurse's house where my child is.'

'Ah, very good! Very good! As for me, I've been here from daybreak, just as you see me; but the weather's so mizzly, that unless you've the feather on the muzzle . . .'

'Good day, Monsieur Binet,' she interrupted, turning on her heel.

'Your servant, Madame,' he resumed in a dry tone.

And he popped back into his tub.

Emma regretted leaving the tax-gatherer so brusquely. He would be making unfavourable conjectures, no doubt. The story of the wet-nurse was the worst excuse, everyone at Yonville knowing full well that the Bovary child had been back at her parents' house for a year. Moreover, nobody lived round about; this path led only to La Huchette; so Binet had guessed where she was coming from, and he would not keep quiet, he would blab, for certain! She continued until dark torturing her mind with all the lying schemes imaginable, and having this imbecile with the game-pouch endlessly before her eyes.

After dinner, Charles, seeing her anxious, wished to divert her by taking her to the pharmacist's; and the first person she noticed in the pharmacy was him again, the tax-gatherer! He was standing before the counter, lit by the glow of the red jar, and was saying:

'Let me have, if you please, a half-ounce of vitriol.'

'Justin,' cried the apothecary, 'bring us some sulphuric acid.'

Then, to Emma, who wished to go up to Madame Homais' room:

'No, stay, it's not worth it, she'll be coming down. Warm yourself by the stove while you wait . . . Excuse me . . . Good day, doctor . . .' (for the pharmacist very much flattered himself in uttering the word *doctor*, as if by addressing another as this, he would have something of the splendour he found therein reflected back on himself) . . . 'But take care not to tip over the mortars! In fact, go and fetch the chairs from the parlour; you know jolly well that the armchairs in the drawing-room are not to be disturbed.'

And Homais was hurrying out from behind the counter to put back his own armchair, when Binet asked him for a half-ounce of sugar acid.

'Sugar acid?' said the pharmacist scornfully. 'Don't know, never heard of it. Perhaps you want some oxalic acid? It's oxalic, isn't that right?'

Binet explained that he needed a mordant to mix his own copper solution with which to rub the rust off various hunting pieces. Emma gave a start. The pharmacist began to say:

'Indeed, the weather is not propitious, on account of the wet.'

'Nevertheless,' said the tax-gatherer with a sly air, 'there are some who put up with it.'

She choked.

'And give me . . .'

'So he's never going to go!' she thought.

'A half-ounce of rosin and turpentine, four ounces of unbleached wax, and three ounces of bone black, please, to clean my equipment's shiny leather parts.'

The apothecary was starting to cut the wax, when Madame Homais appeared with Irma in her arms, Napoléon next to her and Athalie following. She went to sit down on the velvet bench by the window, and the little boy squatted on a stool, while his older sister prowled around the jujube box, next to her dear papa. The latter was filling funnels and corking bottles, he was pasting labels, making up parcels. There was a hush around him; and all that could be heard was the weights jingling in the scales from time to time, with the odd low word from the pharmacist giving advice to his apprentice.

'How is your little one?' asked Madame Homais suddenly.

'Silence!' exclaimed her husband, who was scribbling figures in the rough-book.

'Why haven't you brought her along?' she resumed in a whisper.

'Hush, hush!' said Emma, pointing at the apothecary.

But Binet, completely absorbed in reading the bill, had probably heard nothing. At last he left. Then Emma, rid of him, let out a great sigh.

'What deep breaths you take!' said Madame Homais.

'Oh, it's because it is a little warm,' she responded.

So they considered, the next day, how to arrange their meetings; Emma wanted to bribe her maid with a present; but it would be better to find some discreet house in Yonville.

All winter, three or four times a week, in the darkest night, he would come to the garden. Emma had deliberately taken the key out of the gate, Charles believing it lost.

To alert her, Rodolphe would throw a fistful of sand against the window-blinds. She got up with a start; but sometimes he had to wait for her, as Charles had a mania for prattling by the fire, and he would not finish. She was consumed with impatience; if her eyes could have managed it, they would have thrown him out of the window. At last, she began to prepare for bed; then she took up a book and went on reading quite calmly, as if entertained by the words. But Charles, who was in bed, would appeal to her to turn in.

'Come along, Emma,' he said, 'it's time.'

'Yes, I am coming,' she answered.

However, as the candles dazzled him, he would turn round to face the wall and nod off. She would make her escape with held breath, smilingly, quiveringly, in dishabille.

Rodolphe had a large coat; he wrapped her up in it completely, and, putting his arm around her waist, he hurried her away without a word down to the end of the garden.

It was under the arbour, on that same seat of rotten sticks where in times past Léon would gaze upon her so lovingly, through the summer evenings. She scarcely thought of him now.

The stars glittered through the leafless jasmin branches. They heard the river slipping past behind them, and, from time to time, on the bank, the clapping of dry reeds. Here and there, massed shadows swelled up in the darkness, and sometimes, all shuddering with the same motion, they towered and leaned over like huge black waves advancing to conceal them. The night's cold made them clasp each other the more; the sighs from their lips seemed louder to them; their eyes, though they could barely make them out, appeared to them larger, and, in the midst of the silence, there were words spoken very low that fell on their soul with a crystalline resonance and reverberated there in repeated vibrations.

When the night was wet, they would go and take shelter in the consulting room, between the cart-shed and the stable. She lit one of the kitchen candles, hidden by her behind the books. Rodolphe would make himself at home in there. The sight of the bookcase and the desk, in short of the whole room, fired his high spirits; and he could not stop himself cracking numerous jokes about Charles that troubled Emma. She longed to see him more serious, and even more dramatic on occasion, like that time she thought she could hear the sound of approaching footsteps on the garden path.

'Someone's coming!' she said.

He blew the light out.

'Do you have your pistols?'

'Why?'

'Well . . . to defend yourself,' answered Emma.

'Is it your husband? Ah, the poor fellow!'

And Rodolphe completed his sentence with a gesture that signified: 'I'll crush him with a flick of the nail.'

She was amazed at his courage, although she sensed a kind of indelicacy and natural boorishness which shocked her deeply.

Rodolphe pondered on this pistols business a great deal. If she had spoken seriously, then that was truly ridiculous, he thought, even obnoxious, as he for one had no reason to detest this good Charles, not being consumed, as they say, by jealousy; and, while on the subject, Emma had sworn him a solemn oath that he likewise did not consider to be in the best taste.

Morever, she was becoming frightfully sentimental. Miniatures had had to be exchanged, handfuls of hair cut off and now she was asking for a ring, a real wedding ring, as a token of eternal union. She would often speak to him of evening bells or the *voices of nature*; then chat about her mother and his mother respectively. Rodolphe had lost his twenty years ago. Nevertheless, Emma consoled him with the kind of insipid language you would use on an abandoned little boy, and even said to him sometimes, while gazing at the moon:

'I'm quite certain that together, in Heaven, they approve of our love.'

But she was so pretty! He had possessed so few with such candour! This undebauched love was a new thing for him, and, prising him from his easy ways, it pampered both his pride and his sensuality. Emma's rapturous elation, which his bourgeois common sense disdained, seemed charming to him in his heart of hearts, since it was directed at himself. So, confident of being loved, he did not bother himself unduly, and his attentions imperceptibly changed.

He no longer had, as in times past, those so very sweet words that would make her weep, nor any of those fervent caresses that would drive her wild; so much so that their great love, in which her life was plunged, appeared to diminish beneath her, like the water of a river soaking away into its bed; and she perceived the oozing mud. She did not want to believe it; she was doubly loving; and less and less did Rodolphe conceal his indifference.

She did not know if she regretted having yielded to him, or desired, on the contrary, to cherish him the more. The humiliation of feeling herself weak became a rancour soothed by voluptuousness. It was not affection, it was a sort of permanent seduction. He subdued her. She was almost frightened.

On the surface, however, things were calmer than ever, Rodolphe having successfully steered the adultery according to his own caprice; and, at the end of six months, when spring came, they found themselves, in relation to one another, like a newly married couple keeping the domestic flame alight.

It was the time of year when Père Rouault would send his turkey, in memory of his mended leg. The gift always came with a letter. Emma cut the string securing it to the basket, and read the following lines:

> My dear children,
> I hope that the present letter finds you in good health and that this one is as good as the others; as it seems to me a little softer to the touch, if I may be so bold, and heavier. But the next time, for a change, I'll give you a rooster, unless you prefer *ganny-cocks*;[28] and send me back the basket, if you please, with the two ones previous. I've had a misfortune with the cart-shed, whose covering flew off into the trees when the wind was blowing hard one night. The harvest has not been too famous, neither. In a word, I do not know when I shall be coming to see you. It's so hard for me to leave the house now, since I've been on my own, my poor Emma!

And here there was an interval between the lines, as if the good fellow had let his pen fall in order to dream for a while.

> As for me, I'm well, save for a cold caught the other day at the Yvetot fair, where I went off to hire a shepherd, having

thrown mine out, as a result of his ticklish belly. How we are to
be pitied with all those robbers! Besides he was also dishonest.

I learnt from a pedlar, who had a tooth pulled when travelling
through your country this winter, that Bovary still works hard. That
don't surprise me, and he showed me his tooth; we partook of a
coffee together. I asked him if he had seen you, he said no, but he
had seen two animals in the stable, from which I conclude that
the business bowls along. So much the better, my dear children,
and may the good Lord send you all imaginable happiness.

It grieves me that I don't yet know my beloved
granddaughter Berthe Bovary. I have planted a wild plum-tree
for her, in the garden, under your window, and I don't want
anyone touching it, unless it be to make her fruit-stews later on,
that I shall keep in the cupboard for her, when she comes.

Farewell, my dear children. With love and kisses, my daughter;
you too, my son-in-law, and for the little one, on both cheeks.

I am, with my sincere regards,

    Your loving father,

      THÉODORE ROUAULT

She stayed several minutes holding that coarse sheet of paper
between her fingers. The misspellings[29] twined themselves about each
other, and Emma pursued the gentle thought that cackled all the way
through like a hen half-concealed in a thorny hedge. The writing had
been dried with ashes from the fireplace, for a touch of grey powder
slid from the letter onto her dress, and she believed she could almost
see her father stooping to the hearth to take up the tongs. What a long
time since she had last been there beside him, on the stool, by the great
fireplace, burning the end of a stick in the fierce blaze of the sparkling
sea rushes!. . . She recalled the summer evenings chock full of sunlight.
The foals would whinny when you passed, and gallop about, gallop
about . . . Under her window was a beehive, and sometimes the bees,
whirling in the light, would tap on the panes like bouncing balls of
gold. What happiness in those days! What freedom! What hope! What
abundance of illusions! There were none left now. At every venture

of her soul she had spent them, through every successive state, in maidenhood, in marriage and in love – shedding them thus continually throughout her life, like a traveller who leaves something of his wealth at each of the inns along the way.

But who then was making her so unhappy? Wherein lay the uncommon disaster that had thrown her into turmoil? And she lifted her head, looking all about her, as if seeking out her suffering's cause.

An April sunbeam played its colours over the porcelain figures on the shelves; the fire blazed; she felt the rug's softness under her slippers; the daylight was pale, the air tepid, and she heard her child bursting into laughter.

In fact, the little girl was rolling on the lawn at that point, amid the grass that was being turned. She lay flat on her stomach, on the top of a mown heap. Her nurse-maid was restraining her by her petticoat. Lestiboudois was raking nearby, and, each time he approached, she would lean down and beat the air with her arms.

'Bring her to me!' said her mother as she rushed up to kiss her. 'How I love you, my poor child! How I love you!'

Then, noticing that the tips of her ears were a little dirty, she rang speedily for some hot water, and cleaned her, changed her linen, stockings, shoes, asked a thousand questions about her health, as though back from a journey, and at last, kissing her again and crying a little, she restored her to the hands of the maid, who was left decidedly amazed before this surfeit of tender love.

Rodolphe, that evening, found her more serious than usual.

'That will pass,' he judged, 'it's a whim.'

And he missed three assignations in succession. When he came back, she appeared cold and almost disdainful.

'Ah! You're wasting your time, my darling . . .'

And he seemed not to notice her melancholy sighs, nor the hand-kerchief she would draw out.

It was then that Emma repented!

She even wondered why she detested Charles so, and whether it would not have been better to be able to love him. But he did not offer much of a hold for this recurrence of feeling, with the result that her wavering desire for sacrifice was decidedly stalled, until the apothecary came pat to provide her with an opportunity.

XI

H E HAD RECENTLY READ AN article praising a new method of curing club foot, and, as he was a devotee of progress, he entertained the patriotic idea that Yonville, so as to *put itself on a par*, should have strephopodic operations.

'For,' he said to Emma, 'what do we risk? Consider . . .' (and he enumerated, on his fingers, the benefits of the endeavour): 'success all but certain, relief and improved looks for the invalid, celebrity speedily attained for the operating surgeon. Why should your husband, for example, not wish to unburden this poor Hippolyte, of the *Lion d'Or*? Observe that he would not fail to recount the story of his cure to every traveller, and then' (Homais lowered his voice and looked about him), 'what is to stop me sending a little note about it to the newspaper? Heh? Good Lord! An article circulates . . . it is talked about . . . and finally it's a rolling snowball! And who knows, who knows?'

Indeed, Bovary might succeed; Emma had no evidence that he was not skilled, and how satisfying for her to have committed him to a step by which his reputation and his fortune would find themselves enhanced. All she was asking for was something to lean on that was more substantial than love.

Charles, entreated by her and the apothecary, let himself be convinced. He sent to Rouen for Doctor Duval's volume,[30] and, every evening, taking his head in his hands, he plunged into his reading.

While he was studying the equinus, the varus and the valgus, that's to say the strephocatopodia, the strephendopodia and the strephexopodia (or, to put it more plainly, the different deviations of the foot, either downwards, inwards or outwards), with the strephypopodia and the strephanopodia (in other words, twisting under and stretching upwards), Monsieur Homais, using all sorts of arguments, was exhorting the inn's stable lad to have himself operated on.

'You might just feel, perhaps, a slight pain; it's a simple puncture like a small bleeding, less than the rooting out of little corns.'

Hippolyte, pondering, rolled his stupid eyes.

'Yet,' the pharmacist continued, 'it's no concern of mine. It's for your own sake. Out of pure humanity! I would like to see you, my friend, unburdened of your dreadful lameness, with this swaying of the lumbar region, which, whatever you say, must be of a considerable disadvantage to you in the exercise of your occupation.'

Then Homais described how much more lively and brisk he would feel afterwards, and even gave him to believe that he would be better off in terms of pleasing the women; and the ostler began to smile dully. Then he assailed him through vanity:

'Good grief, where's the man in you? How would it be, then, if you'd had to serve, going off and fighting under the flag? Oh, Hippolyte!'

And Homais went away, declaring that he could not understand this stubbornness, this blindness in denying himself the benefits of science.

The poor wretch yielded, because it was a sort of conspiracy. Binet, who never troubled his head over another's affairs, Madame Lefrançois, Artémise, the neighbours, and right up to the mayor, Monsieur Tuvache, everyone induced him, lectured him, made him feel ashamed; but what really decided him, *was that this would cost him nothing*. Bovary even took it upon himself to supply the machine for the operation. This act of generosity was Emma's idea; and Charles agreed to it, saying to himself in his heart of hearts that his wife was an angel.

To the promptings of the apothecary, and with three false starts, he had the joiner, helped by the locksmith, put together a kind of box weighing about eight pounds, and for which there was no stinting on iron, wood, canvas, metal plate, leather, screws and nuts.

However, in order to know which of Hippolyte's tendons to cut, they had first of all to establish what type of club-foot he had.

He had a foot that along with the leg described an almost straight line, which did not prevent it from being turned inward, so that was an equinus mixed with a dash of varus, or else a light varus strongly marked by equinus. But, on this equinus, as broad indeed as a horse's hoof, with a roughened skin, dry tendons, big toes, and where the black nails formed a horseshoe's studs, the strephopode himself, from morn till night, galloped about like a stag. You saw him constantly in the square, hopping all around the carts, throwing his uneven prop out in front. He seemed even more vigorous on that leg than on the other. By dint of seeing service, it had acquired, as it were, moral qualities of patience and energy, and when he was given some weighty task, he would shore himself up on it, favouring that side.

Now, since it was an equinus, the Achilles tendon would have to be cut, even if it meant getting to work later on the interior tibial muscle to correct the varus; for the doctor did not dare risk two operations in one go, and he was actually trembling already, for fear of stumbling upon any essential area about which he knew nothing.

Surely neither Ambroise Paré, applying a ligature directly to an artery for the first time since Celsus, after an interval of fifteen hundred years; nor Dupuytren proceeding to open an abscess through a thick layer of encephalitic matter; nor Gensoul,[31] when he carried out the first ablation of the upper maxillary, had such a pounding heart, so trembling a hand, so strained an understanding as Monsieur Bovary when he approached Hippolyte, clutching his *tenotome*[32] between his fingers. And you could see, on a nearby table, as in a hospital, a heap of lint, waxed threads, a lot of bandages, a pyramid of bandages, all that could be had in the way of bandages from the pharmacy. It was Monsieur Homais who, from first thing that morning, had got all these things ready, as much to dazzle the multitude as to delude himself. Charles punctured the skin; a sharp crack was heard. The tendon was cut, the operation was over. Hippolyte could not get over his astonishment; he bent over Bovary's hands and covered them with kisses.

'Come now, calm down,' said the apothecary, 'you may show your gratitude to your benefactor later on!'

And he went down to relate the outcome to five or six onlookers who were standing in the yard, and who imagined that Hippolyte would emerge walking soundly. Then Charles, having buckled his patient into the mechanical apparatus, went back home, where Emma, all anxious-ness, was waiting for him at the door. She flew into his arms; they sat down to table; he ate a great deal, and he even desired a cup of coffee with dessert, a debauch he only permitted himself on a Sunday when there was company.

The evening was delightful, full of prattle, of dreams in common. They talked of their future wealth, changes for the better in their household economy; he saw his esteem expanding, his well-being enlarging, his wife loving him for ever; and she was happy to revive herself on a new, more wholesome, finer feeling, to experience at last some tenderness for this poor boy who cherished her so. The thought of Rodolphe crossed her mind for a moment; but her eyes turned back to Charles; she even observed with surprise that his teeth were not ugly.

They were in bed when Monsieur Homais, despite the best efforts of the cook-maid, burst into their room, holding in his hand a freshly-inscribed sheet of paper. It was the announcement he intended for the *Rouen Beacon*. He had brought it for them to read.

'You read it,' said Bovary.

He read:

'"Despite the prejudices that still cover the face of Europe like a net, enlightenment nevertheless begins to penetrate our country places. So it is that, on Tuesday, our little town of Yonville saw itself the theatre of a surgical experiment that is at the same time an act of lofty philanthropy. Monsieur Bovary, one of our most distinguished practitioners . . ."'

'Oh, that's too much, too much!' said Charles, choking with emotion.

'But no, not at all! How so? ". . . operated on a victim of club-foot . . ." I didn't put the scientific term, because, you know, in a newspaper . . . maybe not everyone would understand; the masses have to . . .'

'Indeed,' said Bovary. 'Go on.'

'I'll resume,' said the pharmacist. '"Monsieur Bovary, one of our most distinguished practitioners, operated on a victim of club-foot by the name of Hippolyte Tautain, stable hand for twenty-five years at the *Lion d'Or* hotel, kept by Madame the widow Lefrançois, on the Place d'Armes. The novelty of the attempt and the interest attendant on the subject had attracted such a throng of the populace, that there was a veritable congestion on the establishment's threshold. The operation, however, was carried out as if by magic, and scarce four drops of blood appeared on the skin, as though confirming that the obstinate tendon had just yielded at last under the exertions of great skill. The patient, oddly enough (we vouch for it *de visu*), did not complain of pain. His state, up until time of writing, leaves nothing to be desired. Everything leads us to believe that the convalescence will be short; and who knows whether, at the next village festival, we will not be seeing our valiant Hippolyte stepping out in the bacchanalian dances, amidst a chorus of jocund fellows, and thus proving to all eyes, through his verve and his capering leaps, his complete recovery? Honour therefore to the noble savants! Honour to these untiring spirits who dedicate their night labours to the betterment or rather the relief of their species! Honour! Thrice honour! Should we not now be crying out that the blind shall see, the deaf shall hear and the lame shall walk? But that which zealotry in times of old promised to its elect, science now accomplishes for all mankind! We will keep our readers informed of the successive phases of this truly remarkable cure.'"

Which did not prevent Mère Lefrancois, five days later, from arriving in a state of wild distress and crying out:

'Help! He's dying . . . ! I'm going to go mad!'

Charles rushed towards the *Lion d'Or*, and the pharmacist seeing him passing by on the square, hatless, deserted the pharmacy. He appeared himself, puffing, red-faced, uneasy, and asking all those going up the stairs:

'So what's the matter with our interesting strephopode?'

The strephopode was writhing about in atrocious spasms, so much so that the mechanical apparatus in which his leg was cooped up kept thumping against the wall with enough force to stave it in.

With a great deal of care, in order not to disturb the position of the limb, they then withdrew the box, and saw a horrible sight. The foot's contours were swallowed up in such a swollen mass, that the entire skin seemed about to rupture, and was covered in bruises caused by the much-vaunted machine. Hippolyte had already complained of it hurting; no one had heeded him; they had to admit that he had not been completely mistaken; and they left him liberated for a few hours. But scarce had the oedema faded a little, than the two savants deemed it proper to restore the limb to the apparatus, clamping it on tighter, to speed things up. Finally, three days later, Hippolyte being unable to bear it any longer, they again withdrew the mechanism, while being very much amazed by the observable result. A livid tumefaction was spread over the leg, with phlyctenae[33] here and there, from which oozed a black fluid. Things had taken a serious turn. Hippolyte was starting to get worried, and Mère Lefrançois installed him in the parlour, next to the kitchen, so that he would have some diversion at least.

But the tax-gatherer, who dined there every day, complained bitterly of such company. So they carried Hippolyte into the billiard room.

There he was, moaning under his thick blankets, pale, unshaven, hollow-eyed, and turning his sweaty head now and again on the soiled pillow where the flies kept settling. Madame Bovary came to see him. She brought him linen for his poultices, and comforted him, encouraged him. Yet he did not lack for company, above all on market days, when the peasants surrounding him knocked their billiard balls, fenced with the cues, smoked, drank, sang, brawled.

'How goes it?' they would say, thumping him on the shoulder. 'Ah, you're not in great spirits, it appears! But it's your own fault. You have to be doing this, doing that . . .'

And they told him stories of folk who had all been cured by other remedies than his; then, by way of consolation, they would add:

'It's on account of you nursing y'self overmuch! Up with you now! Coddling yourself like a king, you are! Ah, never mind, y'old dog, you don't smell too nice!'

The gangrene, indeed, was creeping up and up. Bovary was sick from it himself. He came hourly, at all times. Hippolyte gazed at him, eyes brimming with terror, and sobbingly stammered out:

'When'll I be cured? . . . Oh, save me! . . . I'm that low, I'm that low!'

And the doctor went away, invariably recommending a starvation diet.

'Don't you listen to him, my lad,' chided Mère Lefrançois; 'haven't they made enough of a martyr of you already? You'll grow weaker still. Here, drink up!'

And she would offer him some nice broth, a slice of mutton, a morsel of bacon, and at times a small glass of brandy, that he did not have the courage to bring to his lips.

Abbé Bournisien, hearing he was worsening, desired to see him. He began by pitying him his misfortune, at the same time declaring that he should rejoice in it, since it was the Lord's will, and that he should quickly profit from the occasion to be reconciled with Heaven.

'For,' said the clergyman in a paternal tone, 'you've been a little neglectful of your duties; we rarely see you at the divine service; how many years is it since you approached the communion table? I understand that your work, that the whirlwind of the world may well have diverted you from attending to your salvation. But now, the hour has come for reflection. Do not despair, however; I have known men of heavy guilt who, when their appearance before God was all but nigh (you're not yet there, I'm well aware), had beseeched His forgiveness, and who died in the best frame of mind, to be sure. Let us hope that, just like them, you will show us a fine example! Thus, by way of precaution, what is to stop you from reciting morning and evening a *Hail Mary, full of grace* and an *Our Father, which art in Heaven?* Yes, do it! For my sake, to please me. What would that cost? . . . Do you promise me?'

The poor devil promised. The cleric came back over the following days. He chatted with the landlady and even regaled them with anecdotes mixed in with pleasantries, and puns that Hippolyte did not understand. Then, as soon as circumstances permitted, he reverted to religious matters, adopting a suitable face.

His zeal appeared to succeed; for soon the strephopode expressed a desire to go on pilgrimage to Bon-Secours, were he to recover; to which Monsieur Bournisien replied that he saw nothing against it; two precautions were better than one. *Nothing ventured.*

The apothecary was indignant at what he called *the priest's man-oeuvres*; it was prejudicial, he claimed, to Hippolyte's convalescence, and he kept repeating to Madame Lefrançois:

'Leave him be! Leave him be! You're undermining his morale with your mysticism!'

But the good woman would not hear of it. He was *the cause of it all*. To spite him, she even hooked a brimming holy-water pot onto the patient's bed-head, with a sliver of box-wood.

Yet religion appeared to bring him no more succour than surgery, and the insuperable rot went on spreading up from the extremities to the stomach. In vain they had varied the potions and changed the poultices, each day the muscles were becoming increasingly detached, and at last Charles responded with a nod of the head when Mère Lefrançois asked him if she could not, in desperation, call Monsieur Canivet, of Neufchâtel, who was renowned.

Doctor in medicine, fifty years old, enjoying a good standing and sure of himself, Charles's colleague did not refrain from laughing disdainfully when he exposed that leg gangrened up to the knee. Then, having frankly declared that it would have to be amputated, he went off to the pharmacist's to rail against the dunderheads who could have reduced a wretched man to such a condition. Shaking Monsieur Homais by the coat button, he cried out in the pharmacy:

'There we have it – Paris's inventions! Such are the ideas of these gentlemen from the Capital. It's like strabismus, chloroform, lithotrity, a heap of monstrosities that the government should forbid. But they must always be showing off, and they'll stuff you with remedies without a thought for the consequences. We, though, we are not as clever as that; we are not savants, dandies, lady-killers; we are practitioners, healers, and we wouldn't conceive of operating on someone who was doing perfectly well! Correct the club-footed? Can we correct the club-footed? It's like wishing, let's say, to straighten out a hunchback!'

Homais suffered, listening to this speech, and he concealed his unease beneath a courtier's smile, needing to treat Monsieur Canivet with care, his prescriptions sometimes reaching as far as Yonville; neither did he take Bovary's part, nor make so much as a single observation, and, abandoning his principles, he sacrificed his dignity to the weightier interests of his business.

It was a considerable event in the village, this amputation at the thigh by Doctor Canivet! That day, all the inhabitants turned out at the earliest hour, and the main street, although full of people, had a lugubrious air about it as if what was to take place was a public execution. Hippolyte's sickness was discussed at the grocer's; the shops were selling nothing, and Madame Tuvache, the mayor's wife, did not budge from her window, so eager was she to see the surgeon come.

He arrived in his gig, driving it himself. But, the right-hand spring having long sunk under the weight of his stoutness, the vehicle was a little tilted as it went along, and you could make out beside him on the other cushion a great box, covered in red sheep's leather, whose three brass clasps shone magisterially.

After bowling in under the porch of the *Lion d'Or* like a whirlwind, the doctor, shouting at the top of his voice, ordered his horse to be unhitched, then proceeded into the stable to check if it was properly eating its oats; for, on arrival at his patients' homes, his first thoughts were for his mare and his gig. They would even say, in reference to this, 'Ah, Monsieur Canivet, now he's a queer fellow!' And they rated him the higher for this unwavering self-possession. The universe might have expired to the last man, yet he would not have altered the least of his habits.

Homais appeared.

'I'm counting on you,' the doctor said. 'Are we ready? Forward march!'

But the apothecary, blushing, confessed that he was too sensitive to assist at such an operation.

'When one is simply a spectator,' he said, 'the imagination, you know, impresses one with some sinister thought! And then my nervous system is so . . .'

'Bah, nonsense!' interrupted Canivet. 'Quite the reverse: you seem to me the apoplectic type. Which doesn't surprise me, moreover; for you pharmacy fellows are constantly stuck in your kitchens, which must be damaging to your constitution in the end. Look at me, rather: every day, I get up at four o'clock, I shave in cold water (I'm never cold), and I don't wear flannel, I never catch cold, I've a famous chest on me! I eat sometimes this way, sometimes that, staying philosophical, taking potluck. That's why I'm not a delicate thing like you, and it's all the same to me whether I cut up a Christian or the first fowl to hand. After that, y'know, habit . . . habit . . . !'

Then, without any regard for Hippolyte, who was sweating with anguish between the sheets, these gentlemen entered upon a conversation in which the apothecary likened the surgeon's sang-froid to a general's; and this comparison pleased Canivet, who replied with a torrent of words on the exigencies of his art. He considered it a priestly office, even though medical officers dishonoured the calling. At length, returning to the patient, he examined the bandages brought by Homais, the same that had appeared at the time of the operation, and asked for someone to hold the member for him. They sent for Lestiboudois, and Monsieur Canivet, having rolled up his sleeves, passed into the billiard room, while the apothecary stayed with Artémise and the landlady, both of them paler than their aprons, and with ears strained to the door.

Bovary, during all this time, did not dare move from his house. He stayed below, in the parlour, seated by the unlit hearth, chin on chest, hands clasped, gaze fixed. What misfortune, he thought, what disappointment! Yet he had taken all necessary precautions. Fate had intervened. No matter! If Hippolyte happened to die later, he would be the murderer. And then, what reason was he going to give on his rounds, when asked? Still, had he perhaps not made a mistake with something? He hunted about, found nothing. But the most famous surgeons certainly made mistakes. That was what no one would ever believe. Quite the opposite: they were going to be laughing, gossiping! It would spread all the way to Forges, all the way to Neufchâtel, all the way to Rouen! Everywhere! Who knows if his colleagues might not attack him in writing? There would be an ensuing controversy, he would have to respond in the newspapers. Hippolyte could even prosecute him. He saw himself disgraced, ruined, undone! And his imagination, assailed by numberless suppositions, tossed about amidst them like an empty tub carried off by the sea and rolling in the swell.

Emma, sitting opposite, considered him; she did not share his humiliation, but suffered another: it was to have imagined that such a man could be worth something, as if she had not sufficiently perceived his mediocrity twenty times already.

Charles walked up and down in the room. His boots creaked on the parquet.

'Sit down,' she said, 'you're setting my teeth on edge!'

He sat down again.

She had managed to misjudge things once more, but how? (And she being so intelligent!) And what lamentable madness had driven her to ruin her life thus with constant sacrifice? She called to mind all her instinct for luxury, all her soul's privations, the sordidness of married life, of keeping house, her dreams tumbling into the mud like wounded swallows, everything she had desired, everything she had denied herself, everything she could have had. And why? Why?

In the middle of the silence that filled the village, a rending scream struck through the air. Bovary went pale as if about to faint. She rubbed her eyebrows with a nervous gesture, then carried on. Yet it was for his sake, for this creature, for this man who understood nothing, who felt nothing! – for there he was, completely calm, and without even suspecting that the mockery of his name would, from this time forth, soil her as much as him. She had striven to love him, and had weepingly repented having yielded to another.

'But perhaps it was a valgus!' exclaimed Bovary suddenly, who was deep in thought.

At the unforeseen shock of this sentence falling on her thoughts like a lead ball into a silver dish, Emma gave a start and raised her head to guess what he might mean; and they faced one another in silence, almost amazed to see themselves, so removed were they by their differing realisation each from the other. Charles considered her with the confused gaze of a drunkard, while listening, motionless, to the amputee's last screams succeeding one another in long drawn-out inflections, cut off by shrill bursts, like the distant shrieks of some beast being slaughtered. Emma chewed her wan lips, and, rolling between her fingers one of the bits of coral she had snapped off, fixed on Charles the burning points of her eyes, like two flaming arrows ready to be released. Everything about him irritated her now, his face, his clothes, what he did not say, his whole person, in short his existence. She repented of her past virtuousness as of a felony, and what was left broke up under the furious blows of her pride. She took delight in all the wicked ironies of the triumphant adulteress. The memory of her lover came back to her with giddying charm: she cast her soul upon it, swept towards this image by a fresh enthusiasm; and Charles seemed to her so detached from life, so permanently absent, so ridiculous and crushed, that it was as though he was about to expire and would suffer the pangs of death under her very eyes.

There was the click of a footstep on the pavement. Charles looked out; and, through the lowered blind, he caught sight of Doctor Canivet, by the side of the market-house, in full sun, wiping his brow with a silk handkerchief. Homais, behind him, carried a great red box in his hands, and the two of them were making their way towards the pharmacy.

Then, in a sudden fit of fondness and discouragement, Charles turned to his wife and said to her:

'Kiss me then, my sweet!'

'Leave me alone!' she snapped, red in the face with anger.

'What's the matter with you? What's the matter with you?' he repeated, astonished. 'Calm yourself! Take hold of yourself! . . . Surely you know I love you. Come to me!'

'Enough!' she cried, with a terrible look.

And making her escape from the room, Emma closed the door so hard, that the barometer bounced off the wall and smashed on the floor.

Charles sank down into his chair, thrown into confusion, hunting about for what might be wrong with her, imagining a nervous complaint, weeping, and dimly sensing some baleful and incomprehensible thing circling around him.

When Rodolphe, that evening, came into the garden, he found his mistress waiting for him at the bottom of the flight of steps, on the first stair. They clasped each other tight, and all their rancour melted away like snow under the heat of that kiss.

XII

THEY BEGAN TO LOVE ONE another again. Emma would even write to him all of a sudden, in the middle of the day; then, from the window, signal to Justin, who, untying his thick apron, would fly off to La Huchette. Rodolphe would arrive; it was just to say that she was heartily bored, that her husband was odious and her life dreadful!

'What can I do about it?' he exclaimed one day, quite out of patience.

'Ah, if you were willing . . .'

She was sitting on the ground, between his knees, her drawn-back hair loosened, a lost look in her eyes.

'What then?' said Rodolphe.

She gave a sigh.

'We might go and live together . . . somewhere else . . .'

'You're mad, really you are,' he laughed. 'I don't believe it!'

She came back to the subject; he appeared not to understand and diverted the conversation. What he did not understand, was all this turmoil over something as straightforward as love. Her affection had a motive, a reason, and a kind of auxiliary force.

This fondness was, in fact, gaining more and more ground under the repulsion she felt for her husband. The more she surrendered herself to one, the more she utterly detested the other; never had Charles seemed more disagreeable to her, his fingers so stubby, his mind so dull, his manners so commonplace, as after her assignations with Rodolphe, when they would sit together. Then, ever acting the wife and the woman of virtue, she blazed within at the thought of that head of black hair with its curl falling over the tanned forehead, of that robust and yet so elegant figure, of that man in short who showed so much experience in his judgment, so much wildness in his desire! That she filed her nails with a sculptor's care was for his sake, just as there was never sufficient cream on her skin, nor patchouli on her silk handkerchiefs. She loaded herself with bracelets, rings, necklaces. When he was due to arrive, she filled the two large blue-glass vases with roses, and arranged the room and her person like a courtesan awaiting a prince. The maidservant had to be endlessly washing the linen; and Félicité did not stir all day from the kitchen, where little Justin, who often kept her company, watched her working.

Elbow on the long board where she was ironing, he would greedily contemplate the women's things spread out around him: the dimity petticoats, the fichus, the collars, and the running-string pantaloons, full at the hips and narrowing lower down.

'What's that used for?' the young lad would ask, drawing his hand over the crinoline petticoat or a hook and eye.

'You've never seen nothing, then?' laughed Félicité in reply. 'As if your mistress, Madame Homais, don't wear the like.'

'Oh, yes! Madame Homais!'

And he added meditatively:

'Is she a lady like Madame?'

But Félicité grew impatient to see him twirling all around her like that. She was six years older, and Théodore, Monsieur Guillaumin's servant, had started to court her.

'Leave me in peace!' she said, removing her pot of starch. 'Go off and crush the almonds, rather; always rummaging about next to women, you are; wait till you've whiskers on your jaw, naughty brat, before meddling in that.'

'Come, don't be cross, I'm going to *do her lady-boots* for you.'

And straightaway, he reached up to the mantelpiece for Emma's shoes, all pasted with mud – the mud of assignations – that came off in powder under his fingers, and which he would watch gently float up in a beam of sunlight.

'How scared you are of spoiling them!' said the kitchen-maid, who never took such care when she cleaned them herself, because Madame, as soon as the fabric was no longer fresh and new, left them to her.

Emma had a great number of these in her wardrobe, and she squandered them in proportion, without Charles ever allowing himself the slightest remark.

Thus it was that he spent three hundred francs for a wooden leg which she judged only proper as a present for Hippolyte. The shaft was lined in cork, and it had sprung joints, a complicated mechanism covered in a black trouser leg, ending in a varnished boot. But Hippolyte, not daring to use his handsome leg every day, begged Madame Bovary to obtain him another and more convenient one. The doctor, of course, once again incurred the expense of this purchase.

So, the stable lad went back to his work bit by bit. You could see him getting about the village as before, and when Charles heard, from a distance, the sharp tap of his stick upon the paving-stones, he would very speedily take another route.

It was Monsieur Lheureux, the dealer, who took charge of this order; this gave him the opportunity to associate with Emma. He would prattle to her of the latest deliveries from Paris, of a thousand feminine curios, behaving in a most fawning manner, and never demanding money. Emma surrendered to this easy way of satisfying her whims. And so she wished to have, as a gift for Rodolphe, a very handsome horse-whip to be found in an umbrella shop in Rouen. Monsieur Lheureux, the week after, placed it for her on her table.

But the following day he appeared in person at her house with a bill for two hundred and seventy francs, not counting the centimes. Emma was very embarrassed: all the drawers of her secretaire were empty; they owed Lestiboudois more than fifteen days, the servant two quarters, a deal more of other things, and Bovary was impatiently awaiting the remittance from Monsieur Derozerays, who was in the habit, every year, of paying him around St Peter's Day.

She at first succeeded in refusing Lheureux; at length he lost patience: he was being pressed hard, he had a lack of capital, and, if he couldn't call some of it in, he would be forced to take back from her all the wares she had.

'Well, take them back!'

'Oh, that was a jest,' he replied. 'But I do regret the horse-whip, that's all. I'faith, I shall ask Monsieur to return it.'

'No, no!' she said.

'Ah, now I have you,' thought Lheureux.

And, sure of his discovery, he left, repeating in a low tone and with his habitual little wheeze:

'Very well! We shall see, we shall see!'

She was considering how to extricate herself from this, when the kitchen-maid came in, placing on the chimneypiece a little roll of blue paper, *on the part of Monsieur Derozerays*. Emma leapt on it and opened it. There were fifteen napoleons. It was the right amount. She heard Charles on the stairs; she threw the gold into the back of her drawer and took the key.

Three days later, Lheureux reappeared.

'I've an arrangement to propose to you,' he said; 'if, in place of the agreed sum, you would like to take . . .'

'There we are,' she said, placing fourteen napoleons in his hand.

The dealer was astonished. So, to conceal his disappointment, he poured out excuses and offers of service, all of which Emma refused; then she stayed a few moments fingering the two hundred-sous coins in her apron pocket that he had given to her in change. She resolved to economise, before paying back later . . .

'Nonsense!' she reflected, 'he won't give it another thought.'

IN ADDITION TO THE HORSE-WHIP with its silver-gilt knob, Rodolphe had received a seal with this motto: *Amor nel cor;*[34] plus a scarf to use as a comforter, and lastly a cigar-case identical to the Vicomte's, that Charles had picked up long ago on the road and that Emma had kept. Yet these presents humiliated him. He refused several of them; she was insistent, and Rodolphe ended up obeying, finding her tyrannical and over-encroaching.

Then she would have strange ideas:

'Whenever midnight sounds,' she said, 'you shall think of me!'

And, if he confessed that he had not thought of her then, reproaches would fly in abundance, and always finished on the eternal sentence:

'Do you love me?'

'Why yes, I love you,' he would reply.

'A lot?'

'Most certainly.'

'You haven't loved others then, hmm?'

'You think you took me intact?' he exclaimed, laughing.

Emma wept, and he endeavoured to console her, embellishing his protests with puns.

'Oh, it's because I love you,' she went on, 'I love you so much I can't do without you, don't you know that? Sometimes my longing to see you again tears me apart with all the rages of love. I say to myself: "Where is he? Perhaps he's talking to other women? They smile at him, he draws near . . ." Oh no, not one of them pleases you, do they? There are some more beautiful; but I know better how to love. I'm your servant and concubine. You are my king, my idol, you're good, you're handsome, you're intelligent, you are strong!'

He had heard these things said so many times, that to his ear there was nothing original about them. Emma resembled all his mistresses; and the charm of novelty, dropping away little by little like a garment, left nakedly in view the endless monotony of passion, whose shapes and words are always the same. This man, with so much experience, could not distinguish the differences in feeling beneath the sameness of expression. Because licentious or venal lips had murmured similar phrases to him, he believed only feebly in their innocent candour; one had to beat back, he thought, the exaggerated language under which everyday affections hid themselves; as if the soul's fullness would not at times spill over through the most vacant of metaphors, since no one can ever take the exact measure of his needs, nor of his conceptions, nor of his sorrows, and human utterance is like a cracked kettle on which we beat out tunes to make the bears dance, when we would like to move the stars to pity.

But, with that high-ground of discrimination belonging to those who, whatever the engagement, keep to the rear, Rodolphe perceived in this love other enjoyments to be made the most of. He judged any sense of modesty inconvenient. He treated her without ceremony. He fashioned her into something compliant and corrupt. It was a kind of idiot affection full of admiration on his part, of voluptuousness on hers, a bliss that numbed her; and her soul sank down into this drunkenness and drowned in it, shrivelled up, like the Duke of Clarence[35] in his butt of malmsy.

By virtue of her amorous habits alone, Madame Bovary's

appearance changed. Her looks grew bolder, her words looser; she even had the unseemliness to walk out with Rodolphe, a cigarette in her mouth, *as if to defy the world*; finally, those who doubted still, doubted no longer when she was seen, one day, alighting from the *Hirondelle*, her figure squeezed into a waistcoat, in the manner of a man; and Mère Bovary, who, after a dreadful scene with her husband, had come to take refuge at her son's, was not the least scandalised of the good towns-women. She found much else to displease her: first, Charles had not listened to her advice concerning the prohibition of novels; then, she did not like *the style of the house*; she took the liberty of making some remarks, and they quarrelled, one time especially, over Félicité.

The previous evening, when going along the passage, Mère Bovary had surprised her in the company of a man, a man with a dark collar, of about forty years of age, and who, at the sound of her footsteps, swiftly fled the kitchen. Then Emma began to laugh; but the good woman lost her temper, declaring that, unless morals[36] were to be made a mockery of, one ought to watch over those of the servants.

'What world do you belong to?' said the daughter-in-law, with such an impertinent look that Madame Bovary asked her if she were not in fact defending her own cause.

'Get out!' said the young woman, leaping to her feet.

'Emma! . . . Mother! . . .' cried Charles, in an attempt at reconciliation.

But they had both fled in their exasperation. Emma stamped her feet and kept repeating:

'Ah, what good breeding. What a peasant!'

He ran after his mother, she was beside herself, she stammered out:

'A sauce-box, that's what she is! A feather-brain! Worse, perhaps!'

And she wanted to leave immediately, if the other did not come to apologise. So Charles went back to his wife and entreated her to yield; he got down on his knees; she ended by replying:

'So be it. I'll go.'

Indeed, she held out her hand to her mother-in-law with the dignity of a marquess, saying to her:

'Excuse me, Madame.'

Then, going back upstairs to her own room, Emma threw herself full-length upon the bed, and cried there like a child, her head buried in the pillow.

They had agreed, she and Rodolphe, that in the event of something unusual happening, she would attach a little scrap of white paper to the window-blind, so that, if by chance he was in Yonville, he would hasten into the lane behind the house. Emma prepared the signal; she waited for three-quarters of an hour, when all at once she caught sight of Rodolphe at the corner of the market-house. She was tempted to open the window, to call him; but he had already vanished. She slumped again in despair.

Soon however she thought she heard someone walking on the pavement. Doubtless it was him; she descended the stairs, crossed the yard. He was there, outside. She threw herself into his arms.

'Be careful now,' he said.

'Oh, if only you knew!' came her response.

And she began to tell him everything, in a hurry, disconnectedly, exaggerating the facts, inventing a few, and lavishing digressions in such an abundance that he understood nothing.

'Come now, my poor angel, cheer up, console yourself, patience!'

'But I have been patient and suffering for the past four years . . . A love like ours ought to be declared before Heaven. They are torturing me. I can stand it no longer. Save me!'

She pressed herself close to Rodolphe. Her eyes, full of tears, glistened like flames beneath the waters; her throat pulsed in agitation; he had never loved her so much; to such an extent that he lost his head and said to her:

'What must we do? What is it you want?'

'Take me away!' she cried. 'Carry me off . . . Oh, I beg you!'

And she hurled herself onto his mouth, as if to catch there the unhoped-for consent exhaled in a kiss.

'But . . . ,' Rodolphe resumed.

'What is it?'

'And your daughter?'

She reflected for a few minutes, then replied:

'We will take her, too bad!'

'What a woman,' he said to himself, as he watched her move off.

For she had just slipped away into the garden. They were calling her.

Mère Bovary was most astonished, over the next few days, at the metamorphosis of her daughter-in-law. In fact, Emma was turning out more manageable, and even carried her deference to the point of requesting a recipe for pickled gherkins.

Was it in order to dupe both of them the better? Or did she want to savour more deeply, by a kind of voluptuous stoicism, the bitterness of what she was soon to abandon? But she paid no heed to it, quite the contrary; she lived as if lost in the anticipated first taste of her imminent happiness. This was an eternal topic in her chats with Rodolphe. She would lean on his shoulder, murmuring:

'Ah, when we are in the mail coach . . . Do you think about it? Can it be possible? The very moment, it seems to me, that I feel the carriage spring off, it will be as if we are going up in a balloon, as if we are leaving for the clouds. You know that I'm counting the days? . . . And you?'

Madame Bovary was never so beautiful as at that time; she had that undefinable beauty which results from joy, from enthusiasm, from success, and is but the effect of temperament and circumstances in harmony.[37] Her lustfulness, her sorrows, the experience of pleasure and her still youthful illusions, had developed her by degrees, just as dung, rain, wind and sun bring out flowers, and she was opening at last into the fullness of her nature. Her eyelids seemed expressly shaped for her long, amorous glances in which the pupils would vanish, while each vigorous breath widened her slender nostrils and turned up the fleshy corner of her lips where a slight black down lay shadowed from the light. One would have said that an artist qualified in depravities had arranged her hair's twisted coil over her nape: it rolled itself up in one heavy mass, carelessly, and according to the accidents of adultery, which unravelled it every day. Her voice now took on softer inflexions, as did her figure; you were pierced by something artful that emanated even from the fabric of her dress and the arch of her foot. Charles, as in the early days of his marriage, found her delicious and utterly irresistible.

When he came back in the middle of the night, he did not dare wake her. The porcelain night-lamp cast a round, quivering brightness on the ceiling, and swelling out in the shadows beside the bed, the little cradle's closed curtains formed a kind of white hut. Charles gazed at them. He thought he could hear his child's faint breath. She would grow up now; each month would bring a speedy advance. He already saw her coming back from school at dusk, all laughter, her little smock spotted with ink, and carrying a basket on her arm; then she would have to be sent to boarding-school, and that would cost a great deal; how to do it? So he reflected. He thought of renting a small farm in the neighbourhood, and he would look after it himself, every morning, when going to see his patients. He would put the income by, he would place it in a savings-bank; then he would buy shares, somewhere, no matter where; besides, the practice would grow; he was counting on it, because he wanted Berthe to be well brought up, to have accomplishments, to learn the piano. Ah, how pretty she would be, later, at fifteen, when, looking like her mother, she would wear, like her, big straw hats in summer! They would be taken for sisters, from a distance. He imagined her working in the evenings close to them, under the light of the lamp; she would be embroidering slippers for him; occupying herself with the housekeeping; filling the whole house with her charm and cheerfulness. Finally, they would think about her settling down: they would find her some honest fellow with a solid business; he would make her happy; it would last forever.

Emma was not sleeping, she was pretending to be asleep; and, while he was slumbering at her side, she roused herself with other dreams.

A coach-and-four had been galloping them away for a week towards a new land, whence they would not return. On they went, on they went, arms entwined, their words spent. Often, from a mountain-top, they would suddenly descry some splendid city with domes, bridges, ships, forests of lemon-tree and cathedrals of white marble, whose pointed steeples held storks' nests. The horses went at walking pace, because of the great flag-stones, and on the ground there were bunches of flowers that red-bodiced women would offer you. They heard the peal of bells, the neighing of mules, with the murmur of guitars and the splash of fountains, whose drifting mist cooled the heaps of fruit, arranged in pyramids at the foot of pale statues, smiling under the water-jets. And then they arrived, one night, in a fishing village, where dark nets dried in the wind, along the cliffs and the cottages. This was where they would stop to live; they would dwell in a low house, with a flat roof, shaded by a palm tree, in the remotest part of a bay, on the edge of the sea. They would take rides in a gondola, they would swing in a hammock; and their life would be yielding and generous like their silk clothes, all warm and starry like the mild nights they would gaze upon. Nevertheless, from the immensity of this future that she conjured, no one particular thing emerged; the days, all of them magnificent, were as alike as waves; and they rolled to the horizon, endless, harmonious, bluish and bathed in sun. But the child would begin to cough in her cradle, or Bovary snore louder, and Emma would only nod off in the morning, when dawn blanched the window-panes and young Justin on the square was already opening the shutters of the pharmacy.

She had sent for Monsieur Lheureux and had said to him:

'I shall need a cloak, a big cloak, lined, with a long cape.'

'You're going travelling?'

'No! But . . . no matter, I can rely on you, can't I? And quickly!'

He bowed.

'I will also need,' she went on, 'a chest . . . not too heavy . . . suitable.'

'Yes, yes, I understand, roughly ninety-two by fifty centimetres, like what they make them nowadays.'

'With a carpet-bag.'

'Decidedly,' mused Lheureux to himself, 'there's a rumpus at the back of this.'

'And here,' said Madame Bovary, drawing her watch from her belt, 'take this; pay yourself out of it.'

But the dealer exclaimed that she was mistaken; they knew each other; did he doubt her? What childishness! She insisted however that he take the chain at least, and already Lheureux had put it in his pocket and was going out, when she called him back.

'You will leave everything at your house. As for the cloak – ' she seemed to be reflecting – 'don't bring that either; only, give me the workman's address and let me know when they have it at my disposal.'

It was the next month that they were to elope. She would leave from Yonville as though to run errands in Rouen. Rodolphe would have reserved seats, taken the passports, and even written to Paris, so as to have the mail coach to themselves until Marseilles, where they would buy a carriage and, from there, continue by the Genoa road, without stopping. She would have taken care to send her baggage to Lheureux's house, to be carried straight to the *Hirondelle*, in such a way that no one might suspect; and there was never any question of her child, in all of this. Rodolphe avoided mentioning the subject; perhaps she did not give it a thought.

He wanted to have two more weeks ahead of him, to complete a few arrangements; then, at the end of a week, he asked for another two; then he claimed he was ill; after that he made a trip; the month of August went by, and, after all these delays, they determined that it would be set irrevocably for the fourth of September, a Monday.

At last the Saturday, two days before, came round.

Rodolphe came in the evening, earlier than usual.

'Is everything ready?' she asked him.

'Yes.'

Then they made a tour of a flower-bed, and went to sit down near the terrace, on the curb of the wall.

'You're sad,' said Emma.

'No, why?'

And yet he looked at her peculiarly, in a loving fashion.

'Is it because you're going away?' she pursued, 'leaving what you're fond of, leaving your life? Ah, I understand . . . But I, I have nothing in the world. You're everything to me. Likewise I shall be everything to you, I shall be a family to you, a country; I will look after you, I'll love you.'

'How delightful you are!' he said, clasping her in his arms.

'True?' she said with a voluptuous laugh. 'Do you love me? Swear it then!'

'Indeed I love you. Indeed I love you. Why, I adore you, my sweet!'

The moon, quite round and purple-coloured, rose up level with the ground, at the far end of the field. She climbed swiftly between the poplars' branches that hid her here and there, like a black curtain full of holes. Then she appeared, blazing with whiteness, in the empty sky she had illuminated; and so, slowing on her course, she let fall upon the river a great stain, that made an infinity of stars; and this silvery glimmering seemed to writhe there, down to the depths, as if it were a headless snake covered in luminous scales. And it was not unlike some monstrous candelabra too, from whose whole length streamed drops of melting diamonds. The warm night spread out around them; sheets of shadow filled the foliage. From time to time, he half-opened her dressing gown and revealed just the upper part of her breast, which was whiter still than the moon's wanness.[38] Emma, eyes half-shut, sighed deeply, sucking into her lungs the freshness of the blowing wind. There were no words between them, too lost as they were and overrun by their day-dream. The tenderness of the old days crept back into their hearts, abundant and silent like the flowing river, with the same indolence as the scent of the lilacs brought to them, and that cast across their memory shadows more immeasurable and melancholic than those of the still willows, lengthening on the grass. Often some night animal, a hedgehog or a weasel, beginning to hunt, disturbed the leaves, or else they heard at moments a ripe peach falling all by itself from the espalier.

'Ah, beautiful night,' said Rodolphe.

'We'll have others,' responded Emma.

And, as if talking to herself:

'Yes, it will be good to travel . . . Yet why is my heart so sad? Is it the fear of the unknown . . . the reality of ways forsaken . . . or rather . . . ? No, it's a surfeit of happiness! How weak I am, don't you think? Forgive me!'

'There's still time!' he cried out. 'Reflect on it, you'll rue the day, perhaps.'

'Never!' she returned, vehemently.

And, drawing nearer to him:

'Well, what misfortune might come upon me? There's no desert, no precipice, no ocean that I would not cross in your company. As long as we're living together, it will be like an embrace, each day tighter and more perfect. We will have nothing to trouble us, no worries, no hindrances! We shall be alone, entirely together, for eternity . . . Speak then, answer me.'

He replied at measured intervals: 'Yes . . . Yes! . . .' She had run her hands through his hair, and she kept repeating in a childish voice, despite the fat tears trickling down:

'Rodolphe! Rodolphe! . . . Ah, Rodolphe, dear little Rodolphe!'
Midnight struck.

'Midnight!' she said. 'Come, it's tomorrow. Another day!'

He rose to leave; and, as if this movement of his had been the signal for their elopement, Emma, all of a sudden, adopting a cheerful air:

'You have the passports?'

'Yes.'

'You've not forgotten anything?'

'No.'

'You are sure?'

'Quite sure.'

'You will be waiting for me at the *Hôtel de Provence*, isn't that right? At midday?'

He nodded.

'Until tomorrow, then!' said Emma through a last caress.

And she watched him move off.

He did not turn round. She ran after him, and, stooping at the water's edge between the brush-wood:

'Until tomorrow!' she shouted out.

He was already on the other side of the river and walking quickly over the field.

A few minutes later, Rodolphe stopped; and, when he saw her with her white garment fade away little by little into the shadows like a ghost, he was taken by such a thumping of the heart, that he leaned against a tree to stop himself falling.

'What a fool I am!' he said, cursing tremendously. 'No matter, she was a pretty mistress!'

And Emma's beauty, with all the pleasures of this affair, appeared to him again on the instant. At first he felt moved to pity, then grew indignant against her.

'After all,' he exclaimed, gesticulating, 'I cannot leave my own country, or have a child on my hands.'

He said all this in order to harden himself further.

'And, besides, the fuss, the expense . . . Ah no, no – a thousand times no! That would have been too stupid!'

XIII

As soon as he was back home, Rodolphe sat down brusquely at his desk, under the stag's head set boastfully on the wall. But, when he had the pen in his hand, he could not find a thing to say, so much so that, leaning on his elbows, he began to ponder. Emma seemed to him to have receded into a long-ago past, as if his sworn resolution had just placed between them, all of a sudden, an immense distance.

In order to recapture something of her, he went searching in the cupboard, next to his bed, for an old biscuit tin from Rheims in which he habitually locked away his mistress's letters, and from it there slipped an odour of damp dust and withered roses. At once he spied a pocket handkerchief, covered in pale droplets. It was her own handkerchief, from when she had a nose-bleed one day, on a walk; he remembered nothing more. Near it lay the miniature that Emma had given him, bumping against the corners; her dress struck him as pretentious and her soft-eyed *sideways* look[39] achieved the most pitiful effect; then, by dint of considering this image and evoking the memory of the model, little by little Emma's features grew muddled in his recollection, as if the living face and the painted face, rubbing against each other, had been mutually erased. Finally, he read some of her letters; they were full of explanations relating to their journey, as brief, technical and urgent as business notes. He wanted to look again at the lengthy ones, those of earlier days; to find them at the bottom of the tin, Rodolphe disturbed all the others; and mechanically he began to dig about in this heap of papers and stuff, finding there a jumble of nosegays, a garter, a black mask, pins and locks of hair – hair! Dark hair, fair hair; catching in the hinge of the box, several even broke apart when it was opened.

Thus idling among his keepsakes, he examined the handwriting and the style of the letters, as varied as their spelling. They were fond or joyful, facetious, melancholic; there were some that demanded love and others that demanded money. A single word could bring to mind faces, certain gestures, the ring of a voice; yet sometimes he remembered nothing.

Indeed, these women, hastening all at once through his thoughts, got in each other's way and grew smaller there, as if the levelling of love rendered them equal. So taking fistfuls of mixed-up letters, he amused himself for several minutes letting them fall in cascades, from his right hand to his left hand. At length, bored, drowsy, Rodolphe carried the tin back to the cupboard, saying to himself:

'What a heap of humbug! . . .'

Which summed up his opinion: for pleasures, like schoolboys in the school yard, had so trampled on his heart, that nothing green grew there, and what passed across, giddier than children, would not even do as they would, and leave a name engraved on the wall.

'Come,' he said to himself, 'let's begin!'

He wrote:

"Courage, Emma! Courage! I do not wish to bring unhappiness into your life . . ."

'After all, that's true,' thought Rodolphe; 'I'm working in her interest; I'm being honest.'

"Have you considered your decision in a mature way? Are you aware of the abyss into which I was tempting you, my poor angel? You aren't, are you? You were carrying on fond and trusting, believing in happiness, in the future . . . Ah wretches that we are! Fools!"

Rodolphe paused here to think of some good excuse.

'If I were to say to her that my fortune is lost? . . . Ah no! And besides, that would make no difference. It would simply start up again later. Is it possible to make such women hear reason!'

He thought about it, then added:

"I shall never forget you, believe it truly, and will constantly feel deeply devoted to you; but, one day, sooner or later, this ardour (that being the lot of human affairs) will diminish, without a doubt! Weariness will come upon us, and who knows if I might even have the excruciating pain of being present at your scenes of remorse and of taking part in them myself, because I would have been the cause. The mere idea of the sorrows that will come to you tortures me, Emma! Forget about me! Why did I have to know you? Why were you so beautiful? Is it my fault? Oh my God! No, no, blame only fate!"

'Now there's a word that always produces an effect,' he said to himself.

"Ah, if you had been one of those frivolous-hearted women whom we see about, I might have been able, certainly, out of pure selfishness, to risk the experience without danger to you. But this delightful elation, which is both your charm and your torment, has prevented you from understanding, adorable woman that you are, the falsity of your future position. I too failed to reflect at first, and lay down in the shade of this ideal happiness, as if under the venomous shadow of the manchineel tree,⁴⁰ without foreseeing the consequences."

'She might perhaps think that I'm giving her up through stinginess . . . Ah, no matter. Too bad. It has to be terminated.'

"The world is cruel, Emma. Wherever we might have been, it would have persecuted us. You would have had to endure indiscreet questions, slander, scorn, maybe dishonour. Dishonour to you! Oh! . . . And I who wished but to seat you upon a throne! I who carry away the thought of you like a talisman! For I am punishing myself with exile for all the evil I have done to you. I am leaving. Where? I have no idea, I am mad! Adieu! Be always good! Treasure the memory of the wretch who lost you. Teach your child my name, that she might repeat it in her prayers."

The two candlewicks shivered. Rodolphe got up to close the window, and, when he had sat down again:

'That's everything, it seems to me. Ah, just one more thing, lest she come round to badger me.'

"I will be far away when you read these sad lines; for I wanted to flee as quickly as possible so as to avoid the temptation to see you again. No weakness, mind! I shall come back; and perhaps, later on, we shall chat together very coolly about our old amours. Adieu!"

And there was a final adieu, separated into two words, *A Dieu*, which he judged to be in excellent taste.

'How shall I sign, now?' he said to himself. Your entirely devoted? . . . No. Your friend? . . . Yes, that's it.'

"Your friend."

HE READ OVER HIS LETTER again. He reckoned it a good one.

'Poor little woman!' he thought with some tenderness. 'She will reckon me more insensitive than a rock; it needed a few tears on here; but, for my part, I cannot cry; it's not my fault.'

Then, having poured himself some water into a glass, Rodolphe dipped his finger in it and let a big drop fall from above, which made a pale blot on the ink; then, seeking to seal the letter, he came across the *Amor nel cor* seal.

'That will scarcely do in the circumstances . . . Oh, nonsense! No matter!'

After which, he smoked three pipes and went off to bed.

The next day, when he was up (around two o'clock, having gone to sleep late), Rodolphe had a basket-full of apricots picked.[41] He arranged the letter in the bottom, under some vine leaves, and straightaway ordered Girard, his ploughman, to carry this with all delicacy to Madame Bovary's house. He was in the habit of using this means to correspond with her, sending her either fruit or game, depending on the season.

'If she asks you for news of me,' he said, 'your reply is that I have gone travelling. You must deliver the basket to her personally, and into her own hands . . . Be off, and take care!'

Girard put on his new smock, knotted his handkerchief around the apricots, and taking heavy strides in his big iron-studded overshoes, he quietly took the path to Yonville.

Madame Bovary, when he arrived at her house, was arranging a parcel of linen on the kitchen table, with Félicité.

'See here,' said the servant, 'what our master has sent you.'

She was seized with fear, and, while hunting for some change in her pocket, she gazed at the peasant with a wild look, whereas he for his part gazed at her with amazement, not conceiving how such a gift could stir someone up so much. At length he left. Félicité stayed. She could bear it no longer, she ran into the parlour as if to convey the apricots there, turned the basket over, tore away the vine leaves, found the letter, opened it, and, as if a dreadful fire had broken out behind her, Emma fled to her room, utterly appalled.

Charles was there, she noticed him; he spoke to her, she heard nothing, and she continued hurriedly up the stairs, panting, desperate, frenzied, and still holding this horrible sheet of paper, slapping in her fingers like a plate of sheet-iron. On the second floor, she stopped in front of the attic door, which was closed.

She needed to compose herself, then; she remembered the letter; she had to finish it, she did not dare to. Besides, where, how? They would see her.

'Ah no,' she thought, 'here I'll be safe.'

Emma pushed the door open and went in.

A heavy heat beat straight down from the roof-slates, squeezing her temples and suffocating her; she dragged herself over to the closed garret-window, drawing its bolt, and the dazzling light gushed through in one surge.

Opposite, over the rooves, the open fields stretched away as far as the eye could see. Below, directly beneath her, the village square was empty; the pavement's flints glittered, the weather-cocks were stilled; at the corner of the street, a sort of humming emanated from a lower floor in screaking variations of key. It was Binet turning his lathe.

She had supported herself on the window's embrasure, and she was reading the letter again with snickers of rage. But the more she fixed her mind on it, the more confused her thoughts became. She saw him again, she heard him, she wrapped him in her arms; and the drumming of her heart, beating at her under the breast like a battering ram's heavy blows, came faster and faster, at irregular intervals. She cast her eyes all about, wanting the world to collapse. Why not be finished with it? So what was holding her back? She was free. And she stepped forward, looked at the paving stones, and said to herself:

'Go on! Go on!'

The luminous beam that came up directly from below tugged her body's weight towards the abyss. It seemed to her that the square's rocking ground was rising up along the walls, and that the floor was tilting at one end, in the way a ship pitches. She held on right at the edge, almost hanging, surrounded by a great space. The blue of the sky overran her, the air flowed round inside her hollow head, she had but to give in, to allow herself to be taken; and the lathe's humming did not let up, like a mad voice calling her.

'Wife! Wife!' cried Charles.

She stopped.

'Where are you then? Come along!'

The idea that she had just escaped death made her all but faint in terror; she closed her eyes; then she started at the touch of a hand on her sleeve: it was Félicité.

'Monsieur's waiting for you, Madame; the soup is served.'

And she had to go down! She had to sit at table!

She tried to eat. The morsels choked her. So she unfolded her napkin as if to inspect the darning and truly wished to apply her mind to this work, to count the linen threads. Suddenly, the memory of the letter came back to her. Had she then lost it? Where to find it again? But she felt such a weariness of spirit, that she could never dream up a pretext for leaving the table. She had become cowardly; she was frightened of Charles; he knew everything, for certain! Indeed, he uttered these words, extraordinarily enough:

'We are not, so it appears, about to see Monsieur Rodolphe.'

'Who told you that?' she said, trembling.

'Who told me that?' he repeated, a little surprised at her brusque tone; 'it was Girard, whom I met just now at the door of the *Café Français*. He has left on a trip, or is about to leave.'

She gave a sob.

'Why so amazed? He goes off like that from time to time to amuse himself, and, i'faith, I approve. When you're wealthy and a bachelor! . . . Besides, he entertains himself nicely, does our friend! He's a droll fellow, Monsieur Langlois told me how . . .'

He held his tongue out of decency, for the sake of the maid who was coming in.

The latter put the apricots scattered over the shelf back into the basket; Charles, without noticing his wife's blush, had them brought to him, took one out and bit into it.

'Oh, perfect!' he said. 'Here, have a taste.'

And he held out the basket, which she gently pushed away.

'Have a smell, then: what a fragrance!' he said, waving it under her nose several times.

'I'm choking!' she cried, leaping to her feet.

But, by an effort of will, this spasm passed; then:

'It's nothing!' she said, 'it's nothing! Nerves! Sit down, eat!'

For she dreaded them questioning her, nursing her, never leaving her side.

Charles sat down again obediently, and was spitting out the apricot stones into his hand, depositing them afterwards on his plate.

Suddenly, a blue tilbury went by at full trot on the square. Emma let out a shriek and fell backwards to the floor.

In fact, Rodolphe, after much reflection, had decided to set off for Rouen. Now, as the only road between Huchette to Buchy was the Yonville one, he was forced to pass through the village, and Emma had recognised him by the glimmer of the lanterns that cut the twilight like a lightning flash.

The pharmacist, in response to the uproar taking place in the house, hurried over. The table, with all the plates, was overturned; sauce, meat, the knives, the salt-cellar and the oil cruet were strewn about the room; Charles was calling for help; Berthe, scared, was crying; and Félicité, with trembling hands, was unlacing Madame, who was having convulsions all down her body.

'I'll run to fetch a drop of aromatic vinegar from my laboratory,' said the apothecary.

Then, as she opened her eyes again after inhaling from the bottle: 'I knew it,' he said; 'that would wake a corpse.'

'Talk to us!' said Charles, 'talk to us! Come round! It's me, your Charles who loves you! Don't you recognise me? Look, here is your little girl: so, kiss her!'

The child held out her arms towards her mother to hang round her neck. But, turning her head aside, Emma said in a jerky voice:

'No, no . . . nobody!'

She swooned again. She was conveyed up to her bed.

She remained stretched out, mouth open, eyelids closed, hands laid flat, motionless, and white as a waxen statue. From her eyes two rivulets of tears trickled slowly onto her pillow.

Charles, on his feet, stayed at the back of the alcove, and the apothecary, close by, observed that thoughtful silence proper to life's serious occasions.

'Be comforted,' he said, giving him a nudge with his elbow, 'I believe the fit is over.'

'Yes, she's resting a little now,' replied Charles, watching her sleep. 'Poor woman, poor woman . . . there she is, relapsed!'

Then Homais asked how this accident had occurred. Charles replied that it had come upon her all of a sudden, while she was eating apricots.

'Extraordinary! . . .' the pharmacist went on. 'But it could be the apricots that caused the swoon. Some natures are so sensitive to certain smells. And that would actually make a fine subject for study, as much with regard to pathology as to physiology. Priests recognised its importance, they having always mixed aromatics into their ceremonies. The aim being to stupefy your understanding and encourage a state of ecstasy, something readily obtained anyway among persons of the fairer sex, who are more delicate than the rest. Examples are cited of those who faint at the smell of burnt horn, or soft bread . . .'

'Take care not to wake her,' said Bovary in a low voice.

'And it's not just humans,' continued the apothecary, 'who are exposed to these anomalies, but animals as well. Thus, you cannot be ignorant of the singularly aphrodisiac effect produced by *nepeta cataria*, commonly called cat-mint, on the feline race; and on the other hand, to cite an example whose authenticity I can vouch for, Bridoux (one of my old associates, presently practising on the rue Malpalu) owns a dog who falls into convulsions as soon as he is offered a snuff-box. He has even tried it out time and again in front of his friends, at his wooden summer-house in the Bois Guillaume. Can you believe that a simple sternutatory might exert such depradations in a quadruped's organism? It's extremely curious, don't you find?'

'Yes,' said Charles, who was not listening.

'That proves to us,' the other went on, smiling with an air of benign self-conceit, 'the countless irregularities in the nervous system. As far as Madame is concerned, she has always seemed to me, I confess, the genuinely sensitive type. Therefore I would not recommend to you, my good friend, any of these self-styled remedies which, under the pretext of attacking the symptoms, attack the constitution. No, none of these medicinal trifles! Diet, that's all! Sedatives, emollients, dulcifiers. Then don't you think we should perhaps touch the imagination?'

'How? In what way?' said Bovary.

'Ah, there's the question! Such indeed is the question: "*That is the question!*"[42] as I read recently in the newspaper.'

But Emma, waking up, cried out:

'And the letter? And the letter?'

They thought she was delirious; and she did become so after midnight: brain-fever declared itself.

For forty-three days, Charles did not leave her side. He deserted all his patients; he no longer went to bed, he was continually feeling her pulse, applying mustard poultices and cold-water compresses. He sent Justin as far as Neufchâtel to look for ice; the ice melted on the way; he sent him back. He called Monsieur Canivet for a consultation; he sent for Doctor Larivière, his old teacher, from Rouen; he was desperate. What appalled him most of all was Emma's prostration; for she did not talk, heard nothing and even seemed not to suffer – as if her body and soul had together taken a rest from all their agitation.

Around the middle of October, she could sit upright in her bed, with her pillows behind her. Charles cried when he saw her eat her first slice of bread and jam. Her strength returned; she got up for a few hours in the afternoon, and, one day when she was feeling better, he tried to take her for an airing on his arm in the garden. The paths' sand kept disappearing under the dead leaves; she walked step by step, dragging her slippers, and, leaning her shoulder on Charles, she continued to smile.

They went thus down to the end, near the terrace. Slowly she stood erect again, shielded her eyes, in order to gaze; she gazed a long way, a very long way away; but on the horizon there were only some big grass fires, smoking on the hills.

'You will tire yourself, my darling,' said Bovary.

And, gently pushing her under the arbour:

'Sit down on this bench, now: you'll be comfortable.'

'Oh no, not there, not there!' she said in a faltering voice.

She suffered a giddy spell, and from that evening her illness started up again, with, it is true, a more unsettled turn and a more complex character. One moment she was suffering pains in the heart, then in the chest, in the brain, in the limbs; vomiting fits came over her unexpectedly in which Charles thought he could perceive the first symptoms of cancer.

And the poor fellow, to cap it all, had money worries!

XIV

AT FIRST, HE HAD NO notion of how to repay Monsieur Homais for all the medicines taken from his shop; and, although as a doctor he could have avoided paying, nevertheless he blushed a little at this obligation. Then the household expenses, now that the cook was in charge, were becoming frightful; bills poured into the house; the tradesmen were grumbling; Monsieur Lheureux, above all, was harassing him. In fact, when Emma's illness was at its peak, the former profiting from the circumstances to inflate his invoice, had quickly brought the cloak, the carpet-bag, two chests instead of one, and a deal of other things beside. It was useless Charles stating that he did not need them, the dealer replied arrogantly that all these articles had been ordered and that he would not take them back; moreover, that would be to thwart Madame in her convalescence; Monsieur should think it over; in short, he was resolved to pursue him in the courts rather than abandon his dues and take away the merchandise. In the event, Charles directed them to be sent back to the shop; Félicité forgot; he had other worries; no more thought was given to it; Monsieur Lheureux returned to the charge, and, threatening and complaining by turns, schemed in such a way, that Bovary ended up countersigning a bill payable in six months. But scarce had he signed this bill, than a daring idea struck him: this was to borrow a thousand francs from Monsieur Lheureux. So he asked, with an embarrassed air, if there might not be a way of having them, adding that this would be for a year and at whatever rate desired. Lheureux ran to his shop, returned with the cash and dictated another bill, in which Bovary declared that he must pay to order, on the first of September next, the sum of one thousand and seventy francs; which, with the hundred and eighty already stipulated, came to just twelve hundred and fifty. So, lent at six per cent, increased by commission of a quarter, and the goods supplied yielding a full third at least, that would, in twelve months, give a hundred and thirty francs profit; and he was hoping that the business would not stop there, that the bills would not be payable, that they would be renewed, and that his wretched money, thriving at the doctor's as in a private hospital, would come back to him, one day, considerably plumper, and heavy enough to split the purse.

Besides, he was succeeding in everything. He was contractor for a cider supplier to the hospital in Neufchâtel; Monsieur Guillaumin promised him shares in the Grumesnil turf-pit, and he dreamed of starting up a new stagecoach service between Argueil and Rouen, which would not be long in ruining the *Lion d'Or*'s old van, and that, travelling faster, costing less and carrying more baggage, would also put Yonville's trade entirely into his hands.

Charles asked himself several times how he would manage to pay back such an amount next year; and he sought out, dreamed up short-term measures, such as resorting to his father or selling something. But his father would turn a deaf ear, and he had, for his own part, nothing to sell. Seeing then what financial straits he was in, he swiftly waved so unpleasant a subject of contemplation from his mind. He reproached himself for forgetting Emma; as if, all his thoughts belonging to this woman, not dwelling on her all the time would be to deprive her of something.

It was a harsh winter. Madame's convalescence was a long one. When the weather was fine, she was pushed in her chair close to the window, the one looking over the square; for she now had an antipathy for the garden, and the blind on that side remained always drawn. She wanted the horse to be sold; what she liked in the past, now displeased her. All her thoughts seemed limited to the notion of looking after herself. She stayed in her bed making little meals, rang for her maid to inquire about her tisanes or to chat with her. Meanwhile the snow on the roof of the market-house cast a still, white reflection into the room; then it was the rain that fell. And Emma awaited daily, with a sort of anxiousness, the unerring return of trifling events, which nevertheless mattered little to her. The most significant was the arrival of the *Hirondelle* in the evening. Then the inn's landlady shouted and other voices responded, while Hippolyte's great lantern, seeking out the trunks on the canopy, was like a star in the darkness. At midday, Charles came home again; afterwards he went out; then she had a plate of soup, and, around five o'clock, at the end of the day, the children going home from school, dragging their clogs on the pavement, all rapped the shutter catches with their rulers, one after the other.

It was just at this time of day that Monsieur Bournisien would come to visit her. He would ask after her health, bring her news and urge her to the faith in a short, wheedling prattle that was not without charm. The mere sight of his cassock comforted her.

One day when at the very height of her illness she had believed she was dying, she had asked for communion; and, gradually, all the while they were preparing her room for the sacrament, arranging an altar out of the chest of drawers encumbered with syrups and as Félicité was strewing dahlia flowers on the floor, Emma felt something intense passing over her, that stripped her of her sorrows, of all perception, of all feeling. Her unburdened flesh no longer lay heavy, another life was beginning; it seemed to her that her being, ascending towards God, would vanish utterly in this love like lit incense that disperses into fumes. Her bedsheets were sprayed with holy water; the priest withdrew the white wafer from the ciborium; and it was in a swoon of celestial joy that she put forward her lips to receive the proffered body of the Saviour. The curtains in her alcove swelled out softly, around her, like a great bank of clouds, and the rays of the two tapers burning on the chest of drawers appeared to her in dazzling glory. Then she let her head sink back, believing she could hear in the spaces the strains of seraphic harps and perceive in an azure sky, on a throne of gold, in the midst of saints holding verdant palm-fronds, God the Father blazing forth in majesty, Who at a sign bid angels with wings of flame descend to earth to bear her away in their arms.

This sumptuous vision stayed in her memory as the most beautiful thing possible to dream; so much so that now she strove to seize the sensation anew, and it still continued, less exclusively yet with just as profound a sweetness. Her soul, foundered on pride, was at last reposing in Christian humility; and, relishing the pleasure of her enfeebled state, Emma inwardly meditated on the destruction of her will, that must have left a wide opening for grace to invade. So there existed greater delights in place of happiness, another love beyond all loves, with neither pause nor end, and increasing for ever and ever! She glimpsed, amidst her hope's illusions, a state of innocence floating above the earth, mingling with the sky, and where she aspired to be. She wanted to become a saint. She bought rosary beads, she wore amulets; she desired to have, in her room above her bed, a reliquary set with emeralds, to kiss each night.

The priest was struck with wonder at these tendencies, even though he found Emma's religion might, by dint of fervour, end up bordering on heresy and even folly. But, not being well versed in these matters the moment they exceeded a certain limit, he wrote to Monsieur Boulard, Monseigneur's bookseller to send him *something renowned for a person of the fair sex, who was thoroughly intelligent.* The bookseller, with the indifference of one despatching ironmongery to negroes, packed up higgledy-piggledy everything that was then current in the pious book business. They consisted of little question-and-answer handbooks, haughty-toned pamphlets in the manner of Monsieur de Maistre, and the type of novel with pink boards and an insipidly sweet style, manufactured by troubadour seminarists or penitent bluestockings. There was *Think Well On It*; *The Man of the World at Mary's Feet, by M. de ***, a Member of Several Distinguished Orders*; *Errors of Voltaire for the Use of Young People*, etc.

Madame Bovary's mind was not yet clear enough to apply herself seriously to just anything; moreover, she undertook her reading too hastily. She became exasperated by the creed's prescriptions; the arrogance of polemical works displeased her in their obstinate pursuit of people unknown to her; and the profane tales lofty with religion seemed to her written in such an ignorance of the world, that they imperceptibly kept her away from the truths whose proof she awaited. Still she persisted, and, when the volume slid from her hands, she thought herself seized by the most refined Catholic melancholy that an ethereal soul could possibly conceive.

As for the memory of Rodolphe, it had sunk to the very bottom of her heart; and it remained there, more solemn and still than a royal mummy in a vault. A single breath would escape from this great, embalmed love and, passing through everything, scent with tenderness the unstained atmosphere in which she desired to live. When she kneeled on her Gothic prayer-stool, she offered up to the Lord the same sweet words she would murmur of old to her lover, in the outpourings of adultery. It was intended to summon belief; but no pleasing delight descended from the heavens, and she would stand up, weary of limb, vaguely sensing an immense deception. This seeking, she thought, was all the more to her credit; and in her devotional pride, Emma compared herself to those great ladies of bygone times, of whose glory she had dreamed over a portrait of La Vallière, and who, trailing the lace-trimmed train of their long dresses with such majesty, would withdraw into solitude to shed at Christ's feet the innumerable tears of a heart wounded by existence.

She then devoted herself to an excess of charity. She sewed clothes for the poor; she sent firewood to women in confinement; and Charles, coming home one day, found three good-for-nothings sitting at table in the kitchen, drinking soup. She summoned home her little girl, whom her husband, during her illness, had sent back to the wet-nurse. She wanted to teach her to read; however much Berthe cried, she was no longer irritated. She had made her mind up to be resigned, to be universally indulgent. Her language, whatever the subject, was full of high-flown expressions. She would say to her child:

'Has your colic gone away, my angel?'

Mère Bovary found nothing to censure, except perhaps this passion for knitting night-gowns for orphans, instead of darning dusters. But, worn out by domestic feuds, the simple soul delighted in this unruffled house, and even stayed with them beyond Easter, so as to avoid the sarcastic remarks of Père Bovary, who never failed, every Good Friday, to order a chitterling sausage.

Other than the company of her mother-in-law, who fortified her a little with her sound judgment and solid ways, Emma still enjoyed the society of others almost every day. There was Madame Langlois, Madame Caron, Madame Dubreuil, Madame Tuvache and, regularly, from two to five o'clock, the excellent Madame Homais, who had never wanted to believe, for her part, in any of the tittle-tattle that was spread about concerning her neighbour. The Homais children would come to visit her as well, accompanied by Justin. He went up with them into the room, and stayed standing by the door, motionless, not speaking a word. Often Madame Bovary, not realising, would actually start to dress. She began by removing her comb, tossing her head with an abrupt movement; and, when he observed for the first time that complete head of hair uncoiling its black ringlets and falling as far as the backs of her knees, it was for him, poor boy, like the unexpected entry into something new and extraordinary whose splendour appalled him.

Emma, without doubt, noticed neither his silent ardour nor his timidity. She never suspected that love, vanished from her life, was throbbing there, so close to her, under that shirt of coarse canvas, in that adolescent heart open to her beauty's emanations. Nevertheless, she looked on everything now with such indifference, her words were so fond and her gaze so haughty, her ways so various, that none could make a distinction between her egoism and her charity, her corruption and her virtue. One evening, for instance, she flew at her maidservant, who was asking her leave to go out and stammering as she sought a pretext; then all of a sudden:

'You're in love with him, then?'

And, without waiting for a response from Félicité, who was blushing, she added with a sad look:

'Go on, woo him! Have fun!'

At the beginning of spring, she had the garden turned topsy-turvy from one end to the other, despite Bovary's remarks; he was happy, however, to see her display the tiniest bit of determination at last. This grew in proportion to her recovery. At first, she found the means to throw out Mère Rollet, the wet-nurse, who had got into the habit, during Emma's convalescence, of coming into the kitchen too often with her two nurslings and her boarder, with a bigger appetite than a cannibal. Then she disentangled herself from the Homais family, dismissed in succession all the other callers and even frequented the church with less assiduity, to the loud approval of the apothecary, who then said to her in a friendly manner:

'You were lapsing a little into the cloth!'

Monsieur Bournisien, as before, would pop in every day, when he emerged from catechism. He preferred to stay out of doors, to take the air *in the midst of the grove*, as he termed the arbour. It was the time of day when Charles got back. They were hot; sweet cider was brought, and together they drank to Madame's complete recovery.

Binet was there, that is to say a bit lower down, against the terrace wall, angling for crayfish. Bovary invited him to cool down, and he understood perfectly how to uncork those small jugs.

'You must,' he said, casting a satisfied look around him and out to the farthest points of the landscape, 'hold the bottle upright thus on the table, and, after the wires are cut, push the cork with little thrusts, gently, gently, as you do, may I add, with seltzer water, in restaurants.'

But the cider, during this demonstration, would often gush full into their faces, and then the cleric, with an inscrutable laugh, never let this piece of wit go by:

'Its goodness is evident to the eye!'

He was a decent fellow, indeed, and was not even deeply shocked by the pharmacist, who was advising Charles that, to distract Madame, he should take her to the theatre in Rouen, to see Lagardy, the tenor. Homais being amazed at this silence, wanted to have his opinion, and the priest declared that he regarded music as less dangerous for morals than literature.

But the pharmacist took the defence of letters. The theatre, he maintained, served to lampoon prejudice, and, under pleasure's mask, teach virtue.

'*Castigat ridendo mores*,[43] Monsieur Bournisien! So consider the greater part of Voltaire's tragedies; they are cleverly seeded with philosophical reflections which act as a veritable school of ethics and diplomacy for the people.'

'For my part,' said Binet, 'in the old days I saw a play called *The Urchin of Paris*, in which your attention's drawn to the character of an old general who is awfully well hit off! He sends one of his sons packing who had seduced a factory girl, who at the end . . .'

'Of course!' Homais continued, 'there is bad literature as there is bad pharmacy; but to condemn in one lump the most important of the arts strikes me as doltish, a barbarous notion, worthy of those abominable times when they locked away Galileo.'

'I am well aware,' the priest objected, 'that there exist decent works, decent authors; nevertheless, if only owing to these people of different sexes being thrown together in a bewitching room, adorned with worldly splendours, and then those heathen disguises, that face-paint, those torches, those effeminate voices, all that has to end up spawning a certain debauchery of mind and giving you indecent thoughts, unclean temptations. Such at least is the opinion of every Church Father. After all,' he added, taking on a mystical tone of voice, while rolling a pinch of snuff on his thumb, 'if the Church has condemned these plays, she had reason to; we must submit to her decrees.'

'Why,' demanded the apothecary, 'does it excommunicate actors? Because, in the old days, they openly joined in with the creed's rituals. Yes, they would act, they would perform, in the middle of the choir, types of farces, called mysteries, in which the rules of decency were frequently offended.'

The cleric merely uttered a groan, and the apothecary went on:

'It's the same in the Bible; there is . . . you know . . . more than one . . . titillating detail . . . stuff that is . . . truly . . . bawdy!'

And, following an irritated gesture from Monsieur Bournisien:

'Ah, you will agree that it's not a book to put into a young person's hands, and I'd be sorry if Athalie . . .'

'But it's the Protestants, and not us,' the other shouted, provoked, 'who recommend the Bible!'

'No matter,' said Homais, 'I'm astonished that nowadays, in an enlightened century, we are still obstinately bent on proscribing an intellectual recreation which is inoffensive, morally instructive and even at times health-preserving, isn't that right, doctor?'

'Without doubt,' the doctor replied listlessly, whether because, having the same ideas, he did not want to offend anyone, or because he had none.

The conversation appeared to be over, when the pharmacist judged it the moment to make a final thrust.

'Some I have known, priests that is, who would dress as ordinary citizens to go and see dancing-girls wriggle about.'

'Nonsense!' said the priest.

'Ah, some I have known!'

And, separating the syllables of his sentence, Homais repeated:

'Some-I-have-known.'

'Ah well, they were in the wrong,' said Bournisien, his ears resigned to anything.

'Zounds, they've committed many another!' exclaimed the apothecary.

'Monsieur!' chided the priest, with eyes so fierce that the pharmacist felt intimidated.

'I simply want to say,' he replied then, in a more conciliatory tone, 'that tolerance is the surest way to entice minds to religion.'

'True, true,' conceded the good-natured fellow, settling down again on his chair.

But he stayed only two minutes. Then, as soon as he had left, Monsieur Homais said to the doctor:

'There's what you call a set-to. I took a rise out of him there, somehow, did you see? Well, be advised by me, take Madame to the show, if only to enrage one of those crows just once in your life, by Jove! If someone could replace me, I'd accompany you myself. Hurry up! Lagardy is only giving one performance; he's been invited to England for a considerable fee. He is, the rumour goes, a capital fellow. He's rolling in it. He goes about with three mistresses and a cook. All these great artists burn the candle at both ends; their life has to be one of barefaced licentiousness to stimulate the imagination a little. But they die in the work-house because, being young, they haven't had the wit to save. Well, enjoy your dinner; till tomorrow!'

This theatre idea quickly sprouted in Bovary's head; for he shared it straightaway with his wife, who declined at first, pleading fatigue, the inconvenience, the expense; but, extraordinarily, Charles did not give in, so firm was he in his belief that this diversion would be beneficial to her. He could see no impediment; his mother had despatched them three hundred francs on which he was no longer counting, current debts were not so huge, and the expiration of the bills payable to Monsieur Lheureux was still such a long way off, that there was no need to think about them. Moreover, imagining that she was being considerate, Charles was more and more insistent; so much so that finally, by dint of being beset, she decided. And, the next day, at eight o'clock, they packed themselves off in the *Hirondelle*.

The apothecary, whom nothing detained in Yonville, but who considered himself compelled not to budge, let out a sigh on seeing them leave.

'Well, have a good trip!' he said to them, 'happy mortals that you are!'

Then, addressing himself to Emma, who was wearing a four-flounced dress of blue silk:

'I find you as pretty as a Venus. You'll be cutting a dash in Rouen!'

The stagecoach stopped at the *Hôtel de la Croix Rouge*, in the Place Beauvoisine. It was one of those inns found in the outskirts of all provincial towns, with large stables and small bedrooms, where in the middle of the yard you see hens pecking at oats beneath the squalid gigs of commercial travellers; fine old lodgings with worm-eaten wooden balconies that creak in the wind through the winter nights, always full of people, hubbub and mounds of food, whose black tables are stickied by the laced coffee, the thick window-glass yellowed by flies, the damp napkins stained by the cheap blue wine; and which, still redolent of the village, like farm servants dressed as townsmen, have a café facing the road, and a vegetable garden on the field side. Charles immediately got down to business. He muddled up the front of the stage with the gallery, the orchestra with the boxes, demanded explanations, failed to understand them, was sent from the ticket seller to the manager, came back to the inn, returned to the office, and thus paced the length of the town several times, from the theatre to the boulevard.

Madame bought herself a hat, gloves, a nosegay. Monsieur greatly feared missing the beginning; and, without having had the time to swallow a plate of soup, they appeared before the theatre doors, which were still shut.

XV

THE CROWD STOOD AGAINST THE wall, penned in symmetrically between railings. At the corner of the neighbouring streets, gigantic posters repeated in baroque letters: '*Lucie de Lammermoor* [44]... Lagardy ... Opéra ... etc.' It was fine weather; they were hot, sweat trickled through the curls, the drawn handkerchiefs were all dabbing at flushed foreheads; and at times a warm wind, blowing from the river, feebly stirred the edges of the twill awnings suspended over the tavern doors. A little lower down, however, they were cooled by a current of cold air that smelt of tallow, leather and oil. This was the vaporous breath of the rue des Charrettes, full of big dark warehouses where casks are rolled.

Fearful of appearing ridiculous, Emma wanted to take a turn on foot about the harbour, and Bovary, as a precaution, kept the tickets to hand, in his trouser pocket, pressing it to his stomach.

Her heart began beating hard the moment she entered the vestibule. She smiled involuntarily from vanity, on seeing the crowd rushing to the right by the other corridor, whereas she was climbing the staircase for the *dress circle*. She took a child's pleasure in pushing the wide upholstered doors with her finger; she breathed the dusty odour of the corridors deep into her lungs, and, when she was seated in her box, she threw back her shoulders with the airiness of a duchess.

The theatre began to fill up, the opera glasses were drawn from their cases, and the regular playgoers, catching sight of one another from afar, bowed. They were here to relinquish the anxieties of the market-place for the fine arts; but, not unmindful of *business matters*, they were still talking cotton, spirits or indigo. Old men's heads were to be seen there, blank and peaceable, whitish hair and complexion giving them the appearance of silver medals tarnished by a haze of lead. The young fops strutted in the *pit*, showing off, through open waistcoats, their rosy or apple-green neck-cloths; and from up above Madame Bovary admired them as they rested the stretched palm of their yellow gloves upon gold-knobbed riding-crops.

Meanwhile, the orchestra's candles lit up; the chandelier was lowered from the ceiling, its crystal-faceted radiance shedding a sudden gaiety over the theatre; then the musicians entered one after the other, and at first there was a long discordancy of snoring bass-viols, grating violins, screaming cornets, whining flutes and flageolets. But three thumps were heard on the stage; a rolling of kettle-drums began, the brass struck its chords, and the curtain rose to reveal a country scene.

It was a woodland crossroads, with a fountain on the left, shaded by an oak. Crofters and lairds, plaids on their shoulders, all sang a hunting song together; then a chieftain suddenly appeared and, lifting his arms to the heavens, he called on the angel of evil; another man appeared; they went out, and the hunters resumed.

She found herself back in the reading of her youth, in the middle of Walter Scott. She thought she could hear, through the fog, the sound of Scottish bagpipes echoing over the heather. Moreover, the memory of the novel made it easier to understand the libretto, and she followed the plot phrase by phrase, while fleeting thoughts that came back to her scattered, immediately, under the squalls of the music. She let herself be lulled by the melodies and felt her whole being vibrating as if the bows of the violins were being drawn across her own nerves. Her eyes were barely wide enough to take in the costumes, the scenery, the characters, the painted trees that trembled when anyone strutted, and the velvet caps, the cloaks, the swords, all these chimera stirring in harmony as though in the air of another world. But a young woman stepped forward, throwing a purse to a squire in green. She remained alone, and then a flute was heard that played like a fountain's murmur or the purling of a bird. Lucie began her cavatina in G major valiantly; she complained of love, she yearned for wings. Emma, likewise, would have liked to take flight on an embrace, fleeing life. All of a sudden, Edgar, Lagardy, appeared.

He had that splendid pallor which lends a certain marmoreal majesty to the passionate southern races. His vigorous figure was cased in a brown doublet; a little chased dagger knocked against his thigh, and he rolled his eyes languorously, revealing his white teeth. It was said that a Polish princess, hearing him sing one night on the beach at Biarritz, where he was refitting ship-boats, had fallen in love with him. He had been the cause of her ruin. He had left her there in the lurch for other women, and this sentimental fame merely served his artistic reputation. The diplomatic strolling player would even take care always to have a poetic phrase concerning his fascinating personality and his sensitive soul slipped into the advertisements. A lovely voice, an imperturbable aplomb, more robust than intelligent and more energetic than lyrical, was all that was needed to increase the prestige of this admirable kind of charlatan, who had something of both the hairdresser and the toreador about him.

He enthused from the very first scene. He clasped Lucie in his arms, he left her, he came back, he seemed disconsolate: he had bursts of rage, then elegiac death-rattles of an infinite sweetness, and the notes broke loose from his bare throat, full of sobs and kisses. Emma leaned over to see him, scratching her box's velvet with her nails. She filled her heart with these tuneful lamentations that were drawn out to the accompaniment of the double-basses, like the cries of the drowned in a storm's uproar. She knew again all the intoxication and the anguish that she had been like to die from. The singer's voice seemed to her no more than the echo of her mind, and this illusion that held her spellbound something actually drawn from her life. But nobody on earth had loved her with such a love. He did not weep like Edgar, on the last night, in the light of the moon, when they said to each other, 'Till tomorrow! Till tomorrow . . . !' The theatre cracked open with cheers; the whole *stretta* was repeated; the lovers spoke of the flowers on their graves, of oaths, of exile, of fatality, of hopes, and when they uttered the last farewell, Emma let out a shrill cry, which was lost in the quivering of the final chords.

'So why,' Bovary asked, 'is this lord persecuting her?'

'Oh no,' she replied; 'he's her lover.'

'Even so he swears to avenge himself on her family, while the other, the one who came on just now, said: "I love Lucie and I believe I am loved by her." Moreover, he left with her father, arm in arm. Because it's definitely her father, isn't it, the little ugly one who wears a cock's feather in his hat?'

Despite Emma's explanations, from the recitative and duet in which Gilbert reveals his abominable manoeuvrings to his master Ashton, Charles, on seeing the false betrothal ring intended to deceive Lucie, believed it to be a memento of love sent by Edgar. He admitted, however, that he did not understand the story – because of the music – which was very detrimental to the words.

'What does it matter?' said Emma; 'Hush!'

'It's just that I do like,' he began again, leaning on her shoulder, 'to have some idea, as you well know.'

'Hush! Hush!' she said, provoked.

Lucie came forward, partly borne up by her servants, a crown of orange-blossom in her hair, and paler than the white satin of her dress. Emma dreamed of her marriage day; and she saw herself back there, in the midst of the cornfields, on the little path, when they were walking to the church. Why then had she not similarly resisted, entreated, like this woman? On the contrary, she was glad, not perceiving the abyss she was throwing herself into. Ah! If, in the bloom of her beauty, before the stain of marriage and the disillusion of adultery, she had been able to lay her life upon some great, stout heart, thus mingling virtue, love, voluptuousness and duty, never would she have fallen from so supreme a bliss. But that happiness was doubtless a lie contrived as the despair of all desire. She knew now the pettiness of passions that art exaggerated. Forcing herself therefore to avert her thoughts, Emma no longer wished to see in this reproduction of her sorrows anything but an artificial fancy fit for keeping the eye entertained, and she was even smiling inwardly out of scornful pity, when at the back of the stage, beneath the velvet curtain, a man appeared in a black cloak.

With a single movement he swept off his great Spanish hat; and immediately the instruments and the singers began the sextet. Edgar, flashing with fury, dominated everyone else with his clearer voice. Ashton hurled murderous, deep-noted provocations at him, Lucie sang her high-pitched plaint, Arthur intoned to one side in the middle range, and the minister's bass-baritone pealed like a church organ, while the women's voices, reprising their words, resumed deliciously, in chorus. They were all in a line, gesticulating; and anger, vengeance, jealousy, terror, forgiveness and stupefaction breathed simultaneously from their half-open mouths. The outraged lover brandished his naked sword; his lace collar rose in jerks, to the movements of his chest, and he strode from right to left, making the gilded ankle-spurs on his soft flared boots ring against the boards. He must, she thought, bear an inexhaustible love, to cast it upon the crowd in such vast outpourings. All her feeble desire to be disparaging faded away under the poetry of the role breaking in upon her, and, impelled towards the man by the illusion of the character, she strove to imagine his life, this resounding, extraordinary, splendid life, and which she might yet have led, if chance had ordained it. They would have known each other, they would have loved each other! She might have travelled with him through all the kingdoms of Europe, from capital to capital, sharing his hardships and his pride, gathering up the flowers tossed to him, embroidering his costumes herself; then, each evening, in the depths of a theatre-box, behind the gold-lattice of a balustrade, she would have gathered, wide-eyed, the grand effusions of this heart singing for her alone; from the stage, acting all the while, he would have gazed up at her. But a madness gripped her: he was gazing at her, for certain! She longed to run into his arms to take shelter in his strength, as in the embodiment of love itself, and to say to him, to cry out: 'Take me away, bear me away, let us begone! Yours, yours, all my fervour and all my dreams!'

The curtain fell.

The smell of the gas mingled with people's breath; the breeze from the fans rendered the atmosphere more stifling. Emma wanted to go out; the crowd was blocking the corridors, and she fell back into her chair suffocating under the pounding of her heart. Charles, fearful that she was about to faint, ran to the refreshment-room to fetch her a glass of orgeat syrup.

He had great difficulty in returning to his seat, being struck on the elbows at every step, because of the glass he was holding with both hands, and he even spilt three-quarters of it over the shoulders of a Rouen lady in short sleeves, who, feeling the cold liquid trickling down her back, shrieked like a peacock, as though someone were intent on murdering her. Her husband, owner of a spinning-mill, railed against the clumsy fellow; and, while she was dabbing with her handkerchief at the stains on her lovely, cherry-taffeta dress, he was testily muttering the words indemnity, charges, reimbursement. At length, Charles reached his wife, all out of breath and saying to her:

'I thought, well, that I would be stopping there. There were so many people . . . so many people . . .'

He added:

'Just guess who I met upstairs? Monsieur Léon!'

'Léon?'

'The self-same! He's coming to pay his compliments.'

And, as he finished his words, the former clerk of Yonville entered the box.

He held out his hand in the casual manner of a gentleman: and Madame Bovary advanced her own mechanically, no doubt obedient to the attraction of a stronger will. She had not felt it since that spring evening when it rained on the green leaves, and they bid each other goodbye, standing at the window. But, quickly, recalled to propriety, with an effort she shook herself free of this torpor of memories and began to stammer out rapid phrases.

'Ah, good day . . . What! Is it you?'

'Silence!' shouted a voice in the pit, for the third act was under way.

'So you're in Rouen?'

'Yes.'

'And since when?'

'Out with them! Out with them!'

People were turning to look at them; they held their tongues.

But, from this moment, she no longer listened; and the chorus of wedding-guests, the scene with Ashton and his lackey, the great duet in D major, everything went by for her at a distance, as if the instruments had become less sonorous and the characters more remote; she remembered the card games at the pharmacist's, and the walk to the wet-nurse's house, the readings in the arbour, the tête-à-têtes by the fireside, all that wretched love, so calm and so slow, so discreet, so tender, and that she had nevertheless forgotten. Why then had he returned? What combination of fortune was placing him back in her life? He stayed behind her, his shoulder leaning against the partition; and, from time to time, she felt herself shiver in the warm breath from his nostrils falling on her hair.

'Do you find that entertaining?' he said, stooping over her so close, that the tip of his moustache grazed her jaw.

She replied nonchalantly:

'Oh, dear God, no. Not very.'

So he suggested they leave the theatre, to go and get ices somewhere.

'Ah, not yet! Let's stay,' said Bovary. 'Her hair is untied: that promises to be tragic.'

But the mad scene did not interest Emma, and the singer's acting seemed to her overdone.

'She's squealing too loudly,' she said, turning to Charles who was listening.

'Yes . . . maybe . . . a bit,' he replied, wavering between the frankness of his enjoyment and the respect he showed for his wife's opinions.

Then Léon said with a sigh:

'The heat is . . .'

'Unbearable! That's true.'

'Are you uncomfortable?' asked Bovary

'Yes, I'm suffocating: let us go.'

Monsieur Léon set her long lace shawl delicately upon her shoulders, and they all three went to sit by the harbour, in the open air, before a café window.

The first subject was her illness, although Emma interrupted Charles from time to time, from fear, she said, of wearying Monsieur Léon; and the latter told them that he had come to Rouen to spend two years in a large law practice, to be broken in with cases which in Normandy were unlike those handled in Paris. Then he inquired about Berthe, the Homais family, Mère Lefrançois; and, as they had no more to say to each other in the presence of the husband, the conversation soon came to an end.

People coming out of the show went by on the pavement, all humming or bawling out *O lovely angel, my Lucie!* at full throat. Then Léon, acting the amateur connoisseur, began to talk music. He had seen Tamburini, Rubini, Persiani, Grisi; and compared to them, Lagardy, for all his great booming, was good for nothing.

'Nevertheless,' interrupted Charles, taking little bites at his rum sherbet, 'they claim he's really to be admired in the final act; I regret leaving before the end, as I was starting to enjoy it.'

'Anyway,' the clerk continued, 'he'll be giving another performance soon.'

But Charles replied that they were off and away the next morning.

'Unless,' he added, turning towards his wife, 'you might not want to stay on your own, my kitten?'

And, presented with this unexpectedly promising opportunity, the young man changed stratagem, starting to eulogise Lagardy in the final section. It was something superb, sublime! So Charles insisted:

'You might return on Sunday. Come, make up your mind! You're wrong not to do so, if you feel in the least bit that it will do you good.'

Meanwhile the surrounding tables were emptying; a waiter came to station himself discreetly near them; Charles, who understood, drew his purse out; the clerk held him back by the arm, and even remembered to leave, in addition, two silver coins, that he chinked against the marble.

'I am angry, really I am,' muttered Bovary, 'about the money that you . . .'

The other made a dismissive, thoroughly cordial gesture, and, taking up his hat:

'It's agreed, is it, tomorrow, at six o'clock?'

Charles exclaimed yet again that he could not stay away any longer; but nothing was preventing Emma . . .

'It's just that . . .' she stammered with a peculiar smile, 'I am not too sure . . .'

'Ah well! Think on it, we shall see, seek advice with your pillow . . .'

Then to Léon, who was accompanying them:

'Now you are here in our region, you'll call from time to time, I hope, to dine with us?'

The clerk affirmed that he would not fail to, being required more-over to go to Yonville on a legal case for his practice. And they parted in front of the Passage Saint-Herbland, just as half-past eleven was tolling from the cathedral bells.

PART THREE

PART THREE

Monsieur Léon, while studying the law, was a not infrequent regular at the *Chaumière*, where he was remarkably successful with the grisettes,[1] who thought he looked *distinguished*. He was the most proper of students: his hair was neither too long nor too short, he did not run through his term's allowance on the first of the month, and he kept on good terms with his teachers. As for overindulging, he had always refrained from doing so, as much out of faint-heartedness as from scruples.

Often, while he stayed reading in his room, or else seated in the evening under the Luxembourg's linden trees, he would let his law book fall to the ground, and the memory of Emma came back to him. But, little by little, this feeling grew weaker, and other lusts accumulated on top, even though it still persisted through them; for Léon did not entirely lose hope, and he felt a kind of uncertain promise that swung in the future, like a golden fruit hanging from some chimerical foliage.

Then, when he saw her again after three years' absence, his passion revived. He must, he thought, finally make up his mind to try to possess her. Moreover, contact with wanton company had worn away his shyness, and he returned to the provinces, scornful of whatever did not graze the asphalt[2] of the boulevard with a patent-leather boot. Around a Parisienne in lace, in the salon of some illustrious doctor, a personage with medals and coach, the wretched clerk would doubtless have trembled like a child; but here, in Rouen, on the waterfront, before the wife of this insignificant doctor, he felt comfortable, certain in advance that he would dazzle. Aplomb depends on the milieu into which it pitches itself; the idiom of the mezzanine is not that of the fourth floor, and the wealthy woman, to preserve her virtue, seems to have all her bank-notes around her, like a breast-plate, inside the lining of her corset.

On leaving Monsieur and Madame Bovary the previous evening, Léon had followed them along the street, from afar; then having seen them stop at the *Croix Rouge*, he turned on his heels and spent the entire night contemplating a plan.

So the next day, at about five o'clock, he entered the inn's kitchen, a lump in his throat, cheeks pale, and with that coward's resolve that nothing holds back.

'Monsieur is no longer here,' a servant replied.

That seemed to him a good omen. He went up.

She was unperturbed at his approach; on the contrary, she offered her excuses for having forgotten to tell him where they were staying.

'Oh, I guessed it,' answered Léon.

'What?'

He pretended to have been guided towards her, by chance, by an instinct. She began to smile, and at once, to make up for his nonsense, Léon related how he had spent his morning searching for her successively in all the city's hotels.

'So you've decided to stay?' he added.

'Yes,' she said, 'and I was wrong to. One mustn't grow used to unfeasible pleasures, surrounded as one is by a thousand pressing demands . . .'

'Oh, I can imagine . . .'

'Ah no, for you are not a woman.'

But men also had their sorrows, and the conversation began with a few philosophical reflections. Emma expatiated a great deal on the wretchedness of earthly affections and the eternal loneliness in which the heart remained entombed.

To show himself to advantage, or by an unaffected imitation of this melancholy that in turn provoked his own, the young man declared himself to have been prodigiously bored throughout his studies. Legal procedings irritated him, other vocations attracted him, and his mother never left off tormenting him in each letter. They were growing more and more explicit about the grounds for their suffering, each of them, the more they talked, becoming increasingly over-excited by the progressive confiding of their secrets. But sometimes they came to a stop before the full exposure of a thought, and then endeavoured to contrive a phrase which might yet explain it. She did not own to her passion for another; he did not say that he had forgotten her.

Perhaps he no longer recalled his suppers after the dance, with the stevedore-trousered girls; and she doubtless did not remember the assignations of former times, when she would run through the morning pastures, towards her lover's chateau. The noises of the city scarcely reached them; and the room seemed small, expressly to keep their solitude in even closer confinement. Emma, in a dimity dressing gown, rested her chignon against the back of an old armchair; the wall's yellow paper made a kind of golden ground beyond her; and her bare head repeated itself in the mirror with the white parting in the middle, and the tips of her ears peeping below her bandeaux.

'But, forgive me,' she said, 'this is wrong of me. I'm boring you with my endless complaints.'

'No, never. Never!'

'If you knew,' she went on, lifting to the ceiling her lovely eyes with their trickle of a tear, 'all that I had dreamed of.'

'And me, too. Oh, I have truly suffered! I would go out, I'd sneak out, I'd trudge along the quayside, deafening myself in the noise of the crowd without being able to banish the obsession that pursued me. In a print-seller's on the boulevard, there's an Italian engraving depicting a Muse. She's draped in a tunic and she's gazing at the moon, with forget-me-nots in her loose hair. Something urged me there incessantly; I stayed whole hours.'

Then, in a trembling voice:

'She looked a little like you.'

Madame Bovary turned her head away, so he might not see on her lips the irresistible smile she could feel rising there.

'Often,' he continued, 'I would write letters to you that I then tore up.'

She made no reply. He went on:

'Sometimes I'd imagine that chance would bring you. I thought I recognised you at street corners: and I would run after all the coaches where a shawl fluttered from the door, a veil matching yours . . .'

She seemed determined to let him talk without interrupting him. Crossing her arms and lowering her head, she contemplated the bows on her slippers, and made little movements in their satin interior, at intervals, with her toes.

Still, she sighed:

'Is it not quite the saddest thing, to be spinning out, as I am doing, a useless existence? If our sorrows could be of use to someone, we might console ourselves with thoughts of sacrifice.'

He began to praise virtuousness, duty and mute self-immolation, having himself an incredible need for devotion that he could not assuage.

'I would very much like,' she said, 'to be a hospital nun.'

'Alas!' he replied, 'men have no such saintly missions, and I see no calling anywhere . . . save perhaps that of doctor . . .'

With a little shrug of her shoulders, Emma interrupted him to complain of her illness from which she had almost died; what a shame! She would no longer be suffering now. Léon immediately desired *the quiet of the tomb*, and one night he had even written his will, requesting that he be buried in that lovely coverlet, striped with velvet, that he had received from her; for this is how they would have wished to be, each setting up an ideal against which they were now adjusting their past life. Besides, words are a rolling-mill that always stretch out one's feelings.

But at this contrivance of the coverlet:

'Why so?' she asked.

'Why?'

He hesitated.

'Because I truly loved you!'

And, congratulating himself on having surmounted the obstacle, Léon, out of the corner of his eye, spied on her expression.

It was like the sky, when a gust chases away the clouds. The massed banks of sad thoughts that had cast a gloom seemed to withdraw from her blue eyes;[3] her whole face beamed.

He waited. At last she replied:

'I had always suspected it . . .'

They then recounted to one another the little happenings of that far-off existence, whose pleasures and dejections they had just summed up in a single word. They remembered the clematis arbour, the dresses she wore, her room's furniture, the whole house.

'And our poor cactus plants, where are they?'

'The cold killed them this last winter.'

'Ah, how I thought of them, did you know that? Often I used to see them again as in the old days, when, on summer mornings, the sun struck the window-blinds . . . and I glimpsed your two bare arms slipping between the flowers.'

'My poor friend!' she said, holding out her hand to him.

Léon quickly fixed his lips there. Then, drawing a deep breath:

'At that time, you were, for me, an indescribable, incomprehensible force that took my life captive. For instance, I came to your house, once; but you probably have no recollection?'

'Yes,' she said. 'Continue.'

'You were down below, in the anteroom, ready to go out, on the lowest step; you even had a hat with little blue flowers; and, without any invitation on your part, in spite of myself, I accompanied you. At each moment, however, I was more and more conscious of my foolishness, and I continued to walk near you, not daring quite to follow you, and not wanting to leave you. When you went into a shop, I'd stay in the street, I watched you through the glass as you took off your gloves and counted the change on the counter. Afterwards you rang Madame Tuvache's bell, someone opened up for you, and I stayed like an idiot in front of the great heavy door, which had closed upon you again.'

Listening to him, Madame Bovary was amazed at being so old; all these things reappearing seemed to broaden her existence; they made a kind of emotional vastness on which she was being transported back; and she said from time to time, in a low voice and with her eyelids half-closed:

'Yes, it's true . . . It's true . . . It's true . . .'

They heard eight o'clock chime from all the different clocks in the Beauvoisine quarter, which is full of boarding-schools, churches and large abandoned mansions. They were no longer speaking; but they felt, looking at each other, a roaring in their heads, as if a clear loud

225

sound was mutually bursting from eyes fixed on one another. They had just joined hands; and the past, the future, reminiscences and dreams, all were mingled in the sweetness of that rapture. Night thickened on the walls, on which there still shone, half lost in the shadow, the coarse colours of four prints depicting four scenes from *The Tower of Nesle*,⁴ with an inscription at the bottom, in Spanish and French. From the sash-window, you could see a wedge of black sky, between pointed rooves.

She rose to light two candles on the chest of drawers, then came and sat down again.

'Well . . .' said Léon.

'Well . . . ?' she replied.

And he was seeking a way to renew the broken-off dialogue, when she said to him:

'Why is it that no one, up to now, has ever expressed similar sentiments?'

The clerk cried out that ideal natures were hard to understand. He, for his part, had been in love with her from the first glance; and he was in despair, thinking of the happiness they might have had if, by a stroke of fortune, meeting each other earlier on, they might have been bound indissolubly together.

'I dreamed of it sometimes,' she answered.

'What a dream,' murmured Léon.

And, delicately handling the blue piping of his long white waistband, he added:

'So who's preventing us from starting again?'

'No, my friend,' she replied. 'I am too old . . . you are too young . . . forget me! Others will love you . . . you'll love them.'

'Not as I do you!' he cried out.

'What a child you are! Come, let's be sensible. I mean it!'

She impressed upon him the insuperable obstacles facing their love, and that they must behave, as in former times, within the simple limits of a brotherly affection.

Was she speaking thus in earnest? Doubtless Emma herself had no idea, completely taken up by the appeal of the seduction and the need to defend herself against it; and, gazing on the young man with melting eyes, she gently spurned the shy caresses attempted by his trembling hands.

'Ah, forgive me!' he said, drawing back.

And Emma was seized by a vague dread, before this shyness, more dangerous to her than Rodolphe's boldness when he advanced with open arms. Never had any man seemed so handsome to her. There was an exquisite openness about him. He lowered his long, delicate, curving lashes. His cheek's smooth skin blushed – she thought – out of desire for her person, and Emma felt an irresistible longing to plant her lips there. So, leaning towards the clock as if to check the time:

'Dear me, how late it is!' she said; 'how we let our tongues run!'

He took the hint and fetched his hat.

'I've even forgotten the performance! Poor Bovary, leaving me behind especially. Monsieur Lormaux, of the rue Grand-Pont, was supposed to take me there with his wife.'

And the opportunity was lost, for she was leaving tomorrow.

'Truly?' said Léon.

'Yes.'

'Nevertheless I must see you again,' he continued, 'I had something to tell you . . .'

'What?'

'Something . . . grave, serious. Ah no – you can't be leaving, anyway, it isn't possible! If you knew . . . Listen . . . Then you haven't understood me? You haven't guessed, then . . . ?'

'Yet you're a good speaker,' said Emma.

'Ah, jokes! Enough, enough! Allow me to see you again, for pity's sake . . . one time . . . only one.'

'Well . . . !'

She paused; then, as if thinking better of it:

'Oh, not here.'

'Wherever you please.'

'Would you like . . .'

She appeared to reflect, then, curtly:

'Tomorrow, at eleven o'clock, in the cathedral.'

'I'll be there!' he cried, seizing her hands, which she withdrew.

And, as they found themselves both on their feet, he standing behind her and Emma lowering her head, he stooped over her neck and kissed her lengthily on the nape.

'But you're mad! Oh, you're mad!' she said through little ringing peals of laughter, while the kisses intensified.

Then, thrusting his head over her shoulder, he appeared to be seeking consent from her eyes. These fell upon him, full of a glacial majesty.

Léon took three steps back, in order to leave. He stopped on the threshold. Then he whispered in a trembling voice:

'Till tomorrow.'

She answered with a nod, and vanished like a bird into the adjoining room.

That evening, Emma wrote an interminable letter to the clerk in which she extricated herself from the assignation: all was now over, and they should no longer meet each other, for their own good. But, when the letter was sealed, since she did not know Léon's address, she found herself in a most awkward position.

'I shall give it to him myself,' she said; 'he'll come.'

The following day, Léon, window open and humming a tune on the balcony, polished his pumps himself, using several coats. He slipped on a pair of white trousers, fine-knit socks, a green coat, poured into his handkerchief everything he owned in the way of scent, then, having had his hair curled, uncurled it, to give it a more natural elegance.

'It's still too early,' he thought, looking at the wig-maker's cuckoo clock, which was showing nine.

He read an old fashion journal, stepped out, smoked a cigar, went up three streets, considered it was time and slowly made his way towards the porch of Notre Dame.

It was a lovely summer morning. Silversmiths' wares glittered in their shops, and the light falling aslant onto the cathedral set the breaks in the grey stones glistening; a flock of birds whirled in the blue sky, around the trefoil bell-turrets; the square, echoing with cries, was fragrant with the flowers that bordered the paving, roses, jasmin, carnations, narcissus and tuberose, unequally spaced between moist pot-herbs, cat-mint and chickweed for the birds; the fountain gurgled in the middle, and under broad umbrellas, among the tiered pyramids of melons, the market-traders, bare-headed, were twirling paper round bunches of violets.

The young man took one. It was the first time he had bought flowers for a woman; and his breast, as he breathed in their scent, swelled with pride, as if this tribute intended for another had reverted to him.

Nevertheless he was fearful of being spotted; he entered the church with a determined air.

Then there was the beadle standing on the threshold, in the middle of the left-hand doorway, under the dancing Marianne,¹ plume on head, rapier at his side, cane in his hand, more majestic than a cardinal and glittering like a holy chalice.

He approached Léon, and, with that smile of wheedling benignity that clergymen adopt when they question children:

'Monsieur, doubtless, is not from these parts? Monsieur wishes to visit the church's curiosities?'

'No,' said the other.

And he went round the aisles first of all. He then proceeded to take a peep at the square. Emma had not arrived. He went back in as far as the choir.

The nave was mirrored in the brimming fonts, with the first of the lancet windows and some sections of stained glass. But the reflection of the paintings, breaking up on the marble's lip, continued further off, on the flag-stones, like a motley carpet. The broad daylight from outside extended into the church on three enormous beams, through the three open portals. From time to time, at the far end, a sacristan passed across, making the oblique genuflection of the hurried devotee. The crystal chandeliers hung motionless. In the choir, a silver lamp burned; and, from the side-chapels, the gloomy parts of the church, there seemed to breathe an occasional sigh, with the sound of a grill falling back, reverberating its echo under the lofty vault.

Léon, with an earnest stride, walked close to the walls. Never had life seemed to him so good. She would be coming in a little while, delightful, uneasy, watching out behind her for eyes that might be following – and in her flounced dress, with her gold lorgnon, her slender ladies' boots, all sorts of elegant touches that he had not yet relished, and with the ineffable allure of the virtuous woman who succumbs. The church, like a gigantic boudoir, would array itself around her; the vaulted ceiling bow down to receive in the shadows the confession of her love; the stained-glass windows shine brilliantly to illumine her face, and the censers would burn that she might appear like an angel, in the smoke of the incense.

Yet she was not coming. He sat on a chair and his eyes alighted on a blue window in which boatmen can be seen, carrying baskets. He looked at it for a long time, attentively, and he counted the scales of the fish and the doublets' button-holes, while his thoughts roamed in search of Emma.

The beadle, excluded, was inwardly indignant with this individual, who took the liberty of admiring the cathedral on his own. He seemed to be conducting himself in a monstrous fashion, stealing it in a way, and all but committing a sacrilege.

But a rustle of silk on the flagstones, the edging of a hat, a black cope . . . it was her! Léon rose and ran to meet her.

Emma looked pale. She was walking quickly.

'Read it!' she said, holding out a paper for him . . . 'Oh, no.'

And she withdrew her hand abruptly, to enter the Chapel of the Virgin, where, kneeling against a chair, she began to pray.

The young man was irritated by this over-pious whim; then he found a certain charm in seeing her, in the middle of the assignation, thus lost in prayer like an Andalusian marquess; then he grew weary soon enough, for she was taking an age.

Emma prayed, or rather forced herself to pray, hoping that some unexpected resolve would descend upon her from the heavens; and, so as to entice divine aid, she filled her sight with the splendours of the tabernacle, she breathed in the fragrance of the white dame's-violet spreading wide in the great vases, and listened to the church's silence, which merely increased the tumult of her heart.

She got up, and they were about to leave, when the beadle hastily drew near, saying:

'Madame, doubtless, is not from these parts? Madame wishes to visit the church's curiosities?'

'Ah no!' cried the clerk.

'Why not?' she rejoined.

For she clung with her wavering virtue to the Virgin, to the sculptures, to the tombs, to every opportunity.

Then, so as to proceed *in order*, the beadle led them up to the entrance, near the square, where, showing them with his cane a great circle of black flag-stones, with neither inscription nor carving:

'Behold,' he declared majestically, 'the circumference of the beautiful Amboise bell. It weighed forty thousand pounds. It was unequalled in all Europe. The artisan who cast it died of joy . . .'

'Let's go,' said Léon.

The good old gentleman set off again; then, back at the Chapel of the Virgin, he stretched out his arms in a unifying gesture of display, and, prouder than a rustic landowner showing you his espalier:

'This simple slab covers the remains of Pierre de Brézé, Lord of Varenne and Brissac, Grand Marshal of Poitou and Governor of Normandy, who fell at the battle of Montlhéry, on the sixteenth of July 1465.'

Léon, gnawing at his lip, stamped his feet.

'And, to the right, this gentleman, entirely clad in steel, on a prancing horse, is his grandson Louis de Brézé, Lord of Breval and of Montchauvet, Count of Maulevrier, Baron of Mauny, King's Chamberlain, Knight of the Maltese Order and likewise Governor of Normandy, died on the twenty-third of July 1531, a Sunday, as the inscription states; and, below, this man ready to descend into the tomb shows you precisely the same person. Impossible, is it not, to imagine a more perfect representation of nothingness?'

Madame Bovary took up her lorgnon. Léon, stock-still, gazed at her, not attempting to say so much as a single word, to make a single gesture, so discouraged did he feel before this dual obstinacy of loquacity and indifference.

The everlasting guide continued:

'Near him, this kneeling woman in tears is his wife Diane de Poitiers, Countess of Brézé, Duchess of Valentinois, born in 1499, died in 1566; and, to the left, the one carrying a child, the Holy Virgin. Now, turn to this side: here are the Amboise tombs. Both of them were cardinals and archbishops of Rouen. That one was King Louis XII's minister. He did much good for the cathedral. In his will we have found a bequest of thirty thousand crowns for the poor.'

And, without stopping, speaking all the while, he ushered them into a chapel cluttered with railings, disturbed a few, and revealed a kind of block, that could well have been a badly-made statue.

'In former times it embellished,' he said, with a lengthy groan, 'the tomb of Richard the Lionheart, King of England and Duke of Normandy. It is the Calvinists, Monsieur, who reduced it to this state. They had, out of malice, buried it in some earth, under His Grace's episcopal throne. Look, here is the door by which His Grace repaired to his dwelling. Let us go and view the Gargoyle windows.'

But Léon hastily pulled out a silver coin from his pocket and seized Emma by the arm. The beadle remained utterly astonished, unable to comprehend this untimely munificence, while the stranger still had so many things to see. Then, remembering:

'Ah, Monsieur! The spire! The spire . . .'

'Thank you,' said Léon.

'Monsieur is wrong! It weighs four hundred and forty pounds, nine less than Egypt's Great Pyramid. It is all cast-iron,[6] it . . .'

Léon fled; for it seemed to him that his love, which, for almost two hours, had stood as still in the church as the stones, would now evaporate like steam up this truncated funnel, this oblong cage, this open chimney, which exposes itself so grotesquely on top of the cathedral like the wild endeavour of some whimsical tinker.

'Where are we going then?' she said.

Without replying, he continued to walk with a rapid step, and Madame Bovary was already dipping her finger in the holy water, when they heard behind them a great puffing of breath, regularly interspersed with the rebounding of a cane. Léon swerved.

'Monsieur!'

'What?'

And he recognised the beadle, carrying under his arm and holding balanced against his belly about twenty stitched and sturdy volumes. They were the works *that dealt with the cathedral.*

'Idiot!' muttered Léon, dashing out of the church.

An urchin was getting up to mischief in the portico:

'Go and fetch me a hack!'

The child shot off like a bullet, down the rue des Quatre-Vents; so they remained on their own for several minutes, face to face and a little embarrassed.

'Ah, Léon . . . ! Truly . . . I don't know . . . if I should . . . !'

She was affectedly pensive. Then, with a serious air:

'You know this is most improper?'

'How so?' rejoined the clerk. 'They do it in Paris!'

And this utterance, like an irresistible argument, decided her.

The hackney-coach did not come, however. Léon was fearful lest she go back into the church. At last the coach appeared.

'At least leave by the north portal!' the beadle shouted after them, having stayed in the doorway, 'to view the *Resurrection*, the *Last Judgment*, the *Paradise*, the *King David*, and the *Reprobates* in the fires of Hell.'

'Where's Monsieur going?' asked the coachman.

'Wherever you like!' said Léon, pushing Emma into the carriage.

And the conveyance lumbered off.[7]

It went down the rue Grand-Pont, crossed the place des Arts, the quai Napoléon, the pont Neuf and stopped short in front of the statue of Pierre Corneille.

'Carry on!' came a voice from within.

The carriage set off again, and, borne along, from the La Fayette crossroads, by the downward slope, it penetrated the railway terminus at full gallop.

'No! Straight on!' cried the same voice.

The coach emerged from the iron gates, and soon, reaching the park walk, trotted gently, amidst the tall elms. The coachman wiped his forehead, put his leather hat between his knees and urged the vehicle beyond the side paths, to the water's edge, close to the turf.

It proceeded along the river, on the tow-path laid with dry pebbles, and, for a good while, towards Oyssel, beyond the islands.

But all of a sudden, it shot in one bound through Quatremares, Sotteville, la Grande-Chaussée, the rue Elbeuf, and came to its third halt in front of the Botanical Gardens.

'Well, go on!' the voice shouted out, more furious than ever.

And straightaway, resuming its fare, it went by way of Saint-Sever, the quai des Curandiers, the quai aux Meules, once again over the bridge, by the place du Champ-de-Mars and the back of the hospital gardens, where old men in black jackets take a stroll in the sun, along a terrace turned completely green by ivy. It ascended the boulevard Bouvreuil, ran along the boulevard Cauchoise, then the whole of Mont-Riboudet up to the Côte de Deville.

It returned; and then, with neither decision nor direction, haphazardly, it roved. It was seen at Saint-Pol, at Lescure, at Mont Gargan, at La Rouge-Mare, and the Place du Gaillard-Bois; rue Maladrerie, rue Dinanderie, in front of Saint-Romain, Saint-Vivien, Saint-Maclou, Saint-Nicaise – before the Customs House – at the Basse-Vieille-Tour, at the Trois-Pipes and at the Monumental Cemetery. From time to time, the coachman on his box threw despairing glances at the tap-houses. He could not comprehend what mania for locomotion drove these individuals not to want to stop. Sometimes he tried, and immediately he heard furious exclamations burst out behind him. So more than ever he would lash his two sweating nags, but without heeding the jolts, catching on this and that, not caring about it, demoralised, and all but weeping from thirst, fatigue and dreariness.

And on the port, amid drays and casks, and on the streets, standing by the spur-stones,[8] the citizens opened their amazed eyes wide before so extraordinary a thing in the provinces, a carriage with drawn blinds, and which kept re-appearing thus, more sealed than a tomb and tossed about like a ship.

Once, in the middle of the day, in the open level country, at the moment when the sun at its fiercest beat down upon the old silvered lanterns, a bare hand slipped under the little curtains of yellow linen and threw out some torn scraps of paper, that scattered on the wind and alighted further away, like white butterflies, on a field of red clover all in flower.

Then, at about six o'clock, the carriage drew up in a lane in the Beauvoisine quarter, and a woman stepped down, walking on with her veil lowered, without turning her head.

II

ARRIVING AT THE INN, MADAME Bovary was astonished not to see the diligence. Hivert, who had waited fifty-three minutes for her, had finally driven off.

Nothing was forcing her to leave, however; but she had given her word that she would return the same evening. Moreover, Charles was waiting for her; and already she felt in her heart that sluggish docility which is, for so many women, at one and the same time both the punishment and the price for adultery.

Hastily she packed her trunk, paid the bill, took a cab in the courtyard, and, urging on the groom, encouraging him, inquiring at every moment about the time and the number of kilometres travelled, succeeded in overtaking the *Hirondelle* as the first houses of Quincampoix appeared.

Scarcely seated in her corner, she closed her eyes and opened them again at the bottom of the hill, where she recognised Félicité from afar, keeping a look-out in front of the farrier's house. Hivert reined in his horses, and the cook-maid, raising herself up to the carriage-window, said mysteriously:

'Madame you've to go straight off to Monsieur Homais' house. It's for something urgent.'

The village was as silent as ever. At the street corners, there were little rosy heaps steaming in the air, as it was jam-making time, and everyone in Yonville was making their own supply on the same day. But one could admire, in front of the apothecary's shop, a much bigger heap, surpassing the others with the superiority that a laboratory must have over common stoves, a general necessity over individual whims.

She went in. The big chair was tipped over, and even the *Rouen Beacon* lay around on the floor, spread out between the two pestles. She pushed open the passage door; and, in the middle of the kitchen, between the brown jars full of picked redcurrants, ground sugar, lump sugar, the scales on the table, basins on the fire, she saw all the Homais, big and small, with aprons tied up to the chin and holding forks in their hands. Justin stood hanging his head, and the apothecary was shouting:

'Who told you to go and fetch it in the capernaum?'

'What is it? What's the matter?'

'The matter?' replied the apothecary. 'We are making jam: it is cooking; but it was about to run over on account of an over-vigorous ebullition, and I demand another basin. So he through indolence, through sloth, goes and takes, hanging from its nail in my laboratory, the key to the capernaum!'

The apothecary gave this name to a private room, under the roof, full of the implements and wares of his profession. He would often spend long hours there alone, labelling, decanting, retying; and he considered it not as a simple store-room, but as a veritable sanctuary, whence burst forth afterwards, wrought by his hands, all kinds of pill, bolus, tisane, lotion and potion, which went on spreading his fame through the neighbourhood. Nobody alive set foot there; and he revered it so intensely, that he swept it out himself. In short, if the pharmacy, open to all-comers, was the place where he displayed his pride, the capernaum was the retreat where, selfishly retiring, Homais delighted in practising his predilections; in addition, Justin's thoughtlessness appeared to him a monstrous irreverence; and, turning redder than the currants, he repeated:

'Yes, of the capernaum! The key which locks away the acids and the caustic alkalis! To go and get a store-room basin! A basin with a lid! And which I may never perhaps make use of. Everything is of consequence in the delicate operations of our art. But what the devil! One has to maintain distinctions and not employ for virtually domestic use what is intended for pharmaceutics! It's like carving a fat pullet with a scalpel, like a magistrate . . .'

'Do calm down!' said Madame Homais.

And Athalie, tugging him by his frock coat:

'Papa! Papa!'

'No, leave me!' continued the apothecary, 'leave me! The deuce! One might as well set up as a grocer, I swear to you! Go on, off with you! Respect nothing! Break it, smash it! Let the leeches out! Burn the marsh-mallow! Pickle the gherkins in the specimen jars! Tear up the bandages!'

'You did however . . .' said Emma.

'In a moment! Do you know what you were exposing yourself to? Did you not see anything, in the corner, on the left, on the third shelf? Speak, answer, articulate something!'

'I . . . don't know,' stammered the young lad.

'Ah! You don't know! Well, I know, for one! You saw a bottle, of blue glass, sealed with yellow wax, which contains a white powder, on which I had even written: *Dangerous!* And do you know what there was inside? Arsenic! And you're about to meddle with that! To take down a basin next to it!'

'Next to it!' exclaimed Madame Homais, clasping her hands. 'Arsenic? You could have poisoned us all!'

And the children began to cry out, as if they had already felt exquisite pains in their bowels.

'Or else poison a patient!' continued the apothecary. 'So you want me to end up in dock, in the court of assize? To see me dragged to the scaffold? Are you unaware of the care I take in handling these materials, even though I am so tremendously used to it? I often terrify myself, when I think of my responsibility. For the government persecutes us, and the absurd legislation which rules us is like a veritable sword of Damocles hanging over our heads!'

Emma no longer considered asking what they wanted of her, and the pharmacist went on in breathless sentences:

'This is how you recognise the kindnesses we've shown to you! This is how you reward me for the entirely paternal attentions I've lavished on you! Without me, where would you be? What would you be doing? Who supplies you with food, education, clothing, and all the means by which to cut an honourable figure one day, in society's ranks! But, for that, one has to toil at the oars, and gain, as the saying goes, from blistered hands, *Fabricando fit faber, age quod agis.*[9]

He quoted Latin, he was so exasperated. He would have quoted Chinese or Greenlandese, if he had known these two languages; for he was undergoing one of those crises by which the whole mind gives up hints of what it conceals, like the ocean, which, in a storm, parts from the sea-wrack of its shore to the sand of its unfathomable depths.

And he went on:

'I am beginning to rue, with a vengeance, having burdened myself with your person. I would have done better to have left you in the filth in which you were born. All you'll ever be good for is herding horned cattle. You've no talent for the sciences. You scarcely know how to stick a label! And you live there, in my house, like an honorary canon, like a cow in clover, pampering yourself!'

But Emma, turning towards Madame Homais:

'I was sent for . . .'

'Ah, dear God!' the good woman interrupted with a sad air, 'how should I put it to you exactly? It's a tragedy!'

She did not finish. The apothecary thundered:

'Empty it! Scour it! Take it back! Look sharp now!'

And, shaking Justin by the collar of his cotton smock, he caused a book to fall out of his pocket.

The child stooped down. Homais was quicker, and, having picked the volume up, he gazed upon it, eyes wide, jaw dropped.

'*Conjugal . . . Love!*'[10] he said, slowly separating these two words. 'Ah! Very fine. Very fine. Very pretty. And engravings . . . ! Ah, that's too much!'

Madame Homais came forward.

'No! Don't touch it!'

The children wanted to see the pictures.

'Leave!' he said imperiously

And they left.

He walked up and down at first, in long strides, keeping the volume open in his hands, rolling his eyes, choked, swollen-faced, apoplectic. Then he came straight up to his pupil, and, planting himself in front of him with arms crossed:

'So you've every vice then, little wretch . . . ? Take care, you're on the slippery slope . . . ! So you never considered that this, this infamous book, might have fallen into the hands of my children, striking a spark in their brains, tarnishing the purity of Athalie, corrupting Napoléon! He is already formed like a man. Are you certain, at least, that they haven't read it? Can you assure me . . . ?'

'But, Monsieur,' said Emma, 'you had something to tell me?'

'True enough, Madame . . . Your father-in-law is dead!'

In fact, Père Bovary had expired just two days before, quite suddenly, from an apoplectic stroke, getting up from the table; and, out of excessive care for Emma's feelings, Charles had begged Monsieur Homais to apprise her gently of this horrid news.

He had pondered over his sentence, he had smoothed it, polished it, given it a certain rhythm; it was a masterpiece of discretion and transition, of fine turns of style, of fastidiousness; but rage had swept away the rhetoric.

Emma, giving up the idea of getting any details, left the pharmacy; for Monsieur Homais had once more resumed his vituperative flow. He calmed down, however, and was now grumbling on in a fatherly tone, all the while fanning himself with his bonnet-grec:

'It's not that I disapprove entirely of the work. The author was a doctor. It includes certain scientific aspects that it would not be amiss for a man to know and, dare I say it, that a man must know. But later, later! At least wait until you're a man and your character is established.'

On Emma's hammering at the door, Charles, who was waiting for her, came forward with arms spread and said to her in a tearful voice:

'Ah, my dearest . . .'

And he bowed softly to kiss her. But, at the touch of his lips, she was gripped by the memory of the other, and she passed her hand over her face, shuddering.

Nevertheless she replied:

'Yes, I know . . . I know . . .'

He showed her the letter in which his mother recounted the news, without any sentimental hypocrisy. She merely regretted that her husband had not received the succour of religion, having died in Doudeville, in the street, on the threshold of a café, after a patriotic meal with former officers.

Emma returned the letter; then, over dinner, out of decency, she feigned a brief loss of appetite. But as he kept on obliging her, she resolutely set about eating, while Charles, opposite, sat motionless, looking crushed.

From time to time, raising his head, he cast her a long glance full of anguish. Once he sighed:

'I would have liked to see him once more.'

She remained silent. At length, realising that she had to speak:

'How old was he? Your father?'

'Fifty-eight!'

'Ah.'

And that was all.

A quarter of an hour later, he added:

'My poor mother . . . What will become of her, now?'

She gestured that she did not know.

Seeing her so taciturn, Charles inferred she was distressed and forced himself to say nothing, so as not to heighten this grief affecting her. Nevertheless, shaking off his own:

'You had good fun yesterday?' he asked.

'Yes.'

When the table-cloth was removed, Bovary did not stand up, neither did Emma; and, as she considered him, the dreariness of the sight progressively banished all pity from her heart. He seemed to her paltry, weak, useless, in short a wretched man, in every way. How to get rid of him? What an interminable evening! Something stupefying like an opium haze benumbed her.

They heard in the hall the hard sound of a stick on the floorboards. It was Hippolyte bringing Madame's luggage. To put it down, he laboriously described a half-circle with his wooden leg.

'He doesn't even think of it any longer,' she said to herself as she watched the poor devil, his thick red hair dripping with sweat.

Bovary searched for a tiny coin in the bottom of his purse; and, without appearing to take in what humiliation there was for him in the mere presence of this man standing there, the personified reproach of his incurable ineptitude:

'Here, you've a pretty bouquet,' he said, noticing Léon's violets on the chimney-piece.

'Yes,' she said indifferently; 'it's a bouquet I bought just now . . . from a beggar-woman.'

Charles took the violets, and, refreshing his tear-reddened eyes on them, he delicately inhaled their scent. She took them quickly from his hand, and went off to put them in a glass of water.

The next day, Madame Bovary senior arrived. She and her son cried a lot. Emma, under the pretext of giving orders, disappeared.

The day after, they had to see to the mourning arrangements together. They went to sit down, with the work-boxes, by the river, under the arbour.

Charles thought about his father, and he marvelled at feeling so much affection for this man whom he had believed he loved only very middlingly up till now. Madame Bovary senior thought about her husband. The worst times of the old days appeared desirable to her again. Everything was obliterated beneath the instinctive regret of so long a habit; and, now and again, while she plied her needle, a fat tear descended the length of her nose and remained hanging there a moment. Emma thought how not even forty-eight hours ago, they were together, far from the world, heady with ecstasy, and eyes not wide enough to gaze their fill of one another. She strove to seize again the least perceptible details of that vanished day. But the presence of mother-in-law and husband cramped her. She would have liked to hear nothing, see nothing, so as not to disturb the contemplation of her love which would disappear, whatever she did, beneath external impressions.

She was unstitching the lining of a dress, whose scraps lay scattered about her; Mère Bovary, without looking up, kept making her scissors squeal, and Charles, with his list slippers and his old brown frock-coat that served as a dressing gown, kept his hands in his pockets and likewise did not speak; near them, Berthe, in a little white apron, was scraping the sand on the path with her spade.

Suddenly, they saw Monsieur Lheureux, the cloth-dealer, enter by the gate.

He was come to offer his services, *regardful of the fatal circumstance*. Emma replied that she thought she could manage without. The dealer did not consider himself beaten.

'A thousand apologies,' he said; 'I wish to have a private chat.'

Then, in a low voice:

'It's with reference to this business . . . you know?'

Charles turned scarlet to the ear-lobes.

'Ah yes . . . indeed.'

And, in his confusion, turning to his wife:

'Couldn't you . . . my dearest . . . ?'

She appeared to understand him, for she rose, and Charles said to his mother:

'It's nothing. Doubtless some domestic trifle.'

He did not want her to know about the bill business, dreading her comments.

As soon as they were alone, Monsieur Lheureux began, in fairly clear terms, to congratulate Emma on her inheritance, then to chat of unimportant things, the espaliers, the harvest and his own health, which was *middling as ever, neither foul nor fair*. Indeed, he was taking the devil's-own pains, although he did not have the simple wherewithal, despite folk's tattle, to put butter on his bread.

Emma let him talk. The last two days had been so prodigiously weary!

'And here you are altogether recovered?' he continued. 'My word, I saw your poor husband in a nice mess. He's a valiant fellow, even though we've had our difficulties together.'

She asked which ones, as Charles had concealed from her the dispute over the supplies.

'But you know all about it,' said Lheureux. 'It was for your little fancies, the travelling cases.'

He had lowered his hat over his eyes, and, hands behind his back, smiling and wheezing, he looked straight at her, in an insufferable manner. Did he suspect something? She was left plunged in all kinds of fears. In the end, however, he went on:

'We have made it up, and I've just proposed a further settlement.'

It was to renew the bill signed by Bovary. Monsieur, however, would proceed as he thought best; he must not go tormenting himself, above all now that he was going to have a swarm of money worries.

'And what's more it would be better to entrust them to someone, to you, for example; with a power of attorney, that would be comfortable, and then we could do a little business together . . .'

She did not understand. He held his tongue. Then, switching to matters of trade, Lheureux declared that Madame could not avoid purchasing something from him. He would send her twelve metres of black barège wool, from which to make a dress.

'What you have there is fine when you're at home. You need another one for calls. I saw that straight off when I came in, I did. I keep my eyes peeled.'

He did not send her the cloth, he brought it round. Then he returned for the measurements; he returned on further pretexts, endeavouring each time to make himself agreeable, serviceable, enfeoffing himself, as Homais would have said, and forever slipping Emma some piece of advice about power of attorney. He did not bring up the bill. She did not consider it; Charles, at the beginning of her convalescence, had certainly told her some story about it; but her mind had been so tossed about since, that she no longer had any recollection. In addition to which, she was careful not to start any discussion about money; Mère Bovary was surprised, and attributed her change of mood to the religious feelings she had contracted when ill.

But, as soon as she had left, Emma lost no time in amazing Bovary with her practical good sense. They would have to make inquiries, examine the mortgages, see if a co-proprietorial sale or settlement had taken place. She cited technical terms, at random, talked big words about order, prospects, foresight, and continually exaggerated the intricacies of the inheritance; so skilfully that one day she showed him the proof of a general authorisation 'to manage and administer his affairs, carry out all borrowings, sign and endorse all bills, pay all sums, etc.' She had benefited from Lheureux's lessons.

Charles asked her, naively, where this paper came from.

'From Monsieur Guillaumin.'

And, with the utmost cool, she added:

'I don't trust him too much. Solicitors have such a bad reputation. Perhaps we need to take advice . . . We know only . . . Oh, nobody!'

'Unless Léon . . .' replied Charles, ruminating.

But it was hard to make arrangements by correspondence. So she offered to make the trip herself. He declined the offer. She insisted. It was a fencing-match of considerateness. Finally, she cried out in an artificially mutinous tone:

'No, I beg you, I am going.'

'How good you are!' he said, kissing her forehead.

The very next day, she embarked on the *Hirondelle* to go to Rouen and seek the opinion of Monsieur Léon; and she stayed there three days.

III

THEY WERE THREE FULL, EXQUISITE, sumptuous days, a true honeymoon.

They were at the *Hôtel de Boulogne*, on the quay. And they lived there, shutters shut, doors closed, with flowers on the floor and iced syrups, that they were brought first thing in the morning.

Towards evening, they would take a covered boat and go off to dine on an island.

It was the time of day when you hear, along the dock-side, the echoing of the calkers' mallets against the ships' hulls. The smoke from the tar crept away though the trees, and large greasy drops were to be seen on the river, rippling unevenly under the sun's purple colouring, like floating plaques of Florentine bronze.

They sailed down between moored barks, whose long oblique cables just grazed the boat's keel.

The noises of the city imperceptibly withdrew, the rolling of carts, the din of voices, the yelping of dogs on the ships' decks. She untied her hat and they landed at their island.

They took a seat in the low-ceilinged room of an ale-house, which had black nets draped at its door. They ate fried sprats, cream and cherries. They lay down on the grass; they embraced one another in a secluded spot under the poplars; and, like two castaways, they wished to live forever in this little place, which seemed to them, in their bliss, the most magnificent on earth. It was not the first time they had observed trees, blue sky, turf, that they had heard water gliding and a breeze whispering in the leaves; but they had doubtless never wondered at it all, as if Nature had not existed until now, or had only begun to be lovely since the glutting of their desires.

At nightfall, they would set off again. The bark followed the edge of the islands. They lay at one end, both of them concealed in the shadows, without speaking. The square oars rang between the iron tholes, and this marked the silence like the beating of a metronome, while from the stern the hawser would not leave off its soft little plashing as it trailed through the water.

Once, the moon appeared; then they made sure to use flowery phrases, finding the celestial body melancholy and full of poetry; she even began to sing:

One evening, do you remember? We sailed, etc.[11]

Her thin and melodious voice lost itself on the waters; and the wind bore away the roulades that he heard passing around him like the fluttering of wings.

She sat opposite, leaning against the long-boat's partition, the moon stealing in by one of its open shutters. Her black dress, whose draperies spread out in a fan shape, made her thinner, taller. She was looking up, her hands clasped and her gaze skywards. Sometimes the shadows of the willows would wholly hide her, then she would reappear all of a sudden, like a vision, in the moonlight.

Léon, on the deck next to her, found a flame-coloured silk ribbon beneath his hand.

The boatman examined it and said finally:

'Ah, it's maybe from that party I took out the other day. A load of jolly jokers they were, gents and ladies, with cakes, champagne, cornets, the whole shakes! There was one especially, a tall handsome fellow, thin moustache, good fun he was! And they said like so: "Come on, tell us a good story . . . Adolphe . . . Dodolphe . . . I think."'

She shuddered.

'You're not well?' said Léon, drawing nearer to her.

'Oh, it's nothing. The coolness of the night, no doubt.'

'And who can't be lacking for women, neither,' the old sailor softly added, thinking he was being polite to the stranger.

Then, spitting on his hands, he took up the oars once more.

And yet they had to part! The farewell was painful. He must send his letters to Mère Rolet's house; and she gave him such precise advice concerning the double envelope, that he greatly admired her lover's guile.

'In this way, you'll assure me that all's well?'

'Yes, of course!' But then why, he reflected afterwards as he returned alone through the streets, did she care so much about this power of attorney?

IV

BEFORE LONG, LÉON ADOPTED A superior air in front of his friends, abstained from their company, and totally neglected his case papers.

He awaited her letters; he reread them. He wrote to her. He called her to mind with all the force of his memories and his desire. Instead of lessening with absence, this longing to see her again increased, so much so that one Saturday morning he slipped away from the practice.

When, from the hill's height, he descried down in the valley the church tower with its tin flag turning in the wind, he felt that same delight mingled with triumphant vanity and selfish emotion that millionaires must have, when they come back to visit their village.

He went to prowl about her house. A light shone in the kitchen. He looked out for her shadow behind the curtains. Nothing appeared.

On seeing him, Mère Lefrançois made a great fuss, and she found him 'taller and thinner', whereas Artémise, on the contrary, found him 'broader and darker'.

He dined in the parlour, as before, but alone, without the tax-gatherer; for Binet, *weary* of waiting for the *Hirondelle*, had definitively brought forward his meal by an hour, and now he dined at precisely five o'clock, still claiming more often than not that *the old gimcrack was late*.

Léon nevertheless made up his mind; he went to knock on the doctor's door. Madame was in her room, from which she only came down a quarter of an hour later. Monsieur seemed delighted to see him again; but he stayed put the whole evening, and the entire day following.

He saw her alone, very late at night, behind the garden, in the lane – in the lane, as with the other! It was stormy, and they chatted under an umbrella in the glimmer of lightning.

Their leavetaking became unbearable.

'It is better to die!' said Emma.

She writhed on his arm, crying all the while.

'Farewell . . . ! Farewell . . . ! When will I see you again?'

They retraced their steps to kiss once more; and it was then that she made him promise to find, by whatever means and soon, a permanent opportunity to see each other freely, at least once a week. Emma did not doubt it. She was, moreover, full of hope. Money would be coming to her.

Then, she bought for her room a pair of broad-striped, yellow curtains, whose cheapness Monsieur Lheureux had extolled to her; she longed for a carpet, and Lheureux, asserting 'that it was not asking the impossible', politely pledged to supply her one. She could no longer do without his services. Twenty times a day she would send for him, and straightaway he would set out his bargains there, without so much as a murmur. One no more understood why Mère Rolet dined at Emma's every day, and even called upon her privately.

It was at about this period, that is to say near the beginning of winter, when she appeared to be gripped by a great fervour for music.

One evening when Charles was listening to her, she started the same piece again four times running, and each time getting into a fret, while, not noticing any difference, he would cry out:

'Bravo . . . ! Very good . . . ! You're mistaken! Carry on now!'

'No! It's atrocious. My fingers are rusty.'

The next day, he begged her *to play him something more*.

'Oh very well, just to please you.'

And Charles admitted that she had got out of practice. She mistook her place on the stave, slurred the notes; then, abruptly stopping:

'Oh, that's enough. I need to take lessons; but . . .'

She chewed her lip and added:

'Twenty francs for a private lesson, that's too dear.'

'Yes, indeed . . . a little . . .' said Charles, with a silly snigger. 'Still, it seems to me that we could maybe do it for less; as there are players of no repute who are often better than the famous ones.'

'Look for them,' said Emma.

The next day, on his return, he gave her a sly look, and was unable in the end to hold back these words:

'How stubborn you are at times! I was in Barfeuchères today. Well, Madame Liégeard assured me that her three daughters, who are at the Miséricorde, were having lessons for fifty sous the session, and from a famous teacher besides.'

She shrugged, and did not open her instrument again.

But, when she went near it (if Bovary chanced to be there), she would sigh:

'Ah, my poor piano!'

And when you visited her, she was sure to let you know that she had abandoned music and could not take it up again, for important reasons. So she was pitied. What a shame, she with such a fine talent! Bovary was even talked to about it. He was made to feel ashamed, and above all by the pharmacist.

'You are mistaken. Nature's abilities must never be left to lie fallow. Moreover, consider, my good friend, that in obliging Madame to practise music, you economise later on the musical education of your child. I for one deem that mothers themselves should instruct their children. It's a notion of Rousseau's, perhaps still a little new, but which will triumph in the end, I am sure of it, like mothers giving suck and like vaccination.'

So Charles returned once more to this piano question. Emma replied churlishly that it would be best to sell it. This poor piano, which had given him so much vainglorious satisfaction, to see it go off, would have been for Bovary like watching the indefinable suicide of a part of herself!

'If you want . . .' he said, 'from time to time, a single lesson, that might not, after all, be exceedingly ruinous.'

'But lessons,' she retorted, 'are only any use when regular.'

And that is how she set about procuring permission from her husband to go to town, once a week, to see her lover. They even reckoned, after one month, that she had made considerable progress.

V

I T WAS THURSDAY. SHE ROSE, and she dressed silently so as not to wake Charles, who would have pointed out that she was getting ready too early. Then she walked up and down; she stood in front of the windows, she gazed down at the village square. The faint light of day would be creeping between the pillars of the market-place, and the apothecary's house, whose shutters were closed, showed a glimpse of its sign's capital letters in the wan colours of dawn.

When the clock chimed a quarter past seven, she set off for the *Lion d'Or*, whose door had just been opened by a yawning Artémise. The latter was digging out the embers buried under the ashes. Emma stayed on her own in the kitchen. From time to time, she would go out. Hivert was unhurriedly putting the horses to, and listening moreover to Mère Lefrançois, who, slipping her cotton-bonneted head through a hatch, was burdening him with errands along with explanations that would have muddled any other man. Emma tapped the sole of her boots against the yard's paving.

At last, once he had eaten his soup, donned his long woollen cape, lit his pipe and gripped his horse-whip, he settled himself calmly on his seat.

The *Hirondelle* set off at a gentle trot, and, for the first couple of miles, would stop here and there to take on passengers, who would stand on the side of the road by their gates, looking out for it. Those who had let the driver know the day before had him wait; several were still actually abed in their houses; Hivert would call, shout, fling curses, then climb down from his seat, to go and thump on the doors. The wind blew through the cracked casement windows.

Nevertheless the four benches filled, the carriage rolled on, the rows of apple-trees followed one upon another; and the road, between its two long ditches brimming with yellow water, went on ever narrowing towards the horizon.

Emma knew it from one end to the other; she knew that after a meadow there would be a post, then an elm, a barn or a road-labourer's hut; sometimes, to surprise herself, she even closed her eyes. But she would never lose the clear sense of the distance left to run.

At last, the brick houses drew near, the ground rang under the wheels, the *Hirondelle* glided between gardens in which, through an opening in the wall, statues, an ornamental hillock, pruned yews and a swing seat were discernible. Then, at a single glance, the town would appear.

Descending just like an amphitheatre and drowned in the fog, it spread confusedly beyond the bridges. The open countryside then rose in a monotonous rise and fall, until it touched in the distance the sky's pale wavering base. Thus viewed from on high, the entire landscape had the motionless look of a painting; the ships at anchor were bunched in one corner; the river rounded off its curve at the foot of the green hills, and the islands, oblong-shaped, looked like great black fish stilled on the water. The factory chimneys were sprouting immense brown plumes which blew away at the tips. The roaring of the foundries could be heard against the clear pealing of bells from the churches poking up through the mist. The boulevards' trees, leafless, formed a violet brushwood amidst the houses, and the rooves, all glittery with rain, shimmered unevenly, according to the height of the district. Occasionally a gust of wind would bear the clouds away towards Sainte-Catherine hill, like airy billows shattering silently against a cliff.

Something emanated from these packed lives that made her giddy, and her heart would swell with abundance, as if the hundred and twenty thousand souls throbbing there had all sent out to her at once the heady fumes of passion that she imagined they felt. Her love would expand with the space, and fill with tumult from the distant hum coming up. She poured it forth again outside, on the squares, on the walks, on the streets, and the old Norman city sprawled before her gaze like an enormous capital, like a Babylon she was entering into. She leaned on two hands out of the window, breathing in the breeze; the three horses galloped, the stones grated in the mud, the stagecoach rocked, and Hivert, from afar, hailed the carts on the road, while the townsfolk who had spent the night in the Bois Guillaume came peacefully down the hill, in their little family carriages.

They stopped at the gate; Emma unbuckled her overshoes, donned other gloves, rearranged her shawl, and, twenty paces further on, she alighted from the *Hirondelle*.

The town would be stirring then. Shop-boys, in bonnet-grecs, rubbed down the shop-fronts, and women on street corners, with baskets on their hips, would now and again give a high cry. She walked with eyes down, brushing the walls, and smiling with pleasure under her lowered black veil.

For fear of being seen, she did not usually take the shortest route. She would dive into gloomy streets, and arrive bathed in sweat near the lower end of the rue Nationale, by the fountain there. This is the area known for its theatre, taverns and girls. Often a waggon would pass close to her, carrying some quivering piece of scenery. Aproned waiters would throw sand on the flagstones, between green shrubs. There was a smell of absinthe, cigars and oysters.

She turned down a street; she recognised him by his curly hair which poked out from his hat.

Léon, on the pavement, would continue walking. She followed him to the hotel; he climbed the stairs, he opened the door, he went in . . . What clasping!

Then, after the kisses, the words would come in a rush. They told each other of the week's sorrows, the misgivings, the uneasiness over the letters; but now all was forgotten, and they would gaze at each other face to face, with voluptuous giggles and fond names.

The bed was a large mahogany bed shaped like a skiff. The red silk drapes, falling from the ceiling, were gathered in too low over the broad bolster – and nothing in the world was as lovely as her dark head and white skin standing out against that crimson colour, when, in a gesture of modesty, she would draw her naked arms together, burying her face in her hands.

The warm apartment, with its discreet carpet, its frolicsome ornaments and calm light, seemed entirely suited to the intimacies of passion. If the sun penetrated, then the curtains' spear-headed rods, brass tie-backs and the great balls of the firedogs would glitter all of a sudden. On the chimneypiece, between the candelabra, there were two of those big pink conch-shells in which the sound of the sea can be heard when you put them to your ear.

How they loved that simple room, cheerful despite its somewhat faded splendour! They always found the furniture in the same position, and the occasional hair-pin that she had forgotten, on a previous Thursday, under the base of the clock. They would have a fireside breakfast, on a little round table inlaid with rosewood. Emma carved, laid the morsels on his plate while babbling all sorts of kittenish things;

and she laughed a high and licentious laugh when the froth from the champagne overflowed the slender glass onto the rings on her fingers. So completely lost were they in possession of each other, they believed themselves to be in their very own house, living there to the end of their days, like an ever-youthful husband and wife. They would say 'our' bedroom, 'our' carpet, 'our' chairs, she even said 'my' slippers, a present from Léon, a whim she had had. These were slippers of pink satin, trimmed with swansdown. When she sat on his knees, her leg, now too short, swung in the air; and the delicate shoe, which had no heel-strap, clung on only by the toes to her bare foot.

He savoured for the first time the inexpressible refinement of feminine elegance. Never had he encountered such gracefulness of language, such coyness in dress, such drowsy, dove-like postures. He admired the exaltation of her soul and the lacework of her skirt. Moreover, was she not a woman of the world, and a married woman! A true mistress, in short?

Through the variety of her mood, by turns mystical or joyous, chattering, reserved, carried away, listless, she would recall to him a thousand desires, conjuring up instincts or recollections. She was the lover from every novel, the heroine of every play, the vague *she* of every book of verse. He would recognise on her shoulders the amber colour of *the odalisque bathing*;[12] she had the elongated body of feudal chatelaines; she also resembled *the pale woman of Barcelona*, but above all she was wholly Angel!

Often, when gazing at her, it seemed to him that his soul, escaping towards her, spread like a wave over the curve of her head, to be dragged down into her breast's whiteness.

He would fall at her feet; and, his elbows on her knees, he would contemplate her with a smile, his brow taut.

She would lean towards him and murmur, as if elation had taken her breath away:

'Oh! Don't move! Don't speak! Look at me! Something so soft is coming from your eyes, which does me so much good!'

She would call him 'child':

'Child, do you love me?'

And she would scarcely catch his answer, in the rush of her lips up to his mouth.

There was a little bronze Cupid on the clock, mincing as it rounded its arms below a gilded wreath. They laughed at it many times; but, when the time came to part, everything seemed serious.

Motionless, facing one another, they would repeat:

'Till Thursday! Till Thursday!'

All of a sudden she would take his head in her hands, kiss him swiftly on the forehead and, crying out 'Farewell!', would dash down the stairs.

She would go to the rue de la Comédie, to a hairdresser's, to have her bandeaux[13] put to rights. Night fell: they lit the gas-lights in the shop.

She heard the theatre hand-bell calling the strolling players to the performance; and she saw, opposite, men with white faces and women in faded dress go by, entering by the stage door.

It was hot in this little low-ceilinged room, its stove humming amidst wigs and pomades. It was not long before the odour of the curling-irons, with those greasy hands touching her head, began to make her dizzy, and she slept a little under her gown. The boy, while dressing her hair, would frequently offer her tickets for the masked ball.

Then she would be off! She would retrace her steps along the streets; arrive at the *Croix Rouge*; retrieve her overshoes, which she had hidden that morning under a bench, and settle in her place among the impatient travellers. Several alighted at the foot of the hill. She remained on her own in the carriage.

At each turn of the road, all the lights of the city became more and more visible, making a great luminous vapour over the huddled houses. Emma kneeled on the cushions, and blinded herself with the dazzle. She sobbed, called out Léon's name, and sent him loving words and kisses that were whirled away on the wind.

There was a poor devil on the hill, roaming about with his staff, right in among the stagecoaches. A pile of rags covered his shoulders, and his face was concealed by an old stove-in beaver hat, rounded like a bowl; but, when he took it off, he exposed, where the eyelids should be, two bloodied and gaping sockets. The flesh ravelled out into red tatters; and fluids trickled to stiffen into green scabs down to the nose, its black nostrils sniffing convulsively. To speak to you, he would throw back his head with an idiot laugh – then his blueish eyeballs, constantly rolling up towards the temples, would proceed to knock against the rim of the open sore.

He sang a little song as he followed the carriages:

> *A fair day's heat does often move*
> *The thoughts of some young lass to love.*[14]

And the rest was all birds, sun and leafage.

Sometimes, he would appear behind Emma quite suddenly, bareheaded. She would draw back with a cry. Hivert would proceed to joke with him. He urged him to rent a booth at the Saint-Romain fair, or else asked him, laughing, how fared his sweetheart.

Often, when they were on their way, his hat, with an abrupt movement, would poke through the carriage-blind into the coach, while he clung, with the other arm, to the foot-board, between the mud-splash of the wheels. His voice, feeble at first and wailing, grew shrill. It lingered in the night, like the indistinct lamentation of a dim distress; and, through the jingling of the harness bells, the murmur of the trees and the drone of the hollow box, it had something faraway about it that troubled Emma. Down it went into the depths of her soul like a whirlpool in an abyss, sweeping her off amid the spaces of a limitless melancholy. But Hivert, aware of a shift in weight, would deal the blind man fierce blows with his whip. The lash stung against his sores, and he would fall howling into the mud.

Then the passengers on the *Hirondelle* would end up going to sleep, some with mouth open, others with chin lowered, resting on their neighbour's shoulder, or else with an arm slipped through the leather strap, swinging steadily to the motion of the carriage; and the lamp's reflection rocking outside, on the rumps of the shaft-horses, penetrating the interior through the chocolate-coloured calico of the curtains, laid ruddy shadows on all these motionless individuals. Emma, drunk with sadness, shivered with cold in her clothes; and her feet would grow colder and colder, as she inwardly grieved.

Charles was waiting for her, back at the house; the *Hirondelle* was always late on Thursdays. Madame was here at last! Although she hardly kissed the little one. Dinner was not ready, no matter! She forgave the cook. All seemed permitted to this girl.

Often her husband, noting her pallor, would ask her if she was not ill.

'No,' said Emma.

'But,' he answered, 'you are odd tonight . . .'

'Oh, it is nothing, nothing!'

There were even some days when, scarcely returned, she went up to her room; and Justin, happening to be there, padded silently about, more skilful at serving her than a superior lady-in-waiting. He set out the matches, the candlestick, a book, arranged her night-dress, turned back the sheets.

'Come,' she would say, 'that will do, be off now!'

For he would remain standing, hands dangling and eyes wide open, as if entangled in the innumerable threads of a sudden daydream.

The day after was dreadful, and those following were made even more intolerable by Emma's longing to seize her happiness once more – an ardent lustfulness, inflamed by familiar images, and which, on the seventh day, burst with such ease under Léon's fondlings. His own burning heat was half-hidden under effusions of wonder and gratitude. Emma tasted this passion in a discreet and absorbed manner, kept it alive with all the guile of her soft caresses, and trembled a little lest it be lost later.

Often she would say, with the soft voice of melancholy:

'Ah, you'll leave me, you will. You'll marry! You'll be just like the others.'

He would ask:

'What others?'

'Why men, in short,' she replied.

Then, pushing him off with a languorous gesture, she would add:

'Vile wretches, all of you.'

One day when they were chatting philosophically of earthly disillusions, she happened to say (testing his jealousy or perhaps yielding to an over-powerful desire to unburden herself) that in times past, before him, she had loved someone, 'not like you!' she hastily resumed, protesting on her daughter's life *that nothing had happened!*

The young man believed her, and asked her questions nevertheless to find out what it was *he* did.

'He was a ship's captain, my darling.'

Was this not to hinder further inquiry, and at the same time set herself on a truly elevated level, through a feigned fascination for a man who ought by nature to be warlike and accustomed to respect?

So the clerk felt the lowliness of his position; he desired epaulettes, orders, titles. All that sort of thing must please her: he suspected it from her expensive habits.

Nevertheless Emma kept quiet about a host of her extravagances, such as the desire to have a blue tilbury to take her to Rouen, drawn by an English horse, and driven by a groom in top-boots. It was Justin who had prompted this whim in her, by begging her to take him on in the house as a footman; and, if this privation did not dilute, at each assignation, the pleasure of arrival, it certainly increased the bitterness of return.

Frequently when they talked to one another about Paris, she would finish by murmuring:

'Ah, how good things would be for us, living there!'

'Are we not happy?' the young man softly chided, smoothing the sides of her hair with his hand.

'Yes, that is true,' she said, 'I'm mad; kiss me.'

For her husband she was more charming than ever, making him pistachio-creams and playing waltzes after dinner. He reckoned himself the luckiest of mortals, and Emma lived free from anxiety, when one evening, all of a sudden:

'It is Mademoiselle Lempereur who gives you lessons, isn't it?'

'Yes.'

'Well, I saw her just now,' Charles went on, 'at Madame Liégard's. I spoke of you to her; she'd no knowledge of you.'

It was like a lightning-bolt. Nevertheless she answered with a genial air:

'Oh. No doubt she forgot my name?'

'Perhaps there are,' said the doctor, 'several young ladies in Rouen who go by the name of Lempereur and are piano teachers?'

'Quite possible.'

Then, sharply:

'Yet I have her receipts, here, look!'

And she went to the writing-table, rummaged through all the drawers, muddled the papers and ended by losing her head so completely, that Charles strongly urged her not to give herself so much trouble over these wretched receipts.

'Oh, I shall find them,' she said.

Indeed, the very next Friday, Charles, placing one of his boots in the dark closet where his clothes were put away, felt a sheet of paper between the leather and his sock, took it out and read:

'Received, for three months of lessons, plus various materials, the sum of sixty-five francs. FELICIE LEMPEREUR, music teacher.'

'How the devil did it get into my boots?'

'No doubt,' she replied, 'it fell out of the old bill box, which is on the edge of the shelf.'

From that moment on, her existence was no more than a jumble of lies, in which she would shroud her love as if with veils, to conceal it.

This was a need, a mania, a pleasure, to the extent that if she said that yesterday she had gone down a street on the right-hand side, you would have to believe that she had taken the left-hand side.

One morning when she had just set out, as usual, rather lightly dressed, there was a sudden fall of snow; and as Charles was checking the weather through the window, he spotted Monsieur Bournisien in Monsieur Tuvache's gig, being driven to Rouen. So he went down to entrust the cleric with a large shawl to give to Madame, as soon as he arrived at the *Croix Rouge*. No sooner was he at the inn than Bournisien asked for the whereabouts of the Yonville doctor's wife. The landlady replied that she very seldom frequented her establishment. Then, that evening, on recognising Madame Bovary in the *Hirondelle*, the priest recounted his embarrassment to her, without appearing, however, to attach any importance thereby; for he began to sing the praises of a preacher who was working wonders in the cathedral at that time, and whom all the women were hastening to hear.

Never mind that he had not asked for an explanation, others might prove less discreet later on. She also judged it useful to alight each time at the *Croix Rouge*, so that the good folk of the village who saw her on the stairs would suspect nothing.

Yet the day came when Monsieur Lheureux met her leaving the Hôtel de Boulogne on Léon's arm; and she was fearful, imagining that he would blab. He was not so stupid.

But three days later, he came into her room, shut the door and said: 'I shall need money.'

She declared that she could not give him any. Lheureux burst into a groan, and recalled how indulgent he had been.

In fact, of the two bills signed by Charles, Emma had only paid one of them up until now. As for the second, the dealer, at her entreaty, had agreed to replace it with two others, which had even been renewed on a very long expiry date. Then he pulled from his pocket a list of unpaid supplies, viz.: the curtains, the carpet, the cloth for the chairs, several gowns and sundry dressing items for her toilette, whose value came to the sum of about two thousand francs.

She lowered her head; he went on:

'But, if you don't have hard cash, you have *property*.'

And he indicated a wretched hovel situated in Barneville, near Aumale, which yielded nothing much. This was once a dependency of a little farm sold by Père Bovary, for Lheureux knew everything, down to the number of hectares, along with the neighbours' names.

'If I were in your shoes,' he said, 'I would clear my debts, and I'd still have what was left over.'

She argued that it would be hard to find a purchaser; he gave her hope of finding one; but she asked how she might go about selling it.

'Don't you have the power of attorney?' he replied.

This term reached her like a puff of fresh air.

'Leave me the bill,' said Emma.

'Oh, it's not worth the trouble,' answered Lheureux.

He returned the following week, and boasted of having finally unearthed, after many proceedings, a certain Langlois who, for quite a time, had had an eye on the property without naming his price.

'Never mind the price!' she cried.

On the contrary, they must wait, sound the fellow out. The matter was worth the trouble of a journey, and, as she could not make the journey, he offered to go on the spot himself, to make contact with Langlois. On his return, he announced that the purchaser was offering four thousand francs.

Emma's face lit up at the news.

'Frankly,' he added, 'it's a good price.'

She drew on half the amount immediately, and, when she made to settle her bill, the dealer said to her:

'It grieves me, upon my honour, to see you part so promptly with such a *considerable* sum.'

She looked then at the bank notes; and, dreaming of the unlimited number of assignations those two thousand francs represented:

'How? How?' she stammered.

'Oh,' he continued, laughing with a genial air, 'we can put anything we want on the bills. Don't I know a bit about husbands and wives?'

And he gazed at her fixedly, holding in his hand two long documents that he slid between his nails. At length, opening his bill-case, he spread out on the table four promissory notes, for a thousand francs each.

'Sign that for me,' he said, 'and keep everything.'

She cried out, scandalised.

'But, if I'm giving you the surplus,' Monsieur Lheureux brazenly replied, 'is it not to do you, you personally, a service?'

And, taking a pen, he wrote at the bottom of the bill:

Received from Madame Bovary the sum of four thousand francs.

'Why worry, since in six months you can collect the arrears on your hut, and I'm placing your final bill's settlement for after the payment?'

Emma got a little tangled up in his calculations, and her ears rang as if the gold coins, disembowelled from their bags, were clinking all about her on the floor. At length Lheureux explained that he had a friend, Vinçart, a banker in Rouen, who would discount these four notes, then he himself would hand over to Madame the surplus of the actual debt.

But instead of two thousand francs, he brought along only eighteen hundred, as his friend Vinçart (as was *proper*), had deducted two hundred, in commission and discount charges.

Then he casually asked for a receipt.

'You know how it is . . . in business . . . sometimes . . . And the date, please, the date.'

A vista of obtainable extravagances then opened up before Emma. She was prudent enough to place a thousand crowns in reserve, with which the first three bills, when they were due, were paid off; but the fourth, by chance, dropped into the house on a Thursday, and Charles, upset, waited patiently for his wife's return and an explanation.

If she had not made him privy to this bill, it was in order to spare him domestic worries; she sat on his knees, stroked him, cooed, made a long enumeration of all the indispensable things purchased on credit.

'You'll agree that, given the quantity, it's not so expensive, after all.'

Charles, at his wit's end, soon had recourse to the eternal Lheureux, who swore to calm things down, if Monsieur would sign two bills for him, one being for seven hundred francs, payable in three months. To achieve this, he wrote his mother a moving letter. Instead of sending a reply, she came herself; and, when Emma wanted to know if he had got something out of her:

'Yes,' he replied. 'But she demands to see the invoice.'

The next day, at first light, Emma ran to Monsieur Lheureux's house and begged him to write another bill, which would not exceed a thousand francs; for if she were to show the one for four thousand, she would have to say that she had paid two-thirds, consequently admitting to the sale of the property, a transaction the dealer had carried out skilfully, and which would only be known about later.

Despite the very low price of each article, Mère Bovary could not help finding the expense extravagant.

'Could you not have done without a carpet? Why renew the covers on the armchairs? In my day, there was just one armchair, for the old folk – at least, that's how it was at my mother's, who was a respectable lady, I can assure you. It's not given to everyone to be rich. No fortune can hold out against waste. I'd blush to coddle myself as you do! And yet look at me, I'm old, I need care and attention. Here we go, here we go: trickings out, showings off! What's this? Silk for lining, at two francs . . . when you can find jaconet at ten sous and even at eight sous, which would do the business perfectly!'

Emma, lolling on the small sofa, replied as calmly as she could:

'Ah, Madame, enough, enough.'

The other went on lecturing her, predicting that they would finish in the alms-house. Moreover, it was Bovary's fault. Fortunate it was that he had promised to destroy that power of attorney . . .

'What?'

'Oh, he swore to me he would,' continued the good lady.

Emma opened the window, called Charles, and the poor fellow had to acknowledge the promise wrenched from him by his mother.

Emma disappeared, then was swiftly back, majestically tendering her a large sheet of paper.

'Thank you,' said the old lady.

And she threw the power of attorney on the fire.

Emma began to laugh a harsh laugh, loud, going on and on: she was having hysterics.

'Oh, dear God!' cried Charles. 'Well, you're in the wrong, too. It's you who's just worked her up!'

His mother, giving a shrug, maintained that *it was all affectation*.

But Charles, rebelling for the first time, took his wife's side, so much so that Mère Bovary wanted to be off. She left first thing the following day, and on the threshold, as he was trying to keep her back, she replied:

'No, no! You love her more than me, and you are right, it's only natural. For the rest, too bad. You'll see . . . ! Your very good health! . . . because I'm not prepared to come here and work her up, as you put it.'

Charles did not remain a jot less sheepish when it came to Emma, the latter making no effort to conceal the rancour that she reserved for him as a result of his mistrust; a lot of pleading was required before she agreed to resume her power of attorney, and he even accompanied her to Monsieur Guillaumin's to have another drawn up, exactly the same.

'I quite understand,' said the notary; 'a man of science cannot go troubling his head over life's practical details.'

And Charles felt comforted by this wheedling consideration, which gave to his feebleness the flattering guise of a superior preoccupation.

What debauchery, the Thursday following, at the hotel, in their room, with Léon! She laughed, cried, sang, danced, had sorbets brought up, desired to smoke cigarettes, seemed to him wild, but adorable, magnificent.

He did not know what reaction of her entire being was urging her on to rush at life's enjoyments. She became irritable, greedy, and voluptuous; and she walked with him through the streets, head held high, without fear, she said, of compromising herself. Sometimes, however, Emma trembled at the sudden idea of meeting Rodolphe; for it seemed to her, even though they had parted for ever, that she was not entirely freed from her dependency.

One evening, she did not return to Yonville. Charles was out of his wits, and the little Berthe, not wanting to go to bed without her mamma, sobbed fit to burst. Justin had set off aimlessly down the road. Monsieur Homais had left the pharmacy.

Finally, at eleven o'clock, unable to bear it any longer, Charles hitched his gig, leapt in, lashed his beast and arrived at about two o'clock at the *Croix Rouge*. Nobody. He thought that maybe the clerk had seen her; but where did he live? Happily, Charles remembered his master's address. He ran there.

Daylight was beginning to appear. He could make out escutcheons over a door; he knocked. Without opening up, someone shouted out the information required, while embellishing it with violent abuse against those who disturbed people during the night.

The house where the clerk lived had neither bell, nor knocker, nor porter. Charles thumped his fists against the shutters. A police-officer happened to be passing; so he took fright and slipped away.

'I'm mad,' he said to himself; 'doubtless, they've kept her back to dine at Monsieur Lormeaux's house.'

The Lormeaux family no longer lived in Rouen.

'She'll have stayed to nurse Madame Dubreuil. Ah, Madame Dubreuil died ten months ago . . . ! So where can she be?'

An idea occurred to him. He asked in a café for the town directory; and hurriedly looked up the name of Mademoiselle Lempereur, who lived at number 74, rue de la Renelle-des-Maroquiniers.

As he came into this street, Emma herself appeared at the other end; he threw himself upon her rather than kissing her, crying out:

'What kept you yesterday?'

'I have been ill.'

'And what with . . . ? Where . . . ? How . . . ?'

She swept a hand across her forehead, and replied:

'At Mademoiselle Lempereur's.'

'I was certain of it! I'll go there.'

'Oh, it's not worth it,' said Emma. 'She's just this minute gone out; but, in future, be more calm; I am not free, you understand, if I know that the slightest delay upsets you so.'

She was giving herself a sort of permission not to cramp herself in her escapades. And amply did she take advantage of it, just as she liked. When the desire took her to see Léon, she left under any pretext, and, as he was not expecting her that particular day, she would go looking for him at his practice.

This was a great joy the first few times; but soon he revealed the truth, namely: that his master was grumbling vociferously about these disturbances.

'Nonsense! Now come,' she said.

And he sneaked out.

She wanted him to dress all in black and leave a pointy beard on his chin, so as to resemble the portraits of Louis XIII. She desired to be acquainted with his lodgings, found them ordinary; he blushed, she took no notice, then advised him to buy curtains like her own, and as he objected to the expense:

'Well, well! You hold tight to your little coin,' she said, laughing.

Each time, Léon had to recount to her everything he had done, since the last meeting. She wanted verses, verses to her, a *love poem* in her honour; he could never manage to find a rhyme for the second line, and he ended up copying a sonnet out of a keepsake book.

This was less through vanity than from the sole aim of pleasing her. He did not argue with her ideas; he accepted all her inclinations; he became her mistress rather than she being his. Her tender words together with her kisses would sweep his soul away. Where then had she learned that corruption, almost ethereal by dint of being deep and concealed?

VI

ON THE TRIPS HE MADE to see her, Léon would often dine at the pharmacist's, and politeness dictated that he should invite him in turn.

'Willingly!' Monsieur Homais had replied; 'besides, I'm in need of a little reinvigoration, for I'm stultifying here. We'll go to the theatre, to the restaurant, we shall go wild!'

'Oh, dearest!' murmured Madame Homais tenderly, appalled by the vague dangers he was prepared to run.

'Well, what of it? You find I am not ruining my health enough as it is, living amongst the pharmacy's continual emanations? Such, however, is the character of women: they are jealous of Science, then object to you taking the most legitimate diversion. Never mind, count on me: one of these days, I'll come to Rouen and together we'll spend it like water.'

The apothecary, in former times, would have refrained from using such an expression; but these days he was fond of a frolicsome, Parisian style that he would find in the best taste; and, like Madame Bovary, his neighbour, he would question the clerk carefully on the capital's manners, even speaking slang with the aim of dazzling . . . the bourgeoisie, saying *pad*, *crib*, *swellish*, *awful swellish*, *Breda Street*[15] and *I'll be cutting along* for: 'I'll be off'.

So, one Thursday, Emma was surprised to meet, in the kitchen of the *Lion d'Or*, Monsieur Homais dressed to travel, in other words in an old coat not seen on him before, while in one hand he carried a valise, and, in the other, the foot warmer[16] belonging to his business. He had confided his project to no one, apprehensive of worrying the public with his absence.

The idea of seeing again the places where he had spent his youth undoubtedly fired him up, for all the journey long he did not cease expatiating; then, he had scarce arrived, when he leapt vigorously out of the carriage to go in search of Léon; and the clerk struggled in vain, Monsieur Homais dragging him off to the large *Café de Normandie*, where he entered majestically without removing his hat, reckoning it decidedly provincial to bare his head in a public place.

Emma waited three-quarters of an hour for Léon. At last she ran to his office, and, lost in all kinds of conjecture, accusing him of indifference and reproaching herself for her weakness, she spent the afternoon with her forehead glued to the window-pane.

The two men were a further two hours at table facing one another. The large room emptied; the stove-pipe, in the shape of a palm-tree, rounded off its gilded spray against the white ceiling; and close to them, behind the glass partition, in full sun, a little jet of water splashed in a marble basin where, amongst cress and asparagus, three torpid lobsters stretched themselves out as far as some quails, all piled up on the side.

Homais was revelling in it. Although the sumptuousness of the place intoxicated him even more than its fine fare, the Pomard wine was nevertheless exciting his faculties, and, when the rum omelette appeared, he set forth some immoral theories about women. What seduced him above all, was *style*. He adored an elegant dress in a nicely-furnished drawing-room, and, as for corporeal qualities, did not abhor the *crummy*[17] type.

Léon regarded the clock with despair. The apothecary drank, ate, talked.

'You must,' he said all of a sudden, 'be very cut off in Rouen. Yet your amours do not live far.'

And, as the other was blushing:

'Come, be frank! Would you deny that at Yonville . . . ?'

The young man stammered.

'At Madame Bovary's, you are not courting . . . ?'

'Who then?'

'The maid!'

He was not joking; but, vanity outstripping discretion, Léon, despite himself, cried out. Besides, he only liked dark-haired women.

'I approve of your taste,' said the pharmacist; 'they are hotter-blooded.'

And leaning to his friend's ear, he outlined the symptoms by which one could recognise that a woman was hot-blooded. He even launched into an ethnographic digression: the German female was vapourish, the French debauched, the Italian passionate.

'And negresses?' asked the clerk.

'An artist's taste,' said Homais. 'Waiter! Two small coffees!'

'Are we leaving?' resumed the clerk at last, losing patience.

'*Yes.*'[18]

But, before going off, he wanted to see the landlord of the place and offer his congratulations.

Then the young man, in order to be alone, alleged he had business to deal with.

'Ah, I shall escort you!' said Homais.

And, while walking down the streets with him, he spoke of his wife, of his children, of their future and of his pharmacy, recounted how much it was on the decline in the past, and the state of perfection to which he had raised it.

Arrived in front of the *Hôtel de Boulogne*, Léon abruptly left him, scaled the stairs, and found his mistress in a great flutter.

At the pharmacist's name, she flew into a passion. He had a heap of good reasons, however; it wasn't his fault, didn't she know Monsieur

Homais? Could she really believe that he preferred his company? But she turned away; he checked her; and, sinking to his knees, he encircled her waist with both his arms, in a languid pose full of lust and supplication.

She was standing; her large bright-burning eyes gazed on him gravely and in a fashion that was almost dreadful. Then tears dimmed them, her rosy eyelids fell, she surrendered her hands, and Léon was carrying them up to his mouth when a servant appeared, informing Monsieur that he was being asked for below.

'You'll come back?' she said.

'Yes.'

'But when?'

'Right away.'

'It's a *dodge*,' said the pharmacist on spotting Léon. 'I wanted to interrupt what seemed to me to be a bothersome call for you. Let's go to Bridoux' place and have a glass of *garus*.'[19]

Léon swore that he must return to his office. Then the apothecary joked about waste paper and pleadings.

'So leave off Cujas and Barthole[20] for a bit, what the devil! Who's stopping you? Be a brave fellow! Let's go to Bridoux's; you'll see his dog. It's the strangest thing!'

And as the clerk was still holding out:

'I shall go too. I'll read a paper while waiting for you, or leaf through a law-book.'

Léon, stunned by Emma's rage, Monsieur Homais' prattle and perhaps the meal's heaviness, stood wavering and as if under the spell of the pharmacist who kept repeating:

'Let's go to Bridoux's! It's just round the corner, rue Malpalu.'

Then, through cowardice, through folly, through that unnameable feeling which tempts us into the most repugnant acts, he let himself be conducted to the place; and there they found Bridoux in the little courtyard, watching over three waiters puffing away as they turned the large wheel of a machine for making seltzer-water. Homais gave them advice; he put his arms around Bridoux; they drank *garus*. Léon wanted to leave twenty times; but the other would hold him back by the arm, telling him:

'I'm off in a jiffy. We'll make for the *Rouen Beacon*, see those fine gentlemen. I'll present you to Thomassin.'

Nevertheless the clerk shook him off and ran in one bound to the hotel. Emma was no longer there.

She had just left, exasperated. She now detested him. This breaking of his word over the assignation seemed to her a gross insult, and she sought yet further reasons to disengage herself from him; he was incapable of heroism, feeble, commonplace, more spineless than a woman, stingy with it and faint of heart.

Then, calming herself down, she concluded by perceiving that she had doubtless slandered him. But the vilifying of those we still love loosens us from them a little. Idols should not be touched: the gilt comes off on the hands.

They were reduced to speaking more often of matters that had nothing to do with their love; and, in the letters that Emma sent him, there was mention of flowers, of verses, of the moon and stars, artless expedients of a weakened passion, trying to revive itself by means of any possible outward aid. For the next trip, she would keep promising herself a consummate bliss; then admit to having felt nothing extraordinary. This disappointment was quickly erased by a new hope, and Emma returned to him yet more inflamed, more eager. She undressed violently, tearing away the slender laces of her corset, which would hiss about her hips like a creeping snake. She would go up on her naked tip-toes to check yet again if the door was properly closed, then slip off all her clothes in a single movement; and, pale, speechlessly, in earnest, she would fall upon his chest, with a slow shudder.

Yet on this forehead bathed in cold sweat, on these stammering lips, in these wild eyes, in the clasp of these arms, there lay something extreme, vague and dismal which seemed to Léon to slide between them, cunningly, as if to sunder them.

He did not dare ask her questions; but, seeing her so experienced, he told himself that she must have submitted to every test of suffering and pleasure. What charmed him before now faintly scared him. And he rebelled against the absorption, greater each day, of his personality. He begrudged Emma her constant victory. He even strove not to love her; then, at the creak of her boots, he felt himself waver, like drunkards at the sight of strong drink.

She did not fail, it is true, to lavish all sorts of attention on him, from refinements at the dinner-table to affectations of dress and languishing looks. In her bosom she brought roses from Yonville, tossing them in his face, was solicitous about his health, gave him advice on his conduct; and, so as to bridle him further, hoping that heaven would take a hand, she hung a Virgin medallion around his neck. She asked after his comrades, like a virtuous mother. She told him:

'Don't see them, don't go out, think only of us; love me!'

She would have liked to watch over his life, and the idea occurred to her to have him followed in the streets. There was always a kind of vagrant near the hotel, who accosted travellers and would not refuse . . . But her pride rebelled.

'Ah, too bad! If he's cheating on me, what does it matter! Do I care?'

One day when they had parted from each other at the proper time, and she was returning alone by the boulevard, she noticed the walls of her convent; so she sat on a bench, in the elm-trees' shade. How calm it was back then! How she longed for love's unutterable feelings, striving to conjure them up from books!

The first months of her marriage, her rides in the forest, the Vicomte's waltz, and Lagardy singing, all passed again before her eyes . . . And Léon suddenly appeared to her at the same distance as the others.

'Yet I love him!' she told herself.

No matter! She wasn't happy, had never been so. From where did it come then – this deficiency of life, this instantaneous decay of everything she leaned upon? But, if only somewhere there were a manly and handsome being, valiant by nature, full of both high spirits and breeding, a poet's heart in the guise of an angel, lyre strung with bronze, sounding its elegiac epithalamia to the heavens, why might she not accidentally meet him? Oh, impossible thought! Nothing, anyway, was worth the looking for; everything lied! Each smile concealed a yawn of tedium, each joy a curse, every pleasure its disgust, and the finest kisses left you nothing on the lips but the unattainable desire for a voluptuousness still more sublime.

A metallic rattle dragged itself out on high and four strokes were heard from the convent bell. Four o'clock! And she felt as though she had been there, on that bench, for ever. But an infinity of passions can be contained in a single minute, like a crowd in a small room. Emma lived entirely taken up by her own, and no more concerned herself with money than would an archduchess.

Once, nevertheless, a mean-looking man, red-faced and bald, came to her house, professing to have been sent by Monsieur Vinçart, of Rouen. He withdrew the pins that fastened the side pocket of his long green riding-coat, stuck them in his sleeve and politely held out a paper.

It was a bill for seven hundred francs, signed by her, and that Lheureux, despite all his protestations, had passed over to Vinçart.

She despatched her maid to his house. He was unable to come.

Then the stranger, who had remained on his feet, casting curious glances right and left that his coarse flaxen eyebrows concealed, asked with an innocent air:

'What answer to take to Monsieur Vinçart?'

'Well,' replied Emma, 'tell him . . . that I haven't one . . . It will be there next week . . . That he wait . . . yes, until next week.'

And the fellow went off without another word.

But, the following day, at twelve o'clock, she received a notarised protest for non-payment; and the sight of the stamped paper, where *Maître Hareng, bailiff at Buchy* was displayed several times and in bold letters, affrighted her so much, that she ran as fast as she could to the cloth-dealer's house.

She found him in his shop, tying up a package with string.

'Your humble servant,' he said.

Lheureux carried on with his task none the less, helped by a young girl of about thirteen, a little crook-backed, employed by him as both clerk and cook.

Then, smacking his clogs against the shop's floorboards, he led Madame up to the first floor, and showed her into a narrow study, where a large desk in pinewood bore up several registers, protected crosswise by a padlocked iron bar. Against the wall, under remnants of printed cotton, could be glimpsed a strong-box, but of such dimensions, that it must have contained other than bills and money. Monsieur Lheureux was, in fact, a pawnbroker, and it was there that he had deposited Madame Bovary's gold chain, with the earrings belonging to poor old Tellier, who, finally forced to sell up, had bought a meagre grocery business, where he was dying of his catarrh, amidst candles less yellow than his face.

Lheureux sat down in his large straw-bottomed armchair, saying: 'What news?'

'Here.'

And she showed him the paper.

'Well, what can I do about it?'

Then she flew into a passion, reminding him of the promise he had given not to pass the bills round; he admitted it.

'But I was forced to on my own behalf, I had the knife at my throat.'

'And what is going to happen, now?' she went on.

'Oh, it's very simple: a court verdict, and then the seizure . . . *not a hope!*'

Emma forbore from hitting him. She asked him gently if there was not a way of soothing Monsieur Vinçart.

'Well well, yes, soothing Vinçart! You scarce know him; fiercer than an Arab, he is.'

Yet Monsieur Lheureux had to take a hand in this.

'Now listen! It seems to me that, up until now, I have been rather good to you.'

And, laying out one of his registers:

'Here!'

Then, moving his finger up the page:

'Let's see . . . let's see . . . The third of August, two hundred francs . . . On the seventeenth of June, one hundred and fifty . . . Twenty-third of March, forty-six . . . In April . . .'

He stopped, as though fearing to do something foolish.

'And I've not mentioned the bills signed by Monsieur, one for seven hundred francs, another for three hundred! As for your petty instalments, at interest, those are never-ending, we're in a complete muddle. I'll not take a hand in this any longer!'

She wept, she even called him 'good Monsieur Lheureux'. But he kept falling back on this 'rascal Vinçart'. Besides, he had not a centime, nobody was paying him at present, they were having the shirt off his back, a poor shopkeeper like him could not make advances.

Emma held her tongue; and Monsieur Lheureux, who was nibbling the vane of a quill, doubtless grew uneasy over her silence, for he resumed:

'At least, if one of these days I were to have a few payments . . . I could . . .'

'What's more,' she said, 'as soon as Barneville's arrears . . .'

'What?'

And, on being apprised that Langlois had not yet paid up, he seemed most surprised. Then, in honeyed tones:

'And we are agreed, you say . . . ?'

'Oh, whatever you like!'

So, he closed his eyes to reflect, wrote down a few figures, and, declaring that it would be seriously injurious to him, that the matter was shockingly risky and that he was *bleeding* himself, he suggested four bills of two hundred and fifty francs, each, payable at monthly intervals.

'Provided Vinçart chooses to hear me! For the rest it's agreed, I'm not the trifling sort, I'm as sound as a bell.'

Then he carelessly showed her several new wares, but not one of which, in his opinion, were worthy of Madame.

'When I consider that here's a dress at seven sous the yard, and certified fast dye! Yet they swallow it! We don't tell them what it really is, of course — ' intending by this admission of roguery towards the others to convince her entirely of his fair dealing.

Then he called her back, to show her three ells of silk lace that he had found recently 'in an *auction*'.

'Isn't it smart!' said Lheureux; 'they use it a lot these days, for the tops of armchairs, it's the fashion.'

And, quicker than a conjurer, he wrapped the silk lace in blue paper and placed it in Emma's hands.

'But if I at least know how . . . ?'

'Oh, later,' he replied, turning on his heels.

That very evening, she urged Bovary to write to his mother so she might speedily send him all the unclaimed inheritance. The mother-in-law replied that she no longer had anything: the settlement was concluded, and there remained to them, other than Barneville, six hundred francs a year, that she would send to them promptly.

Then Madame despatched bills to two or three clients, and soon made copious use of this means, and successfully. She always took care to add as a postscript: *Do not mention it to my husband, you know how proud he is . . . My apologies . . . Your servant . . .* There were a few complaints; she intercepted them.

In order to make herself some money, she set about selling her old gloves, her old hats, the old silver-plate; and she haggled rapaciously – her peasant blood urging her to a profit. Then, on her trips to town, she would buy secondhand trifles, that Monsieur Lheureux, for want of others, would certainly take. She bought herself ostrich feathers, china-ware and chests; she borrowed from Félicité, from Madame Lefrançois, from the landlady of the *Croix Rouge*, from everyone, anywhere. With the money she finally received from Barneville, she paid two bills; the other fifteen hundred francs drained away. She committed herself anew, and always in this manner!

At times, certainly, she tried to do her sums; but she unearthed doings that were so excessive, she could not believe it. So she began again, fast embroiled herself, walked away from it all and gave it not another thought.

How very sad the house was, now! Tradesmen with furious faces were to be seen leaving. There were handkerchiefs drooping from the stoves; and little Berthe, much to the alarm of Madame Homais, wore stockings with holes in. If Charles, albeit timidly, ventured an observation, she brutally replied that it was not her fault!

Why these fits of anger? He let her old nervous illness explain it all; and, reproaching himself for having taken her frailties as failings, he accused himself of selfishness, had a mind to go over and kiss her.

'Oh, no,' he said, 'I'll annoy her.'

And he stayed where he was.

After dinner, he walked alone in the garden; he would take little Berthe on his knees, and, spreading out his medical journal, try to teach her to read. Soon enough the child, who had never studied, would open her sad eyes wide and start to cry. Then he would comfort her; he would go off to fetch her some water in the watering-can to make rivers in the sand, or break branches off the privet bushes to plant trees in the flower-beds, which hardly spoilt the garden, all congested as it was with long grass; Lestiboudois was owed so many days' wages! Then the child would feel cold and ask for her mother.

'Call your nurse-maid,' said Charles. 'Surely you know, my little one, that your mamma doesn't want us to disturb her.'

It was the beginning of autumn and already the leaves were falling – just like two years ago, when she was ill! So when would all this be over! . . . And he went on walking, hands behind his back.

Madame was in her room. No one went up. She stayed there all day long, in a state of torpor, barely dressed, and, from time to time, burning pastilles of harem incense that she had bought in Rouen, from an Algerian's shop. So as not to have, close to her at night, this spread-eagled and slumbering man, she ended up, by dint of pulling faces, relegating him to the second floor; and right through to the morning she read lurid books full of orgiastic scenes and blood-soaked plots. Frequently gripped by terror, she would let out a scream. Charles came running.

'Oh, go away!' she would say.

Or, at other times, scorched more fiercely by that intimate flame brightened by adultery, panting for breath, aroused, full of desire, she would open her window, suck in the cold air, scatter her too-heavy hair in the wind, and, gazing at the stars, long for a prince's love. She thought of him, of Léon. She would have given anything for a single one of those meetings, sating her as they did.

Those were her gala days. She wanted them to be sumptuous! And, whenever he was unable to afford an expense, she made up the difference liberally, something that happened almost every time. He tried to make her understand that they would be just as fine elsewhere, in some more modest hotel; but she found objections.

One day, she pulled from her bag six little silver-gilt spoons (they were Père Rouault's wedding present) begging him to go immediately and take them, on her behalf, to the pawnbroker; and Léon obeyed, even though he disliked taking this step. He was afraid of compromising himself.

Then, on thinking it over, he felt that his mistress was behaving strangely, and that people were perhaps not amiss in wanting to disengage him from her.

In fact, someone had sent his mother a long anonymous letter, to warn her that he was going to wrack and ruin with a married woman; and straightaway the good lady, glimpsing every family's nightmare, that vague and pernicious creature, the siren, the monster, which dwells phantasmagorically in love's depths, wrote to his master, Maître Dubocage, who dealt with the matter impeccably. He kept him for three-quarters of an hour, wishing to open his eyes, warn him of the whirlpool. Such an intrigue would harm his business later on. He beseeched him to break off, and, if he would not make this sacrifice in his own interest, that he would at least do it for his, Dubocage's, sake!

Léon had finally sworn not to see Emma any longer; and he reproached himself for not having kept his word, considering all that this woman might still provoke by way of embarrassment and idle talk, not to mention his comrades' pleasantries, which poured out every morning, around the stove. Moreover, he was going to be made senior clerk: now was the moment to be serious. He was also renouncing the flute, and exalted feelings, and the imagination; for every bourgeois, in the over-excitement of his youth, if but for a day, a minute, has believed himself capable of immense passions, of lofty undertakings. The most ordinary rake has dreamed of sultans' consorts; each notary bears within him the remnants of a poet.

He grew weary now when Emma, all of a sudden, would sob on his chest; and his heart, like people who can only put up with a certain quantity of music, drowsed indifferently in the tumult of a love whose niceties he could no longer distinguish.

They knew each other too well to feel that astonished sense of possession which increases joy a hundred-fold. She was as tired of him as he was weary of her. Emma found in adultery all the same dullnesses of marriage.

But how to get rid of him? Besides, however much she felt humiliated by the sordid nature of such happiness, she held on to it out of habit or depravity; and, each day, she hung on more fiercely, exhausting any bliss by wanting it too vast. She blamed Léon for her dashed hopes, as if he had betrayed her; and she even wished for a catastrophe to bring about their separation, since she had not the courage to resolve it herself.

She carried on writing him love letters none the less, by virtue of this idea, that a woman must always write to her lover.

But, as she wrote, she perceived another man, a phantom made up of her most fervid memories, her most beautiful readings, her strongest lusts; and he became so real, and approachable, that her heart beat wildly over him, wonder-struck, without however being able to imagine him distinctly, so much had he vanished, like a god, under the abundance of his attributes. He dwelt in the blue-tinted country where ladders of silk swing from balconies, under the breath of flowers, in the brightness of the moon. She felt him near her, he was about to come and carry her away entire on a kiss. Then she would fall flat again, shattered; for these bursts of hazy love wore her out more than any grand debauch.

She now experienced an incessant and universal ache. Emma would even receive frequent summonses, on stamped paper which she scarcely looked at. She would have liked to stop living, or uninterruptedly to sleep.

On the middle day of Lent, she did not come back to Yonville; she went in the evening to the masked ball. She put on a pair of felt trousers and red stockings, with a pigtailed wig and a single lantern earring. She skipped all night to the furious sound of trombones; they gathered round her in a circle; and in the morning she found herself in the theatre's colonnade among five or six masquers, stevedore-trousered girls and sailors, friends of Léon, who were talking about going off to eat something.

The neighbouring cafés were full. In the harbour they spied the most mediocre of restaurants, whose landlord opened a little room for them on the fourth floor.

The men whispered in a corner, doubtless consulting on the expenditure. They consisted of a clerk, two medical students and a shop-boy: what company for her! As for the women, Emma rapidly perceived, by the tone of their voices, that almost all must be of the lowest rank. She felt frightened then, withdrew her chair and lowered her eyes.

The others began to eat. She did not eat: she felt her face on fire, her eyelids tingling and an icy cold on her skin. She felt the ballroom floor in her head, rebounding still under the rhythmic pulse of the thousand dancing feet. Then the smell of the punch along with the cigar smoke made her giddy. She swooned; they carried her to the window.

Day was breaking, and a great stain of purple was spreading in the pale sky beyond Sainte Catherine. The livid river shivered in the wind; there was no one on the bridges; the street-lamps were going out.

She revived nonetheless, and happened to think of Berthe, who was sleeping way over there, in her nurse-maid's bedroom. But a waggon full of long strips of iron passed by, hurling a deafening metallic shudder against the walls of the houses.

She slipped away brusquely, got rid of her costume, told Léon that she had to return home, and finally stayed alone at the *Hôtel de Boulogne*. Everything and herself felt insufferable. She would have liked, vanishing like a bird, to be renewed somewhere, a great way off, in undefiled spaces.

She went out, crossed the boulevard, the place Cauchoise and the outlying part of town, to an open road that looked down upon gardens. She walked quickly, the fresh air soothed her: and little by little the faces of the crowd, the quadrilles, the chandeliers, the supper, those women, all vanished like blown-away mists. Then, returning to the *Croix Rouge*, she threw herself on her bed, in the little room on the second floor, where there were images from *The Tower of Nesle*. At four o'clock in the afternoon, Hivert woke her up.

When she got back home, Félicité showed her a grey paper behind the clock. She read:

By order, in execution of a judgment . . .

What judgment? In fact, the previous day they had delivered another paper she knew nothing about; she was just as stupefied by these words:

Order in the name of the king, the law and justice, to Madame Bovary . . .

Then, jumping a few lines, she saw:

In twenty-four hours, without any delay.— What now? *To pay the total sum of eight thousand francs.* And, lower down, there was even: *She will be constrained thereto by all due course of law, and notably by the seizure of her furniture and effects.*

What to do? This was within twenty-four hours; tomorrow! No doubt Lheureux wanted to scare her again; for now at a stroke she guessed at all his schemes, the goal of his panderings. What reassured her, was the exaggerating of the amount.

Yet, by dint of buying, not settling, borrowing, signing bills, then renewing bills, which rose at each new date of payment, she had ended up providing a capital for Monsieur Lheureux, which he was impatiently awaiting for his speculations.

She called on him with a free and easy manner.

'Do you know what has happened to me? It's a joke, no doubt!'

'No.'

'How so?'

He slowly turned, crossed his arms and said to her:

'Do you think, my little lady, that I would be your supplier and banker until the end of the world, for goodness' sake? I do have to recover what I lay out, let's be fair.'

She protested about the debt.

'Ah, too bad! The court has upheld it. Judgment has been given, and served on you. Besides, it's not me, it's Vinçart.'

'Could you not . . . ?'

'Oh, nothing at all.'

'But . . . still . . . let us be reasonable.'

And she searched out every excuse; she had had no idea . . . it was a surprise . . .

'Whose fault is it?' said Lheureux, bowing ironically to her. 'While I, for my part, am working away like the devil, you're having yourself a fine time.'

'No lectures, now!'

'It never does any harm,' he replied.

She played the coward, she implored him; and she even pressed her pretty, slender white hand upon the dealer's lap.

'Now leave me be! Anyone would think you wanted to seduce me!'

'You're a wretch!' she cried.

'Oh, how you do go on,' he answered with a laugh.

'I shall make it known what you are. I will tell my husband . . .'

'Well, and I will show him something in turn, this husband of yours.'

And Lheureux took out from his strong-box the receipt for eighteen hundred francs, that she had given him at the time of the Vinçart discount.

'Do you think,' he added, 'that he won't make out your little theft, this poor dear man?'

She sank back, felled more surely than if she had been hit by a bludgeon. He walked from the window to the desk, all the while repeating:

'Ah, I will show him all right, I will show him all right . . .'

Then he drew nearer to her, and in a gentle voice:

'It's not amusing, I know; no one's died, everything considered, and, since it's the only way remaining for you to repay my money . . .'

'But where shall I ever find it?' said Emma, twisting her arms about.

'Oh fiddlesticks, when you have friends as you do!'

And he looked at her in such a shrewd and terrible manner, that she shuddered to the very core.

'I promise you,' she said, 'I shall sign . . .'

'I've had enough of your signatures!'

'I will sell some more . . .'

'Nonsense,' he said with a shrug, 'you have nothing left.'

And he shouted through the spy-hole that opened onto the shop.

'Annette! Don't forget the three off-cuts for number 14.'

The servant appeared; Emma understood and asked 'what in the way of money was needed to stop all the suits.'

'It's too late.'

'But if I brought you several thousand francs, a quarter of the amount, a third?'

'No, a waste of time.'

He pushed her gently towards the stairs.

'I entreat you, Monsieur Lheureux, just a few more days!'

She sobbed.

'Well, well. Tears.'

'You're driving me to despair!'

'What do I care for that!' he said, closing the door.

VII

SHE WAS STOICAL, THE NEXT day, when Maître Hareng, the bailiff, accompanied by two witnesses, called on her to conduct the inventory for the seizure.

They started with Bovary's consulting room and did not record the phrenological skull, which was considered a *tool of his profession*; but in the kitchen they counted the plates, the cooking-pots, the chairs, the candlesticks, and, in her bedroom, all the knick-knacks on the shelves. They scrutinised her dresses, the linen, the dressing-room; and her existence, down to her most intimate secret recesses, was, like a corpse at an autopsy, laid out at full length under the gaze of these three men.

Maître Hareng, buttoned up in a thin black coat, with a white cravat, and sporting extremely taut foot-straps, kept repeating from time to time:

'May I, Madame? May I?'

Often, he would exclaim:

'Charming! Most pretty!'

Then he would start writing again, dipping his quill in the horn ink-pot that he held in his left hand.

When they had finished with the rooms, they went up to the attic. She kept a desk there in which Rodolphe's letters were locked up. It had to be opened.

'Ah, a correspondence,' said Maître Hareng with a discreet smile. 'But allow me, as I must make certain that the box does not contain anything else.'

And he tilted the papers, just slightly, as if to make napoleons drop out of them. Then she was seized with indignation, on seeing that plump hand, with its flabby red fingers like slugs, settle on those pages where her heart had throbbed.

They left at last! Félicité came back. She had been sent as a look-out to divert Bovary; and they briskly installed the bailiff's man under the roof, where he swore to stay put.

Charles appeared anxious to her during the evening. Emma kept watching him with a look full of distress, fancying she could read accusations in the lines of his face. Then, when her eyes returned to the chimneypiece protected by Chinese fire-screens, to the broad curtains, to the armchairs, in short to all those things that had sweetened her life's bitterness, she was seized by remorse, or rather by an immense regret and which, far from quelling her passion, inflamed it. Charles placidly poked the fire, his feet on the fire-dogs.

A moment came when the bailiff's man, no doubt growing bored in his hiding-place, made a little noise.

'Is someone walking about up there?'

'No!' she replied. 'It's an attic window left open that the wind is rattling.'

She left for Rouen, the Sunday after, in order to call on all the bankers whose names she knew. They were in the country or travelling.

She would not be disheartened; and from those she did manage to meet, she requested money, protesting that she needed some, that she would pay it back. Several laughed in her face; all refused.

At two o'clock, she ran to Léon's house, knocked on his door. It was not opened. At last he appeared.

'What brings you?'

'Am I bothering you?'

'No . . . but . . .'

And he admitted that the landlord did not like anyone entertaining 'women'.

'I need to talk to you about something,' she went on.

So he reached for his key. She stopped him.

'No, over there, at our place.'

And they went up to their room, at the *Hôtel de Boulogne*.

She drank a big glass of water on arriving. She was very pale. She said to him:

'Léon, you are going to do something for me.'

And, shaking him by both hands, squeezing them tightly, she added:

'Listen, I need eight thousand francs.'

'But you're mad!'

'Not yet!'

And, straightaway, recounting to him the business of the seizure, she laid bare her financial distress; for Charles was ignorant of it all: her mother-in-law hated her; Père Rouault could do nothing; but Léon, for his part, could set about finding this absolutely essential sum . . .

'How do you want me to . . . ?'

'What a coward you are!'

Then he said stupidly:

'You're overstating the mischief. Perhaps with a thousand crowns your gentleman would calm down.'

Yet another reason to do something; it was impossible not to secure three thousand francs! Moreover, Léon could pledge himself in place of her.

'Go on. Try. You must. Run . . . ! Oh, do your best! Do your best! I will love you so much!'

He went out, came back after an hour, and said with a solemn face: 'I have called on three people . . . in vain.'

Then they stayed seated opposite each other, either side of the fireplace, motionless, without speaking. Emma was shrugging her shoulders as she stamped her foot. He heard her murmuring:

'If I were in your place, I would certainly find some.'

'Where then?'

'At your office!'

And she looked at him.

A diabolical boldness escaped from her blazing eyes, and the lids narrowed in a lewd and inciting way – so much so that the young man felt himself weakening under the mute will of this woman who was counselling him to commit a crime. Then he felt frightened, and, to avoid any elucidation, he struck his forehead and cried out:

'Morel must be returning tonight! He won't refuse me, I hope.' (This was one of his friends, the son of an extremely rich merchant.) 'And I shall bring it along tomorrow,' he added.

Emma did not seem to welcome this hope with as much joy as he had imagined. Did she suspect the lie? Blushing, he went on:

'However, if you don't see me at three o'clock, don't wait for me, my beloved. I must be off. Farewell!'

He took her hand, but it felt completely inert. Emma no longer had the strength to feel anything.

Four o'clock rang out; and she got up to return to Yonville, obeying the impulse of habit like an automaton.

It was fine weather; one of those clear, sharp March days, when the sun gleams in an all-white sky. The Rouennais in their Sunday best were strolling with a happy air. She reached the cathedral square. They were coming out of vespers; the crowd flowed out by the three portals, like a river by the three arches of a bridge, and, in the middle, more motionless than a rock, stood the beadle.

Then she recalled that day when, all anxious and full of hope, she had entered in under this great nave which extended before her less abyssal than her love; and she continued walking, weeping under her veil, dizzy, tottering, near-swooning.

'Look out!' cried a voice coming out from a carriage gateway as it opened.

She stopped to let a black horse go by, that was pawing the ground between the shafts of a tilbury driven by a gentleman in sable fur. Now who was it? She knew him . . . The carriage shot forth and disappeared.

But it was him, the Vicomte! She turned round; the street was deserted. And she was so dejected, so sad, that she leaned against a wall so as not to fall.

Then she thought she had been mistaken. Besides, she had no idea. Everything was deserting her, within and without. She felt cast away, wandering at random in undefinable depths; and it was almost with joy that she glimpsed, on arriving at the *Croix Rouge*, that good Homais surveying the loading onto the *Hirondelle* of a large box full of pharmaceutical supplies; he was holding in his hand, wrapped in a silk handkerchief, six *cheminots* for his wife.

Madame Homais loved these heavy, turban-shaped rolls, that are eaten at Lent with salted butter: last specimen of the Gothic diet, perhaps going back to the Crusades, and with which the robust Normans filled themselves up in former times, thinking they could see upon the table, by the glimmer of yellow torches, between the jugs of aromatic wine and the gigantic hunks of pork, the heads of Saracens ready to be devoured. The apothecary's wife crunched them as they had done, heroically, despite her terrible teeth; and, every time Monsieur Homais made the trip to town, he never failed to bring some back for her, always buying them at the main producer in rue Massacre.

'Charmed to see you!' he said, offering Emma his hand to help her up into the *Hirondelle*.

Then he hung the *cheminots* on the netting's straps, and remained bare-headed and with arms folded, in a thoughtful and Napoleonic posture.

But, when the blind man appeared as usual at the bottom of the hill, he shouted:

'I do not understand why the authorities go on tolerating such disreputable trades! We should shut these unfortunates up, get them to do some sort of forced labour. Progress, upon my word, proceeds at a snail's pace! We're floundering about in complete barbarism!'

The blind man held out his hat, which tossed about alongside the door, like an unnailed portion of the upholstery.

'There we are,' said the pharmacist, 'a scrofulous affection!'

And, although he knew this poor devil, he pretended to see him for the first time, murmured the words *cornea, opaque cornea, sclerotic, facies*, then asked him in a fatherly tone:

'Have you had this dreadful infirmity for a long time, my friend? Instead of making yourself tipsy in the tavern, you'd do better following a diet.'

He urged him to buy good wine, good beer, good roast meat. The blind man went on with his song; he seemed, anyway, almost imbecilic. At last, Monsieur Homais opened his purse.

'Look, here's a *sou*, give me back two *liards*: and don't forget my recommendations, you will find them beneficial.'

Hivert took the liberty of expressing aloud some doubt as to their virtue. But the apothecary assured him that he would cure the fellow himself, with an anti-inflammatory salve of his own composition, and he gave his address:

'Monsieur Homais, near the market-house, well enough known.'

'And now, for our trouble,' said Hivert, 'you're going to *show us your act*.'

The blind man sank down onto his knees and, with head thrown back, rolling his greenish eyes and sticking out his tongue, he rubbed his belly with both hands, while he let out a sort of muffled howl, like a famished hound. Emma, seized with disgust, flung him a five-franc piece over her shoulder. It was her entire fortune. It seemed to her glorious to cast it away thus.

The vehicle had set off again when, suddenly, Monsieur Homais leaned out beyond the carriage-blind and shouted:

'Nothing farinaceous nor dairy! Wear wool next to the skin and expose the diseased parts to the smoke of juniper-berries!'

The sight of familiar things passing before her eyes averted Emma bit by bit from her present grief. An unbearable weariness overwhelmed her, and she arrived home stupefied, disheartened, all but asleep.

'Come what may!' she said to herself.

And then, who knows? Why might some extraordinary event not arise, at any moment? Lheureux could even die.

At nine o'clock in the morning, she was woken by the sound of voices in the square. There was a mob around the market-house, reading a large bill pasted on one of the pillars, and she saw Justin who stepped up onto a spur-stone and tore down the bill. But, at that moment, the village guard collared him. Monsieur Homais emerged from the pharmacy, and Mère Lefrançois seemed to be holding forth in the middle of the crowd.

'Madame! Madame!' cried out Félicité as she came in, 'it's abominable!'

And the poor girl, upset, handed her a yellow piece of paper that she had just torn from the door. Emma read in a flash that all her personal chattels were for sale.

Then they gazed at each other in silence. Servant and mistress, they had no secrets between them. At last Félicité sighed:

'If I were you, Madame, I would call on Monsieur Guillaumin.'

'You think so . . . ?'

And this question meant:

'Knowing the house through the manservant as you do, does the master speak of me now and again?'

'Yes, go along, you'd do well to.'

She changed, put on her black dress with her hooded gown beaded with jet; and, so that no one would see her (there were always a lot of people in the square), she skirted the village, by the river-path.

She arrived completely out of breath in front of the notary's railing; the sky was overcast and there was a touch of snow.

At the sound of the bell, Théodore, in a red waistcoat, appeared on the steps; he came to let her in almost familiarly, as though for an acquaintance, and showed her into the dining room.

A large porcelain stove hummed beneath a cactus filling the niche, and, in frames of black wood, against the oak-coloured wall-paper, there was Steuben's *Esmeralda*, with *Potiphar* by Schopin.[21] The laid table, two silver chafing-dishes, the crystal door-knobs, the parquet and the furniture, all shone with a meticulous, English cleanliness; the panes were embellished, at each corner, with coloured glass.

'Here's the sort of dining room,' thought Emma, 'that I ought to have.'

The notary came in, left arm clasping his palm-patterned dressing gown against his body, while the other hand raised and briskly lowered his brown felt cap, affectedly set on the right side, where the ends of three blond locks dangled, drawn from the back of the head and around his bald skull.

After he had proffered a seat, he sat down to dine, all the while profusely apologising for the incivility.

'Monsieur,' she said, 'I beg you . . .'

'For what, Madame? I'm listening.'

She began to reveal her situation to him.

Maître Guillaumin knew all about it, being secretly connected with the cloth merchant, with whom he always found capital for mortgage loans that he was asked to contract.

Therefore, he knew (and better than she did) the long story of these bills, trifling at first, bearing various names as endorsers, payable at long intervals and continually renewed, up to the day when, gathering together all the protests for non-payment, the merchant had charged his friend Vinçart to instigate the necessary proceedings in his own name, not wanting to play the tiger amongst his fellow citizens.

She mingled her account with recriminations against Lheureux, recriminations to which the notary responded from time to time with insignificant comments. Eating his cutlet and drinking his tea, he lowered his chin into his sky-blue cravat, pricked by two diamond pins linked by a little gold chain; and he smiled a peculiar smile, insipidly sweet and ambiguous. But, perceiving that she had wet feet:

'Come nearer to the stove, now . . . higher . . . against the porcelain.'

She was afraid of dirtying it. The notary answered in a gallant tone:

'Nothing is spoilt by beauty.'

So she tried to touch his feelings, and, growing emotional herself, she recounted to him the straitness of her domestic economy, her pains, her needs. He understood this: a fashionable lady! And, without breaking off from his meal, he turned fully towards her, so that his knee lightly grazed her little boot, whose sole curved back as it steamed against the stove.

But, when she asked him for a thousand crowns, he pursed his lips, then declared himself most grieved not to have had the management of her fortune in times past, for there were a hundred extremely convenient ways, even for a married woman, to make the most of her money. It would have been possible, either in the turf-pit of Grumesnil or the Havre plots, to venture some excellent speculations with a near certainty of success; and he let her be consumed with rage at the idea of the fantastic sums she would most probably have made.

'How was it,' he went on, 'that you did not call on me?'

'I'm not sure,' she said.

'Why? Do I frighten you then? On the contrary, it is I who should be complaining. We scarcely know one another! Yet I am devoted to you; you no longer doubt it, I hope?'

He held out his hand, seized hers, covered it with ravenous kisses, then kept it on his knee, and he delicately dabbled with her fingers, all the while talking blandishments to her by the thousand.

His insipid voice murmured, like a stream gliding past; a spark flashed from his eye through the gleam of his spectacles, and his hands advanced into Emma's sleeve, to examine her arm. She felt the puff of a panting breath against her cheek. This man was bothering her horribly.

She leapt to her feet and said to him:

'Monsieur, I am waiting!'

'What for?' said the notary, who grew extremely pale all of a sudden.

'That money.'

'But . . .'

Then, giving in to the irruption of an overpowering desire:

'Well, yes . . . !'

He was crawling on his knees towards her, without regard for his dressing gown.

'For mercy's sake, stay! I love you!'

He clasped her about the waist.

A tide of crimson surged swiftly over Madame Bovary's face. She drew back with a terrible look, shouting:

'You are taking shameless advantage of my distress, Monsieur! I am to be pitied, but not to be sold!'

And she left.

The notary remained decidedly stupefied, eyes fixed on his handsome needle-work slippers. They were a love token. This sight finally consoled him. In addition to which, he considered that such an adventure would have drawn him in too far.

'What a wretch! What a blackguard! What ignominy!' she said to herself, dashing away beneath the aspens by the road. The disappointment of failure strengthened the indignation of outraged modesty; it seemed to her that Providence was implacable in its pursuit of her, and, self-worth appreciating with pride, never had she held herself in so much esteem nor others in so much contempt. Something warlike was enrapturing her. She would have liked to batter the race of men, to spit in their faces, pulverise them all; and she continued to walk speedily onward, pale, quivering, enraged, ferreting the empty horizon with tearful eyes, and as if relishing the hatred which choked her.

When she caught sight of her house, a torpor took hold. She could not go on any more; yet she must; besides, where flee?

Félicité was waiting for her at the door.

'Well?'

'No!' said Emma.

And, for quarter of an hour, the two of them considered the various people in Yonville prepared perhaps to come to her aid. But, each time Félicité named someone, Emma replied:

'Is it likely? They wouldn't want to.'

'And Monsieur on his way home!'

'I know . . . Leave me on my own.'

She had tried everything. There was nothing more to do now; and so when Charles appeared, she would say to him:

'Step back. This carpet you tread is no longer yours. Of your house, you do not have a stick of furniture, a pin, a straw, and it is I who have ruined you, poor man!'

So there would be a great sobbing, then he would cry a great deal, and at length, the surprise over, he would forgive her.

'Yes,' she murmured as she ground her teeth, 'he'll forgive me, the one who has not millions enough to offer me that I might pardon him for having known me . . . Never! Never!'

It was exasperating, this notion of Bovary's superiority over her. Then, whether she confessed or did not confess, presently, soon, tomorrow, he would not know any the less of the catastrophe; so she must await this horrible scene and suffer the burden of his magnanimity. She felt a desire to go back to Lheureux's – to what end? To write to her father: it was too late; and perhaps she would now rue not having yielded to that other, when she heard a horse's trot on the path. It was him, he was opening the gate, he was paler than the plaster wall. Leaping down the stairs, she made her escape smartly by the square; and the mayor's wife, who was chatting in front of the church with Lestiboudois, saw her go into the tax-gatherer's house.

She ran to tell Madame Caron. These two ladies went up into the attic; and, hidden by laundry spread out on poles, stationed themselves conveniently to see full into Binet's home.

He was alone, in his garret, in the process of imitating, in wood, one of those undescribable ivories, made up of crescents, spheres hollowed from one another, the whole as straight as an obelisk and of no earthly use; and he was attacking the last piece, the end was in sight! In the workshop's half-light, the flaxen dust flew from his lathe like a tuft of sparks under the shod hooves of a galloping horse: the two wheels were turning, were humming; Binet was smiling, chin lowered, nostrils flared, and seemed lost at last in one of those perfect joys, doubtless belonging only to mediocre occupations, that tickle the intelligence through simple difficulties, and satisfy it with an accomplishment beyond which there is nothing to dream.

'Ah there she is,' said Madame Tuvache.

But it was scarcely possible, on account of the lathe, to hear what she was saying.

At last, these ladies thought they could make out the word *francs*, and Mère Tuvache whispered very low:

'She's begging him in order to get a deferment of her tax payments.'

'On the surface!' replied the other.

They saw her walking up and down, inspecting the napkin rings, the candlesticks, the baluster knobs against the walls, while Binet stroked his beard in satisfaction.

'Might she have come to order something?' said Madame Tuvache.

'But he doesn't sell anything,' her neighbour objected.

The tax-gatherer looked to be listening, though with wide eyes, as if he did not understand. She went on in a tender, beseeching manner. She drew nearer; her breast heaved; they were no longer talking.

'Is she making advances to him?' said Madame Tuvache.

Binet was red up to the ears. She clasped his hands.

'Oh, that's too much!'

And without question she was offering him something disgusting; for the tax-gatherer – he was valiant, all the same, he had fought at Bautzen and at Lutzen, he had served in the French campaign, and had even been *recommended for a medal*– all of a sudden, as at the sight of a snake, drew well away, shouting:

'Madame! What are you thinking of . . . ?'

'Women like that should be horse-whipped!' said Madame Tuvache.

'Where is she now?' resumed Madame Caron.

For she had disappeared during these words; then, glimpsing her as she threaded her way up the Grande-Rue and turned right as though to reach the cemetery, they lost themselves in conjecture.

'MÈRE ROLET,' SHE SAID ON her arrival at the wet-nurse's, 'I'm choking . . . Unlace me.'

She fell upon the bed; she sobbed. Mère Rolet covered her with a petticoat and remained standing near her. Then, as she did not reply, the good woman moved away, took up her wheel and began to spin flax.

'Oh, have done!' she murmured, believing she could hear Binet's lathe.

'What's bothering her?' the wet-nurse asked herself. 'Why has she come here?'

She had hastened there, driven by a sort of dread that banished her from home.

Lying on her back, motionless and with unblinking eyes, she discerned things vaguely, even though she gave them her attention with an idiot persistence. She studied the wall's peeling flakes, two fire-brands smoking end to end, and a long spider crawling above her head in the cleft of a beam. At last she gathered her ideas together. She remembered . . . One day, with Léon . . . Oh, how far away it was . . . The sun shone on the river and the scent of clematis hung sweet . . . Then, swept away by her memories as by a bubbling torrent, she soon came to recall the previous day.

'What time is it?' she asked.

Mère Rolet went out, raised the fingers of her right hand up towards where the sky was clearest, and slowly came back in, saying:

'Three o'clock, shortly.'

'Ah thank you! Thank you!'

For he was going to come. It was certain! He would have found the money. But he would perhaps go over there, not doubting she was there; and she bid the wet-nurse to run to her house and fetch him.

'Hurry!'

'But, my dear lady, I'm going, I'm going!'

She was amazed, now, that she had not thought of him straightaway; yesterday, he had given his word, he would not fail; and she saw herself already at Lheureux's house, spreading out the three bank-notes on his desk. Then she would have to invent a story to explain things to Bovary. Which one?

Yet the wet-nurse was a long time coming back. But, as there was no clock in the thatched cottage, Emma feared she was perhaps exaggerating the length of time. She began to walk around the garden, a step at a time; she went along the hedge-side path, and turned back smartly, hoping that the good woman would have returned by another route. Finally, weary of waiting, assailed by suspicions that she beat back, no longer knowing whether she had been there for a century or a minute, she sat in a corner and closed her eyes, blocked her ears. The gate creaked: she leapt up: before she had spoken, Mère Rolet said to her:

'There's no one at your house.'

'What?'

'Oh, no one! And the master's crying. He's calling for you. They're looking for you.'

Emma said nothing in reply. She was panting, rolling her eyes all about her, while the peasant woman, frightened by her face, stepped back instinctively, believing her to be mad. All of a sudden she slapped her brow, let out a cry, for the memory of Rodolphe, like a great flash of lightning on a gloomy night, had slipped into her mind. He was so good, so nice, so generous! And, what is more, if he should hesitate to do her this service, she would know how to compel him into it by calling up their lost love at a single glance. So she left for La Huchette, not perceiving that she was rushing to yield to what had so greatly incensed her a little while ago, nor suspecting herself in the slightest of this prostitution.

VIII

WALKING ALONG SHE ASKED HERSELF: 'What shall I say? How shall I begin?' And according as she advanced, she recognised the bushes, the trees, the sea rushes on the hill, the chateau over there. She found herself returned to the sensations of her first tender love, and her poor flattened heart swelled lovingly. A warm wind blew against her face; the snow, melting, fell drop by drop from the buds onto the grass.

She entered, as in former times, by the park's little door, then reached the main courtyard, lined by a double row of bushy lindens. They waved their long branches, hissing. All the kennelled dogs barked, and the explosion of their baying resounded without anyone appearing.

She climbed the broad, straight, wooden-balustered staircase, that led to the corridor paved with dusty flagstones onto which several bedrooms opened in a row, as in a monastery or an inn. His was right at the end, furthest off, to the left. When she came to place her fingers on the lock, her strength unexpectedly forsook her. She was fearful that he might not be there, all but desired it, and yet this was her only hope, the last chance of salvation. She collected herself for a moment, and, tempering her courage in the consciousness of present necessity, she went in.

He was in front of the fire, both feet on the mantelpiece, smoking his pipe.

'Well! It's you!' he said, abruptly starting up.

'Yes, it's me. I would like to ask you, Rodolphe, for a bit of advice.'

And, despite all her efforts, it proved impossible for her to open her lips.

'You haven't changed. You are still charming.'

'Oh,' she answered bitterly, 'those are sad charms, my friend, seeing how you have scorned them.'

Then he entered upon an explanation of his conduct, excusing himself in vague terms, for want of being able to invent better ones.

She let herself be carried away by his words, yet more by his voice and by the sight of his person; so much so that she pretended to believe, or perhaps did believe, in the pretext for their rupture; it was a secret on which the honour and even the life of a third person depended.

'Never mind,' she said, looking at him sadly, 'I have suffered so!'

He replied in a philosophical tone:

'Life is like that.'

'Has it,' replied Emma, 'at least been good to you since our separation?'

'Oh, neither good . . . nor bad.'

'It would perhaps have been better never to have left each other.'

'Yes . . . perhaps.'

'You think so?' she said, drawing nearer.

And she sighed:

'O Rodolphe! If you knew . . . I loved you very much!'

It was then that she took his hand, and they remained a little while with fingers entwined – as on the first day, at the agricultural show! Out of a residue of pride,[22] he floundered under the emotion. But, collapsing against his chest, she said to him:

'How do you want me to live without you? Happiness can't be broken like a habit! I was in despair. I thought I would die. I'll tell you all about it, you'll see. And you, you ran away from me . . . !'

Because, for three years, he had studiously avoided her, in consequence of that natural cowardice by which the stronger sex is characterised; and Emma went on with pretty movements of the head, more wheedling than a loving cat:

'You love others, admit it. Oh, I understand them, agreed – I forgive them; you'll have seduced them, as you seduced me. You, you're a man. You have all that's needed to make you beloved. But we'll begin again, shan't we? We will love one another! Hey, I'm laughing, I'm happy . . . ! Speak, then!'

And she was ravishing to see, with her gaze in which a tear quivered, like the rain from a storm in a blue flower-cup.

He drew her onto his knees, and with the back of his hand he stroked her smooth bandeaux, where, in the light of dusk, a last ray of sun shimmered like a golden arrow. She inclined her brow; he finished by kissing her on the eyelids, very gently, with a brush of his lips.

'But you've been crying!' he said. 'Why?'

She burst into sobs. Rodolphe thought it was the bursting of her love; as she said nothing, he took this silence for a final modesty, and so he cried out:

'Ah forgive me! You are the only one who pleases me. I've been idiotic and wicked. I love you, I shall love you for ever . . . What is the matter with you? Tell me now!'

He knelt down.

'Well . . . I am ruined, Rodolphe. You are going to lend me three thousand francs.'

'But . . . but . . .' he said, getting to his feet by degrees, while his face took on a solemn expression.

'You know,' she speedily continued, 'that my husband placed his entire fortune with a notary; he ran away. We took out loans; the clients were not paying. The settlement is not done, however; we will have something later. But, today, for want of three thousand francs, they are going to seize our goods; it is happening now, at this very instant; and counting on your friendship, I have come.'

'Ah,' thought Rodolphe, growing very pale all of a sudden, 'that's why she has come!'

Finally he said with an air of great calm:

'I don't have it, dear lady.'

He was not lying. Had he had it he would doubtless have given it to her, even though it was generally disagreeable to carry out such fine deeds: a demand for money, of all the squalls that fall upon love, being the coldest and the most uprooting.

At first she stayed staring at him for some minutes.

'You don't have it!'

Several times she repeated:

'You don't have it . . . I might have spared myself this final shame. You've never loved me! You are no better than the others!'

She was giving herself away, she was growing confused.

Rodolphe interrupted her, maintaining that he was somewhat 'short of cash' himself.

'Oh, I pity you!' said Emma. 'Yes, so very much!'

And, her eyes fastening on an elaborately embossed musket glittering in the armour display:

'But, when someone's poor, he does not invest money in the butt-end of his gun! He does not buy an ornamental clock with tortoiseshell inlays,' she went on, indicating the Boulle clock; 'nor silver-gilt whistles for his whips – ' she touched them! ' – nor charms for his watch. Oh, he lacks for nothing! Even a liquor-frame in his bedroom; for you love yourself, you live well, you have a chateau, farms, woods; you hunt with the hounds, you take trips to Paris . . . Well, when all it is is that,' she cried, seizing his sleeve buttons from the chimney-piece, 'but the least of these baubles, money can be got from it . . . Oh, I don't want any! Keep them!'

And she hurled the two buttons a fair distance, so that the gold chain between them snapped on hitting the wall.

'But as for me, I would have given you everything, would have sold everything, would have laboured with my hands, would have begged in the streets, for a smile, for a glance, to hear you say, "Thank you." And you stay there calmly in your armchair, as if you haven't already made me suffer enough? Without you, as well you know, I could have lived quite happily. Who forced you into it? Was it a wager? Yet you loved me, you said so yourself . . . And again just now . . . Ah, it would have been better to drive me away. My hands are warm from your kisses, and there's the very spot, on the carpet, where you fell at my feet and swore everlasting love. You made me believe it: for two years you dragged me along in the sweetest and most magnificent dream . . . Well? Our plans to travel, do you remember? Oh, your letter, your letter. It tore my heart apart. And then, when I come back to him – to him – he being rich, happy, free – to implore the kind of help that anyone would have given, beseeching and yielding him all my tender love, he spurns me, because that would cost him three thousand francs!'

'I don't have it,' replied Rodolphe in that perfect calm with which a resigned fury masks itself as though behind a shield.

She left. The walls shook, the ceiling bore down on her; and she passed again by the long alley, tripping up on the piles of dead leaves that the wind was scattering. At last she arrived at the ha-ha before the gate; she broke her nails on the lock, she was in such haste to open it. Then, a hundred paces further on, out of breath, near collapse, she stopped. And so, turning round, she saw once again the impassive chateau, with the park, the gardens, the three courtyards, and all the windows of the façade.

She remained lost in a stupor, and had no more consciousness of herself than through the throb of her arteries, thinking she could hear it burst forth like a deafening music that filled the countryside. The earth under her feet was softer than a wave, and the furrows appeared to her as immense brown billows, unfurling. All that was in her head, those reminiscences, ideas, broke loose at once, in a single leap, like the thousand parts in a firework. She saw her father, Lheureux's study, their bedroom over there, another landscape. Madness seized her, she grew scared, and managed to recover herself, in truth confusedly; for she could not remember the reason for her horrible state, that is to say the question of money. She suffered only from her love, and felt her soul abandoning her through this memory, as the wounded, in the pangs of death, feel life slipping away through their bleeding hurt.

The night was falling, crows took wing.

It seemed all of a sudden that little fire-coloured globes were bursting in the air like explosive shot flattening out, and were reeling round, reeling round, eventually to melt on the snow, between the branches of the trees. In the middle of each one, Rodolphe's face would appear. They multiplied, and they came closer, penetrated her; everything vanished. She recognised the lights of houses, beaming from afar in the fog.

And, like an abyss, her situation appeared before her. She was panting sufficient to rupture her chest. Then, in an heroic delirium that turned her almost joyous, she ran down the hill, crossed the cattle-board, the path, the alley, the market-house, and arrived in front of the pharmacist's shop.

No one was around. She was about to enter; but, at the sound of the bell, someone could come; and, creeping in by the gate, holding her breath, feeling the walls, she made it up to the threshold of the kitchen, where a candle burned on the stove. Justin, in shirt-sleeves, was carrying a dish.

'Ah, they're at dinner. Let's wait.'

He returned. She knocked on the glass. He came out.

'The key! The one high up, where the . . .'

'What?'

And he stared at her, completely astonished by the pallor of her face, which stood out against the night's blackness beyond. She appeared extraordinarily beautiful to him, and as majestic as a phantom; without understanding what she wanted, he had a presentiment of something terrible.

But she continued eagerly, in a low voice, with a sweet, deliquescent voice:

'I want it. Give it to me.'

As the wall was thin, you could hear the clicking of forks on the plates in the dining-room.

She pretended that she had to kill the rats that stopped her sleeping.

'I must inform Monsieur.'

'No! Stay!'

Then, with an air of indifference:

'Well, it's not worth it, I'll tell him presently. Come, light my way!'

She entered the corridor onto which the laboratory door opened. On the wall there was a key labelled *capernaum*.

'Justin!' roared the apothecary, growing impatient.

'Coming up!'

And he followed her.

The key turned in the lock, and she went straight to the third shelf, so well did her memory guide her, seized the blue jar, tore the stopper out, thrust her hand inside, and, withdrawing it full of a white powder, she began to eat then and there.

'Stop!' he shouted, throwing himself upon her.

'Hush, they'll come . . .'

He grew desperate, wanted to call out.

'Say nothing about this, it will all be laid at your master's door.'

Then she went back home unexpectedly soothed, and in the near serenity of a duty fulfilled.

WHEN CHARLES, THROWN INTO CONFUSION by the news of the seizure, had returned to the house, Emma had just left. Where could she be? He sent Félicité to Homais' house, Monsieur Tuvache's house, Lheureux's house, to the *Lion d'Or*, everywhere; and, in the pauses of his anguish, he saw his respectability destroyed, their fortune lost,

Berthe's future shattered. From what cause? Not a word! He waited until six o'clock in the evening. Finally, able to hold out no longer, and imagining that she had left for Rouen, he went out onto the highway, walked a mile and a half, met no one, waited some more and returned.

She was back.

'What was the matter . . . ? Why . . . ? Will you tell me . . . ?'

She sat down at her writing-table, and wrote a letter that she slowly sealed, adding the day's date and the hour. Then she said in a solemn tone:

'You will read it tomorrow; from now until then, I beg you, do not address a single question to me . . . No, not one!'

'But . . .'

'Oh, leave me alone!'

And she lay down full length on her bed.

An acrid taste that she could sense in her mouth woke her up. She caught sight of Charles and closed her eyes again.

She watched herself closely and carefully, to discern whether she was suffering pain. But no! Nothing yet. She could hear the beat of the clock, the crackle of the fire, and Charles, standing near her bed, breathing.

'Ah it's really nothing much, death,' she thought; 'I'll go to sleep, and it will all be over.'

She drank a mouthful of water and turned to the wall.

This horrible taste of ink continued.

'I'm thirsty . . . ! Oh, I'm really thirsty!' she sighed.

'What is the matter with you?' said Charles, holding out a glass for her.

'It's nothing . . . Open the window . . . I am choking!'

And she was taken with a fit of nausea so sudden, that she hardly had time to grab hold of her handkerchief under the pillow.

'Take it away!' she said sharply; 'throw it away!'

He asked her questions; she did not answer. She stayed stock-still, for fear that the least disturbance might make her vomit. Nevertheless, she felt an icy cold rising from her feet to her heart.

'Ah, now it's beginning!' she murmured.

'What did you say?'

She rolled her head with a gentle movement full of anguish, while at the same time continually opening her jaws, as if she were carrying something very heavy on her tongue. At eight o'clock, the vomitings came back.

Charles observed that at the bottom of the basin there was a sort of white grit, stuck to the inner sides of the porcelain.

'It's extraordinary, it's peculiar,' he repeated.

But she said in a loud voice:

'No, you're mistaken!'

Then, delicately and all but caressing her, he passed his hand over her stomach. She let forth a shrill scream. He retreated, utterly appalled.

Then she began to moan, feebly at first. A great shuddering rocked her shoulders, and she became paler than the sheet in which her tensed fingers were buried. Her pulse, become irregular, was almost imperceptible now.

Drops oozed over her bluish face, that seemed frozen with the exhalation of a metallic vapour. Her teeth chattered, her widened eyes gazed vaguely about her, and to every question, she would only answer by shaking her head; she even smiled two or three times. Little by little, her moans grew louder. A muffled howl escaped her; she maintained that she was feeling better and would get up by and by. But the convulsions took hold; she shouted out:

'Ah, it's dreadful, my God!'

He fell upon his knees against her bed.

'Speak! What have you eaten? Answer, in heaven's name!'

And he looked at her with eyes of a tender lovingness such as she had never seen.

'Ah well, there . . . there . . .' she said in a faltering voice.

He leapt to the writing-desk, broke the seal and read out loud. *No one is to blame . . .* He stopped, passed his hand over his eyes, and read over it again.

'What? Oh, help! Help!'

And he could only repeat this word: 'Poisoned! Poisoned!' Félicité ran to Homais' house, who shouted it out in the square; Madame

Lefrançois heard it at the *Lion d'Or*; several people got out of bed to tell their neighbours, and all night the village was on the alert.

Desperate, stammering, near collapse, Charles paced round and round in the bedroom. He knocked against the furniture, tore his hair out, and the pharmacist would never have believed such a frightful sight possible.

He went back home to write to Monsieur Canivet and to Doctor Larivière. He was out of his wits; he got through more than fifteen drafts. Hippolyte set off for Neufchâtel, and Justin pressed Bovary's horse so hard, that he left it on the hill at Bois Guillaume, badly lamed and three-quarters done for.

Charles wanted to leaf through his medical dictionary; he could not see it, the words danced.

'Calm down!' said the apothecary. 'The question is simply to administer some powerful antidote. What is the poison?'

Charles showed the letter. It was arsenic.

'Right then,' Homais went on, 'we must make an analysis.'

For he knew that one must, in all cases of poisoning, make an analysis; and the other, not understanding, replied:

'Ah, make it, make it, save her . . .'

Then, returning to her side, he sank down onto the carpet, and he stayed with his head leaning on the side of her bed, sobbing.

'Don't cry,' she told him. 'Soon I'll torment you no longer.'

'Why? What drove you to it?'

She replied:

'It had to be done, my dear.'

'Weren't you happy? Is it my fault? Yet I did everything I could!'

'Yes . . . that's true . . . you, you are good!'

And she ran her hand through his hair, slowly. The sweet pleasure of this sensation overburdened his sadness; he felt his entire being collapse in despair at the idea that he must lose her, when, on the contrary, she was acknowledging more love for him than ever; and he could think of nothing, did not dare to, the urgency of an immediate solution bringing him to a state of utter distraction.

She had finished, she reflected, with all the treachery, the sordidness and the innumerable lusts that tortured her. She hated no one, now; a twilight confusion fell on her thoughts, and of all the sounds of the earth Emma heard nothing but the intermittent lamentation of this poor heart, soft and indistinct, like the last echo of a symphony growing ever fainter.

'Bring me the little one,' she said, raising herself on one elbow.

'You're not worse, are you?' asked Charles.

'No, no.'

The child, serious and still half-dreaming, came on the arm of her nurse-maid, in her long night-shift, from which her bare feet poked out. She considered the room in its state of complete disorder with astonishment, and blinked her eyes, dazzled by the lighted candles on the furniture. They doubtless reminded her of New Year or mid-Lent feastday mornings, when, woken up early like this by flamelight, she came into her mother's bed to receive her presents, for she began to say:

'Where is it then, Mamma?'

And, as everyone held their tongue:

'But I can't see my little stocking!'

Félicité tilted her towards the bed, while she was still looking in the direction of the fireplace.

'Has nurse taken it?' she asked.

And, at this name, which took her back to the memory of her adulteries and her afflictions, Madame Bovary turned her head aside, as if in disgust at the taste of another, stronger poison coming up into her mouth. Berthe, meanwhile, stayed where she was put on the bed.

'Oh, how big your eyes are, Mamma! How pale you are! How you sweat so . . . !'

Her mother looked at her.

'I'm frightened!' said the little girl, retreating.

Emma took her hand to kiss it; she struggled.

'Enough! Take her away!' cried Charles, sobbing in the alcove.

Then the symptoms were allayed for a moment; she appeared less agitated; and, at each insignificant word, at each slightly-calmer swell and fall of her breast, he recovered hope. At last, when Canivet came in, he threw himself weeping into his arms.

'Ah, it's you! Thank you! You are good! But it's all getting better. Here, look at her . . .'

His colleague was not at all of this opinion, and, not wishing, as he put it, to *beat about the bush*, he prescribed an emetic, in order to clear the stomach completely.

She was not long in vomiting blood. Her lips were increasingly clamped. She had twitching limbs, a body covered in brown spots, and her pulse slid between the fingers like a stretched thread, like a harp chord ready to snap.

Then she began to shout, horribly. She cursed the poison, inveighed against it, begged it to make haste, and pushed away with her arms all that Charles, more in the throes of death than she was, struggled to make her drink. He was standing, his handkerchief over his lips, groaning, weeping, and suffocated by the sobs that shook him right down to his toes; Félicité ran hither and thither in the room; Homais, immovable, let out great sighs, and Monsieur Canivet, still maintaining his self-possession, began however to feel perturbed.

'The devil . . . ! Yet . . . she has been purged, and, from the moment the cause ceases . . .'

'The effect should cease,' said Homais; 'it is obvious.'

'But save her!' shouted Bovary.

Then, without listening to the pharmacist who was still hasarding this hypothesis: 'It is perhaps a beneficial paroxysm', Canivet was about to administer an opiate, when the crack of a whip was heard; all the window-panes trembled, and a post-chaise, urged on at full stretch by three horses spattered in mud up to their ears, emerged in a bound from the corner of the market-house. It was Doctor Larivière.

The appearance of a god would not have caused more of a stir. Bovary raised his hands, Canivet stopped short, and Homais removed his bonnet-grec long before the doctor made his entry.

He belonged to the great school of surgeons issuing from Bichat's leather apron, to that generation, now vanished, of practising philosophers who, cherishing their art with a fanatical ardour, would exercise it exultantly and shrewdly. Everyone in his hospital trembled when he got into a rage, and his pupils venerated him so much that, scarce set up in business, they strove to imitate him as closely as possible; so that you would recognise them, in the neighbouring towns, by his long wadded great-coat of merino wool and his large black dress-coat, whose unbuttoned cuffs partly covered his brawny hands, very handsome hands, and which never wore gloves, as if to be readier to plunge into pain. Disdainful of medals, of titles and academies, hospitable, liberal, fatherly to the poor and practising virtue without being aware of it, he would have passed almost for a saint if the subtlety of his mind had not made him feared as a demon. His gaze, sharper than his scalpel, sank straight down into your soul and unjointed every lie through its assertions and coynesses. And thus he would proceed, full of that easy grandeur imparted by the consciousness of a great talent, wealth, and forty years of a hard-working and irreproachable life.

He frowned from the door, on seeing the cadaverous face of Emma, stretched out on her back, mouth open. Then, while appearing to be listening to Canivet, he passed his forefinger under his nose and repeated:

'Good, good.'

But his shoulders made their slow sign. Bovary noticed it; they looked at one another; and this man, so accustomed to the sight of sorrow, could not restrain a tear that dropped onto his shirt-frill.

He wished to take Canivet away into the adjoining room. Charles followed him.

'She's very bad, isn't she? If we were to apply mustard poultices? – I don't know what! Then think of something, you who have saved so many!'

Charles wrapped his arms about the doctor's frame, and gazed at him wildly, beseechingly, half-swooning against his chest.

'Come, my poor boy, cheer up. There is nothing more to be done.'

And Doctor Larivière turned away.

'You're leaving?'

'I shall return.'

He left as though to give an order to the postillion, along with Monsieur Canivet, who did not care to see Emma die in his hands.

The pharmacist joined them in the square. He was, by disposition, incapable of parting company from celebrated persons. And he entreated

Monsieur Larivière to grant him the honour of accepting an invitation to dine.

Pigeons were sent for at the *Lion d'Or*, everything in the way of cutlets at the butcher's, cream from Tuvache, eggs from Lestiboudois, and the apothecary himself helped with the preparations, while Madame Homais said, tightening the strings on her gown:

'You must beg our pardon, Monsieur; for, in our wretched part of the country, if it happens that notice isn't given the day before . . .'

'The wine glasses!!!' whispered Homais.

'At least, if we were in town, we could make shift with stuffed trotters.'

'Hold your tongue! Dinner's ready, doctor.'

He thought it proper, after the first morsels, to provide a few details on the catastrophe:

'Initially we had a feeling of dryness in the pharynx, followed by intolerable pains in the epigastrium, superpurgation, coma.'

'How did she poison herself?'

'I have no idea, doctor, and I'm not even too sure where she could have come by this arsenical acid.'

Justin, who was just then carrying a pile of plates, started to tremble.

'What's the matter with you?' said the pharmacist.

In reply, the young man dropped everything on the floor, with a great crash.

'Idiot!' yelled Homais. 'Butterfingers! Blockhead! Deuced ass!'

But, controlling himself suddenly:

'I wanted, Doctor, to attempt an analysis, and *primo*, I delicately introduced a tube . . .'

'It would have been of more value,' said the surgeon, 'to have introduced your fingers into the throat.'

His colleague kept quiet, having only a few moments ago received in confidence a serious reprimand concerning his emetic, so that this good Canivet, so arrogant and verbose at the time of the club-foot, was very unassuming today; he smiled without pause, in an approving manner.

Homais was full-blown in his pride as host, and the distressing notion of Bovary vaguely contributed to his pleasure, through some egoistical reflection on himself. And the doctor's presence enraptured him. He made a show of his erudition, he cited a hotchpotch of Spanish-fly, poison-tree, manchineel-tree, viper.

'And I have even read that various people have been found poisoned, Doctor, and as if struck by a thunder-bolt, due to blood-puddings that had been too vehemently smoked. At least, it was in a very fine report, composed by one of our pharmaceutical leading lights, one of our masters, the illustrious Cadet de Gassicourt!'

Madame Homais reappeared, bearing one of those shaky machines that are heated with spirits; for Homais liked to make his coffee on the dining-table, having, moreover, roasted it himself, ground it himself, blended it himself.

'*Saccharum*, Doctor,' he said, offering some sugar.

Then he had all his children come downstairs, eager to have the surgeon's opinion on their constitution.

Finally, Monsieur Larivière was about to leave, when Madame Homais asked him for an opinion concerning her husband. His nodding-off each evening after dinner might encourage thickening of the vein.

'Oh, it's not the *vain* that is bothering him.'

And, smiling a little at this unheeded pun, the doctor opened the door. But the pharmacy was overflowing with people; and he had much trouble in disentangling himself from Monsieur Tuvache, who feared his wife had an inflammation on the chest, because she had a habit of spitting in the embers; then from Monsieur Binet, who would feel a sudden great hunger from time to time, and from Madame Caron, who had tinglings; from Lheureux, who had trouble with giddiness; from Lestiboudois, who had rheumatism; from Madame Lefrançois, who had stomach acid. At last the three horses scampered away, and it was generally thought that he had not shown himself very obliging.

Public attention was distracted by the appearance of Monsieur Bournisien, who passed through the market-house with the holy oils.

Homais, as he had to by his principles, compared priests to crows drawn by the odour of death; the sight of a clergyman was personally obnoxious to him, for the cassock made him muse on the winding-sheet, and he cursed the one partly out of terror of the other.

Nevertheless, not recoiling from what he called *his mission*, he returned to Bovary's house in the company of Canivet, whom Monsieur Larivière, before leaving, had vigorously bound to this action; and, but for his wife's protests, he would even have brought his two sons along with him, so as to habituate them to serious cases, that it should be a lesson, an example, a solemn picture that would remain in their heads later on.

The bedroom, when they entered, was full of a dismal solemnity. On the work-table, covered in a white napkin, there were five or six little balls of cotton in a silver plate, beside a large crucifix, between two burning candlesticks. Emma, chin on her chest, had her eyes open extravagantly wide: and her poor hands crawled over the sheets, with that dreadful and gentle movement of the dying who seem to want to cover themselves over already with the shroud. Pale as a statue, and eyes red as coals, Charles, without weeping, stood opposite her, at the foot of the bed, while the priest, down on one knee, mumbled words in a low tone.

She slowly turned her face, and appeared struck with joy at suddenly seeing the violet stole, doubtless recognising in the midst of an extraordinary calm the lost voluptuousness of her first mystical yearnings, together with incipient glimpses of eternal happiness.

The priest got to his feet to take the crucifix; then she stretched forth her neck like someone thirsty, and, pressing her lips on the body of the man-God, she planted there with all her expiring force the most intense kiss of love that she had ever given. Then he recited the *Misereatur* and the *Indulgentiam*, dipping his right thumb in the oil and beginning the extreme unction: first on the eyes, that had lusted so after all the sumptuous things of earth; then on the nostrils, fond of warm breezes and the fragrances of love; then on the mouth, which had opened to lies, which had groaned with pride and shrieked in abandon; then on the hands, which would revel at each sweet touch, and finally on the soles of the feet, so swift in times past when she would run to glut her desires, and which walked no longer now.

The cleric wiped his fingers, threw the oil-soaked bits of cotton into the fire, and came back to sit next to the dying woman to tell her that she must presently join her sufferings to those of Jesus Christ and to surrender herself to the Divine mercy.

Concluding these exhortations, he tried to place a consecrated taper in her hands, a symbol of the celestial glories by which she would shortly be encompassed. Emma, too weak, could not close her fingers, and the taper, without Monsieur Bournisien, would have fallen to the floor.

Nevertheless she was no longer so pale, and her face bore a serene expression, as if the sacrament had healed her.

The priest did not fail to observe this; he even explained to Bovary that the Lord, sometimes, prolonged the life of people when He judged it expedient for their salvation; and Charles recalled a day when, likewise close to death, she had received communion.

'Perhaps we must not give ourselves up to despair,' he thought.

Indeed, she was looking all about her, slowly, like someone waking from a dream; then, in a clear voice, she asked for her mirror, and she stayed bent over it for some time, up to the moment when large tears trickled from her eyes. Then she threw her head back with a sigh and fell against her pillow again.

At once her chest began to heave rapidly. The whole of her tongue emerged from her mouth; her eyes, rolling, turned pale like two lamp-globes being dimmed, so she might have been considered dead already, were it not for the dreadful accelerating movement of her ribs, racked by a furious breathing, as if the soul were skipping about to loosen itself. Félicité kneeled before the crucifix, and the pharmacist himself flexed his hams a little, while Monsieur Canivet gazed vaguely out upon the square. Bournisien set to praying again, face inclined against the edge of the bed, with his long cassock trailing behind him in the room. Charles was on the other side, kneeling, arms stretched towards Emma. He had taken her hands and was clasping them, starting at every beat of her heart, as if at the reverberation of a tumbling ruin. As the death-rattle grew louder, the clergyman hastened on with his orisons; they mingled with Bovary's stifled sobs, and sometimes everything seemed to vanish in the dull murmur of the Latin syllables, that tolled like a passing-bell.

All of a sudden, the sound of heavy clogs could be heard on the pavement, along with the scrape of a stick; and a voice rose, a hoarse voice, singing:

> *A fair day's heat does often move*
> *The thoughts of some young lass to love.*

Emma rose like a corpse galvanised by an electric current, hair unravelled, eyes staring, agape.

> *So to gather with all care*
> *The ears of corn where sweeps the blade*
> *My Nanette shall be bending o'er*
> *The furrowed earth wherein they're made.*

'The blind man!' she screamed.

And Emma began to laugh, a dreadful laugh, frantic, despairing, thinking she could see the wretch's hideous face, which reared up out of the eternal gloom like some appalling terror.

> *It blew so hard that very day*
> *And the petticoat did fly away!*

A convulsion knocked her back onto the mattress. Everyone drew nearer. She no longer existed.

IX

THERE IS ALWAYS, AFTER SOMEONE'S death, a kind of stupefaction given off, so hard is it to take in this abrupt coming of nothingness and to resign oneself to believing it. But, when he nevertheless became aware of her stillness, Charles threw himself upon her and cried:

'Goodbye! Goodbye!'

Homais and Canivet dragged him out of the bedroom.

'Restrain yourself!'

'Yes,' he said as he struggled, 'I shall be reasonable, I won't do anything wrong. But let me be. I want to see her. She's my wife!'

And he wept.

'Weep,' replied the pharmacist, 'give vent to nature, it will ease the pain.'

Grown feebler than a child, Charles suffered himself to be led downstairs, into the parlour, and before long Monsieur Homais went back home.

On the square he was accosted by the blind man, who, dragging himself as far as Yonville, hoping for the anti-inflammatory ointment, was asking each passer-by where the apothecary lived.

'Well, fine! As if I didn't have other fish to fry. Ah, too bad, come back later!'

And he hurried into the pharmacy.

He had two letters to write, a calming draught to prepare for Bovary, a lie to think up that might conceal the poisoning and an article for the *Beacon* to compose, not counting the people awaiting him, for news; and, when the Yonvillais had all heard his story of the arsenic which she had mistaken for sugar, when making vanilla custard, Homais returned again to Bovary's house.

He found him alone (Monsieur Canivet had just left), seated in the easy-chair, by the window, and contemplating the room's flagstones with an idiot gaze.

'You must now,' said the pharmacist, 'fix an hour for the ceremony yourself.'

'Why? What ceremony?'

Then, in a stammering and appalled voice:

'Oh no, surely not! No, I want to keep her.'

Homais, to hide his confusion, took down a carafe from the shelf to water the geraniums.

'Oh, thank you,' said Charles, 'you are good!'

And he did not finish, suffocating under a wealth of recollections that the pharmacist's action brought to his mind.

Then, to distract him, Homais deemed it fitting to talk about gardening a little; the plants needed to be kept moist. Charles lowered his head as a sign of approval.

'What's more, fine days will be back again now.'

'Ah,' said Bovary.

The apothecary, out of ideas, gradually began to open the window's little curtains.

'Look, there's Monsieur Tuvache passing by.'

Charles repeated like a machine:

'Monsieur Tuvache passing by.'

Homais did not dare speak to him again of funeral arrangements; it was the clergyman who succeeded in persuading him to it.

He shut himself up in his surgery, took a pen, and, after having sobbed for a while, he wrote:

I want her to be buried in her wedding dress, with her white slippers, a crown. Her hair should be spread out on her shoulders; three coffins, one of oak, one of mahogany, one of lead. As long as no one says anything to me, I shall be strong. A great piece of green velvet should be lain over everything. I wish it. Do it.

These gentlemen were most astonished at Bovary's romantic ideas, and straightaway the pharmacist went to tell him:

'This velvet seems to me a superfluity. The expense, moreover . . .'

'Is that any of your business?' shouted Charles. 'Leave me be! You did not love her! Go away!'

The clergyman took him by the arm for a turn in the garden. He expounded on the vanity of earthly things. God was very great, very good; one must submit to his decrees without a murmur, even thank him.

Charles exploded into blasphemy.

'I curse him, your God!'

'The spirit of revolt is within you still,' sighed the clergyman.

Bovary was off. He took great strides beside the wall, near the espalier, and he ground his teeth, he raised cursing eyes to heaven; but not a single leaf stirred.

A light rain fell. Charles, who was bare-chested, ended up shivering with cold; he went inside to sit in the kitchen.

At six o'clock, a rattling noise could be heard in the square: it was the *Hirondelle* arriving; and he stayed with his forehead pressed to the window-pane, to see all the passengers alight one after the other. Félicité spread a mattress for him in the sitting room; he threw himself on it and fell asleep.

ALTHOUGH A PHILOSOPHER, MONSIEUR HOMAIS respected the dead. And, without bearing any ill-will towards poor Charles, he came back in the evening to keep vigil over the body, bearing with him three volumes, and a pocket-book, in order to make notes.

Monsieur Bournisien was there, and two tall tapers burned at the head of the bed, which had been pulled out of the alcove.

The apothecary, for whom the silence weighed, was not long in formulating a few doleful words concerning this 'unhappy young woman'; and the priest replied that there was nothing left now but to pray for her.

'Nevertheless,' continued Homais, 'it is one of two things: either she died in a state of grace (as the Church puts it), and so she has no need for our prayers; or else she died impenitent (I believe that's the ecclesiastical term), and so . . .'

Bournisien interrupted him, replying in a testy tone that it was no less necessary to pray.

'But,' the pharmacist objected, 'since God knoweth all our need, what profiteth prayer?'[23]

'What! Prayer!' said the clergyman. 'You are not Christian then?'

'Forgive me,' said Homais. 'I admire Christianity. First of all it freed the slaves, brought a morality into the world . . .'

'That is not the question. All the texts . . .'

'Oh, oh! As for the texts, open the history books; we know that they were falsified by the Jesuits.'

Charles came in, and, moving towards the bed, he slowly drew back the curtains.

Emma's head was resting on her right shoulder. The corner of her mouth, which was held open, made a sort of black hole in her lower face, the two thumbs remained inflected in the palms of her hands; a kind of white dust was sprinkled over her lashes, and her eyes were beginning to disappear into a viscous wanness that was like a fine web, as if spiders had been spinning over them. The sheet was hollowed out from the breasts to the knees, then rose again at the tips of the toes; and to Charles it seemed that infinite weights lay heavy upon her, an enormous load.

The church clock struck two. The loud murmur of the river could be heard flowing through the darkness, at the foot of the terrace. Monsieur Bournisien, from time to time, noisily blew his nose, and Homais scratched his pen across the paper.

'Now then, my good friend,' he said, 'come away, this sight is tearing you apart!'

Once Charles had left, the pharmacist and the priest started their discussion once more.

'Read Voltaire!' said one; 'read some Holbach, read the *Encyclopedia*!'

'Read the *Letters of Certain Portuguese Jews*!' said the other; 'read *The Proof of Christianity*, by Nicolas,[24] former justice of the peace!'

They were becoming heated, they were red-faced, they spoke at the same time, without listening to each other; Bournisien was scandalised by such audacity; Homais was amazed at such stupidity; and they were not far off calling each other names, when all of a sudden Charles reappeared. A fascination drew him. He was continually coming up the stairs.

He positioned himself opposite her to see better, and he lost himself in this contemplation, which by virtue of its profundity was no longer painful.

He remembered stories of catalepsy, the miracles of magnetism; and he told himself that by willing it to the extreme, he might succeed

315

in raising her from the dead. One time he even leaned towards her, and he cried out very softly, 'Emma! Emma!' His breath, blowing hard, made the tapers' flame tremble on the wall.

In the small hours, Madame Bovary senior arrived; Charles, when he embraced her, had a fresh overflow of tears. She attempted, just as the pharmacist had tried, to make a few observations on the funeral expenses. He flew into such a rage that she held her tongue, and he even charged her with heading off immediately to the town to buy what was needed.

Charles stayed on his own all afternoon; Berthe had been taken to Madame Homais' house; Félicité stayed upstairs, in the bedroom, with Mère Lefrançois.

In the evening, he received visitors. He would get up, clasp your hands without being able to speak, then one would sit down with the others, who formed a semi-circle in front of the fire. With lowered faces and knees crossed, they jiggled one leg from side to side, while intermittently heaving a great sigh; and each was inordinately bored; yet no one would be the first to leave.

Homais, when he returned at nine o'clock (he would be all you saw on the square, for the last two days), was loaded with a supply of camphor, gum benjamin and aromatic herbs. He was also carrying a vase full of chlorine, to dismiss noxious vapours. At that moment, the maid, Madame Lefrançois and Mère Bovary were moving about Emma, to finish dressing her; and they lowered the long stiff veil, that covered her down to her satin slippers.

Félicité was sobbing:

'Ah! My poor mistress! My poor mistress!'

'Look at her,' said the inn-keeper, sighing, 'how pretty she still is! If you wouldn't swear she's about to get up.'

Then they leaned over, to put her crown on.

They had to lift her head a little, and so a torrent of black fluids poured, like a vomiting, out of her mouth.

'Ah, dear God! Mind the dress!' shouted Madame Lefrançois. 'Help us then!' she said to the pharmacist. 'Are you frightened, by chance?'

'Me, frightened?' he replied, shrugging his shoulders. 'Ah well, yes!

I saw the like at the Hôtel-Dieu, when I was studying pharmacy. We prepared punch in the dissecting theatre. Nothingness does not scare a philosopher; and, I often say it, I even intend to bequeath my body to a hospital, to be of some use later on to Science.'

On arrival, the priest asked how Monsieur was; and, when the apothecary replied, he resumed:

'The blow, you understand, is still too recent!'

Then Homais congratulated him on not being exposed, like everyone else, to the loss of a loved partner; from which ensued a discussion on the celibacy of priests.

'For,' said the pharmacist, 'it is not natural for a man to dispense with women! We have witnessed crimes . . .'

'But, good grief!' cried the ecclesiastic, 'how do you suppose an individual contracted in marriage might keep, for example, the secrets of confession?'

Homais attacked confession. Bournisien defended it; he expanded on the rehabilitations it had brought about. He cited various anecdotes of thieves suddenly turned honest. Soldiers, having stepped up to the penitential judgment-seat, had felt the scales fall from their eyes. At Fribourg there was a minister . . .

His companion was asleep. Then, feeling a little suffocated in the bedroom's stuffy atmosphere, he opened the window, which woke up the pharmacist.

'Come, a pinch of snuff,' he said to him. 'Do accept, it kills the time.'

A continuous barking dragged on a long way off, somewhere.

'Can you hear a dog howling?' said the pharmacist.

'It's alleged they smell the dead,' replied the ecclesiastic. 'Likewise with bees: they fly away from the hive when someone dies.'

Homais did not react to these prejudices, as he had fallen asleep again.

Monsieur Bournisien, more robust, continued now and again to move his lips in a whisper; then, imperceptibly, he lowered his chin, let slip his great black book and began to snore.

They were facing one another, bellies prominent, faces bloated, with a scowling look, after so much disagreement joined at last in the same human frailty; and they stirred no more than the body beside them with its air of being asleep.

Charles, coming in, did not wake them. It was the last time. He was come to bid her farewell.

The aromatic herbs still smoked, and the eddies of blue vapours blended with the fog that came in. There were a few stars, and the night was mild.

The wax from the tapers fell in great drops on the bed's sheets. Charles watched them burn, wearying his eyes against the radiance of their yellow flame.

Moiré patterns shivered on the satin dress, white as moonlight. Emma vanished away under it; and it seemed to him that, spreading outside herself, she was disappearing confusedly into the surrounding things, into the silence, into the night, into the wind blowing past, into the moist smells wafting up.

Then, all of a sudden, he saw her in the garden at Tostes, on the bench, against the thorn hedge, or else at Rouen, in the streets, at the door of their house, in the farmyard at Les Bertaux. He heard once more the laughter of the merry lads dancing under the apple trees; the room was full of the scent of her hair, and her dress shivered in his arms with a crackle of sparks. This, this was the very same!

He spent a long time thus, remembering all the vanished delights, her postures, her gestures, the timbre of her voice. After one despair, another came and always, inexhaustibly, like the waves of a bursting flood.

He felt a terrible curiosity: slowly, with his fingertips, heart pounding, he raised her veil. But he let out a scream of horror that woke the other two. They dragged him away downstairs, into the parlour.

Then Félicité came to say that he was asking for some locks of hair.

'Cut them!' replied the apothecary.

And, as she did not dare to, he came forward himself, scissors in hand. He was trembling so hard, that he punctured the temple's skin in a number of places. At last, stiffening himself against the emotion, Homais administered two or three great thrusts at random, which left white dints[25] in that beautiful head of black hair.

The pharmacist and the priest plunged anew into their affairs, not without slumbering from time to time, which they accused one another of doing each time they woke up. Then Monsieur Bournisien sprinkled the room with holy water and Homais tossed a bit of chlorine on the floor.

Félicité had been careful to leave them a bottle of eau-de-vie, a cheese and a plump brioche on the chest of drawers. And, at about four o'clock in the morning, the apothecary, who was exhausted, sighed:

'My word, I'll take sustenance with pleasure!'

The clergyman needed no persuasion; he went out to say his mass, returned; then they ate and touched glasses, all the while sniggering a little, without knowing why, inflamed by that vague cheerfulness that takes hold of you after a heavy-hearted session; and, over the last little glass, the priest said to the pharmacist, slapping his shoulder all the while:

'We shall end up understanding each other!'

Downstairs in the hallway they met the workmen arriving. So, for two hours, Charles had to endure the torment of the hammer resounding on the boards. Then they brought her down in her oak coffin which they fitted into the two others; but, as the outer coffin was too big, the gaps had to be stopped up with the wool from a mattress. Finally, when the three lids were planed, nailed, soldered, she was laid in state before the door; the house was opened wide, and the folk of Yonville began to flock.

Père Rouault arrived. He fainted in the square when he saw the black pall.

X

HE HAD ONLY RECEIVED THE pharmacist's letter thirty-six hours after the event; and, out of respect for his feelings, Monsieur Homais had written it in such a way that it was impossible to know how things stood.

The good fellow collapsed at first as if hit by a stroke. Then he understood that she was not dead. But she might be . . . At length he had slipped on his smock-frock, donned his hat, hooked a spur on his shoe and had left at full speed; and, for the whole journey, Père Rouault, panting for breath, was consumed with anguish. Once, he even had to dismount. He could no longer see a thing, he kept hearing voices around him, he felt he was going mad.

The day broke, he saw three black hens sleeping in a tree; he gave a start, terrified by this omen. So he promised the Holy Virgin three chasubles for the church, and that he would go barefoot from the cemetery at Les Bertaux to the chapel at Vassonville.

He rode into Maromme hailing the people from the inn, forced the door open with a blow from his shoulder, leapt to the sack of oats, poured a bottle of sweet cider into the feeding trough, and again straddled his nag, whose hooves struck sparks from the stones.

He said to himself that they would no doubt save her; the doctors would find a remedy, for certain. He called to mind all the miraculous cures recounted to him.

Then she appeared to him, dead. She was there, in front of him, in the middle of the road. He pulled on the reins and the hallucination vanished.

At Quincampoix, to give himself courage, he drank three coffees straight off.

He thought they had made a mistake in writing her name. He looked for the letter in his pocket, felt it there, but did not dare open it.

He was reduced to conjecturing that it was perhaps a *prank*, someone's revenge, the whim of a man on a spree; and, besides, if she were dead, would you not know it? But no! the countryside had nothing extraordinary about it: the sky was blue, the trees swayed; a flock of sheep passed. He glimpsed the village; they saw him rushing up, bent right over his horse, which he was drubbing with heavy blows, and whose saddle-girths were trickling blood.

When he recovered consciousness, he fell all in tears into Bovary's arms:

'My daughter! Emma! My child! Explain to me . . . ?'

And the other replied through sobs:

'I don't know, I don't know! It is a curse!'

The apothecary separated them.

'These horrible details are useless. I will apprise Monsieur. There are people coming. Dignity, the deuce! Philosophy!'

The poor boy wanted to appear strong, and he repeated several times:

'Yes, courage!'

'Ah well,' cried the good fellow, 'I'll have it, in the name of God's thunder! See if I shan't be bearing her right to the end!'

The bell tolled. Everything was ready. They must be setting off.

And, seated in a choir stall, one next to the other, they saw the three precentors continually passing back and forth in front of them, chanting psalms. The serpent-player blew with all his might. Monsieur Bournisien, in full apparel, sang in a shrill voice; he bowed to the tabernacle, raised his hands, stretched his arms out. Lestiboudois went round the church with his whalebone staff; near the lectern, the coffin lay between four rows of tapers. Charles had a mind to get up and put them out.

He strove nevertheless to stir himself to his devotions, to lift himself up into the hope of a life to come when he would see her again. He imagined that she had gone on a voyage, far away, for a long time. But, when he considered that she was under there, and that everything was finished, that they would carry her into the earth, he got caught in a fierce, black, despairing rage. Sometimes, he thought he felt nothing; and he enjoyed this soothing of his sorrow, reproaching himself all the while for being a miserable wretch.

They heard on the flagstones something like the sharp click of an iron-shod pole tapping them with even strokes. It came from the back, and stopped abruptly in the church's side aisle. A man in a coarse brown jacket kneeled painfully. It was Hippolyte, the servant from the *Lion d'Or*. He had put on his new leg.

One of the precentors was walking up the nave for the collection, and the two-sous coins chinked in the silver dish, one after the other.

'Hurry up now! I'm suffering. I am!' cried Bovary, as he threw a five-franc coin at it in anger.

The churchman thanked him with a slow bow.

They sang, they knelt, they got up, it never ended! He remembered how once, in the early times, they had attended mass together, and they were on the other side, to the right, against the wall. The bell began again. There was a great stirring of chairs. The bearers slipped their three poles under the coffin, and it was carried out of the church.

Justin then appeared at the door of the pharmacy. He went back inside all of a sudden, pale, tottering.

They stood at windows to watch the procession pass. Charles, in front, threw back his shoulders. He put on an appearance of courage and nodded at those who, emptying out of lanes and doors, found a place in the crowd.

The six men, three on each side, were walking with short steps and puffing a little. The priests, the precentors and the two choirboys were performing the *De Profundis*; and their voices dwindled away over the fields, rising and falling in waves. Sometimes they disappeared from sight with the track's windings; but the great silver cross stood erect still between the trees.

The women followed, covered in black mantles with lowered hoods; each carried in her hands a big lighted candle, and Charles felt himself swooning at this continual repetition of prayer and flame, under these cloying smells of wax and cassock. A fresh breeze blew, the rye and the rape were verdant, the dewdrops trembled on the sides of the path, on the thorn hedges. All kinds of joyous sounds filled the horizon: the banging of a cart rolling at a distance over the ruts, the cockerel's crow repeating itself or the scamper of a hen that you could see fleeing under the apple-trees. The clear sky was speckled with pink clouds; curls of smoke fell back upon the thatched rooves covered in irises; Charles, as he passed, recognised the yards. He remembered mornings like this, when, having visited some sick patient or other, he left them, and went back to her.

The black cloth, sprinkled with white teardrops, rose up from time to time and revealed the coffin. The weary bearers were slowing down, and it advanced by continual jerks, like a launch that pitches at every wave.

They arrived.

The men continued further down, to a spot in the grass where the ditch had been dug.

They lined up all round; and, while the priest spoke, the red earth, thrown up on the sides, was trickling at the corners noiselessly, on and on.

Then, when the four ropes were ready, the coffin was heaved on top. He watched it descend. It was descending for ever.

At last they heard a thud; squeaking, the ropes came back up. Then Bournisien took the spade that Lestiboudois held out to him; with his left hand, as he went on sprinkling with the right, he pushed in a large shovelful with vigour; and the coffin's wood, clipped by the pebbles, made that tremendous noise that seems to us to be the resounding of eternity.

The clergyman passed the aspergill to his neighbour. It was Monsieur Homais. He shook it solemnly, then held it out to Charles, who sank down onto his knees in the earth, and was casting in handfuls of it as he called out: 'Adieu!' He blew kisses at her; he crawled to the grave to be swallowed up with her.

They led him away; and he was not long in calming down, experiencing, perhaps, like all the others, the vague satisfaction of having done with it.[26]

Père Rouault, on the way back, began quietly smoking a pipe; something Homais, in his heart of hearts, deemed improper. He noted likewise that Monsieur Binet had refrained from appearing, that Tuvache had 'made off' after the mass, and that Théodore, the notary's servant, wore a blue coat, 'as if they couldn't find him a black coat, seeing it's the custom, devil take it!' And to impart his observations, he went from one group to the other. They deplored Emma's death, and above all Lheureux, who had not failed to come to the funeral.

'That poor little woman. What woe for her husband.'

The apothecary answered:

'Without me, I'll have you know, he'd have carried out some fatal attempt on himself.'

'Such a good person she was. And to think that it was only last Saturday that I saw her again in my shop!'

'I didn't have the leisure,' said Homais, 'to prepare a few words for me to cast on her tomb.'

Back home, Charles undressed, and Père Rouault donned his blue smock again. It was new, and, as he had, along the way, wiped his eyes often on the sleeves, its colour had come off on his face; and there the trace of tears made lines in the layer of dust by which it was soiled.

Madame Bovary senior was with them. All three kept quiet. At length the good old fellow sighed:

'Do you remember, my friend, me coming to Tostes that time, when you'd just lost your first deceased. I comforted you back then. I found what to say; but right now . . .'

Then, with a slow groan that raised his entire chest:

'Ah, it's the end for me, y'know. I've seen my wife depart . . . my son after . . . and here's my daughter, today!'

He wanted to head back to Les Bertaux straightaway, saying that he could not sleep in that there house. He even refused to see his granddaughter.

'No, no. That'd be too much grief for me. Just give her a fine kiss. Farewell! You're a good lad! And besides, I'll never forget this,' he said, slapping his thigh, 'never fear! You'll always have your turkey.'

But, when he reached the top of the hill, he turned round, as before he had turned round on the Saint-Victor road, on parting from her. The windows of the village were all aflame in the sun's slanting rays as it sank into the meadow. He put his hand in front of his eyes; and he glimpsed on the horizon an enclosure of walls where, here and there, trees formed dark tufts between white stones, then he carried on at a gentle trot, for his nag was lame.

Charles and his mother, despite their weariness, stayed chatting together for a very long time that evening. They spoke of days past and of the future. She would come to live in Yonville, she would run the house, they would never more leave one another. She was ingenious and fawning, inwardly delighted to retake possession of an affection that had evaded her for so many years. Midnight rang out. The village, as usual, was silent, and Charles, wide awake, still thought of her.

Rodolphe, who, to distract himself, had beaten the wood for game all day long, slept peacefully in his chateau; and Léon, further away, slept as well.

There was someone else who, at that hour, was not asleep.

On the grave, between the pines, a child wept on his knees, and his breast, made sore with sobbing, heaved in the shadows, under the pressure of an immense regret gentler than the moon and more unfathomable than the night. All of a sudden the gate creaked. It was Lestiboudois; he was coming to look for his spade that he had forgotten earlier. He recognised Justin scaling the wall, and now knew just who the evil-doer was that kept stealing his potatoes.

XI

CHARLES, THE NEXT DAY, HAD the little one returned home. She asked for her mamma. They told her that she was away, that she would bring her back some toys. Berthe spoke of her again a few times; then, in the end, thought no more of it. This child's cheerfulness broke Bovary's heart, and he had to suffer the pharmacist's unbearable consolings.

Soon the money business began afresh, Monsieur Lheureux stirring up his friend Vinçart again, and Charles pledged himself to exorbitant amounts; for he would never consent to allow the least stick of furniture to be sold that had belonged to *her*. His mother grew exasperated with him. He waxed more indignant than she did. He had quite changed. She quit the house.

Then each person set about *profiting*. Mademoiselle Lempereur claimed six months of lessons, even though Emma had never taken a single one (despite that paid-off bill she had shown Bovary): it was an agreement between the two women; the book-lender claimed three years of subscription; Mère Rolet claimed the postage for a score of letters; and, as Charles asked for an explanation, she had the decency to reply:

'Ah, I don't know anything about it. It was to do with her transactions.'

With each debt he paid off, Charles thought he had done with them. Others kept arriving unexpectedly, over and over.

He demanded that the arrears of former consultations be paid. He was shown the letters his wife had sent. Then he had to apologise.

Félicité now wore Madame's dresses; not all, as he had kept some, and he would go to examine them in his dressing-room, secluding himself there; as she was roughly her size, Charles, on catching sight of her from behind, would frequently be gripped by delusion, and shout out:

'Oh! Stay! Stay!'

But, at Pentecost, she decamped from Yonville, carried off by Théodore, and stealing everything that remained in the wardrobe.

It was at about this time that the widow Dupuis had the honour to inform him of the 'marriage of Monsieur Léon Dupuis, her son, notary at Yvetot, to Mademoiselle Léocadie Leboeuf, of Bondeville.' Among the congratulations that he conveyed to her, Charles wrote this sentence:

'How happy my poor wife would have been!'

One day when wandering aimlessly through the house, he had climbed right up to the attic, he felt under his slipper a ball of thin paper. He opened it out and read: 'Courage, Emma! Courage! I do not wish to be your life's misfortune.' It was Rodolphe's letter, fallen to the floor between some boxes, that had lain there, and that the wind from the dormer-window had blown towards the door. And Charles stayed motionless and gaping on that same spot where long ago, even paler than he, Emma, in despair, had wanted to die. At last, he discovered a little R at the bottom of the second page. Who was it? He recalled the attentiveness of Rodolphe, his sudden disappearance and the constrained manner he had showed on meeting him two or three times since. But the respectful tone of the letter deceived him.

'They perhaps loved each other platonically,' he told himself.

Moreover, Charles was not the type to go to the bottom of things; he recoiled from evidence, and his uncertain jealousy was carried away in the immensity of his grief.

They must, he thought, have adored her. All the men, most certainly, had hankered after her. She appeared to him more beautiful; and he conceived a permanent, furious desire for her, which inflamed his despair and was limitless, because it could not be realised.

For his own pleasure, as if she were still alive, he adopted her partialities, her ideas; he bought himself polished boots, he took to wearing white neck-cloths. He applied cosmetics on his moustaches, like her he signed promissory notes. She corrupted him from beyond the grave.

He was obliged to sell the silver-plate piece by piece, then he sold the sitting-room furniture. All the rooms were stripped; but the bedroom, her own bedroom, stayed as before. After his dinner, Charles would go up there. He pushed the round table in front of the fire, and he approached *her* arm-chair. He sat down facing it. A candle burned in one of the gilded candlesticks. Berthe, close by him, would colour in some prints.

He suffered, the poor man, to see her so badly dressed, with her laceless boots and her blouses' arm-holes torn down to the hips, for the housekeeper took but little care. But she was so sweet, so pretty, and her little head would lean so gracefully, letting her full blonde hair fall over her pink cheeks, that an infinite delight broke upon him, a pleasure entirely mixed with bitterness like those badly made wines that smell of resin. He repaired her playthings, made her dancing puppets out of card, or sewed up her dolls' torn stomachs. Then, if his eyes lighted on the work-box, a ribbon lying about or even a pin remaining in a crack in the table, he began to dream, and he looked so sad, that she became sad with him.

Nobody now came to see them; for Justin had fled to Rouen, where he had become a grocer's boy, and the apothecary's children associated less and less with the little girl, Monsieur Homais not caring for the close connection to be prolonged, given the difference in their social conditions.

The blind man, whom he had not been able to cure with his salve, had gone back to the hill at Bois-Guillaume, where he related to travellers the fruitless attempt of the pharmacist, to the point where

Homais, when he went to town, hid behind the curtains of the *Hirondelle*, in order to avoid meeting him. He cursed the fellow; and, in the interests of his own reputation, wanting to be absolutely rid of him, he swung all his guns upon him in secret, revealing the depth of his own intellect and the nefariousness of his vanity. So for six consecutive months, you could read in the *Rouen Beacon* paragraphs conceived thus:

'Whoever proceeds towards the fertile lands of Picardy has doubtless observed, upon the hill at Bois-Guillaume, a wretch suffering from a loathsome facial sore. He plagues you to death, persistently follows you and levies a veritable tax on the traveller. Are we yet in those monstrous times of the Middle Ages, when vagabonds were permitted to show off in our public places the leprosy and the scrofula that they had carried back from the Crusades?'

Or else:

'In spite of the laws against vagabondage, the approaches to our great towns continue to be infested by gangs of paupers. Some are to be seen going about on their own, these being, perhaps, not the least dangerous. What are our magistrates thinking of?'

Then Homais would make up anecdotes:

'Yesterday, on the hill at Bois-Guillaume, a skittish horse . . .' And an account would follow of an accident caused by the presence of the blind man.

He did so well that they imprisoned the fellow. But they let him go. He began again, and Homais also began again. It was a battle. He won the day; for his enemy was sentenced to life confinement in an alms-house.

This success emboldened him; and not a dog was run over, a barn burnt down, a wife beaten in the district, that he did not immediately apprise the public of it, ever guided by a love of progress and a loathing of priests. He made comparisons between elementary schools and the Ignorantine brothers, to the detriment of these latter, called to mind Saint Bartholomew in reference to a grant of a hundred francs made to the Church, and denounced abuses, shot forth sallies. He was having his say. Homais kept on undermining; he was becoming dangerous.

Nevertheless, he was suffocating in the narrow confines of

journalism, and soon he must have the book, the literary work! So he composed *General Statistics of the Canton of Yonville, followed by Some Climatological Observations*, and the statistics pushed him on towards philosophy. He engrossed himself in the big questions: the social problem, the moralisation of the poorer classes, pisciculture, India rubber, railways, etc. He came to feel ashamed at being a bourgeois. He affected *the artistic manner*, he smoked! He bought himself two *chic* Pompadour statuettes, to adorn his drawing-room.

He did not give up the pharmacy; quite the contrary! He kept up with the latest discoveries. He followed the great advance in chocolates. He was the first who brought *cho-ca* and *revalenta* into the Seine-Inférieure. He was smitten with enthusiasm for the Pulvermacher hydro-electric body-chains; he wore one himself; and, in the evening, when he removed his flannel vest, Madame Homais remained utterly dazzled before the gold spiral beneath which he would disappear, and felt her ardour double for this man pinioned tighter than a Scythian and as splendid as a magus.

He had some fine ideas concerning Emma's tomb. At first he proposed a stump of pillar with a piece of drapery, then a pyramid, then a temple of Vesta, a sort of rotunda . . . or else 'a heap of ruins'. And, in all these plans, he stuck to the weeping willow, considering it the required symbol of sadness.

Charles and he took a trip together to Rouen, to view tombs at a monumental mason's – accompanied by a painter, one Vaufrylard by name, friend of Bridoux, and who kept making puns all the time. At last, having examined a hundred drawings, ordered an estimate and made a second trip to Rouen, Charles settled on a mausoleum which would bear on its two principal facets 'a guardian spirit holding a snuffed torch'.

As for the inscription, Homais found nothing fitter than *Sta viator*, and he stopped there; he racked his brains; he continually repeated *Sta viator* . . . At last, he hit on *amabilem conjugem calcas!*[27] Which was taken up.

One strange thing, was that Bovary, while continually thinking on Emma, was forgetting her; and he was in despair at feeling this image escaping his memory amidst the efforts he was making to retain it. Yet each night he would dream of her; it was always the same dream: he would approach her; but, when he was on the point of clasping her, she fell to rottenness in his arms.

They saw him entering the church in the evening for a week. Monsieur Bournisien even called on him two or three times, then gave him up. Besides, the old fellow was becoming intolerant, fanatical, Homais said; he would fulminate against the spirit of the age, and never failed, every fortnight, in his sermon, to relate the death-struggle of Voltaire, who died eating his own faeces, as everyone knows.

Despite the thriftiness with which Bovary lived, he was far from being able to pay off his debts. Lheureux refused to renew any promissory note. The seizure grew imminent. So he had recourse to his mother, who agreed to let him take out a mortgage on her property, while pouring out violent recriminations against Emma; and, in return for her sacrifice, she asked for a shawl, which had escaped Félicité's pillagings. Charles refused. They fell out.

She made the first overtures towards a reconciliation, by proposing to take in the little girl, who would comfort her in her home. Charles consented. But, at the moment of parting, all courage forsook him. So there was a definitive, total rupture.

According as his affections disappeared, the more narrowly did he confine himself to the love of his child. She worried him, however; for she would cough sometimes, and had red blotches on her cheeks.

Opposite him sprawled, blooming and merry, the family of the pharmacist, whom all earthly things conduced to satisfy. Napoléon helped him in the laboratory, Athalie embroidered him a bonnet-grec, Irma cut out paper circles to cover the jams, and Franklin recited the multiplication table in a single breath. He was the happiest of fathers, the most fortunate of men.

Illusion! One secret ambition gnawed at him: Homais longed for the cross. He did not lack for claims:

1° Being distinguished by a boundless devotion at the time of the cholera; 2° having published, at my own expense, various works of public benefit, such as . . . (and he called to mind his dissertation entitled: '*On cider, of its manufacture and effects*'; plus, some observations on the apple plant-louse, sent to the Academy; his book of statistics, and even his pharmaceutical thesis); not to mention the fact that I am a member of several learned societies (he belonged to only one).

'Lastly,' he cried, with a cunning side-step, 'even if it's only for distinguishing myself at the fires!'

So Homais bent to the Powers that be. He privately did Monsieur le Préfet great services in the elections. In short he sold himself, he prostituted himself. He even addressed a petition to the sovereign in which he entreated him *to do him justice*; he called him *our good king* and compared him to Henri IV.

And, each morning, the apothecary threw himself on the newspaper to behold his nomination within: it did not come. Finally, unable to contain himself any longer, he had a turf plot designed in his garden representing the star of honour, with two little grassed twists springing from the top to imitate the ribbon. He would stroll around it, arms folded, reflecting on the government's folly and man's ingratitude.

Out of respect, or a kind of sensuality that made him slow down his investigations, Charles had not yet opened the secret compartment of an ebony desk that Emma habitually used. One day, at last, he sat before it, turned the key and pressed the spring. All Léon's letters lay within. No doubting it, this time! He devoured them to the last one, rummaged in every corner, every piece of furniture, every drawer, behind the walls, sobbing, howling, desperate, mad. He discovered a box, staved it in with a single kick. Rodolphe's portrait leapt at him full in the face, amidst a confusion of love letters.

People were astonished at his despondency. He no longer left the house, received no one, refused even to go and see his patients. So they maintained that he *shut himself up to drink*.

Sometimes, however, a busybody would raise himself above the garden hedge, and discern with amazement this long-bearded man, muffled up in sordid clothes, wild-looking, and weeping loudly as he paced.

In the evening, through the summer, he would take his little girl with him and convey her to the cemetery. They would return from there in the dark of night, when the square was lit by no more than Binet's garret-window.

Nevertheless, the voluptuousness of his grief was incomplete, for he had no one around him who shared it; and he would call on Mère Lefrançois so that he could talk about *her*. But the landlady would only listen with half an ear, having heart-aches like him, for Monsieur Lheureux had just set up *Les Favorites du Commerce* at last, and Hivert, who enjoyed a high reputation for running errands, exacted an increase in salary and threatened to hire himself out '*to the Competition*'.

One day when he had gone to the market in Argueil in order to sell his horse – last resort – he met Rodolphe.

They paled on perceiving each other. Rodolphe, who had only sent his card, stammered the odd excuse to begin with, then grew bolder and even stretched his self-possession (it was very hot, this now being August) to the point of inviting him to the tavern for a bottle of beer.

Leaning on his elbow opposite him, he chewed his cigar while he chatted, and Charles lost himself in reverie before this face that she had loved. He seemed to see something of her again. It was a wonder. He would have liked to be this man.

The other continued to talk cultivation, cattle, manure, stopping up with banal phrases any little space between where a hint might slip in. Charles was not listening to him; Rodolphe noticed this, and he followed the memories fleeting past in the motions of his face. Little by little it turned crimson, the nostrils palpitating fast, the lips quivering; there was even a moment when Charles, full of a dark rage, fixed his gaze on Rodolphe who, in a kind of fright, broke off. But soon the same mournful weariness reappeared on his countenance.

'I hold nothing against you,' he said.

Rodolphe remained speechless. And Charles, his head in his hands, repeated in a feeble voice and in the resigned tone of numberless sorrows:

'No, I hold nothing against you any more!'

He even added a high-flown phrase, the only one he had ever uttered:

'It is the fault of fate!'

Rodolphe, who had driven this fate, thought him too easy-going and weak for a man in his situation, comic even, and a little contemptible.

The next day, Charles went to sit on the bench, in the arbour. Daylight filtered through the trellis[28]; the vine-leaves drew their shadows on the sand, the jasmin gave out its fragrance, the sky was blue, the Spanish-flies hummed around the flowering lilies, and Charles choked like an adolescent under the vague exhalations of love that swelled his grief-stricken heart.

At seven o'clock, little Berthe, who had not seen him all afternoon, came to fetch him for dinner.

His head was tipped back against the wall, eyes closed, mouth open, and he was holding in his hands a long lock of black hair.

'Papa, come now!' she said.

And, thinking that he wanted to play, she gently pushed him. He fell on the ground. He was dead.

Thirty-six hours later, at the apothecary's request, Monsieur Canivet hastened in. He opened him up and found nothing.

When everything was sold, there remained twelve francs and seventy-five centimes that served to pay for Mademoiselle Bovary's journey to her grandmother's. The good woman died that same year; Père Rouault being paralysed, it fell to an aunt to take charge of her. She is poor and sends her, to earn her bread, to a cotton mill.

Since Bovary's death, three doctors have succeeded one another at Yonville without managing to prosper there, Monsieur Homais so instantly demolishing them. He has a hellishly fine clientele; authority treats him with care and public opinion protects him.

He has just received the cross of the Legion of Honour.

NOTES

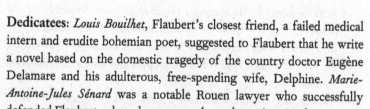

Dedicatees: *Louis Bouilhet*, Flaubert's closest friend, a failed medical intern and erudite bohemian poet, suggested to Flaubert that he write a novel based on the domestic tragedy of the country doctor Eugène Delamare and his adulterous, free-spending wife, Delphine. *Marie-Antoine-Jules Sénard* was a notable Rouen lawyer who successfully defended Flaubert, when charges were brought against *Madame Bovary* for affronting public morals, by suggesting it was an astringent warning to young girls.

PART ONE

1. **chapka**: a 19th-century Polish cavalryman's hat; this celebrated description of Charles Bovary's composite headgear introduces him as a dull-witted, bovine grotesque. It will take the length of the novel to turn him into a much more complex and sympathetic character.

2. **the *Quos ego***: the command by which Neptune calms the storm in Virgil's *Aeneid* (1, 135), a passage familiar as a set text to the 19th-century pupil.

3. ***ridiculus sum***: 'I am ridiculous'. A definition which holds true for Bovary during much of the novel.

4. **innumerable cringings**: the original '*servilités*' is an abstract noun and never usually in the plural, thus sounding similarly odd to a French ear.

5. **It would be impossible now for any of us**: the reappearance of the opening voice, Charles's schoolfellow; he recalls the cap in meticulous detail, yet has no memory of Charles himself, and subsequently dissolves as a narratological device. Authorial lapse, or modernist irony?

6. *Anacharsis*: the *Voyage du jeune Anacharsis en Grèce* by Abbé Barthélemy (1716–95), a work much used in 19th–century French education.

7. **the river**: the Robec, then flowing through one of the poorest, most industrialised areas of Rouen, changed colour according to the dyes jettisoned into it. Its symbolic possibilities seem (typically of the novel) to be outweighed by its matter-of-fact presentation.

8. **infatuated with Béranger**: Pierre-Jean de Béranger (1780–1857), the proto-socialist, highly influential poet and songwriter, despised by Flaubert.

9. **the medical officer**: Charles is a mere *officier de santé* in the strict medical hierarchy of the time; as such, he was not allowed to practise outside his department, and could carry out only minor operations unless supervised by a qualified doctor.

10. **ivories of Dieppe**: from the 17th-century on, Dieppe was an important ivory-carving centre, reaching its apogee in the mid 19th-century when it produced everything from crucifixes to snuffboxes.

11. **bandeaux**: this confusing hairdressing term from the 1830s (borrowed by the English) appears several times in the original. It can either refer to a hair-tie or, as always in *Madame Bovary*, the sides of the hair when drawn smoothly across the ears into a knot or chignon at the back. The side hair does then resemble 'bands' or, as here, a single swathe.

12. **lashed whip**: in French, '*nerf de boeuf*'; this highly charged scene climaxes on a term which also meant 'bull's pizzle'.

13. **barton-yard**: southern English dialect for 'farmyard', reflecting Flaubert's Norman term, *masure*.

14. **And besides . . . heart?**: this passage is present in the final manuscript copy and the first edition, but missing in all subsequent editions, perhaps due to a misreading of the repeated '*la veuve*'; its restoration gives a sequential logic to the physical description that follows.

15. **long, hungry teeth**: the figurative expression '*avoir les dents longues*' means to be ambitious or ravenous. Here, Flaubert seems to be playing with both the literal and the figurative meanings.

16. **The base . . . at the summit**: This famous description of the suggestive and top-heavy wedding cake is a stylistic echo of both the wedding procession and, in the opening chapter, Charles's schoolboy cap. In this scene, by contrast, we have no description of Charles's dress: he is described only as 'empty-handed'.

17. **pebble-stone heaps**: used for road-mending: called in French *mètres de caillou*, being a cubic metre in size.

18. **He felt as sad as an unfurnished house**: similes outnumber metaphors in *Madame Bovary*, and take a variety of forms, from the parodic to the down-to-earth.

19. **shivered all over**: a cut line in the manuscript makes clear that the canvas-hung wallpaper was shivering because of a draught through the open door.

20. **the *Dictionnaire des sciences médicales***: Flaubert took copious notes from this, the first encyclopedic dictionary of medicine (1812–22).

21. **silk kerchief**: the kerchief usually covered the head, being drawn over the nightcap.

22. **he stepped up . . . she cried out**: an example of Flaubert's characteristic ternary (threefold) structure, often used within a single sentence.

23. ***Paul et Virginie***: a popular Enlightenment novel by Bernardin de Saint-Pierre, published in 1787. Much influenced by Rousseau, it is set on the island of Mauritius and pitches nature's utopic innocence against upper-class corruption.

24. **Mademoiselle de La Vallière**: Louis XIV's mistress, Louise de la Vallière (1644–1710) became a Carmelite nun and a favourite 19th-century example of pious conversion.

25. **Abbé Frayssinous's *Conférences***: these lectures were published under the title *Défense du Christianisme* (1825; 'A Defence of Christianity'), and helped inaugurate the restoration of religion following the Revolution. The royalist François-René Chateaubriand's *Le Génie du Christianisme* (1802; 'The Genius of Christianity') played a similar role, but in a poetic style that Flaubert much admired.

26. **Mary Stuart . . . Jeanne d'Arc, Héloïse, Agnès Sorel, *La Belle* Ferronière and Clémence Isaure**: Mary Stuart (1542–87): Queen of Scotland and Queen consort of France, eventually executed for treason by Elizabeth I. Jeanne d'Arc, or Joan of Arc (1412–31), the illiterate farm girl who led the French army to victory during the Hundred Years' War, burned as a heretic in Rouen by the English, canonised in 1920. Héloïse d'Argenteuil (1101–64): the ill-fated mutual passion of the scholars Héloïse and Abelard has been called the first modern love affair, documented by their remarkable letters. Agnès Sorel (1422–50) was the favourite mistress of Charles VII; she died – possibly murdered – from mercury poisoning. La Belle Ferronnière was a mistress of François I, via whom the revengeful husband was said to have passed on syphilis to the king. Clémence Isaure, a medieval poetess of Toulouse, revealed in Flaubert's time to have been an invention of the troubadours, devoted herself to poetry after her lover was killed in battle.

27. **Saint Louis . . . Louis XIV**: 19th-century French schoolchildren would have been familiar with these anecdotal snippets of history. The pious King Louis IX (1214–70) was said to have administered justice under a vast oak tree; Pierre Terrail, seigneur de Bayard (1476–1524), was known as the fearless and faultless knight, famous for his magnanimity and strategic brilliance in battle. The cunning and ruthlessness of Louis XI (1423–83) earned him the sobriquet 'The Spider King', but unified France; the St Bartholomew's Day Massacre (*Massacre de la Saint-Barthélemy*), in which thousands of French Protestants were slaughtered by the Catholic majority, began on the night of 23–24 August 1572. The Béarnais crest refers to the white plume on the helmet of Henri of Navarre (1553–1610), under which the king rode into battle. Louis XIV (1638–1715), the absolute monarch known as the Sun King, builder of the lavish Palace of Versailles.

28. **bonnet-grecs**: the bonnet-grec is a tasselled, fez-like cap, appearing with this name in, for instance, Charlotte Brontë's *Villette* (1853). 'Indispensable to the studious man. Lends majesty to the face' (Flaubert, *Dictionary of Received Ideas*).

29. **Lamartinian**: the poet Alphonse de Lamartine (1790–1869) was a deeply influential figure in the French romantic movement, and detested by Flaubert for having 'no ear'.

30. **pellets of breadcrumbs**: used at the time as pencil erasers.

31. **mouthwash bowls**: known euphemistically in English as finger bowls, they were little bowls of rosewater with a cup, to rinse one's mouth for the dessert.

32. *quite good enough for the country*: Flaubert uses italics not only in the usual way, but also when he wishes to draw attention to the manner in which a consumerist society saturates its discourse with received ideas, recycled phrases, banal epithets. Here, as elsewhere, the italicised phrase lies somewhere between *style indirect libre* and direct dialogue: or is reported speech not quite in quotation marks.

33. **She called Djali**: Emma's greyhound bitch (a breed made fashionable by Lamartine) is named after Esmeralda's goat in Victor Hugo's *The Hunchback of Notre-Dame* (1831). This celebrated scene includes the first time we hear Emma's voice since her single question to Charles ('Are you looking for something?' p.15). Here she again poses a question, but an interior and more essential one.

34. **several ladies had not put their gloves in their glass**: a woman put her glove in her glass to signal that she would not be drinking wine, as was expected in polite society.

35. **Trafalgar puddings**: *pudding à la Trafalgar*, or jam roly-poly and custard.

36. *La Marjolaine*: the medieval love-song '*Compagnons de la Marjolaine*' ('Fellowship of the Marjoram'). Young men and women would go in a group to dance in the meadow where the marjoram flowers: a knight asks them for a girl to marry.

37. **the Bois**: familiar term for the Bois de Boulogne, on the outskirts of Paris.

38. **Eugène Sue**: a socialist dandy, Sue (1804–57) exposed the seamy side of the Industrial Revolution in popular, serialised melodramas.

PART TWO

1. **Yonville-l'Abbaye**: said to be based on the village of Ry, the Normandy home of the unfortunate Delphine Delamare, the town's lengthy opening documentation is essential to our understanding of Emma's plight. Flaubert himself insisted the 'place *does not exist*'; Ry now does its best to conform to the fictive version.

2. **Cupid, finger to his lips**: probably a reproduction of Étienne-Maurice Falconet's famous *Seated Cupid* (1757), reaching for an arrow as he urges secrecy.

3. **Charles X's reign**: an ultra-reactionary Catholic, Charles-Philippe reigned from 1824 until the July Revolution of 1830.

4. **the Charter**: the constitution of the new monarchy of 1830, the 'Gallic cock' being the ancient symbol of Gaul.

5. **The *Hirondelle***: the Swallow, the name of Flaubert's fictional stagecoach from Rouen.

6. **the selfishness of a bourgeois**: 'I make Literature for myself as a bourgeois turns napkin rings in his attic.' (Flaubert, letter to George Sand, 6 September 1871)

7. **My God ... principles of '89!**: Homais' list glibly lumps together the key reference points for an enlightened rationalism: Socrates, the father of Western philosophy (469–399 BC); Benjamin Franklin (1706–90), the inventor, diplomat, statesman of genius and New World hero to the French; François-Marie Arouet de Voltaire (1694–1778), the anti-clerical Enlightenment writer and philosopher; Béranger, the subversive songwriter (see previous note to p.10); and Jean-Jacques Rousseau (1712 –78), whose educational treatise *Émile: or, On Education* was banned and then burnt in 1762 due to the cited 'Profession' section, which promoted a revolutionary 'natural religion'. The 'immortal principles' are those of the French Revolution (1789), during which the infamous Robespierre inaugurated the Festival of the Supreme Being (obliquely referred to by Homais) and a new state religion based on rational devotion. No one is listening to Homais, of course.

8. **news, explanations and baskets**: Flaubert is fond of the comically disparate triplet, mixing abstract and concrete nouns.

9. **a young man with fair hair**: like Emma's eyes, Léon's hair is inconsistent, passing from blonde to 'auburn' (see p.90).

10. **fifty-four Fahrenheit**: this should be eighty-six Fahrenheit.

11. **'Isn't it?'**: the dissonance in the reply, resulting from a late authorial cut, happily reflects Emma's dreamy state. Flaubert commented on this 'grotesque' duet: 'The irony takes nothing away from the pathos, on the contrary it exaggerates it.' (Letter to Louise Colet, 9 October 1852.)

12. **the *Rouen Beacon***: when the editors asked Flaubert to swap the real *Journal de Rouen* for an invented name, he wrote agonisedly to Louis Bouilhet: 'I don't know what to do . . . it will break the rhythm of my poor phrases!' Thus *Fanal* (Beacon).

13. **until the end of dinner**: 'Never in my life have I written anything more difficult than what I am doing now – trivial dialogue. This inn scene may take me three months... but I'd die rather than skirt round it.' (Flaubert, letter to Louise Colet, 19 September 1852.)

14. **the 19th *Ventôse*, Year XI, Article 1**: this being 3 March 1803 in the Republican calendar (1793–1806). Flaubert took much trouble with his research into pharmaceutical legislation.

15. **Athalie**: the eponymous heroine of Racine's last play (1691).

16. ***The God of the Simple Folk***: an anti-clerical song by Béranger (see note above to p.10).

17. ***The War of the Gods***: a violently anti-Christian poem by the influential libertine poet Chevalier de Parny (1753–1814).

18. **the six weeks of the Virgin**: the customary lying-in period after a birth.

19. **a Mathieu Laensberg almanac**: these were hugely popular almanacs with a touch of the arcane, produced in Liège, sold door-to-door by pedlars.

20. ***L'Illustration***: the most celebrated 19th-century quality journal began publication in 1843; therefore it was, according to the novel's (fluctuating) internal chronology, brand new.

21. **'My respects to your husband!'**: 'Frankly there are moments when I almost feel like vomiting, *physically*... This [direct dialogue] must be no more than six or seven pages long, and without a single reflection or analysis...' (Flaubert, letter to Louise Colet, 13 April 1853)

22. **to the Arts**: here Flaubert cut an extended and much-drafted description of an Italian master of fireworks setting out lamps on the Mairie.

23. **rat in his cheese**: a literary reference to one of Jean La Fontaine's Fables (VII, 3, 'The Rat Who Retired from the World') lost on the inn's landlady and so self-confirming Homais' superiority.

24. **the counsel of science!**: Homais is in the vanguard; France was a leading exponent of *la chimie agricole* – agricultural chemistry – from the mid-century onwards, with experimental farms like Georges Ville's at Vincennes analysing manure. Flaubert, while acutely suspicious of technological progress and regarding science as another 'superstition', claimed that 'poetry is as exact a science as geometry' and demanded of the writer the same objectivity and rigour as was found in the laboratory.

25. **half-century of servitude**: 'For half a century, the housewives of Pont-l'Evêque envied Madame Aubain her servant, Félicité.' The famous opening sentence of Flaubert's late masterpiece, *Un coeur simple* (1877; *A Simple Heart*), whose obscure heroine seems an intentional counterpoint to Emma.

26. **staddles**: trees whose stumps were reserved for coppicing (*baliveaux*).

27. **in the evening's blush**: Speaking of this scene (which he called 'their Fuck'), Flaubert said 'It is a delicious thing to write, no longer to be *oneself*... Today, for instance, as man and woman together, both lover and mistress, I rode in a forest, on an autumn afternoon, under yellow leaves, and I was the horses, the leaves, the wind, the words they uttered and the red sun that half closed their love-drowned eyes...' (Letter to Louise Colet, 23 December 1853)

28. *ganny-cocks*: a turkey-cock in southern English dialect, reflecting Flaubert's Normandy term, *picots*.

29. **the misspellings**: Flaubert chose not to reproduce them in the embedded text.

30. **Doctor Duval's volume**: Flaubert made copious notes from Vincent Duval's *Traité pratique du pied-bot* (1839; *A Practical Treatise on the Treatment of Clubfoot*). Duval corrected a patient's club-foot that Flaubert's surgeon father had been unable to treat.

31. **Ambroise Paré . . . Celsus . . . Dupuytren . . . Gensoul**: the list of these famous surgeons includes Achille-Cléophas Flaubert's remarkable tutor and friend, Guillaume Dupuytren (1777–1835), chiefly known for inventing the artificial anus.

32. *tenotome*: a narrow-bladed surgical instrument for cutting tendons. Charles is not authorised to carry out this type of serious operation on his own.

33. **phlyctenae**: fluid-filled blisters.

34. *Amor nel cor*: 'Love in my heart.' Louise Colet gave a cigarette case engraved with this motto to Flaubert; in a furious, revengeful poem of the same name, she wrote: 'Ah well! in a novel of commercial traveller style,/As nauseating as unwholesome air,/He mocked the gift in a flat-footed phrase,/Yet kept the handsome agate seal.'

35. **Duke of Clarence**: in Shakespeare's *Richard III*, the wicked Richard has his brother stabbed and then drowned in a butt of malmsey wine.

36. **morals**: the one instance when the sub-title's key word, the multivalent *'moeurs'*, is used. Here it clearly means 'morals' rather than 'manners', 'customs' or 'mores'.

37. **Madame Bovary . . . in harmony**: perhaps the most shocking aspect of the novel for its contemporaries was the notion that adultery beautifies.

38. **From time to time . . . wanness**: this passage was cut by the *Revue de Paris*, and not put back despite Flaubert's express wishes. Left out in the 'definitive' 1873 edition, it still seems (at least to this translator) too crucial to omit.

39. *sideways* **look**: a favourite pose in portraiture – flirtatious, inviting the viewer in.

40. **manchineel tree**: a poisonous tree native to the Americas, so deadly that standing beneath it in the rain causes skin blisters.

41. **apricots picked**: the fruit is symbolically associated with both love and, particularly in the 19th-century, the female genitals; it is likely to have been the Biblical 'apple' of Genesis.

42. *That is the question!*: Homais reduces Hamlet's 'To be or not to be, that is the question' to the level of a newspaper snippet.

43. *Castigat ridendo mores*: 'It [comedy] amends morals by laughing at them,' a phrase coined by Molière's contemporary, Jean de Santeuil (1630–97).

44. *Lucie de Lammermoor*: the tragic opera by Donizetti, *Lucia di Lammermoor* (1836), based on Sir Walter Scott's novel *The Bride of Lammermoor* (1819), was performed in this French version in 1839, supervised by the composer: the major changes include a frailer Lucie, manipulated by the more brutish men around her.

PART THREE

1. *Chaumière . . .* **grisettes**: *La Grande Chaumière* was a popular Paris dance hall, opened in 1788, already closed when Flaubert was writing this part of the novel. The grisette was an integral feature of bohemian Paris, being an independent working-class woman who combined the roles of artist's model, multiple lover and, if things went badly, prostitute. Renowned for their beauty and overt sexuality, the grisettes were dismissed by a disappointed Mark Twain as 'another romantic fraud'. They were immortalised in the character of Mimi in Puccini's opera *La Bohème*.

2. **whatever did not graze the asphalt**: asphalt, a new invention, had an erotic significance at this period, attracting an excited response from writers such as Mallarmé or Zola. The bituminous, slippery, dust-free and brightly lit boulevards were a pick-up point for prostitutes: the boot clearly belongs to one of the latter.

3. **her blue eyes**: there has been much critical debate on why Flaubert gave Emma changeable eyes: earlier they are 'brown' but seem black (p.15), then 'black in the shadow and deep blue in daylight'

(p.31), and here simply 'blue'. Flaubert was the least careless writer imaginable: it seems he is deliberately subverting a conventional part of any character description, but to what end? To make Emma yet more ungraspable, and therefore even closer to reality? That the gift Léon gives Emma changes from a 'rug' or a 'tablecloth' to a 'coverlet' is more likely to be an oversight.

4. *The Tower of Nesle*: *La Tour de Nesle*, a five-act melodrama of royal medieval adultery and murder by Alexandre Dumas (1802–70), first performed to enormous acclaim in 1832, it serves as an ironic counterpoint to Emma's modern affair in a hotel room.

5. **the dancing Marianne**: the local misnomer for a carving depicting Salomé (symbol of female seductiveness) dancing before her stepfather, Herod; Mariamne (sic) was Herod's mother. Flaubert used the figure, who is shown walking on her hands, to depict Salomé in his short story *Hérodias* (1877).

6. **it is all cast-iron**: the original stone spire of Rouen cathedral having been destroyed by a lightning bolt in 1822.

7. **the conveyance lumbered off**: the famous ensuing passage was cut by the *Revue de Paris*, who were praised at Flaubert's trial for 'lowering the coach's blinds', but criticised for still allowing us 'into the bedroom'. It is possible to trace the carriage's itinerary on an old map of Rouen. The railway station that features had only recently been opened (in 1843).

8. **spur-stones**: a rounded stone block set at the angles of buildings or the corners of archways to protect them from damage by wagon or carriage wheels.

9. *Fabricando fit faber, age quod agis*: 'Practice makes perfect, whatever you do.'

10. *Conjugal . . . Love!*: *The Mysteries of Conjugal Love Revealed* (*Le Tableau de l'amour conjugal*) by Nicolas Venette was published in 1686: an enlightened, scientific approach to sex education, it ran through numerous editions. Flaubert thought it 'inept'.

11. **One evening . . .**: A line from Lamartine's (see note to p.36) elegiac poem 'Le Lac', his most famous.

12. *the odalisque bathing*: Jean Auguste Dominique Ingres's painting

La Grande Odalisque (1814) depicts a naked courtesan whose sensuous back has been anatomically elongated – with five extra vertebrae. The work's overt eroticism caused a scandal. *The pale woman of Barcelona* reflects Romanticism's attraction to all things Spanish, while the 'Angel' was a familiar trope in romantic literature. Léon can only view his lover through current stereotypes.

13. **bandeaux**: see earlier note to p.15.

14. *A fair day's heat . . .* : from a poem by the extraordinary proto-communist writer Rétif de la Bretonne (1734–1806).

15. *Breda Street*: in English in the original text, referring to any street where prostitutes plied their trade – the actual Breda Street being situated in the once-bohemian area around Notre-Dame-de-Lorette (Paris, 9th arrondissement).

16. **foot warmer**: a fur-lined box or bag for both feet.

17. *crummy*: early 19th-century slang for 'fleshy' or 'buxom', the nearest equivalent to the original French '*morceau*'.

18. *Yes*: in English in the original.

19. *garus*: elixir of Garus, tonic and digestive stimulant, made mainly from aloes, myrrh and saffron.

20. **Cujas and Barthole**: Jacques Cujas (1522–90), French legal humanist; Bartole (1313–56), Italian lawyer and professor: both specialists in Roman law.

21. **Steuben's *Esmeralda*, with *Potiphar* by Schopin**: *Esmeralda* would be an engraving from the much-reproduced painting by Charles von Steuben (1788–1856), showing the scantily clad gipsy heroine of Hugo's *The Hunchback of Notre-Dame* cuddling her pet goat, Djali. Henri-Frédérick Schopin (1804–80) was the brother of Chopin: he painted no known image of Potiphar, whose wife attempted to trap Joseph by seduction. The notary's choice of art (see also note to p.68) is signalled as being conventionally bourgeois.

22. **a residue of pride**: Flaubert wrote 'un reste d'orgueil', rendered correctly in the first edition – but in all subsequent editions as the curious '*un geste* [a gesture] *d'orgueil*'. I have restored what appears to be the correct version.

23. **since God . . . prayer?:** Homais lumps together citations from Habakkuk (2:18), Philippians (4:19) and Matthew (7:32).

24. **Holbach . . . Nicolas!:** the atheist Baron d'Holbach's *Encylo-pédie* (1751–65) included Diderot, Voltaire and Montesquieu as contributors. Abbé Guenée's *Lettres de quelques juifs portugais, allemands et polonais à M. De Voltaire* (1769) defended Biblical truth. Auguste Nicolas' *Etudes philosophiques sur le christianisme* (1845) offered a rational defence of Christianity which had considerable contemporary influence.

25. **white dints:** in an earlier draft, this was the crueller and more graphic 'scars of ringworm'.

26. **done with it:** Flaubert paid close attention to a funeral he attended while working on this scene: 'One must . . . *profit from everything* . . . I will perhaps find things there for my *Bovary* . . . I hope to make others cry with the tears of one man, to go on afterwards to the chemistry of style.' (Letter to Louise Colet, 6 June 1853)

27. *Sta viator . . . calcas:* 'Stay, traveller, you tread upon a wife worthy of love.'

28. **Daylight filtered through the trellis:** *'Des jours passaient par le treillis'.* This is awkward (or highly poetic) French, likely to be misread as 'days passed by [or through] the trellis'. An earlier draft has Charles sitting there 'for such a long time' that 'all the sorrows of his life revisited him . . . from the first day to the last,' contrasting with the precise 'seven o'clock' of Berthe's discovery. Sadly, the dappled effect of the misreading – possibly intended – cannot be reproduced in translation.

This book is set in FOURNIER. Pierre Simon Fournier (1712–1768) was a French punch-cutter, type-founder and typographic theoretician who produced some of the most influential type designs of the eighteenth century. In 1924, the Monotype foundry produced the Fournier typeface, based on types cut by Pierre Simon Fournier circa. 1742.

THE HISTORY OF VINTAGE

The famous American publisher Alfred A. Knopf (1892–1984) founded Vintage Books in the United States in 1954 as a paperback home for the authors published by his company. Vintage was launched in the United Kingdom in 1990 and works independently from the American imprint although both are part of the international publishing group, Random House.

Vintage in the United Kingdom was initially created to publish paper-back editions of books acquired by the prestigious hardback imprints in the Random House Group such as Jonathan Cape, Chatto & Windus, Hutchinson and later William Heinemann, Secker & Warburg and The Harvill Press. There are many Booker and Nobel Prize-winning authors on the Vintage list and the imprint publishes a huge variety of fiction and non-fiction. Over the years Vintage has expanded and the list now includes great authors of the past – who are published under the Vintage Classics imprint – as well as many of the most influential authors of the present.

For a full list of the books Vintage publishes, please visit our website www.vintage-books.co.uk

For book details and other information about the classic authors we publish, please visit the Vintage Classics website www.vintage-classics.info